THE BRIARS

Stephanie Parent

CEMETERY GATES
MEDIA

The Briars
Published by Cemetery Gates Media
Binghamton, New York

ISBN: 9798377131946

For more information about this book and other Cemetery Gates
Media publications, visit us at:

cemeterygatesmedia.com
twitter.com/cemeterygatesm
instagram.com/cemeterygatesm

Cover Design: Claire L. Smith

Content Warning: This story contains strong depictions of
BDSM and has scenes with sexual assault.

"Stephanie Parent's *THE BRIARS* is both haunting and lyrical, a gripping blend of the macabre and the romantic. Set in a BDSM dungeon where the women are expected to be subservient and the men catered to at all costs, Parent's story is a dazzling and subversive upending of expectations. A stunning affirmation of female empowerment and solidarity, even in the darkest of places."

—Claire C. Holland, author of *I Am Not Your Final Girl*

"With *THE BRIARS*, Stephanie Parent delves fearlessly into an exploration of desire and darkness, deftly weaving threads of urban modernity, folklore, mystery, and romance into a tapestry that is both compelling and harrowing. In a world dominated by men's wishes, Parent brings female relationships to the forefront, celebrating love, sisterhood and women's strength. Superb and spellbinding!"

—Antonia Rachel Ward, author of *Marionette*

"Stephanie Parent's *THE BRIARS* will completely decimate you."

—Robert P. Ottone, author of *The Vile Thing We Created* and *Nocturnal Creatures*

"*THE BRIARS* is a novel of rare quality. Equal parts raw, thrilling and brilliant, Stephanie Parent crafts a thoroughly unique ghost story told in a BDSM dungeon where some of the most terrifying ghosts are the phantoms of who its employees used to be. Haunting, romantic, and exquisitely beautiful, do not dare to skip this book."

—Zach Rosenberg, author of *Hungers as Old as This Land* and *The Long Shalom*

3

"Nobody even spoke of burying the woman… It would have been useless to bury her—because the last undying wish of a dying person for vengeance can burst asunder any tomb and lift the heaviest graveyard stone."

—*"The Corpse Rider" Lafcadio Hearn*

We all knew a ghost haunted the dungeon's attic, but the phantom coexisted peacefully with us. She sent us playful messages, showing herself in the wink-like flickering of a candle, the giggling trickle of a faucet that no one had turned on—until Mara arrived. That was when the ghost turned, like the moment the warm water of a shower runs out and becomes cold as needles. Cold as knives.

How could a dungeon have an attic, you might ask? Well, this wasn't a dungeon made of iron, the kind that stank of damp earth and echoed with the rattle of old bones, the kind buried deep beneath the ground. This was an S&M dungeon, where men slapped their hard-earned (or well-hoarded, or slyly swindled) hundred-dollar bills down on the front desk in exchange for an hour with the mistress or submissive of their choice. It looked like just another house from the outside, on a quiet street off of Santa Monica Boulevard in Los Angeles, only a few miles from the ocean so when the wind blew just right, you could taste a hint of salt in the air. An ordinary little cottage, except for the red roses and briars threading along the front gate and climbing the walls, flashing their grinning red mouths. Unless you bothered to look closely, you'd never notice that all the windows beneath those roses were covered with black curtains, to bar any curious eyes.

The roses were a lot of work to maintain, and during the cooler months when even in Los Angeles, the blossoms hid their heads, the thorns could turn foreboding; but they were on brand. The dungeon, which had tucked itself away in this little house on this little side street since 1983, was officially known as Briars & Roses, though these days everyone simply called it "The Briars." And nestled beneath the peaked roof of the cottage, where the thorns ascended all the way up the gables as if they were reaching for the moon, was the attic where the ghost lived. Her home base from which she played her little tricks and sometimes sent us the sparks of ideas, or encouragement when we needed it.

When Nadia's last client of the night gave her a thousand spankings and made her count each one, and the numbers dissolved beneath yawns and thoughts of soft blankets waiting for her at home, the ghost kept her awake and helped her count. The electric candelabras in the alcoves of the room began to blink on and off—once for the first ten spankings, twice for the second ten, all the way up to a hundred flashes by the time they were through. Even her client said, "Someone needs to replace those bulbs."

When Ruby had a three-hour session with a man who wanted only to be tied up and teased, who kept saying, "no pain, no pain," like a desperate prayer until Ruby thought she'd lose her mind with boredom, the ghost made the nipple clamps hanging on a rack in the corner sway and tinkle as if caught by an errant breeze. Ruby blindfolded her client and fastened those metal vices around his nipples, even as he whined *"no pain, no pain,"* and only moments later he gasped in surprised ecstasy. The client fell in love with her and came back to see her every week, leaving a larger tip each time.

When Gabriella and Luna had a double session with portly Joshua, who wanted to see the most "exotic" ladies on the shift— by which he meant the ones with skin the most different from his own pasty, bloodless flesh—the ghost made the old CD player skip all through the striptease Joshua asked both women to perform. He grumbled at their jerky movements and Luna reminded him this was a house of BDSM, a place for roleplay, spanking and bondage, and not a strip club. They ended up paddling him until his white ass turned red and his mind was too muddled to call Luna a Mexican or ask Gabriella what country she was from for the third time.

When Claire had to close up Lady Lilith's room—the very room where the stairs to the attic, and the ghost's residence, were located—alone on a rainy night, and she shivered at the thought of driving through slick streets to the apartment where Danny waited for her, she heard a humming from above. It sounded like the half-remembered melody of a lullaby, from some warm, safe night years and years ago, and a calm washed over her as the downpour outside slowed to a drizzle.

Though we referred to our dungeon phantom simply as "the ghost"—*the ghost left the water running again; the ghost made that old door stick, until I thought I might be locked in*—we all knew this was the ghost of the Briars' original owner, Lady Lilith, and that her spirit now guarded the attic above the room that bore her name. Lady Lilith had always kept a watchful eye over every inch of her dungeon, from the roses topping the roof to the spiders that occasionally crept in through a crack in the floorboards. Why wouldn't she maintain that same vigilance even after death? Working at a dungeon could be a difficult job, and we were grateful for her presence.

Grateful, that is, until the strange, quiet girl named Mara came to work at the Briars, and the ghost's tricks turned dark.

ONE: CLAIRE

Of course, on the morning Claire walked into the dungeon prepared to quit her job as a professional submissive, her boss would ask her to show a new girl the ropes.

It wasn't that different from any other workplace, Claire supposed. As a secretary she would have to demonstrate the filing system to her replacement, when all she wanted was to wipe the hours she'd wasted organizing memos and invoices from her mind. If she'd waited tables for a living, she'd be forced to recount the quirks of regular diners she hoped never to lay eyes on again. But instead, Claire was about to show some wide-eyed ingenue the bondage beds and crosses she'd be strapped to while men spanked and flogged and tickled her. She'd have to warn this new girl which of those clients would hit too hard, or yank her underwear down, or plant an unexpected wet smooch on her cheek—or worse, her lips.

In some ways, it might be just like the final day of any other job; but at the same time, it was so very different. And to complicate matters, Claire wasn't sure how *she* felt about leaving. She couldn't shake Danny's heated words from the night before, the curses her boyfriend had hurled at her like a handful of stones, until at last she agreed: she'd stop working at a dungeon where men left bruises and rope marks on her flesh. Yet even after she'd appeased him, those stones smoldered in the pit of her belly, coals that wouldn't burn themselves out. They niggled at Claire, insisting she might be making a mistake.

And then there was the fact that Lady Eva, the Briars' owner who sat behind the lacquered lobby desk like a queen on her throne, had no idea Claire planned to quit. Minutes earlier, Claire had stepped carefully through the dungeon's rose-covered gates, trying not to jostle those stones of frustration and confusion and some other, unnamable emotion that hung heavy in her stomach. She changed into her crop top and schoolgirl skirt in the dressing room, steeling herself to deliver the news; but before she had a chance Lady Eva announced that a new girl was starting that day, and Claire would be giving her the tour. Now the new hire waited by the desk, so slender and quiet that she seemed no more than another shadow in the dim velvet-lined lobby, until Lady Eva pointed her out.

"Sorry," Claire asked the girl who stood playing with her long black hair, "can you tell me your name again?" Claire tried to learn new submissives' names right away, but her current agitation didn't help. The girl had said Mira, or Moira, or—

"Mara." She clasped her hands in front of her, worrying her unpolished fingers against each other, her voice so soft Claire had to lean close to hear it.

"You'll have to speak up, dear," Lady Eva said from behind the desk. The dungeon owner's own voice came out high-pitched, and a bit more forceful than necessary. "Some of our clients are on the older side, and a little hard of hearing."

On the older side was putting it mildly. Lady Eva, in her early sixties with hair swept into a blonde updo among which she'd permitted a few elegant strands of gray, was "on the older side." Some of the Briars' clients were downright ancient. There were younger men too, of course, though not as many as they hoped for these days. Lady Eva had lamented a thousand times: with BDSM going mainstream, the younger generations un-abashedly proclaimed their fetishes online and found willing partners. They didn't need to spend two hundred bucks an hour to satisfy their sadomasochistic urges in secret. Dungeons were a dying business, drooping like the last roses left on the Briars' roof in late winter. Another year without fresh blood, and they'd have to close.

Not that Claire should care—after today, she'd be gone and wouldn't have to watch the dungeon crumble, as Lady Eva so dramatically proclaimed it might.

Beside Claire, Mara cleared her throat, a sound like the rustle of water over stones. "All right. I'll be louder, then," the girl managed—in a whisper Claire could barely make out. Claire couldn't help smiling a little. Maybe showing this shy new arrival around would distract her from her own troubles.

"All right," Claire echoed Mara's words, as she ducked into the hallway behind the desk and grabbed one of the keys hanging on the wall, "I'll show you the rooms where we session first. Does she have any sessions booked yet, Lady Eva?"

"Not yet," Lady Eva said, scribbling something on a note-card. Each lady who worked at the dungeon had her own card, listing whether she was submissive or switch or dominant, her height, body type, bra and shoe size... Lady Eva wouldn't inundate Mara with all those questions yet, but she did say,

"Where are you from, dear? You have such striking features—Russian, perhaps? The clients will wonder…"

"Oh—" Mara tried to grab the lace that fluttered below her white corset, but her fingers only clutched air. She tottered in pink heels that left a half-inch of space between her feet and the ankle straps, and Claire hoped she wouldn't walk right out of them. Only a year ago, Claire had been just as awkward in her new dungeon costumes, and now that she belonged here, she had to go…

"I'm"—Mara cut through Claire's thoughts—"I'm not entirely sure where I'm from. I didn't know my parents, so…"

"I don't need your life history, Mara," Lady Eva said brusquely but not unkindly, "I just need to know how you'll represent yourself to clients. I'll give you time to think about it." With that, Lady Eva ducked behind the desk and retrieved a dozen fake roses from the bottom drawer. She brushed a delicate finger across red petals studded with jeweled dewdrops, before handing them to Claire. "Can you replace the ones in the vase while you're up there?"

"Yes, Lady Eva." Even on her final day, Claire wouldn't dare to question her boss's ritual. Flowers in hand, Claire led Mara out the front door, along a stone walkway lined with potted spider plants and ivy, and around the corner where an exterior staircase rose to the second floor. "I hope Lady Eva didn't make you uncomfortable," Claire glanced back at Mara, who looked down at each stair as she climbed, "it's just that a lot of the clients here have, well—types…"

Mara lifted her gaze as they reached the top of the stairs, and Claire lost her train of thought. She wasn't sure how Lady Eva would describe Mara to the clients, because the girl's dark, liquid-looking eyes drew Claire in until she could see nothing else. The stair lurched under her heels, and she grabbed the banister with her free hand to keep from tumbling. Mara wobbled too, her all-white outfit fluttering as if she were a blossom insubstantial enough for a breeze to carry off.

Claire shook off the strange slant to her thoughts, and the step steadied beneath her. She had a dungeon tour to get through. "So, you'll unlock this door for your client and lead them into the hallway…" She did so, asking Mara, "Did Lady Eva go over the rules when she hired you?"

"No sex or…" She paused as if trying to remember the exact words. "…sexual touching, and underwear stays on?"

12

"That's the most important part," Claire agreed. She opened the first door to her left and stepped inside, turning the lights up halfway. "This is Lady Lilith's room," she said, "named after the dungeon's original owner. It's one of two rooms up here, then there's also the annex. That's the building on the other side of the parking lot, for dommes and switches." She braced herself for the question almost everyone asked so eagerly—*How long before I can become one of those dominatrixes and, you know, spank and tie up men?*—but it didn't come. Instead, Mara simply followed her into Lady Lilith's room, a shadowy space that would intimidate any newcomer. Yet on her last day, Claire saw the room through fond, wistful eyes—even if it might be the home of a dungeon-owner-turned-ghost.

There was the six-foot-tall St. Andrew's Cross in one corner, the black leather bondage bed lined with silver rings along the opposite wall. The cage with its dull metal bars, just large enough to hold one crouching man or, as Claire knew intimately, two kneeling girls. A zebra-striped carpet zigzagged across the floor, cheetah-printed pillows and blankets covered the bed, and sheepskin rugs sploshed like spots of cream here and there across the carpet. *The meat room*, Claire secretly called it; a space tantalizing and disquieting at once, where bare flesh was offered up and consumed. But this morning, the familiar surroundings brought only a dull pang in her chest, an anticipation of loss.

Could she really leave, just like that? Never saying goodbye to the clients who'd become something close to friends, Tickle Thomas and Spanking Eric and especially Yarik, who brought her treasures from his trips to foreign lands? She had to go, though—she loved Danny, and if she didn't quit, her boyfriend would leave *her.* At that thought, dread awoke inside her, a *drip-drip* like—

"Oh, shoot!" Claire scurried into the bathroom at the far end of the room, where water drops clinked against porcelain, and jiggled the faucet until it shut off. "Lady Eva must have left this on. Okay," she said as she emerged, "the intercom is over here, and you'll press it to start a session..."

She spent a few minutes on practicalities, pointing out the equipment and how it might be used. Cautioning Mara not to let a client tie her to the suspension bar and crank it up until she dangled off the floor, or she could damage those fragile-looking wrists. Warning her never to stand on the bondage bed with her heels on—a few duct tape-patched tears already marred the leather, and as Lady Eva frequently reminded them, the dungeon couldn't afford to replace it.

Mara, however, seemed more interested in the mirrors: she wandered silently from one to the next, gazing at her wide-eyed reflection. The long, horizontal glass above the bondage bed; the full-length style you might find in a closet, lining the adjacent wall; the oval that watched them like a big drooping eye from the third wall. A carnival funhouse, reflections reflecting reflections.

Claire said without thinking, "I try not to look in those most of the time."

"Why?" Mara asked. "You're so pretty."

Claire didn't feel pretty that morning—she'd lacked the energy to tame her light-brown curls, and her bare stomach and legs appeared far too pale and soft. Claire had once flattered herself that she had a dancer's body, but she hadn't done a *rond de jambe* or *grand battement* since she'd dropped out of the Dancers' Institute at age twenty-two; only three years ago, but it somehow seemed longer.

Besides, all the Hollywood apartments she'd lived in since then were so small and cluttered, she couldn't lift her leg in an arabesque without knocking something over.

Claire was petite, barely taller than tiny Mara; but if the new girl was a long-stemmed flower, Claire, after abandoning ballet, had become a wilting shrub. Still, dissatisfaction with her appearance wasn't the reason she kept her gaze from the mirrors and sometimes closed her eyes altogether. "To be honest," she told Mara, "it's more about avoiding the guys' reflections than my own."

Without so much as a shrug in response, Mara headed toward the back alcove with its leather sofa and faux-animal-skin pillows—*the meat room*—the vanity lined with garish makeup, '80s-style electric-blue eyeshadow that might actually *be* from the '80s, tubes of Wet 'n' Wild lipstick, and above it all the room's final mirror—

Claire gasped like a wounded animal. Across the mirror someone had written in big lipstick letters, red gashes in the glass, bleeding blurred edges:

SHOW ME WHAT A WHORE YOU ARE

Claire's hands fell open, and the plastic roses plummeted to the floor.

14

"What is it?" Mara asked, the placidity of her voice now more irritating than endearing. Claire glanced over to her, but the new girl's head was tilted downward, and her hair hid her expression. Claire turned back to the vanity, and—

It was just an empty mirror with black carvings around the edges like a tangle of thorns. The lipstick words were gone.

"Nothing," Claire said quickly. The fight with Danny must have left her more tired than she'd thought.

Claire knelt to pick up the roses while Mara swept her hands across the makeup-strewn table, unscrewing a deformed finger of lipstick, tickling the needle bristles of a hairbrush. "That's all for cross-dressing," Claire spoke quickly, hoping to chase her strange vision off. "There's dresses—well, if you can call those sequined monstrosities *dresses*—in that closet, and the dommes and switches will dress guys up and put makeup on them and parade them around the room." *And, if the guy is really into humiliation, maybe call him a "dirty whore" or even write it in lipstick on the mirror.*

Claire could see someone like Ruby doing that, standing before the vanity in the spiked heels that made her six feet tall, laughing and tossing her long red-tinged hair behind her as she scrawled a lipstick message that told her client just how pathetic he was. Then she would force the guy to wipe off every last trace of the lipstick himself, she'd inspect the mirror and if she saw a single red speck of shame left behind—or only imagined one— her client would pay for it.

Claire grabbed the last of the flowers with their crimson petals, the same shade as those highlights in Ruby's hair. She stood to find Mara's hand hovering over the scissors at one end of the vanity. "Safety scissors," Claire said. "In case someone needs to get out of bondage quick."

Mara lowered one finger to the metal, then pulled back as if she'd been stung. "Don't worry," Claire added, "I've never heard of anyone needing the scissors, the entire year I've been here. Come with me, I've got to put down these flowers..."

Claire headed to the opposite corner from the cross-dressers' alcove, where six black-painted stairs led upward, and a thick metal chain barred entry to the attic above. Halfway up the stairs, Lady Eva had placed a fat vase erupting with artificial roses, and she insisted on replenishing the blossoms every week.

If the dungeon owner was so worried about her business descending into ruin, the flowers were one unnecessary expense she could wipe off the books.

Claire switched out the flowers, avoiding the dust coating the dry insides of the vase, and called back to Mara, "Make sure you stay away from this attic. It's not safe—there was some kind of accident up there." It was the same speech Claire had heard when she started, but after all her time at the Briars, she doubted any danger truly lay at the top of those stairs. Any earthly danger, at least.

"*We can't disturb Lady Lilith*," Lady Eva would say, if someone suggested rearranging the furniture or, God forbid, repainting those bleak black stairs. And then there were the new flowers every week, an offering that would never wither or droop. Lady Eva had her reasons for keeping the women away from the attic, for taking care to replace the air fresheners and burnt-out bulbs in Lady Lilith's room, but refusing to get rid of the faded pillows and vintage makeup that had sat here since Lady Lilith herself tortured men between these walls. It was one of the Briars' unspoken truths:

Lady Eva believed Lady Lilith's spirit lingered in the attic above them, unwilling to abandon the dungeon she'd built, even after her death. And while Claire herself wasn't so certain of the existence of ghosts, she wouldn't risk disturbing one.

Maybe she would even sneak up there after her shift ended and say goodbye to Lady Lilith, just in case.

Her task complete, Claire deposited the old roses in the trash can by the vanity. The petals slid down the sides of the can like bits of congealed blood, and beneath a few cotton balls and candy wrappers, a silver edge shined. Was that— She wormed her fingers into the bottom of the trash and, sure enough, her thumbpad met the sharp point of the scissors. Had Mara thrown them away?

Claire glanced over to the girl, who was gazing up toward the attic, reaching one pale arm over the stairs. Claire pulled the scissors from the trash and debated whether to say anything—

When a burst of static sizzled into the room, jolting through her and making Mara jump.

The crackle resolved into the crisp, composed tone Lady Eva used in front of clients. "Excuse me, ladies," her voice echoed over the intercom, "Gunther is here and he would like to meet Mara."

Oh no. Gunther was one of those misbehaving clients Claire needed to warn Mara about, but there was no time now.

They hustled downstairs, where Lady Eva asked Claire to sit in on Mara and Gunther's interview. Claire leaned on an armchair at the back of the "parlor"—the little room beside the lobby that was claustrophobic enough to feel like a converted closet—while Gunther sat on the couch beneath the crystal chandelier, his elbows perched on long legs that rose up awkwardly like a grasshopper's appendages.

Mara, on the other hand, had folded herself elegantly onto the paisley rug, her hair flowing down her back like a waterfall. Her first interview, her first session, while Claire was so close to her last.

Emotion swelled in Claire's chest, but she forced it down as Gunther prodded: "Tell me, Mara, where are you from? That dark hair and eyes...you look like a gypsy girl."

Mara glanced back toward Claire, and those wide eyes looked lost, somehow—not as if she were offended, but more as if she didn't understand the question. Who would help Mara find her feet after today?

No, that was a silly worry. There were plenty of women here to guide her.

Then Mara's lips tilted up into a little red smile, as if she were putting on a mask, and when she turned toward Gunther her voice was louder than it had been all morning.

"I'm from wherever you want me to be, sir."

Perhaps Mara didn't need Claire's help after all.

Claire let Mara and Gunther leave the parlor before her, and as Gunther slipped by with his deceptively wholesome smell of Ivory soap, he whispered, "I'll have to play with you next. That skirt is far too short, and you're not wearing a bra. I'm going to have to punish you for that inappropriate outfit."

Of course Claire would have to see *Gunther* on her last day. Well, she'd take whatever sessions she could get—it would be a struggle to pay rent until she found a new job. And as much as Danny wanted her to quit, her boyfriend wasn't in a hurry to get a job himself.

Something sparked inside Claire, a protest fizzing through her veins even as she told Gunther, "I'm looking forward to it, sir."

She was desperate for coffee, but something—those sparks under her skin?—made her stop at the front desk first. "Lady

Eva," she said, "you might have left the faucet on in Lady Lilith's room. It was dripping."

Lady Eva looked up, her blue eyes crinkling at the corners but appearing more amused than concerned. "Oh, I didn't use the sink, dear," she said. "It must have been the ghost."

When Mara and Gunther's session ended, Claire was ready and waiting, fortified with caffeine, her curls tamed into pigtails. She still hadn't mustered the courage to tell anyone she was leaving. Then while Gunther paid at the front desk, Mara touched Claire's hand with fingers almost as cold as the metal of the scissors. "Thanks for helping me," she whispered. "I'm glad you're here."

Claire bit her lip and tried to smile. "Only for today." The words slipped out quiet and coppery as blood. "I...I'm quitting."

Mara's eyes widened, and another wave of dizziness threatened to crash over Claire. She pushed it back and muttered, "Don't tell anyone, okay?"

Mara nodded, and Claire hurried to meet Gunther before Lady Eva could chastise her for making a client wait. Claire wasn't about to tell *Gunther* it was her last day—he would consider it a challenge to spank her harder.

As usual, Gunther grabbed a few peppermints from the bowl on the lobby's end table before making his plodding way upstairs. Trailing behind him, Claire kept her eyes on the shoulders rounding beneath his plaid button-down, a posture that seemed calculated to appear harmless, but brought an uncomfortable sizzling sensation to her veins. Just impatience, she told herself.

Once they entered Lady Lilith's room, Gunther handed her a peppermint and said, "I'd tell you to hide it in your bra, but you aren't wearing one, so you know where it goes." His voice sounded harmless, too, as Claire swallowed the acrid taste in her mouth and stuffed the peppermint into her G-string. The wrapper crunched as she tightened her hand and then released it. Now the candy rested right above her uterus, a cold lump against her bare flesh.

Gunther grinned, becoming the gleeful principal with an excuse to punish his student, as he grabbed Claire's wrist and led her over to the bondage bed. "Claire, one of the teachers saw you smoking outside the gymnasium. You know what that means: I'll have to search you for cigarettes." He spoke slowly, taunting yet patronizing, as though he were addressing a child.

"*Nooo*," Claire's whine grated against her own ears, "it's not *fair*. I wasn't *smoking*."

"Bend over." Gunther pushed her upper half down onto the bed, so one of its metal rings dug into her hipbone. "I'm going to give you the old strip search." He ran his hands over Claire's back, down her ass and legs and up again, groaning when his fingers grazed her underwear before he pulled her upright. "Untie that blouse," he said, "take off that skirt, I'll find what you're hiding."

Claire undressed and before she could finish Gunther's hands were on her again, cupping her bare breasts though it was clear she wasn't hiding any peppermints—er, "cigarettes"—between them. He forced her torso back down on the bed, his hand resting on the thin triangle of her G-string far too long before he finally cried, "*Aha!*" and reached beneath the fabric to pull out the peppermint.

Gunther knew better than to actually grab her pussy. He was one of the Briars' last old faithfuls, the clients who'd frequented the dungeon since before the current submissives had been born. Gunther could probably recite the house rules by heart—but he'd also learned how far he could push them. So he drew out those moments with his fingers creeping inside Claire's underwear, descending until she'd think she ought to say something and then pulling up again, his other hand palming her breast, his breath animal-like behind her.

Claire squeezed her eyes shut and pictured the way Danny's soft, sweet gaze would light up tonight, once she told him it was over, that she'd quit. She conjured his hands on every inch of her, tender and teasing, chasing away the last grasping echoes of this man's—

Gunther reached further down to grab the peppermint, and grazed Claire's pussy along the way. Even as she saw Danny's warm eyes in her mind, even as she imagined his welcome hands on her, her insides throbbed.

Her eyes opened and there it was again, a crimson flash in the mirror:

WHORE

Acid swept up the back of her throat.

"Look what I found." Gunther thrust the candy in her face. "Now it's time to *punish* you."

That meant a quick hand spanking before Claire faced the looming X of the St. Andrew's Cross in the corner, where she stood on tiptoes and raised her wrists so Gunther could cuff them to the wood above her head. Then came the *smack* of the leather paddle against her bare butt cheeks, each impact a flame licking up her skin. Despite herself, she let out a gasp tinged with pleasure. Even with a companion as odious as Gunther, a part of Claire loved this: the sensation that her body was no longer her own, the certainty that no matter how hard she pulled, she could not free her limbs. It brought her back to the days she had strived to become a dancer, the hours with arms reaching, legs stretched, toes pointed; the knowledge that she must not release her muscles however much they throbbed. The hope that if she worked hard enough, all that agony might allow her to fly.

Claire wasn't a dancer leaping across a stage any longer, but she still had this: the magical moment when pain transformed into something else. Anyone looking at her would see a girl bound to a cross, smacked by a paddle until her ass blazed; but inside, Claire was soaring, leaving the boundaries of her body behind.

She'd already given up dancing; would Claire have to lose this as well?

As if the thought had reached Gunther's ears, he paused and pulled back.

"Sir?" Claire asked, but the only response was the crinkling of a wrapper. The peppermint. He must have pulled it from his pocket, though Claire couldn't twist her head far enough to see, and now he was popping it in his mouth. She could hear the candy clacking against his teeth. She gritted her own teeth, and then—

Slam. The paddle wrapped around her hip with a force that pierced through her bones, right at the top of her thigh, where there was no meat to blunt the blow. She let out a high-pitched sound, a prey sound, as her floating body plummeted back to earth. The hip was the wrong place to spank—Gunther knew that. He didn't want her to soar; he only wanted her to hurt.

"This is why I'm leaving—" She whispered the words under her breath, wanting the room to witness them, sure Gunther would be too distracted to hear as—

Slam. The paddle landed in the same spot.

"Gunther," Claire gritted louder, "sir, please don't hit me there. Spank my ass all you want, but it's not safe to hit my hip."

He laughed and cracked the paddle down right on the middle of her ass cheeks. A blow so hard the walls shuddered and the mirrors shook.

Claire glanced into the oval mirror and saw the flash of Gunther's incisors as he clacked the candy between his teeth. "Now, Claire, you know this is for your own good."

The words Danny had spoken last night came back to her, his voice so much younger and more earnest than Gunther's as he'd said, "This job's no good for you—for us."

Gunther smacked her again, the force of it sweeping hot and liquid through her core. "I'm doing this because I care," her client said with theatrical concern. "You need to learn to be a good girl. I only want what's best for you."

Gunther was lying, but Danny wasn't. Danny really did want what was best for her. And what Claire wanted—

Smack. Gunther went for Claire's hip again.

What Claire wanted—

Smack.

That heat surged inside Claire, red and molten, and what Claire wanted, in this moment, was for it to overflow and splash scalding onto Gunther, so he might suffer just one ounce of the pain and powerlessness she felt.

The paddle headed for her thigh again, and she braced herself for the impact—

The leather fell weakly to the carpet. A rubbery hacking erupted from Gunther's throat. And then, silence swallowed the entire room.

"Gunther?" Claire's voice came out in a whisper that the black walls absorbed.

No response.

Claire turned her head slowly toward the mirror, her heart thudding a tempo of impending doom. Inside that droopy glass oval, a miniature version of Gunther clutched desperately at his throat.

He was choking on that stupid peppermint. Maybe he would die.

He deserved it—

No. That horrible thought brought Claire back to her senses. The heat rushed out of her, and she shivered in the sudden cold. Gunther didn't deserve to die. She had to help him. She yanked at the cuffs around her wrists but the binds held fast, two hands clasping until they threatened to snap her bones.

"Hit your stomach against the bed, Gunther," Claire called out. "Force the candy out of your throat."

In the mirror she saw Gunther stagger, and then his spine jerked as though some invisible presence had knocked into him. The peppermint flew from his mouth and landed with a wet *snap* against Claire's scalp. The walls of the room exhaled.

"*Eeew-uhh…,*" she groaned, a mixture of relief and disgust. "Gunther, get me out of these cuffs." But instead he rushed back to her and tugged on her pigtail, where the peppermint was now lodged. "No, Gunther, just untie me."

"Sorry," he sounded a lot sheepish but only a little shaken, "it's sticky. If I can get this…" He yanked harder.

"Gunther, get me out of here!"

"Okay, okay…" He abandoned her pigtail and uncuffed her as Lady Eva's voice came through the intercom: "*Excuse me, your session is ending.*" And not a moment too soon.

Claire ran to the bathroom where she stood above the sink, locating the peppermint at the top of her left pigtail, and began to tug. But the candy wouldn't budge, and with each pull a red line sliced the glass, words carving their way across the mirror.

SHE NEEDS YOU

TELL THE TRUTH

DON'T GO

Claire yanked and yanked, sure that if she could get rid of the candy dripping with Gunther's saliva, the words would vanish too. She had to get it all out, every sticky remnant, every slash of red that pulsed in time with her racing heart…

"Fine," she screamed at the mirror, not caring if Gunther heard. "Fine. I'll tell the truth. I don't want to quit…"

Before her eyes, the words trembled as if the glass might shatter.

"I'll stay."

The lipstick blurred into nothing and the peppermint plunged into her palm.

Claire leaned over the sink, her chest heaving as if she'd spun and spun across a dance floor, as if she were still spinning and she couldn't stop. And then she heard it:

The faucet was *drip, drip, dripping* again. A message meant for Claire.

A message she needed to hear, in a language she feared she'd never understand.

TWO: RUBY

The new girl wouldn't stop playing with that peppermint wrapper. The dark-haired submissive had been perched on the edge of the couch, watching her reflection in the mirror behind the vanity table full of perfume bottles, old-fashioned glass candy jars repurposed to hold Q-tips and bobby pins, and makeup bags that had long since lost their owners, since she'd tiptoed into the dressing room nearly an hour ago. The girl kept worrying the plastic between her fingers, and the crunching sound was about to drive Ruby mad.

"Maybe you should get another one," Ruby finally said, as she touched up her crimson lipstick. She was breaking her rule of never speaking to a new girl—if she did that, she might be expected to remember their names or explain something to one of them—but she couldn't take it anymore.

It took the girl a moment to react, as if her thoughts were somewhere else. Her corset was laced wrong—the ribbon had skipped two or three eyelets entirely. "Another what?" she finally asked, tilting her head toward Ruby. She was a waifish wisp of a thing, and she spoke so quietly Ruby could barely hear her over Nadia and Alice gossiping in the corner.

"Peppermint," Ruby said. "You must have finished that one."

The girl tilted her head further, as though she were trying to look under Ruby's chin, and Ruby whirled away in irritation. After living alone for most of her adult life, Ruby had enough trouble dealing with coworkers who *knew* dungeon protocol. As for the new girls—well, there should be a special room where they had to stay until they'd proven themselves.

Nadia looked up as Ruby's heels clicked along the tile flooring, echoing with disapproval. Then she glanced at the girl on the couch and said, "Hey, you sessioned with Gunther this morning, didn't you? Sorry, that's not a great first session."

Ruby's burgundy-nailed hand stilled on the doorknob. *Gunther.* Her lips curled, and she wished for her own peppermint to soothe the bitter taste in her throat. Ruby had never had the dubious pleasure of sessioning with Gunther—he only liked to spank, not be spanked, and Ruby had never been a submissive at the Briars—but she had overheard enough to know he deserved a few whacks from the paddle himself.

"Yes." The girl was mumbling again, but at least she'd stopped fussing with the wrapper. "He spanked a little hard, but it wasn't too bad."

"He didn't bruise you, did he?" Tucking a stray blonde lock behind one ear, Nadia rose from the table in the corner and sat beside the new girl on the couch. And then jumped up again, leaving behind a scattering of pink sequins, pulling something from between the cushions. "Did you drop this, honey?"

The new sub regarded the hundred-dollar bill in Nadia's hand with the same dazed disinterest as she had the candy wrapper. "Oh," she whispered, "he gave that to me. I'm not sure why."

Could this girl really be *that* naïve?

"That's your tip, sweetie. And you can't leave money out, someone will take it." Nadia sat down for real this time as she handed the hundred to the girl. "I'm sorry," she went on, "we should have introduced ourselves earlier, but Alice and I were so busy with The Book—"

She gestured to the spiral notebook that held a permanent place on the corner table. The Book, where ladies wrote details they thought their coworkers should know. "Watch out for Gunther—he hits the side of your hip on purpose," for instance. Or "The bed in the Enclave has a wonky leg—needs replacing, but should we upset Lady Eva???"

"Anyway," Nadia went on, "I'm Nadia, that's Alice in the corner, and Miss Grouch over by the door is Ruby."

Ruby rolled her eyes and gave a few finger flutters. "That's *Mistress* Ruby," she said. She didn't mind if Nadia called her by her first name, but the new girl should know her title. Ruby turned toward the others—her session wasn't for another ten minutes, and she hadn't had a reason to leave the dressing room anyway.

It took the girl a minute to realize she should respond. Her big, dark eyes made her appear overwhelmed, like a doe caught in headlights—a look that should get her a lot of clients, considering the creeps who went after new submissives around here. Finally she said, "I'm La—" Her forehead creased. "I mean, Mara."

"It's hard to remember your dungeon name at first, isn't it?" Alice stood and strolled to the far side of the couch in her Lucite heels. "But watch out—work here too long and you'll forget your real one!" She rooted around in the pocket of a jacket slung over the edge of the sofa and pulled out a pack of cigarettes. With her angled, flapper-style bob, Alice looked like she should have a cigarette permanently wedged between two fingers, a plume of smoke perpetually floating from her lips— and most of the time, she did.

"So Gunther didn't hurt you?" Nadia persisted. She lifted one of her glowy spray-tanned hands like she wanted to reach for the new girl—Mara—but lowered it again.

"No. He just kept asking me where I was from, and whether schoolgirls got...*corporal punishment* in Russia." Her voice stayed quiet and slow, too, as if it took effort to get each word out, and she wasn't quite sure what they meant. It made Ruby even more impatient; it made her want to shake the girl until she woke up.

"God, he's such a creep," Alice said. "All these guys want innocent little girls. If I had enough hair for pigtails and I'd been willing to play the Asian schoolgirl or Sailor Moon, I'd have booked twice as many sessions as a sub." She shook her head so the fringe of her black bob danced around her face. "I'm going outside for a smoke."

When Alice opened the back door, a gust of unusually cold air swirled in from the gazebo, and Ruby thought of the few straggling roses she'd seen along the gables when she arrived. They'd probably be blown away by the time she left this evening.

Mara's slim shoulders trembled as the door closed, as if she too had felt the cold. "I guess Gunther thought I was Russian, but I'm not really sure where I'm from. My parents weren't in my life, and—I have a hard time remembering... The clients want to know, though?"

"Some of them." Nadia narrowed her eyes on Mara. "You can definitely pass for Slavic, maybe Czech or Romanian. I'm Ukrainian, and some of the guys love it. Others just want to think of me as their basic California blonde, the girl next door." She shrugged. "Whatever they want us to be, right? We're the ones walking away with their money."

That was the truth. Although in Ruby's case, with her not-particularly-remarkable face behind the red lipstick and cat-winged eyeliner, the only thing men asked about was her hair. It looked crimson in some lights, so dark it was nearly black in others, and Ruby was happy to become the redheaded wild woman or the raven-haired seductress depending on her client's desires. So long as she got to punish him, of course.

Mara, though, really did look otherworldly. So slender and pale in her white lace that your eye slipped right over her, unable to see her clearly, to pin her down. She could have come from everywhere and nowhere all at once, Ruby thought, and then wondered why that turn of phrase would have occurred to her. She was no poet. Not with words, at least.

And though Mara had at last abandoned that candy wrapper, Ruby still felt on edge, her fingers itching to wrap around the handle of a riding crop. She glanced at her phone where it lay on the edge of the sofa; only five minutes until her appointment now.

She looked herself over in the mirror one last time, tightening the laces of her black corset, etching out her small waist and becoming a sharp-angled hourglass. Then she headed to the hall where paddles and floggers, wrist and ankle cuffs hung from hooks, and considered what she was in the mood for today. She picked up a cane that lay on a shelf, ran a finger across the wiry surface that could cut right into a man's flesh, if you knew how to use it.

An unpleasant voice came from the front desk. "Tell me, Lady Eva, are any more young ladies looking for a *spanking* today?" She could almost hear Gunther salivating as he spoke, though his tone had a rasp to it, as if he'd lost his voice. Then a presence slipped by her: Claire, hustling toward the dressing room, one half of her curls in a pigtail and the other loose and wild. Ruby had a sudden desire to tug the remaining hair tie free—until Claire looked up at her, her blue eyes half-haunted. Ruby almost asked what was wrong, but swallowed the words. Someone like Nadia would handle this better.

Claire looked away, muttered, "Excuse me, Mistress Ruby," and disappeared into the dressing room, leaving a hint of perfume behind her. Something sweet and floral—cherry blossoms, maybe? Too soft for a girl who'd spent the past hour getting her ass beaten black and blue by Gunther.

Ruby used up a few minutes picking out a flogger with stiff leather strands and a snappy leather paddle, until she heard Gunther again from the lobby: "Well, can I make another appointment with Mara for this weekend? *Two* hours this time." His tone dripped with lust—for violence as much as flesh, Ruby was sure. How would any girl, and especially one as delicate as Mara, survive more than an hour with that man? And Gunther never made appointments—he showed up and took whoever he could get. But Ruby didn't have time to consider the anomaly, because as Gunther shuffled out the front door, another man entered, shorter than Gunther but with a sprightlier step and a more open, confident set to his shoulders. A silver fox, with graying scruff accentuating a sharp jawline.

"I'm Jack," he said as he reached the front desk, tucking his thumbs into jeans pockets below the folds of a V-neck sweater that looked to be cashmere. "I have an appointment with Ruby?" He peered past Lady Eva to where Ruby stood between the lobby and the hallway beyond it, a riding crop in her hand, and he flashed a white-toothed grin. His charm wouldn't work on Ruby, though. He wasn't her type; no man was.

"Shall we talk in the parlor first?" Keeping her expression stern rather than matching his smile, Ruby used the riding crop to invite Jack into the interview room. He sat casually on the sofa, one leather loafer on his opposite knee, as Ruby perched on a footstool and asked what he was looking for. "I'm more of a dominant," Jack said, "but as I get older, I find myself wanting to...test my boundaries, so to speak. See what it feels like from the other side. So I booked a session with a mistress." His foot jiggled with what seemed more anticipation than nerves. "I'll need you to go easy on me this first time around, though." He was still grinning, self-assured—clearly not intending to surrender any real control. "I'd prefer it if you didn't leave any marks."

So none of the cruel toys she'd chosen would work for this session. Damn it. She'd bring them anyway, just in case.

Once Jack had paid for the hour-long session at the front desk—two hundred dollars, a hundred for the house and a hundred for Ruby, and he pulled the bills from his wallet as if they were pennies he'd found on the street—Lady Eva shot Ruby a pointed look. "Now, Mistress Ruby," she said, "don't even think about scaring off our charming guest here." She smiled at Jack as if it were all a joke, but Ruby knew what it really was: a warning, and one Ruby hadn't always heeded before. New clients were hard to come by these days, and Lady Eva would never forgive Ruby if she chased away one who appeared to have money to spare. Ruby tried to shift the cane behind the other, kinder implements she'd chosen, but she was sure her boss's shrewd eyes had already spotted it. "You can have Lady Lilith's room," Lady Eva went on. "Alice's client already requested the Enclave."

Ruby's hand tightened around the cane handle. As a rational adult, Ruby told herself that she didn't believe in ghosts, but she could never shake the superstition that had been ingrained in her since childhood. Strange, that her family had been so sure of the existence of evil spirits as well as good ones. She supposed no one could strive for purity and righteousness without believing the opposite side—the ghostly and the demonic—was just as powerful.

Ruby would never admit to anyone that even the idea of a ghost as benign as Lady Lilith's unsettled her, just a little. Still, she preferred to session in the Enclave next door, where the ghost's messages could only reach her secondhand, like words garbled after an old-fashioned game of telephone. But today, she had no choice.

Once she'd guided her client up the exterior staircase, Ruby arranged the toys in an intimidating row on the edge of the bondage bed while Jack wandered the room, appearing perfectly at ease with his thumbs tucked into his pockets. "In twenty years," he said with a chuckle, "this place hasn't changed much at all."

Ruby paused with her palm above a flogger. "You've been here before?"

He flashed those teeth again. "Oh, so long ago, it hardly seemed relevant. Up here, though..." He reached out and ran a hand over the St. Andrew's Cross, jangling one of its metal rings. "It's all coming back to me."

Ruby wasn't sure how to feel about this revelation, but the solution was obvious: take back the balance of power. "Well, you haven't played with Mistress Ruby before," she told him. "This time is going to be different. Take off your clothes."

Once Jack had revealed his pale skin interrupted only by a pair of boxers, his form impressively maintained but still soft and fleshy and vulnerable, Ruby felt much better. She sat in the throne-like chair at one end of the room and had Jack get over her lap so she could spank him, and they could both see his compromised position in the long mirror opposite. "You know," Jack began, "I wish I could say I didn't deserve to be here..." Another strike to his buttocks, and he paused to catch his breath. "But I've done my fair share of bad deeds in my life. I can't claim I'm not in need of punishment."

His tone was light, flirtatious; he was egging her on. "How intriguing," Ruby spanked harder, "tell me, what sorts of crimes are you guilty of?"

"Well..." She couldn't see his eyes, but Ruby pictured them glinting. "...I might have a bit of an...*unwholesome* appreciation for the female form. When I saw you standing behind the front desk, for instance, I couldn't help imagining how you look under that corset."

Ruby laughed and slapped his rear end again. "Oh, Jack, I can tell you're the kind of man who's used to getting what he wants. You saw submissives when you came here before, didn't you? It doesn't work like that with a mistress."

"Oh really?" Jack stood and turned to face her, and yes, those light-blue eyes that had likely charmed more than a few women were mischievous and teasing. Ruby would never understand what straight women saw in this sort of man. "I'm sure I can get you to show me how hard your nipples are by the end of the session."

"That's it," Ruby rose and tugged his boxers off before he had time to protest, "you're in trouble now. Get on the bondage bed. Lie on your stomach. Not another word out of you." Secretly, she hoped he would say something even more inappropriate—the more reasons he gave her, the more she could punish him. This might not be one of her more serious sessions, but she was still enjoying it.

As Jack climbed onto the bed topped with a leopard-spotted blanket, Ruby grabbed paddles and riding crops and floggers. She introduced them to her client one by one, alternating lively flicks of the riding crop between his thighs with swats to his bare butt cheeks. Letting the softest flogger linger lovingly across his back, then surprising him with a whack from a thick paddle. Jack kept up the commentary for a while—"Are your tits as firm as that paddle?" earned him an extra blow—but eventually, he began to fall under the spell Ruby was weaving. She had warmed him up perfectly, priming his body to accept more pain, varying the sensations between softness and heaviness, punishment and reprieve, until he could barely discern them. His words faded to mumbles and exhalations; his limbs softened into the blanket beneath him, as Ruby's own limbs awoke and made the implements dance in her hands.

Ruby might not be a poet with words, but *this*—this ability to wield power, to enrapture another being—this was her poetry. And as she sensed Jack surrendering to her, she felt, as she only did when her hands held weapons, at peace for the moment.

She paused to choose a new implement, and Jack shifted his head to glance up at her. "What's that under your chin?" he asked.

Ruby froze.

"It looks like a little scar," he said, his voice as carefree as when he'd been speculating about her nipples. And Ruby's peaceful mood evaporated into a sudden storm of anger, as much at herself for believing she'd lulled him into a stupor, as at the man's thoughtless comment.

"It's none of your concern," she said, careful to keep her voice steady, "and *you* need to address your mistress properly. You call me Mistress Ruby"—she reached for another paddle, but her fingers, of their own volition, wrapped around the cane instead—"and when I'm punishing you, you ask if you may speak."

He laughed. "You're a feisty one, aren't you, with those red streaks in your hair? So tell me, did you fall off your bike when you were a kid? Slice your neck against something sharp?"

In a truly poetic world, Ruby's scar would start to throb, now, telling her to hit this impertinent man harder. But in truth, she never felt pain along that line between her throat and her chin, the one you could only see if you were looking up at it from below. She never felt any sensation there at all.

"No," Jack went on, propping himself up on his elbows, his actions echoed in the mirror so that Ruby watched two versions of him mocking her, "it looks too recent to be something from childhood." The Jack in the mirror grinned with teeth, wolflike, his eyes glowing red. Ruby shook her head and the two images matched again, Jack's gaze a clear, brilliant blue as he went on: "It was sex, right? You were lying on your stomach—no, on all fours, with your neck jutting over the headboard, and—"

Ruby lifted the cane and snapped it across Jack's bare ass cheeks, once, twice, three times, each strike slicing the air with a *whoosh* that erased all traces of joking or laughter. Jack's forearms slipped forward across the bed, a marionette with his strings tugged, until he lay flat and she could no longer see his eyes. He breathed out.

Ruby struck once more, lower, in the sensitive spot between his ass and the top of his thighs, and waited for him to use his safe word. He gave another loud exhale, but made no further sound.

"Well," she traced the edge of the cane along his legs, trying to breathe deeply, to calm the pulsing of her heart, "are you ready to apologize now?"

Muffled against the bed, she heard a chuckle. "No."

Ruby caught sight of herself in the mirror. The light from the electric candelabras fell in stripes across her black-clothed form. Her eyes glowed green. At the edge of her vision, something pulsed traffic-light red in the darkest corner of the room. No, not pulsed, wavered—a handful of flower petals, drifting back and forth.

Who would bring flowers up here? She peered into the darkness and remembered: Lady Eva's plastic-stemmed roses guarding the attic. The attic where the ghost lurked.

Ruby hated this room. This was the room where submissive girls sessioned, where sadistic clients brandished floggers they had no idea how to use. Where men with no conscience, like Gunther, punished girls like Claire, who had probably never done anything worth punishing in her entire life. There would always be girls like Claire, taking beating after beating, some with masochistic glee and others coming closer to tears with each impact; there would always be men like Gunther, taking the trust those girls placed in them and battering it with each blow.

Heat crimson as those roses rushed through Ruby's veins, and she told herself to step back, take a breath, cool her blood. A good domme never let her own emotions bleed into her work—and Ruby wanted nothing more than to be a good domme.

Ruby told herself to stop; but in the mirror, she watched her hand squeeze tight around the cane and raise it high. Then she struck.

Ruby brought the cane down on Jack's rear end, again and again, driving the implement deeper into the flesh each time. The second Jack spoke his safe word, or made any noise at all, she would stop. He was a man, a rich, soft-bodied man who was used to getting his way. He wouldn't allow her to split him open. She had one, maybe two more strokes—

Out of the corner of Ruby's eye, the roses pulsed like warning lights. Jack still didn't speak or move; the two of them hung in one distended moment, the limbo between a blow and the pain that would inevitably come. That second when the nerve signals hadn't made it to the brain yet, and reality was water rather than stone.

The air hummed, dull sirens droning against Ruby's ears, so if Jack did cry out she might not have heard. The black walls and the zebra-striped floor twisted and throbbed, her vision warping until the only straight line was that cane in her hand going up and down, up and down. A desire rose red from her heart, a determination to show this man, with his roguish laugh and his blue eyes and his charm, a universal truth: that pain could break anyone.

For a moment that stretched on and on, Ruby caned Jack to the rhythm of that desire beating through her heart. Then a sudden pressure fell onto her shoulders, an invisible weight that shocked her into lowering her arm. The room righted itself around her, and she stopped to gasp for breath—

And couldn't breathe at all.

What had she done? Jack's backside was a mess of welts and blood, a horrifying, haphazard scrawl, lines swerving in all directions like some witch's spell carved into the earth. How could Ruby have created this? She always caned in straight, neat lines, train tracks that never crossed. And—

—oh God—

Jack had said no marks.

Lady Eva would fire her if she saw this. Ruby would lose more than a job; she'd lose the identity she'd worked so hard for. Jack could sue the dungeon, maybe, and considering they were barely turning a profit these days, that would be the Briars' death knell...

Ruby was going to be sick. The inside of her mouth tasted thick and coppery, like the blood she saw before her—saw it twice, since it was reflected in the mirror.

Jack propped himself up again, flipping nimbly over so he was sitting on his ass, as Ruby wondered at how badly it must sting. He grinned, the echo of red blood in his blue eyes. "Why did you stop?" he asked, his voice buoyant as a feather. "I know I said no marks, but I thought a caning was supposed to be painful. The cane is the cruelest of implements, isn't it? The *ne plus ultra* of S&M?"

Ruby was too befuddled to let the pretention of his little speech bother her. "I..."

"Excuse me," Lady Eva's voice intruded over the intercom, far too serene, "your session has ended."

"Thank you," Ruby managed to grit out, though most of her attention was on the grip of her fingers around the cane. If she didn't focus, she would drop it, and maybe fall to the floor herself.

Jack hopped off the bed, landing gracefully on his feet. "Well, that was a fun experiment...but I have to admit I still prefer to be on the other side of things. The one holding the implements." He walked past her toward his abandoned clothing, flashing the perfectly white moon of his backside. Ruby blinked and looked again, but still: no marks.

This time, the cane really did fall from her hands.

As Jack searched for his boxers, then his jeans, Ruby's mind worked. She had hit him, hard, ten or fifteen times. She was certain of that. Each flick of her wrist, each swing of her arm echoed through her bones. She couldn't have imagined it all.

But had she imagined the blood? Could such a soft, wealthy man have skin too tough to break? No, that was impossible. None of this made sense. Those welts she'd seen on Jack's backside loomed before her eyes again, superimposing themselves over the mirrors and the walls.

It was this haunted room—the shadows creeping inside her, twisting her mind. Suddenly Ruby was the child she'd been twenty years ago, that little girl who couldn't stop thinking about ghosts and demons and dark mysteries even as she knew they were wrong, wrong, wrong. Through the haze of her thoughts, she realized Jack was speaking:

"...prefer playing with a submissive. But I may have to session with you one more time, just to see if I can charm you out of your corset."

He expected some clever retort—that future session depended on it—but she couldn't get the words past her clogged throat.

She had to start cleaning the room, but instead Ruby simply stood there, watching Jack dress until his flesh was concealed, searching for one tiny speck of red, one sign that the events of the past hour hadn't occurred entirely in her head. But no matter how closely she looked, all she saw was white.

Looking back, it seems so obvious, the way those first seeds were planted on the morning Mara arrived. In the days that followed, The Book birthed notes like fragile, creeping sprouts, full of equivocations and doubts:

"I think I saw..."

"A weird feeling..."

"Probably imagined it..."

Claire was not the only lady among us who wrote about a strange heat running through her veins, a new irritation with old clients and their familiar tricks, a rising frustration that, for a moment or two, seemed impossible to hold back.

But it was easy for us all to discount an eerie sensation or two, in a place so shadowy, where dust clung to the old furniture no matter how often it was scrubbed. The type of place that played tricks on us, brought us visions that couldn't possibly be true. No, none of us paid enough attention to those first hints of something green and grasping, with a current of crimson beneath the surface, waiting to bloom.

We never imagined all that promise could become something tangible and dangerous and real—

For what sort of seedling could grow in the dark?

THREE: CLAIRE

Danny had *way* too many tie-dyed surfer-boy hoodies, and all of them were at least two sizes too big. They lived too far from the beach for that. And why had he dumped them in the corner of the closet where she kept her extra dungeon outfits? The ones she only had to dig out for special requests, like the email she'd just gotten from Lady Eva—

Because she hadn't quit. That message she'd seen in the mirror—*SHE NEEDS YOU*—had wriggled its way inside her, silencing her every time she imagined voicing the words.

Then there was that other message: *TELL THE TRUTH.* When she'd stood screaming at the dungeon mirror, Claire had been sure of one truth: that she wanted to stay. But then she came home and fell asleep with Danny's warm arms wrapped around her, and the truth changed. She had to quit, had to hold on to what she had with Danny; she just needed one more day to understand what had happened in Lady Lilith's room first. One good day, so she wouldn't leave with dripping faucets and smeared lipstick haunting her thoughts.

"Claire?" She heard Danny's voice and the sound of the apartment door shutting behind him. Band rehearsal must be over.

"In here," she called, as—*aha!*—she spotted the slit of a black pencil skirt protruding from the bag of costumes. Underneath it was the button-down in desperate need of an iron. Well, she'd kill two birds with one stone: this "sexy secretary" costume could become her interview outfit and, perhaps, an *actual* secretary's attire.

Claire held up the ensemble, trying to picture herself as a receptionist at a law firm or hair salon—well, not a hair salon, her crazy curls would scare the customers. But something like that. She wouldn't go back to retail, which she'd done for a few months, after she'd finally accepted she'd never make it as a dancer. After she'd walked out of the Hollywood Dancers' Institute on the spot, halfway through class, before it was her turn to perform the *grand jeté* combination across the floor.

The memory made her legs ache, memory of all that hard work and desire that had filled her muscles for so long, until she couldn't bear to think about it anymore; it made her legs ache more than the hours and hours of standing at Wasteland that had followed, selling overpriced vintage T-shirts to teenagers and tourists on Melrose Avenue. Wondering if this was all she had left to look forward to.

Eventually, she had done what so many young women do, when they see the tiny paycheck with the taxes taken out, their lives measured out in fifteen-minute breaks and half-hour lunches and one-and-a-half-pay overtime: She answered an ad on Craigslist. And then another. And another. She met men in sketchy motels, and a few times in their apartments, though she knew that was dangerous. She thought about looking for an agency, but worried about having her picture on some website, about getting arrested; she thought about auditioning at a strip club, but if she was no ballerina, she was no pole dancer either.

And then, like an unexpected gift, she'd seen the ad for the Briars at the back of the *LA Weekly*. A commercial dungeon, a place where she wouldn't be expected to have sex, or even take her underwear off; a place where she simply got spanked and tied up in a safe space and, most of the time, enjoyed it. She'd chosen her new name, Claire, and started to use it outside the dungeon too, and tried her best to forget that she'd once been a dreaming, dancing girl named Anna. To forget everything about the person she'd been before. And a few months after she'd found the Briars, she'd found Danny, and her life had begun to feel like a new sort of dream.

But dreams were always in danger of becoming nightmares.

Or, maybe worse, you might have to wake up and face the real world.

"Babe?" Danny's big hands with those guitar-player callouses slid around her waist, under her tank top. One touch, and all the stress of the past few days started to slip away beneath his fingers.

He flipped her around to face him, and she let the wrinkled shirt drop. Danny's brown eyes peered into her, so soft and smooth he appeared lost in his own dream-state, that place he went when he worked on his music. It was the same warm gaze he'd wrapped her up in when they'd first met, after he'd played an acoustic set at the Roxy. Claire wasn't a clubgoer, but she was glad some of her old classmates from the Dancers' Institute had coaxed her out. She hadn't bothered to stay in touch with the classmates after that—but she had definitely stayed in touch with Danny.

"What are you looking for?" he asked.

"Uh...job interview outfits." Wanting to change the subject, she added, "Why do you have all these hoodies back here?"

"Ricky gave some to me when he moved," Danny said. "He didn't have space in his new place."

That made sense—Ricky was one of Danny's stoner bandmates who actually did surf at Venice Beach every day, and his "new place" was probably, like most of his former places, someone's couch.

"Got an interview lined up already, huh?" Danny said. "You *are* industrious." His hands inched beneath her tank top as he added, "But we can take some time to celebrate too." His lips ghosted against hers until she could taste the sweet echo of marijuana, then he pulled back with a self-satisfied grin. "A new start for us, right?"

Danny's fingers trailed over her skin and sparks rose, prickling until she wanted to jerk away. If it was a new start for both of them, why was *she* the one who had to change?

But then Danny's palms rested against her sides, just warm enough to assure her she was safe in his arms. His lips pressed against hers, his tongue slipped inside her mouth, and she tumbled into Danny's world where everything was smooth and supple, like a song crooned under a spotlight, and the practicalities of life held no urgency. His arms snaked around her, landing in the notch of her waist where they fit perfectly, and she followed his lead and wrapped her legs around his hips.

Danny carried her into the bedroom without breaking the kiss, like a scene from a movie. Claire felt like she was floating, even as he lowered her onto the bed with its pilling sheets she needed to replace, as soon as she had the money. That rough fabric didn't matter when he pulled off her top and leaned over her, not bothering to brush back the shaggy brown hair that fell into his eyes; all his attention was on her, adoration in every touch of his fingers. No other man had made her feel that way. She would do anything to hold on to it.

Claire arched off the bed to return the kiss more deeply. Minutes melted away; the sun sank into the horizon outside the closed blinds. On the seedier side of Hollywood, where a drunk might mistake the tiny patch of grass out front for his toilet, they had to keep the blinds shut all the time. Keep themselves closed in, tucked away in their own little world.

Danny reached over to the bedside table and switched on the lamp, bathing the room in soft light. He teased his fingers around the waistband of Claire's sweatpants, tickling a little, making her giggle. Flipped her onto her stomach and gave a light swat to her ass. She wanted him to pull the pants down, and her underwear, and bury himself inside her, but something penetrated through the haze. Words scrawled on a mirror in lipstick red as blood.

Show me what a whore you are.

Suddenly, she knew what would happen when Danny pulled her pants down, but it was too late. She felt cold air against her bare skin, the absence of Danny's touch.

"Shit, Claire, what the fuck?"

At least he sounded more worried than angry. "It's just a few bruises, Danny."

"No, Claire, this is— Someone went to *town* on your ass. The whole thing is purple."

She should have warned him. But last evening when she'd arrived home from the dungeon, the bruises had only been faint blue ghosts, just coming to life; and this morning she'd showered and dressed before Danny awoke.

She breathed out as his hand reached for her again. But his touch was tentative, now, just the tips of his fingers tracing her backside. As if he had suddenly become aware that she didn't belong to him. "Jesus Christ, Claire, you let some creep do this to you on your *last day*? Thank god you're out of there."

That crackle of heat raced across her flesh again, so quick she might have imagined it. She should be happy he cared about her, she should be sinking further into their shared dream—

"You might as well have still been escorting," he went on, his voice walking the line between dismay and disgust. And then, almost smugly, "That place is so sleazy. It was no good for you."

The sparks were back, dancing into her veins. What did *Danny* know about what was good for her? Shouldn't that be up to her? And before Claire could stop herself, she flung the words out:

"The Briars is not sleazy. And I didn't quit."

Danny jolted, as if a few of those sparks had landed on him. "*What?*"

"*Yet*," she added quickly, the fire fading, already regretting her words, "I didn't quit *yet*. I just—" She turned onto her back to face him again. "—it was the weirdest day ever. There was this energy in the room, like...like it was *angry*, and my client almost choked on a peppermint and—" She tripped over herself in the rush to explain. "There wasn't a good time to tell my boss, and I wanted to come back one more time and make sure everything's okay and—"

"You don't owe them anything!" Danny's eyes narrowed as she looked up at him. "Damn it, Claire, it seems like you care more about the dungeon than you do about us!"

Claire watched Danny closing himself off, crossing his arms, and the last embers on her skin fizzled out. Her voice became a whine as she mumbled, "You didn't mind the dungeon when we met."

Danny tugged at the collar of his Led Zeppelin T-shirt, as though the fabric constricted his throat. "I just don't get why you want to stay so much."

Claire sat up, reaching for her tank top and pulling it back on. "For one thing, all my friends work there. Besides, the business isn't doing so well—financially, I mean. I'm worried, and Lady Eva can be a pain, but she'd be so devastated if we had to close—"

Danny leveled those now painfully dark eyes on her. "Again, what does that matter to you?"

Claire clutched the worn fabric of the sheets in her hand, wishing it was Danny's flesh, that she could hold tight to him and somehow make him understand. "It matters because the dungeon is...it's like my home."

"This—*us*—should be your home," Danny said in a voice that hurt more for how quiet it was. He turned and walked out of the room, and a moment later Claire heard the accusatory clink of bottles in the kitchen. She sat there, unable to move, wondering if he'd come back, and trying to remember where she had stashed the ironing board.

Danny did come back a few minutes later, lingering in the bedroom doorway and chugging his half-finished beer. His lips remained parted as he lowered the bottle, as if he wanted to offer some apology but couldn't quite get it out. And Claire, sitting straight and rigid on the bed, her own words trapped in her throat, could only wonder: *What happened?*

When she'd first met Danny, he'd insisted he didn't mind the dungeon, or even the former escorting, though he was glad she'd found a safer place to work. He'd laughed at her stories of clients who called the Briars asking which of the girls were "acting up" and needed to be "taught a lesson."

"As long as I'm the only one spanking you in bed at night," he'd said with a gleam in his eyes. And now, less than a year later, he demanded she quit?

The lipstick words scrolled across the screen of her mind: *Show me what a whore you are.*

Somehow, even in those early days when she and Danny spent all their time off in bed together, when Claire told stories of being spanked and tied up at work, and Danny recreated them with more exciting endings, she'd known not to mention certain things. Gunther's hands creeping inside her panties, for instance. Kenny, who insisted on bringing his own ropes—and always snuck a vibrator in with them. The men who bent down and bit her nipples or slobbered along her collarbone before she could stop them.

But men would be men. They were as badly behaved in dance studios and in dark alleys as they were at the dungeon. There was no escaping it. Still, Claire wished she could have that softer, sweeter Danny back, for more than a few moments.

"Come back to bed," she told him, though she knew it was too late. The last hints of sunshine had faded beyond the blinds, and with the light had gone their yearning for each other. At least for tonight. "Nah," Danny said, lifting the now-empty beer bottle, "I've got to get some more of this. We're all out."

The next morning, Claire stood before the Briars' dressing-room mirror, trying vainly to smooth the wrinkles from her button-up shirt. She'd never found the ironing board. It shouldn't matter if she displeased Lady Eva on her last day—for real, this time—but for some reason, Claire suspected her boss's long-suffering sigh would hurt more this morning.

On the other hand, maybe Lady Eva would be so distracted by Mara that she wouldn't even notice Claire. Today Mara wore a white slip with a rip in the hem and lace-up black boots, as if she had fallen back in time twenty years and was ready to join some '90s grunge band. Her limbs were so thin, her veins so blue they reminded Claire of another term from that decade: heroin chic. Mara seemed too innocent to be a drug addict, though, as she stood beside Claire and grabbed one lipstick after another from the vanity table, unscrewing each cap and regarding the makeup with confused wonder. She looked like a little girl who'd snuck into her mother's bedroom and was planning some forbidden art project in shades of brick and rose, burgundy and scarlet.

"I wouldn't use that," Ruby said from Mara's other side, peering down on the girl's wide-eyed reflection. "It's touched more lips than you'd care to imagine."

Claire couldn't quite put her finger on what made Mara seem...*off*, somehow. But if even Ruby, who couldn't be bothered to look twice at the new girls, felt the need to comment—well, there had to be something.

Mara nodded and, without speaking, put the lipstick down next to a small pair of beauty scissors. Maybe Claire imagined it, but the girl appeared to jerk her hand away from the metal, the way she had the day before.

As Claire straightened her pencil skirt, she caught Gabriella's brown eyes in the mirror—she was watching Mara too. Gabriella leaned in toward Alice on the couch, and Claire heard "just shy" and "doesn't know how to dress." Claire turned to Mara and said loudly, "I have an extra lip gloss you can use if you want. It's pink, not red, but—"

Mara looked straight at Claire, then; the girl's lips already blazed red against the pallor of her skin. She didn't need lipstick at all. Those lips parted, and Claire was sure Mara would ask why she was here, after she'd said she was quitting—

Claire gave a quick, desperate shake of her head, and Mara pressed her mouth closed as if she understood.

Before Claire could decide what to do next, Nadia appeared at the dressing-room door and said, "Claire, your appointment's here." Claire looked herself over one more time in the mirror and added a few bobby pins from the table to her secretary bun. After a twirl to ensure her shirt was, if wrinkled, at least a pristine white, she headed out front.

Claire entered the parlor to find a familiar black-bearded man who had to stoop to keep from colliding with the chandelier. Relief and regret wound together inside her—

She would get to say goodbye.

She would *have* to say goodbye.

"Yarik!" Claire moved forward to hug him. She breathed in his warm, spicy smell, and as he broke the embrace, he showed Claire what he was holding: a leather paddle that was smooth on one side but, when he flipped it over, revealed intricate cut-outs of flowers and vines. "It's beautiful," Claire said. "A souvenir from your latest trip?"

Yarik nodded. "I thought the dungeon could use something new."

"Lady Eva will love it." As long as she didn't realize the clients were aware of how worn-out some of their paddles had become. Last time she and Yarik played, a handle almost broke off in his hand—and he didn't even hit very hard.

As Yarik paid at the front desk, Lady Eva told him, "Thank you for the beautiful gift, Yaroslav."

Claire was sure that, unlike the million and one clients who claimed to be named "John," Yarik wasn't lying about his name. "If I'm going to use a nickname with you, Claire," he had once told her in his thick Russian accent, "it should really be Slava. Now that I'm a grown-up, only my old friends can call me Yarik. But is it too strange for me to consider you an old friend?"

They'd known each other for nearly a year, and Yarik was one of Claire's friendliest clients—so no, she'd assured him, it wasn't strange at all.

They headed up the stairs to Lady Lilith's room—Yarik's usual request, from the first time they'd played together, and she hoped his sturdy presence would scare off any sinister intrusions. "Is the paddle from Russia?" she asked, and Yarik nodded. After his first long absence from the dungeon, Yarik had explained that as a Russian history professor, he often returned to his homeland for research purposes. Claire pictured him wandering amidst the snow-swept spires of Moscow and the wilderness of Siberia, dressed in a fur coat and hat and mittens rather than the suit he always wore at the dungeon, searching for treasures to bring back with him to California. A wildly inaccurate image, she was sure.

As a child, she had read stories of collectors and wanderers and explorers, and she'd imagined the father she'd never known was one of them, and that one day he would return to her bearing wonders. He never had, but now she had Yarik and his tales of far-off places.

"So," she said as they entered, "you wanted me to wear a secretary outfit, huh? What's that about?"

"I thought we could do a..." He twirled his finger in the air like he was either searching for the word, or about to perform a magic trick. "A roleplay."

That was new. But then Yarik had tried almost every-thing—bondage, spanking, tickling—at least once. Claire still wasn't sure what he was *actually* into.

As soon as Claire had placed the paddle down on the bed, Yarik launched into a precise speech: "Claire, look at all those wrinkles in your shirt. And the run in your stockings. Is this an appropriate way to dress for work?"

Claire crossed her arms. "You rehearsed that, Yarik. How did you know my shirt would be wrinkled?"

Yarik's eyes sparked. "Lucky guess. Now, don't distract me." He placed both hands on his hips and peered into every corner of the room, his gaze lingering on the roses in their vase, as if he were buying himself time to remember his next line. "My biggest investor is arriving in one hour, and you..." He frowned and drew closer, peering at the back of her neck. "You have lipstick *all over* the back of your collar."

"I..." Claire tried to think of a clever response, but she couldn't keep her mind on the roleplay. She had to tell Yarik she was quitting, and her vocal cords were constricting again. "I..."

She looked into Yarik's kind, crinkled eyes, and he reached out to straighten her shirt. "I have to say," he said, "adding a real stain was a nice touch."

Yarik had dropped his hands, but the collar of the shirt squeezed Claire like a vice. What was he talking about? She glanced from one mirror to the next until she caught sight of it: a red gash, the same crimson as the lipstick messages two days earlier, marring the back of the shirt.

"I— I didn't do that—" The collar grew tighter, tighter as Claire gasped for air and the room spun. Minutes earlier, in the dressing-room mirror, the shirt had been white as a fresh snowfall. She tried to raise her hands, to pull the fabric off, but her arms seemed bound to her sides. *Yarik, help*, she thought, but her lips moved with no sound. His blurred features lifted into a smile as if he had no idea of her predicament at all.

"Were you fooling around with one of my other em-ployees?" Yarik went on in a light, teasing voice. "Was it Laura, or Lucy, or..." His words took on a more deliberate tone that cut through the panic filling her lungs. "Was it Violet?"

Claire's vision cleared as red words carved themselves across the big horizontal mirror. *DON'T TALK ABOUT HER.* The collar bit deeper into her neck, until she wrenched her arms up with all her might and ripped the shirt off. White buttons scattered like tiny teeth across the zebra-striped carpet. Air rushed into Claire's throat, and she breathed out.

Then held her breath again as new words streaked across the mirror:

FIND THE TRUTH

"Claire!" Concern overtook the playfulness on Yarik's face as he grabbed her hand. "What happened? Are you all right?"

"The collar. It...it was choking me," she gasped. In the mirror the words faded; she saw only her bare chest heaving above her pink bra. "I...I'm sorry, I can't do a roleplay right now. I..."

She released Yarik's hand and slumped until she was half sitting, half leaning against the bed. "It's my last day. I'm quitting."

The room darkened, the air so heavy and silent it might have eaten up her voice. Yarik stepped forward to stand beside her, his presence warm and solid and asking for nothing. "I'm sorry to hear that," he said, "and not a little surprised. But I hope you're going on to somewhere good."

"I'll be looking for a real—er, a different job, I guess." Danny's face filled Claire's mind—the angry Danny, the demand in his eyes—and she wished she could explain it all to Yarik, and maybe to herself, too. How one part of her would do anything to please Danny, while another part wanted—needed—to stay here. But despite their dungeon friendship, she'd never told Yarik much about her life outside these walls. "Anyway," she went on, "I'm glad you came today, so I could say goodbye."

She had barely finished speaking when she saw it again: a streak of red at the corner of her vision. She braced herself for more lipstick words, but no—it was those roses, waving at her from the attic steps. She turned slowly toward them, and as she did so that fiery color seeped inside of her, washing through her bloodstream, drawing her closer. One step, then two.

"Claire...?"

If Lady Lilith's spirit really was here, watching over them all, why wasn't she making things easier for Claire? Why was she scrawling cryptic messages, raising questions when all Claire wanted was answers? She had a mind to stomp upstairs and demand an explanation—

"Claire." Yarik clutched her wrist and pulled her back, but without thinking she jerked her hand away. Yarik couldn't understand what she was feeling. No man could.

One more step and the floor lurched beneath Claire. She fell onto all fours on the staircase; dust and a splinter or two prickled under her palms. But she wouldn't stop now. She reached one hand up to the next stair, then the other. Another run skittered up her stocking like an insidious bug. The roses loomed, a clump of screaming red mouths, and beyond their call came the distant concern in Yarik's voice. Heat radiated from those flowers until she burned—

And then she was cold, and wet, her hair and shoulders drenched. She screamed, jerking herself up to stand, pulling her arms across her bare chest.

The vase at the top of the staircase had tumbled and broken, leaving plastic stems and fabric flowers scattered across the six black steps and the carpet beyond. And despite the fact that the flowers were fake, the entire scene was saturated.

The gutted insides of the vase gleamed, ringed with water droplets like morning dew.

FOUR: RUBY

R uby stood before the dressing-room mirror, white-
knuckling the communal curling iron, shaping her hair
into the Veronica Lake-style waves she often wore. She
was trying not to feel left out because she was the only lady who
wasn't in session at the moment—she should have been
relieved the dungeon was busy for once. She was trying not to
think about those welts on Jack's backside, and the way they'd
disappeared as if they were no more than a bad dream; and most
of all, she was hoping she wouldn't have to go back into Lady
Lilith's room for quite a while. Especially since she'd looked in
The Book this morning and seen the notes from the last few
days. *Sick to my stomach and couldn't shake it off,* Gabriella had
said. *The room spun around me,* Alice wrote, *and only spanking
my client harder made it stop.* Luna, with characteristic drama:
My breath was stolen and my blood ran hot. And all of these from
sessions in Lady Lilith's room.

Considering that The Book was meant for practical advice,
and not as some silly diary for the girls to share Instagram
poetry about their feelings, it was odd to see those types of
entries at all.

"Ruby?" Lady Eva popped her prim chignon-topped head
into the dressing room, startling Ruby so she nearly singed her
forehead with the curling iron. Lady Eva almost never came
back there. The dungeon owner swept her gaze over the purses
and sweaters strewn across the couch, no doubt cringing
internally, although her expression remained as smooth as her
perfectly ironed blouse. "Oh dear," Lady Eva said, "you really are
the only one back here. I was hoping there was a little
submissive hiding in the corner." She shook her head and kicked
a pair of black lace-up boots out of her way. Whoever had left
those where anyone could trip over them would be getting a
chewing out.

"I hate to ask a mistress," Lady Eva went on, "but Claire
called down—she had an accident in session and she needs
some help. She's in Lady Lilith's room."

God damn it.

"She asked for towels," Lady Eva added as she pivoted
toward the hallway. "I do hope nothing was damaged up there.
These girls..." Her heels clip-clopped back up front.

A few minutes later, Ruby shifted the huge stack of bath towels to one arm and knocked tentatively on the closed door of Lady Lilith's room with her free hand. Why was her heart beating so quickly? Claire would be there, and nothing so eerie could happen with a witness, right?

Still, the idea of being alone in a room with Claire didn't make Ruby's heart beat any slower.

The door creaked open, and Ruby took in Claire's silhouette against the dim light inside. She hadn't brought too many towels after all. Claire's hair, freed from the bun she'd confined it in earlier, was soaked, and water dripped down into her lacy pink bra. "Oh my God," Ruby said, "what happened?"

She felt like she should look away, but she could still see Claire's reflection in the mirrors on nearly every wall. Claire wore plenty of skimpy outfits, like that belly-dancer costume, but with the water drops glistening on her chest, this moment seemed more intimate. It was as if she had caught Claire unawares, emerging from the shower and only half-dressed.

Yes, Ruby thought, she should look away—but she didn't want to.

"I— I'm sorry," Claire said, and Ruby realized she was shaking, "I thought Lady Eva would send a submissive to help me. I can clean it myself—"

She reached for the towels, but Ruby turned and put them on the bondage bed. "It's okay," she said, "I'll help." No matter how aloof she acted downstairs, Ruby wouldn't leave a sopping wet, trembling girl to handle whatever had gone wrong by herself. "Are you all right? Was your client an asshole? You look like you're freezing."

Ruby picked the top towel off the stack and tried to wrap it around Claire's shoulders, but Claire must have thought she was going in for a hug, because she fumbled backwards a few steps and the towel landed on the floor between them.

"I'm okay," Claire said, "I don't want to get you wet. Besides," she knelt to pick up the towel before Ruby could do it, "I know you're not a hugger."

Right. Ruby stepped back and asked again, "So what happened?"

Claire shook her head. "It was the weirdest thing. The vase on the attic steps—you know, the one with the fake roses in it— it fell over and broke, even though nothing was touching it." She pointed and Ruby took in the pottery shards, the strewn petals and stems. She shivered, suddenly as cold as Claire seemed to be, and remembered glimpsing that vase two days earlier, the red roses emerging erect from its black mouth.

"And somehow the water soaked my hair," Claire went on, "although it doesn't seem possible that it splashed that high. It all happened so fast..." Claire shook her head as though snapping herself out of a trance and grabbed more towels from the pile. "What am I doing! Lady Eva will lose her mind over the water damage." She ran into the corner and pressed the towels into the stairs and carpet. "And oh my god, that was her special vase..." She dropped the towel and looked at the fragments as if contemplating whether she could glue them back together.

"I think she'll just be relieved you're okay," Ruby said, walking more slowly than she should toward the stairs, and hoping the words were true. She was still trying to process the scene, the strangeness of the limp fabric flowers. "Where did the water come from? Did your client throw a water bottle on you?" It wouldn't be the first time something like that had happened.

Claire turned her head and looked up at Ruby, her eyes big and blue and innocent in the electric candlelight. "No," she said, "it came from the vase."

"But they're *fake* flowers!" It occurred to Ruby that she should help, so she grabbed the trash can from the corner, plucked petals and dropped them inside. At least it gave her something to do with her hands. She didn't want to start shaking too.

"This room gives me the creeps," Ruby muttered, and then cursed herself for having said anything. Claire, who had returned to her frantic water-blotting, paused, and glanced at Ruby again, with what almost looked like a smile.

"I can't imagine you being creeped out by anything," she said, then stood with a pile of wet towels in her arms.

Ruby shrugged and tried to make the gesture appear nonchalant. "Well, you know, all those silly ghost stories... What were you doing so close to the attic anyway? You know it's not safe. There was that accident—"

Claire opened her pink lips and closed them again. She peeked at the mirror as if expecting to see something other than her reflection, before finally saying, "Was there really an accident, though? Or is that Lady Eva's way of keeping us out of the attic because of—because of the ghost?"

Ruby's heartbeat picked up again. She wanted to finish cleaning and get out of there, but Claire went on: "I don't know what it is, but something's going on in this room. It's messing with my head. First I thought my shirt was choking me, so I ripped it off like some lusty madwoman." She pointed toward a piece of crumpled white fabric on the floor. "And I don't even have the excuse of saying it was part of a roleplay.

"My client tried to stay and help me clean it up, but I couldn't make him do that. I wanted us to have a nice goodb—" Her voice cut off as she entered the bathroom, and Ruby heard the hamper swinging open and shut. "He did give me a huge tip though," she called back. "Said it was to replace the vase, but...I doubt Lady Eva would spend two hundred bucks on pottery."

Claire had just left the bathroom when a squeal pierced the room, seeming to echo from the mirror nearest the front door. Ruby nearly dropped the trash can as the noise turned into high-pitched laughter.

Claire laughed a little herself. "That gets me every time," she said. "You know the St. Andrew's Cross in the room next door is right on the other side of that mirror, so if someone's tied to it in session you can hear *everything*."

Since Ruby avoided these upstairs rooms so assiduously, she *hadn't* known that. Then she remembered, about twenty minutes ago, she'd been in the hallway when the new girl—Mara—came to pick out toys with some overly jolly, big-bellied client. He'd chosen a lot of feathers, giggling as he gave each one to Mara to hold. A tickler.

"I think that's Mara in there," Ruby said. "She went into session not long before you called down for help."

"That's *Mara*?" Claire's blue eyes went wide, and Ruby knew exactly what she was thinking.

"Crazy, right? She's so quiet, I didn't think she was capable of making that much noise."

Claire shook her head as she crouched to pluck pieces of something from the carpet. Buttons, Ruby realized. Claire really had been desperate to get that shirt off.

"It TIIICKLES!" they heard, a girlish voice that managed to sound delighted and terrified at once, followed by a pounding as if the St. Andrew's Cross was being smashed repeatedly into the wall.

"I didn't think Mara was that strong, either. Are you *sure* that's her?" Claire asked.

As if they'd heard her from the other room, a male voice boomed, "Watch out, little Mara, the tickle monster is coming!"

Ruby picked up the last plastic stem from the stairs, deposited it in the trash can and then carried it toward Claire. "I don't know how you girls put up with those awful sessions."

Claire glanced away from her handful of buttons, her eyes narrowing at Ruby. "You must have gotten through it, when you first started."

Ruby shook her head. "I had already trained under a dominatrix before I started working here. No submissive sessions for me. Actually..." Ruby tried to remember Claire's arrival at the dungeon. She was pretty sure it had been February or March, almost exactly a year ago. "I only started a few months before you did."

Claire's mouth fell open. "Seriously? I thought you'd been here for years."

"Do I seem that old?" Ruby joked. She knew she didn't appear as young as Claire, who could pass for a teenager when her hair was in pigtails; but at twenty-seven, Ruby had a few years left before she'd start worrying about her age.

"No, of course not, you're just so...confident. And everyone looks up to you." Claire glanced down at the buttons in her hand as if unsure what to do with them, and Ruby held the trash can out to her.

"You mean everyone avoids me?" Ruby countered. When she could see Claire was about to speak again, probably to offer some platitude, she went on, "I just keep to myself. People tend to mistake mystery for confidence."

Another shriek reverberated through the wall, and with a force that seemed physical, it rocketed right into Ruby. Before she could stop herself, she tilted toward Claire, just as Claire swayed toward *her*. Ruby dropped the trash can and reached for Claire, but it was too late: they fell right into each other, the soft, slender line of Claire's arm brushing against Ruby's shoulder before they landed on all fours, their heads only inches apart. Ruby breathed in damp hair and cherry blossoms, and—

"Ah!" Claire yelped and lifted one palm to reveal a tiny bead of blood. Without thinking Ruby grabbed the injured hand, looking for signs of further damage, feeling the frantic beat of Claire's pulse. But Claire gently wiggled her fingers away. "I'm fine," she said. "It was just..."

Ruby followed Claire's gaze down to see a sharp edge poking from the edge of the overturned trash can. Claire lifted the pair of scissors, blades open and facing up; they glinted extra brightly in time with another screech from next door.

"I saw Mara throw these safety scissors in here two days ago," Claire went on, "and I took them out later. I know I did. She must have thrown them away *again*."

"She's had a bunch of sessions up here already, hasn't she?" Ruby asked. "But why would she…"

Claire shook her head, clearly considering Ruby's question an unanswerable one. She returned the scissors to the vanity table, then they both gathered the buttons and flowers that had once again scattered across the floor. When they'd finished, Ruby peered into the trash can as if it might contain some explanation, but she found only flashes of white gleaming atop drowned petals and plastic thorns. Claire stood and tugged her skirt straight and sighed. "I guess I have to go downstairs and face Lady Eva now. It's a good thing I'm quitting anyway, or she might fire me after she finds out what happened here."

All around Ruby, the black walls seemed to tilt. Claire was *quitting*? Maybe she'd heard her wrong— But no, Claire had both hands clasped over her mouth, though she was too late to hold back the words. "You're leaving?" Ruby blurted. "Why? You can't!"

"I…" Claire looked away. "I don't want to, but—"

"Then don't." Ruby couldn't understand the hollow sensation in her chest. It wasn't like she and Claire were friends. Whether Claire stayed or went shouldn't make much difference to her. But as those shadows crept under Claire's eyes again, the same ones she'd noticed in the hallway two days ago, Ruby thought she might do anything to chase them off. "If it's because of Lady Eva," she said impulsively, "don't worry. I'll handle her for you."

Claire raised her eyebrows. "It's not, but I'll take any help I can get."

"Well lucky for you, I've got a plan," Ruby said, and then racked her brain for one. She grabbed Claire's button-down from the floor, ran into the bathroom and wet it in the sink. She noticed a stain at the top of the collar, but decided it was best not to bring that up right now. "Come on," she said, heading back toward the door. When Claire seemed reluctant to follow, Ruby impulsively reached out with her free hand.

Claire took her hand slowly, tentatively, and the sight of her chipped silver nail polish made Ruby smile. Claire was endearingly imperfect. And this time, she didn't pull away.

Ruby squeezed Claire's hand, a brief message of reassurance, before letting her go.

Ruby stood in front of Claire as they entered the lobby, doing her best to shield Claire's dripping hair and bra from view. Scanty outfits were a staple in the dungeon, but Lady Eva did not appreciate her employees parading around the common areas in anything that could be described as *underwear*. Luckily there were no clients in the lobby, but Lady Eva's piercing assessment was bad enough:

"Well, Claire," she said, "I see your presentation has gone from bad to worse this afternoon."

"Oh, Lady Eva," Ruby held out the shirt she'd soaked in the bathroom sink, "Claire's client was so clumsy, he spilled his water bottle *all over* her, and on one of your rugs. The water damage would have been irreparable if Claire hadn't thought fast and used her shirt to sop it up. Now you can't even tell where it happened!"

Lady Eva pursed her lips in disapproval, not yet convinced. "Hmm..."

"What about the vase?" Claire whispered.

"And then...then her client thought he heard some noise in the attic, and he wanted to go up and check it out, but Claire knows how strict you are about keeping *everyone* out of there, so she pulled him back from the stairs and he knocked the vase over. We cleaned it all up, of course." Ruby wasn't used to explaining herself like this—she usually just did what she wanted, and didn't worry what other people might think, or of the consequences.

Lady Eva stood and shook her head. "But Yaroslav is such a polite client! Why would he insist on going up in the attic?"

"He *is* polite," Claire broke in. "But..." Her eyes narrowed as if she were thinking something through. "He's always been interested in that attic..."

"Well," Lady Eva stood straighter, speaking haughtily now, "thank goodness you girls are okay. I will have to head upstairs and ensure that chain over the attic entrance is secure. And maybe add a sign."

"Great idea, Lady Eva." Ruby grabbed Claire's hand again and pulled her past the front desk. "I'm going to help Claire find a new outfit." Best to quit while they were ahead.

The moment they entered the empty dressing room and shut the door behind them, Claire half-fell onto the couch and let out the giggles she'd been struggling to hold back. Ruby soaked in Claire's unguarded expression, the shadows gone from under her eyes, her relief filling the room with sudden warmth. A moment later, Ruby was giggling too. She couldn't remember the last time she'd laughed like that.

"Wow," Claire said, once she caught her breath, "you were great. I've never seen you like that before. You must have been one of those kids who talked the teacher out of sentencing you to detention every time."

"Yeah, pretty much," Ruby admitted. It was true. Although her efforts to avoid discipline hadn't worked so well at home, with her parents. And she'd always had some new offense to get out of.

"Well, thank you," Claire said, and looked up and smiled at Ruby. The tilt of those lips buoyed Ruby's insides, lifting her away from the last lingering heaviness of the haunted room upstairs. "You saved my ass." But then Claire's mouth pressed closed again, her voice deflating as she added, "Not that it matters, if I'm not going to stay here any—"

The door to the dressing room swung open and Luna and Gabriella burst in, talking over each other.

"That client is *so* in love with you, Luna," Gabriella said, adjusting the strap of her Agent Provocateur bustier. "I might as well have worn a garbage bag for the number of times he looked my way. Why'd he bother doing a double?"

"Because I asked him to," Luna said, "and Peter will do whatever I say. So I get a friend to keep me company, we both get paid, it's per—"

Her stiletto caught on the black boot that had somehow made it to the middle of the floor again, although Ruby remembered Lady Eva kicking it to one side. Luna nearly stumbled into the vanity table, and Gabriella reached out one hot-pink-manicured hand to catch her.

"Damn it!" Luna said. "That new girl..." She picked up the chunky boot, regarded it critically, then stomped to the far end of the room, opened the door to the gazebo and flung the shoe outside. She turned to find the other three—even Ruby—watching with disapproval.

"What?" Luna said. "She needs to learn what happens when she leaves her stuff in the middle of the floor. She'll find her shoe sooner or later. It's not like it's raining. Although, Claire, why is your hair wet?"

Claire twisted one damp curl around a finger. "Mara was probably distracted because she's nervous," Claire said, without addressing the wet hair, "and maybe Lady Eva called her into session before she was ready..."

Of course Claire was defending the new girl—Mara—who must have been the one to leave the boot out in the open. Ruby couldn't help smiling.

"Claire's right," Gabriella added, "we were all new once. It's scary to come in here and wear these skimpy outfits and feel judged and..." She placed a hand on her slender waist and grimaced. "Ugh, not my stomach *again*..."

Luna shrugged and turned to the mirror, rearranging her 1950s-style black curls. "Anyway, *this* new girl— What's her name again?" She adjusted her corset with one hand, fumbling for her makeup bag and pulling out a gigantic eyeshadow palette with the other. Luna was always doing three things at once. In session, she could blindfold a guy and cane him while posting a selfie to Instagram and typing a text message.

"She forgot her dungeon name the other day," Gabriella said. "Started to say something with an L—"

The door opened and a pair of skinny legs in white stockings and too-big pink heels walked in, and all noise and motion ceased.

"We weren't talking about you," Luna said without bothering to lower the makeup brush. Ruby cringed.

But where another girl might laugh nervously, or turn and run right out of the room, Mara didn't seem to register what was going on at all. She stepped forward as if in a trance, almost levitating along the narrow path between the vanity table and the sofa, past all four girls, and into the bathroom at the end of the hall.

The new girl had also left the door ajar, and now a clattering came from out front. Ruby's eyes darted to Claire's wide ones, and in unspoken agreement they hurried out into the hall. Sure enough, Lady Eva had deposited all the vase fragments on the front desk. She must have picked them out of the trash.

"What should I do?" she asked the woman beside her—Nadia, her blonde ponytail swinging back and forth. "Those flowers have kept her calm for so long..." Lady Eva's voice rose and then dwindled, with an uncertainty Ruby didn't think she'd ever heard from her before.

"Kept *her* calm?" Claire whispered, as the dungeon owner turned and rushed right back upstairs. She couldn't have been gone more than a few minutes, but it seemed far longer as Nadia and Claire and Ruby stood in silence, watching the broken pottery as if it were a portent of some greater rupture.

But when Lady Eva stepped back into the lobby, she marched calmly, deliberately forward. Ruby and Claire scurried into the hallway where they'd hopefully remain unnoticed. "It's all settled," Lady Eva told Nadia, as she began collecting the fragments. "We don't need the vase and the flowers anymore." She lifted one hand to her face and brushed something away—a stray hair, or perhaps a tear. Redness seeped like a stain from the corners of her boss's eyes; Ruby blinked and it was gone.

Lady Eva gazed into the small mirror on one wall of the lobby, as if she weren't speaking to Nadia any longer, and added, "She'll still watch over us all."

"Is she talking about...Lady Lilith?" Claire whispered.

It certainly sounded like it. But Ruby said only, "See, you can't quit—there's too many mysteries to unravel right now."

Claire gave a small, sad smile. "You're right. I want to stay—I want to find out the truth."

By the time Lady Eva had disposed of the vase, clients had arrived, and everyone scattered into session. Before Ruby knew it most of the day shift had gone, including Claire, and it was time for Ruby to head home too. She always felt a sort of melancholy when she had to leave behind the woman she had worked so hard to become—the woman who wielded floggers and made men bend and kiss her leather-encased toe—and tonight, that sense of dissatisfaction was even worse. She couldn't escape the strange ache of something missing, so she drove around making up errands: a trip to the grocery store just for bananas, a stop at CVS for the tampons she wouldn't need until next week. Starbucks for a latte, decaf because caffeine would keep her mind whirling.

Eventually, though, Ruby had to return to her tiny west side apartment, the quiet street lined with palm trees, the neighbors who smiled as they walked their dogs or strolled home carrying takeout.

Ruby could have found a cheaper apartment in a different neighborhood, like her place in East Hollywood before. But when *it* had happened, when the wound under her chin had healed and she'd had to leave everything behind, she had looked for places not far from the Briars. It was the most respected dungeon in Los Angeles, and though Ruby couldn't aim a flogger properly at that point, she already knew where she wanted to end up.

Ruby found an empty parking spot only half a block from her building—a small miracle—and took a sip of bitter espresso before dumping the rest on the grass. What a waste of money. The sludgy liquid soaked into the soil like the water had into the carpet in Lady Lilith's room. Haunted room, like the haunted look in Claire's eyes, and Ruby couldn't banish either from her mind as she wondered whether she'd ever see Claire again, ever watch relief fill her features the way it had in the dressing room.

Once she reached her own building, a pretty Spanish-style house that had been converted into many tiny homes, Ruby unlocked her door and stepped into the small space that was, in its own way, haunted. Haunted by what wasn't there: no pictures on the wall; no pots or pans to cook with in the miniscule kitchen. She kept it clean, but considering the lack of furniture and visitors, that wasn't difficult. The apartment was a place to sleep and to store her growing collection of corsets and leather and latex, and nothing more.

After a frozen burrito and an episode of *Law & Order* she watched in bed on her laptop, Ruby tried to sleep, but her thoughts kept returning to her encounter with Claire. Claire was right: Ruby had experience getting herself out of trouble. But it was the transgressions she hadn't been able to wriggle her way out of that came back to her now. The early years when she couldn't sit still in church, when she kicked the pews and played with the Bible until she'd made tiny rips in all the pages. When she pushed Billy to the ground after he told her she looked like a show poodle in the frilly dress her mother made her wear. It didn't help that Billy was the reverend's son.

Ruby hadn't been able to escape her parents' punishments, but they'd never been too unreasonable, too extreme. Her parents had never whipped her with a belt or sent her to bed without dinner. They'd simply looked at her with disappointed eyes (her mother) and mouth set in a stoic line (her father), both of their gazes piercing through her skin to see the rebellion swirling like a flame inside her. Sometimes, they called it sin, and they banished her to her room and told her to pray.

Ruby never prayed. She only used those hours alone to tighten her resolve, to sharpen the edges of her will until she had the power to break through any walls that threatened to contain her.

Now, twenty years older than that little girl forced to sit through sermons about evil and sin and the corruption of power, ideas that had lingered like devils wielding whips in her mind even as her child's brain struggled to understand them, Ruby stared at the dark ceiling above her, the dark walls closing her in, and she sharpened her will.

And she wondered why freedom eluded her still.

If it hadn't been for The Book, none of us would have realized how many strange occurrences had taken place, in those weeks after Mara arrived. We wrote words we could not say aloud; we recounted stories that, had we spoken them, we would have discounted as our imaginations running wild. But when our pens met the paper of The Book, the words poured out. And as each woman read the entry of the lady before her, her own story became easier to tell.

First came Luna: as she flogged her devoted client Peter in Lady Lilith's room, she happened to glance at the mirror above the bondage bed. To her astonishment, Peter's hair was no longer dishwater blond, but the exact honey-brown shade of her good-for-nothing, lying, cheating ex-boyfriend's. That caramel color made her long for the taste of something sweet on her lips, something she feared she'd never have again, and she flung the flogger as though she could beat away her desire. With each strike, the cool blue of longing heated toward the urge for revenge, until she wanted only to make her ex-boyfriend hurt the way she did. But Max wasn't here, so this man would have to do.

Luna's client would let her do anything to him, his cries of ecstatic pain spurring her on; still, she had to tear her gaze off the mirror eventually. She had to make Peter kneel so she could look down at him and assure herself his hair was its typical sickly shade, rather than the warm tones of maple syrup. She had to abandon the flogger, for fear she might go too far.

Nadia had to be the most patient switch the Briars had seen in its thirty-some years, and the most elderly, fastidious clients who wanted to be spanked or tied up stuck to Nadia like horse glue. But even Nadia lost her patience one morning, when she'd spent the hour before work commiserating as her boyfriend complained about his unreasonable boss; and the next hour sitting with Lady Eva, listening to her gripe about the girls who always ran late; and now she had to hear some old man grumble about how she was tying the ropes too tight around his wrists, but she couldn't loosen them *that* much, because he needed to believe he truly was helpless beneath her voluptuous figure—Oh, but now, the rope was pinching, and would she adjust her position so he could admire her luscious curves more easily.

Sometime in the middle of Gregory's grousing, the bathroom sink faucet started to drip. The clink of each drop embedded itself in Nadia's brain so that frustration germinated like a foreign substance inside her. It grew and grew in violent shades of red until it exploded. "Shut the fuck up," Nadia yelled, making Gregory flinch beneath her, "it's not my purpose in life to make everyone perfectly comfortable all the time. Be quiet or I'll blindfold you, and you won't get a single glimpse of those 'voluptuous'"—she spat the word, an old-fashioned, old man's word—"curves you're so obsessed with."

Gregory was so stunned, he kept his mouth shut for the rest of the session, and gave Nadia twice his usual, measly twenty-dollar tip. The sink, however, kept dripping.

Gabriella stood before the mirror in Lady Lilith's room late one night, watching her reflection as her client Tim tied her hands together behind her, and she saw the dark brown skin of her waist dissolving into the shadowy contours of the room. Her already slim figure contracted with each pull of the rope around her wrists, growing smaller, smaller, until she was as tiny as she had been back in high school, when she had allowed herself to eat only after nightfall. When she would do anything to become the bone-thin woman the world seemed to want.

As Tim crouched to bind her ankles together, the bathroom sink switched on, a rushing waterfall. Gabriella waited for Tim to say something, but he didn't seem to hear the water, or to notice the fact that the woman he was tying up was shrinking. In her thoughts, Gabriella was back in the pre-dawn darkness of the family bathroom, the sink on so no one would hear her retching up the candy she'd scarfed down in the midnight hours. All that effort, all that pain, so she could live up to some insane ideal...

The memory of it sat in her hungry insides like a clenched fist, like a closed red bud.

Finally, as Gabriella's ribs started to contract, Tim asked calmly, "Is the water on in the bathroom?" He went to check, and Gabriella closed her eyes, and when the sound of the water stopped and she opened them again, she had returned to her normal size.

But that bud remained inside her, waiting to unfurl.

As the days passed, the unsettling entries multiplied to ten, then fifteen—from two-thirds of the Briars' staff, even women who rarely bothered to write in The Book at all. And as the ladies noted, clients were reacting as well: jumping at strange noises, peering suspiciously into corners. Roleplay Mark requested a different room and, when none were available, suddenly remembered an urgent meeting he had to get to. Tickle Rick took a shower in the bathroom of Lady Lilith's room after his session, and emerged looking spooked. Though he was a weekly fixture at the dungeon, since then he hadn't returned.

But not every lady at the dungeon chose to write about her sessions in The Book. Mara, for instance, wasn't any more forthcoming in writing than with spoken words. After her long sessions with Gunther or Spanking Anthony in Lady Lilith's room, Claire and Nadia would ask with concern how Mara was doing. When she responded with a "fine" or "not so bad," they snuck surreptitious glances at her butt. She wore only phantom bruises, small splashes of violet that disappeared in a day or two. However Mara kept the clients from going too far, it was working, and perhaps discouraging the ghost as well. But she never shared her secrets with the rest of us.

And amid all that remained unspoken, one truth was becoming clearer:

Something had made the ghost stir in her attic hideaway, had made her rise and collect herself and begin to take action.

The ghost was speaking to us—and through us—and if we couldn't find a way to interpret her message, who knew how deeply she might penetrate our thoughts.

How much of our actions she might control.

FIVE: CLAIRE

It took an entire week for the bruises Gunther left to fade from ripe plums back to the dull pearl shade of Claire's late-winter skin. As Claire waited for her skin to renew itself, she told Danny she was going on job interviews, or running errands, every time she drove to the Briars for another shift and tried to figure out what to do.

And Danny seemed to be avoiding her as well. He only touched her in darkness; if she turned on a light he looked away, refusing to witness those lingering marks from another man's hands. His practices ran later and later, and Claire knew he was hanging out with his bandmates, getting stoned. She thought about asking if she could watch one of his jam sessions, like she used to in their first months together. When each lyric he sang was a clue to this sweet, soulful man she'd started sharing her life with. He'd written an entire song about Houdini's ghost, haunting the ruins of the magician's mansion in the Hollywood Hills; about sad souls who could free themselves from every trap made of chains and rope, but lost themselves in less visible binds.

He'd promised to drive her out to the ruins one night, but they never got around to it.

When a week had passed, and the deep ache of Gunther's bruises had finally dissolved, Claire awoke early to the sound of rain outside the closed blinds. It was the rainy time in Los Angeles—March, when the preceding months had been too chilly to soak in the sun, and instead of giving everyone the reprieve they'd hoped for, the sky dumped water everywhere.

Danny must have heard the rain too, and his arms curled around Claire's bare waist and pulled her to him. She soaked in the warmth of his body as if it were the sun they all missed, as if it were the only nourishment she needed. This was what she had always wanted—the safety of a body around hers, a place to retreat to when the world outside was dark and cold. Yes, she had wanted to be a dancer too, to perform and expand her limbs, take up space and command the audience's attention from a stage; but maybe she had only wanted that because she hoped it would lead to this. To that one person who would see her, really see her, and hold her close and tight.

But now it seemed that if either of them opened their eyes or spoke, all that closeness would fall away, as precarious as a ballerina balancing on one pointed toe.

No one in Los Angeles could drive in the rain, so Claire had to leave for work early to have any hope of making it on time. She wiggled out of Danny's arms and headed for the bathroom, then turned to see his long guitar-player's hand dangling off the edge of the bed. Reaching for her, but only in his dreams. She dressed in a cardigan and that black secretary skirt, and Danny woke in time to ask sleepily, "Another interview?"

Claire only nodded, unwilling to speak the lie aloud.

An hour later, Claire stood before the dressing-room mirror, trying desperately to flat-iron the frizz out of her curls. Her eyes kept darting to Mara where she sat on the sofa, running a comb through the gleaming hair that fell halfway down her back. The comb slipped right through the strands as if they were silk. How did she manage that in such humid air?

Maybe that hair was one of the reasons Mara had enraptured so many clients. Dominant men loved playing with and pulling on a submissive's hair. And the clients loved something about Mara: after her first shift or two, she'd spent her days flitting from one session to the next. Today, however, no one had sessions yet—aside from Ruby, who was in the building next door, probably stomping on some man's balls. The rain kept all the other clients away, and trapped the women inside, and so the dressing room was crammed with bodies on the sofas and around the little table, all of them scrolling Instagram or tapping away on their laptops. Mara was the only one without a phone in front of her—come to think of it, Claire had never seen her with one—and she just kept combing and combing her hair, though the effort seemed as pointless as polishing a patch of black ice.

A few more minutes passed; then, maybe because she knew everyone's attention would only be half on her, maybe because she couldn't shake the memory of Danny's chest against her back that morning, his heartbeat thrumming into her, Claire spoke into the room:

"Has your boyfriend ever asked you to quit working here?" She directed the words to Gabriella, who she knew actually had a boyfriend, and who was closest to her, perched on the edge of the sofa in a one-shouldered crop top that revealed her impossibly tiny waist. But she was sure the others would chime in too.

"If he does," Luna was the first to answer from the table where she was buried in her laptop, headphones in, so Claire wondered how she'd heard her, "it means *he's* cheating on you. Never trust a jealous man."

"Remy hasn't," Gabriella twirled a black braid around her fingers, "but I'm also strategic about what I tell him. Guys are human, right? Even if they know it's just a job, no red-blooded man is going to like the idea of a bunch of old geezers' hands all over his girlfriend."

Claire gulped, wondering how much she should share. "But if he did ask you to quit, and you really loved him—would you do it?"

The comb froze in the middle of Mara's black locks, and she looked right into Claire's eyes. Probably putting the pieces together, remembering Claire's whispered vow to quit, which neither had mentioned since.

A wave of queasiness swept through Claire, making her drop the flat-iron onto the vanity table. It landed against a container of Q-tips, knocking something loose that had been half-hidden behind them: the beauty scissors. They didn't belong there. Claire almost asked Mara if she had moved them, but—well, she was being paranoid. Anyone could have tossed them in the wrong place.

Claire steadied herself and picked up the iron and clamped it back on her hair.

"I've known a few girls who never told their partners they were working here," Nadia piped in. "They said it was a catering company or something—that explained the random hours, nights and weekends, the need to carry around extra outfits..."

"But what about bruises?" Claire asked. "How would they hide those?" Her hand tightened around the straightening iron and lingered too long in one spot; she released it to a singed smell.

"No clue." Nadia frowned. "Are you trying to hide from someone, Claire? Danny already knows, right?"

"He does, but..." Claire forced the iron past another rebellious curl. She wasn't ready to give up the Briars *or* Danny, and she suspected that hiding the truth from him, for far longer than a week, was exactly what she'd have to do. "How about you,

Mara? Have you told anyone about the dungeon? A boyfriend, or—"

Mara half-dropped her comb onto the trim of her lacy thigh-highs. "I... Uh..." She looked down at her lap and ran her small fingers over the comb's ridges, and guilt pinched at Claire. She'd put Mara on the spot.

"I've never had a boyfriend," Mara finally said. She couldn't be older than her mid-twenties, but still, that seemed odd.

"Girlfriend, then?" Nadia asked.

"No... Well..." Mara paused and her big, dark eyes narrowed. "I mean, there was someone..." She looked down as if an answer might swim up out of the tiled floor.

"I'm sorry," Nadia patted Mara's knee, "I didn't mean to make you uncomfortable. Just wondered if you've told anyone about working here."

Mara shook her head decisively. "No."

"Maybe that's the smart way to do it," Claire said. Her confusion over the whole situation was edging toward frustration, heating like the flat-iron beneath her hands. "Maybe it's crazy to expect a man to accept a place like this. If I'd fudged the truth with Danny from the start, kept him happy and..."

Claire heard the door open and all that heat siphoned out of her, leaving her only with uncertainty, and when she looked toward the doorway she knew who she would find.

Ruby, who must have just returned from her session next door. Her hair was damp from the rain and darker than usual, which only accentuated the piercing green of her eyes. Claire wished she could swallow back her words. She didn't want Ruby, who had probably never worried about making a man happy in her life, witnessing her weakness. But it was too late to undo what she'd said now.

"Claire and Mara," Lady Eva's voice called from the hallway, "there are clients here to see you."

Claire dropped the flat-iron—Lady Eva hated when girls were still primping after the shift began—and tried to smooth her far-from-straight hair into something presentable. Mara, meanwhile, floated out of the dressing room like a nymph descending from a tree, and Claire wondered if the new girl had ever been a ballerina. Claire certainly felt clunky and clumsy beside her, as she so often had among her more talented classmates at the Dancers' Institute. And as she passed Ruby, breathing in a hint of her strong, self-possessed scent, a mixture of smoke and rain, Claire wished again that she had just kept her mouth shut.

Once they reached the lobby, Lady Eva told Mara she was seeing Kenny—or, as the ladies called him behind his back, Cupcake Kenny, because he always brought a box of cupcakes for the girls, and his physique suggested he'd eaten a few too many of them himself. Kenny was an old faithful like Gunther, to the point that he called himself "Lady Eva's old friend." No true "friend," however, would have broken Lady Eva's rules by fondling the new girls' pussies while their arms and legs were bound. Claire wished she could save Mara from the experience, but Kenny sampled every new girl in the dungeon like another flavor of cupcake. Thankfully he'd lost interest in Claire months ago.

While Mara and Kenny headed out of the lobby—oh so slowly, with Kenny leaning heavily on his cane—Claire entered the parlor and almost stumbled over her heels. Not only was her client someone she'd never seen before, a rarity these days, but he was gorgeous too. Blue-eyed and broad-shouldered with hair edged in silver, like an aging movie star with self-assurance radiating from his every pore. He extended a hand to shake and offered what she guessed was his normal smile, but it came with a wink, a little flirtation that said: *This is just for you.*

His handshake was firm, his skin smoother than Danny's as his fingers closed around hers. "Jack," he said. "Pleased to meet you."

When Jack paid at the front desk, Lady Eva offered a rare smile and asked, "You've been here before, haven't you? I mean, before last week, when you came to see Ruby. It took me a while to realize why you looked familiar."

"I have, although I'm afraid my hair was a different color then." He said it with the confidence of someone who knew the graying tips of his close-cut hair and beard only made him more distinguished. The old-fashioned desk phone rang, and Lady Eva shrugged an apology as she answered, while Claire hurried back to the hallway to grab a few paddles.

As she was reaching for the paddle with one leopard-print side and one leather one, a hand closed around Claire's wrist. Ruby's hand, her nails painted a red so dark it was almost black. "What room are you playing in?"

"Lady Lilith's, I think."

"I think you should try to get Lady Eva to let you go next door." Ruby's lips tightened with what seemed like real concern.

"I don't want to cause a fuss," Claire said. "The guy seems nice, anyway. I heard you—"

"I don't trust him," Ruby interjected as Lady Eva's heels clicked toward them along the tiles.

"Girls," she said much more sharply than she had spoken to Jack moments ago, "what on earth is taking so long? Claire's client is waiting."

Ruby stood straighter. "Lady Eva, I don't think Claire should play in Lady Lilith's room with a client we don't know very well. After that difficult session she had last week— And, well, that room *is* supposedly haunted—"

Claire held her breath. Had Ruby really spoken those words aloud? Yes, they had stood in this hallway a week ago and heard Lady Eva talking about the broken vase, about how some mysterious *she* in Lady Lilith's room would watch over them all—

But you didn't use words like *haunted* in front of Lady Eva. Just like you didn't show her all those secrets the women had planted within the pages of The Book.

"*Mistress* Ruby," Lady Eva gritted out, "We can discuss this when there *aren't* clients waiting in the lobby."

Claire shrugged her way out of Ruby's grip, which had only grown more rigid around her wrist, and hurried back to the lobby before she could get a mistress into any more trouble.

The exterior staircase was covered with a tarp, so Claire and Jack stayed dry though the rain had picked up, drenching the roses that wrapped their way around the front gate and soaking the passersby beyond. Inside Lady Lilith's room, the sound of raindrops drumming on the roof penetrated the dim space with its animal prints scattered everywhere, transforming it into a fur-lined womb. Claire turned the lights up a little, set the toys she was carrying down on the bed, and looked up to see the word SLUT, in all-capital lipstick letters, splayed out across the horizontal mirror.

She wasn't even surprised.

Claire squeezed her eyes shut and thought, *Not today, not today*, but when she opened them she found *LIAR* and *WHORE* and finally, *SHE KNOWS THE TRUTH.*

Claire thought of Mara's dark eyes and Ruby's green ones piercing through her this morning—the two women who knew parts of Claire's truth. Both, in their own way, judging her for being so desperate to please Danny, her inability to break out of this terrible limbo.

Or was it only Claire judging herself—was it all in her head, like these lipstick words might be?

With that question, the scrawls across the glass dissolved into dust. And Jack seemed to have noticed nothing at all.

"So," Claire tried to keep her voice light, to distract herself as well as her client, "you've been here before, sir? Before last week, I mean."

"Yes." Jack wandered the room as if he were right at home, although Claire caught a frown as he passed the attic stairs and the missing vase. "Back when I had much less gray hair and, dare I say, your mistress down at the desk did as well. I believe she'd only recently taken over the dungeon when I was last here."

Lady Lilith had passed away and named Lady Eva the dungeon's new owner about twenty years ago. Claire tried to imagine Jack as a dashing, dark-haired younger man. It wasn't difficult. "What kept you away so long?" she asked.

He shrugged as he walked back to the bondage bed and examined the paddles, along with the bundles of rope he'd asked for. "I moved away from Los Angeles for a while." Claire expected that would be his only answer, but to her surprise, he continued: "I'd had my heart broken, had to get away from it all. Young love, you know."

Jack looked to be in his fifties now, so he'd been thirty-something when he left. Not *that* young.

"But I'm back now." Jack grinned and picked up a paddle. "Just moved back a few weeks ago, in fact. New York was a good place for an investment banker, but I'm ready to rest on my laurels and soak up the LA sun. Now, young lady, I think you need to be punished for asking too many questions. Your curiosity is quite impertinent."

Claire thought about pointing out that he had volunteered more information than she'd requested, but it didn't seem like a wise idea. Besides, before she could have gotten the words out, Jack swung himself onto the bed and pulled Claire over his lap. He didn't bother to ask before flipping up her skirt and spanking her bare ass cheeks, his hand practiced and sure. Her self-

68

preserving side forced her to say: "Not too hard, please, sir—I'm trying to avoid bruises right now."

She was trying, really, to figure out what to do—if she could stay here and keep Danny—

As if the room sensed her thoughts, more words rose to blood-red life on the mirror behind Jack:

WE NEED YOU HERE

We? Last time it had been *she*.

After maybe a quarter hour of spanking—she had started to lose track of time—Claire found herself hog-tied on a blanket on the floor, naked except for her G-string, her wrists bound behind her back and ankles wrenched up to meet them. More rope twined up her calves and forearms, a crimson cocoon. She hoped Jack wasn't one of those clients who wanted her to struggle until she managed to wriggle out on her own, because she'd be here for hours. No matter how hard she pressed against the binds, she couldn't move her arms or legs a single inch. Jack knew how to tie a knot, and Claire was thankful to sink into a place where she didn't have to make decisions anymore.

His spanking had lulled her like a lullaby, each sharp impact opening her further. Forcing her to abandon her defenses. Reminding her of all that time spent lifting her legs and rising on her toes and pushing her muscles beyond what they should have been capable of. Submission and dance taught her the same lesson: only when a body had been forced to the breaking point could it truly soar.

And now, she was soaring. Or floating? Or maybe sinking, because the longer the ropes caressed her, the more she felt submerged. Underwater, in some weightless place where she could breathe despite the liquid that crept inside her. Jack walked a tight circle around her, his boots sinking into the carpet as if it were the sludgy silt at the bottom of some ocean. *Lovely little girl*, she thought she heard him whisper. She hoped he would leave her here to rest. She had found a sort of peace, at least for a moment.

And then, she became distantly aware of a pressure looming, as though something had crashed into the surface of the ocean far above, and the impact was rolling its way down to her.

"Fuck!" Jack's voice cut through the murky water of her mind, and she realized that something big and black was careening toward her. She tried to roll over, out of the way, but the ropes wouldn't allow even that. A part of her attempted to awaken into panic, but the watery weight on her was too much to overcome.

And then Jack's face was inches above hers, one arm pulling her tightly to him, his blue eyes looking down at her as if she were something worth safeguarding. His other arm propped up something above them—the *X* of the St. Andrew's Cross, which had to weigh a hundred pounds, and which now hovered inches over their heads. He released his hold on her and pushed himself up to stand, carrying the cross with him, until it thudded back into place. The shelf-like wooden support beneath it should have kept it from tipping in the first place. Especially since no one had touched it.

Dread darkened inside Claire, dissolving the last traces of her dreamlike state.

Jack was crouched down again, now, untying Claire quickly and roughly. "Are you all right?" he asked, his voice as panicked as Ruby's just before the session. Both of them so dominant, so certain of themselves, it felt wrong to hear fear color their words.

"I think so," Claire said slowly, unsure, "are you?"

"Yes, I'm just— I'm so glad I was able to stop it falling in time. I can't imagine what would have happened if..." He stopped untying to squeeze her wrist. When he returned to the ropes, his touch had turned gentle again, the panic gone. "You'll probably be too scared to ever session with me again after this."

"Why would I be scared?" Claire said. "You rescued me." *It's the room I should be frightened of,* she thought but didn't say.

Jack grinned. "I did, didn't I?" The gleam was back in his eye. "But I fear that might be enough ropes for you. It must have been quite a shock, that thing almost falling on your head. And you not able to get out of the way."

Such a shock, in fact, that Claire suspected she hadn't processed it yet. "Someone will be up to check on us, anyway," she said. "That thumping when you put the cross back would have echoed through the entire building." It had probably sounded like the ceiling was splitting in two, considering that just the noise of a girl getting spanked up here ping-ponged and grated on everyone's nerves.

Jack unlooped the last ropes from Claire's ankles and rubbed the warmth back into them. Then he rose and reached a hand down to her, lifting her to stand so the blood rushed through her in a dizzying whirl.

He sat on the bed, legs dangling, and patted the blanket in an invitation for her to hop up beside him. When she did so he kept his hand resting there, almost touching her bare thigh, but otherwise made no move to lessen the space between them. It felt respectful, even though she was naked and he was clothed. Claire breathed in the crisp wool of his sweater, and the faint muskier scent underneath. Here, beside him, no lipstick words could intrude.

"So, Claire," he said, "I told you a bit about my history. Since we have a few minutes left, why don't you return the favor?"

Most ladies at the dungeon made up cover stories for inquisitive clients, changing their hometown and the name of their college, but Claire had always gone for vague but truthful. If she'd started telling tales, she might have been tempted to reimagine the details every time, and then she'd get confused about who she'd told what. Besides, she didn't want to lie to Jack.

"It's pretty much a cliché," she said. "I grew up in a small town in Northern California, got a worthless associate's degree before I came down here searching for fortune and fame. I went to the Dancers' Institute in Hollywood for a year and a half, but—"

She turned her head, not wanting to look into Jack's eyes as she admitted the truth, but found herself gazing at her own reflection in the droopy-eye mirror. That was worse, so she glanced down to study her bare feet, no longer calloused as in her dancing days. "I wasn't good enough. I dropped out."

Shame burned in her belly as she remembered the moment she'd made the decision, the boiling fear and frustration. The way Mr. Rivers' eyes had bored into her from across the studio, challenging and unforgiving, as he'd called her group to perform the combination across the floor. She'd known her legs weren't capable of leaping against gravity any longer, so she spared herself the humiliation and walked out.

"I'm sorry to hear that," Jack said, and placed a warm hand on her thigh. "I suspect you're being hard on yourself. You're quite flexible, if that hog-tie was any indication." He paused. "But you stayed here, I see? The city of angels and devils cast its spell over you?"

"Oh, yes." She shuddered at the idea of retreating to that empty little town of her childhood, a place where the fog hung so low, it threatened to smother your dreams. A place she tried never to think about, but it seemed all the bad memories were coming back now, crashing down like the cross she'd so narrowly avoided. An image of her mother intruded, alone in the small apartment where she'd raised Claire, with only the noise of the television to create some simulacrum of life between the faded walls. But Claire pushed the picture away before guilt could rise up.

Her discomfort must have shone through, because Jack said, "You miss your family, though."

"My mom," Claire said. "I never had a dad. I wish I had enough money to help her move down here, where it's sunny"— she thought of the rain running across the roof and added, "well, usually, and I could take care of her."

Jack gently lifted her chin and turned her face toward his. "You seem like a kind soul, Claire," he said seriously, all hint of flirtation gone as he rested his blue eyes on her. "I'm sure your mom knows how much you love her. You remind me of someone, actually, a girl I played with when I came here before." His gaze clouded. "She was a kind soul, too."

"Excuse me, your session has ended," Lady Eva's voice came through the speaker. Claire wanted to yell back that she had to be mistaken, they needed at least another fifteen minutes. But Jack had already dropped his hand and risen, the mischievous smile back on his face, the spell broken.

"Guess they didn't hear the cross," he said. "No one seems the least bit concerned about us." He chuckled.

"I suppose we could have gotten away with murder."

SIX: RUBY

"Jesus, Ruby, you're going to scratch your skin off," Luna said, pausing the furious typing on her laptop. Ruby wondered if Luna was writing a novel. She lowered her hands to her lap and tried to keep them there, but without a flogger to clutch and a willing victim to use it on, what was she supposed to do with herself? She hated sitting in the dressing room when it was so full of girls, the constant ding of text messages and the odor of competing perfumes, everyone looking over each other's shoulders—Ruby wondered how they managed to breathe. She would have gone outside and huddled under the awning, but the dressing room was right beneath Lady Lilith's room and would be the best place to hear if anything went wrong during Claire's session.

In spite of herself Ruby raised her nails toward the scar under her chin, and once more the clacking of the computer keyboard stopped. Luna leveled serious eyes on her. "Are you worried about...Lady Lilith's room?" She inclined her head toward The Book on the table beside her, where new entries about the "haunted" room, as Ruby had so unwisely called it, were appearing every day.

"No," Ruby said automatically, forcing her hands down. "Are you?"

"I wouldn't say *worried*, but..." Luna opened the notebook and flipped through it with a frown. Ruby doubted Luna would be any more willing to admit true fear than she herself was able to. "It intrigues me. A mystery, for sure."

On the sofa, Gabriella shivered, her goose-bumped arms appearing almost frail. "It was so cold and dark up there yesterday..."

"Well turn the lights on!" Lucy said.

"No— A different kind of dark..."

Ruby started to tune the voices out, mindful to keep her attention on any noises from upstairs. She was still waiting for a bang or cry when she heard Claire's voice itself, coming from around the corner, and—giggling? "Thanks again for the session, Jack," she was saying. "I hope to see you again soon."

It took all of Ruby's willpower to keep her black fishnetted-thighs glued to the sofa when she wanted to run into the hallway and see for herself that Claire was whole and smiling and unbroken. She fidgeted along to the jangle of Claire hanging the paddles back on their rack, her heels clicking on the tiles and then, finally, walking all the way into the dressing room. Claire really was smiling, almost glowing, like she had after Ruby had gotten her out of trouble with Lady Eva the week before. The day she'd vowed to quit, but had, apparently, changed her mind.

"All good?" Ruby asked, and Claire nodded before qualifying:

"Well, actually—" She glanced around the room of women and asked, "Want to go out back for a minute?"

Ruby followed Claire out the back door and watched her spring across the three feet of open space, landing under the canopy and out of the torrential rain. Ruby made the same trip much less gracefully and wrung the water out of her hair as she asked, "So, what happened?"

"Jack was a perfect gentleman!" Claire said far too cheerfully for the weather. "I don't know why you were so worried about him."

"But?" There had to be a but.

"Well..." Claire bit her lip and when she continued, she strung the words together so quickly Ruby struggled to understand them. "There may have been a moment when the St. Andrew's Cross fell and almost landed on me, and I might have been tied up so I couldn't get out of the way."

"Fuck!" Ruby barely restrained herself from grabbing Claire's hand. She was close enough to smell the rain clinging to Claire's hair, mingling with the cherry blossoms of her perfume.

"But I'm fine," Claire added, "Jack caught it and rescued me."

Something about her choice of words grated on Ruby's nerves. "Are you sure he didn't make it fall in the first place?"

"Positive," Claire said, "he wasn't anywhere near it. Didn't you hear it downstairs? It boomed when Jack set it back into place..."

"No," Ruby clenched her fingers, "I didn't hear anything." She chose not to mention how closely she'd been listening. "But, look— I still think you should be careful around Jack. If you're not—" She took a breath to steady herself, before asking: "If you're not quitting, if you're going to see him again..."

The afterglow surrounding Claire faded as she said softly, "I'm not quitting." Relief washed over Ruby, surprising her in its power, until Claire added, "—*yet*," and the relief drew back into disappointment like a wave retreating from the shore. "But as far as Jack goes," Claire went on, "did something happen during your session with him?"

Ruby remembered Jack's blue eyes narrowing on her scar, the way he'd taunted her. The bitter taste of blood emerged from underneath her tongue. But she couldn't bear to explain all that. She didn't want Claire to know she was scarred. So she simply said, "I caned him hard enough to bleed. I saw the broken skin. I thought I'd gone too far. But then"—she took a deep breath— "then he jumped up without a mark on him, like the cane hadn't touched him at all. It was like…like he was unnatural, somehow. Inhuman."

Claire frowned. "Ruby—Mistress Ruby—I don't want to be disrespectful, but are you sure you saw the marks on his skin? Or…did you only see them in the mirror? There's something going on with the mirrors in that room. I've seen things in them, this past week or so. Things that didn't make sense…" She shook her head.

Ruby wanted to ask Claire to elaborate, but she was stuck on the question. *Had* she only seen Jack's bloody backside in the mirror? It had seemed so real, the swollen welts, the shiny red smears— But now, when she strained to recapture the details, where she'd stood and which direction she'd been looking, she couldn't recall them. Was it possible she'd imagined it?

"Claire," Ruby said, before she could second-guess herself, "do you believe in ghosts?"

Claire opened her pink lips to answer, but then Luna stuck her head out the back door. "Ruby!" she yelled through the rain. "You have another session. Some client wants to do a double with you and Mara."

A few minutes later, Ruby sat on the stool in the parlor, tapping her toes as Mara kneeled on the rug and gray-haired Gregory hemmed and hawed on the low sofa in front of them. She'd never gotten to hear Claire's opinion on ghosts, and now Gregory would spend an hour painstakingly describing his perfect session if she let him. He usually played with Nadia; Ruby had no idea how the blonde switch found the patience to deal with him. "I want Ruby to spank Mara for the first ten minutes…," Gregory was saying.

"That sounds like a good start." Ruby stood. "We'd better get next door before the rain picks up a—"

"We-*ell*," Gregory went on, "since this is my first time playing with you, Mara, I should get to know you first. Do you like a good spanking, Mara?"

Ruby crossed her arms and resumed tapping her toes.

"Yes, sir," Mara said softly, "I'm a light to medium player," as if she were reciting a script Lady Eva had given her.

"Can you speak up?" Gregory yelled. Why did old men think *they* needed to talk louder because they couldn't hear? Then, before Mara could repeat her words, he added, "Are you sure you're old enough to work here? You should put that beautiful hair of yours in two braids like a schoolgirl."

If Gregory asked Mara to redo her hair, Ruby was going to punch something.

"I'm afraid my schoolgirl days are over," Mara spoke louder. "If only my teachers could see me now. I just know they would be so proud!"

Ruby's gaze darted back to Gregory, wondering how he'd react, but the furrows in his face didn't budge; he didn't seem to have heard Mara's last words at all. And then Mara turned her head back toward Ruby, and actually winked at her.

Ruby thought back to Mara's first day, when she'd abandoned her hundred-dollar tip without seeming to know what it was. Could she *really* be that naïve? Ruby had wondered.

The more time Ruby spent around Mara, the more questions she had—and no answers at all.

Ruby and Mara put on the long coats Lady Eva kept in the laundry room to hide their skimpy outfits, then the three crossed the parking lot to the low, squatting building next door. It was a painstakingly slow trip, with Gregory acting as if the slick pavement were an ice-skating rink, while also insisting on shielding Mara beneath his umbrella. Once they were finally inside, Ruby led them to the big back room known as the Enclave. This was Ruby's domain, this wide space with its plush crimson carpet and furniture decorated in shades of black and red. Those splashes of color brought out the red highlights in Ruby's hair when she glanced at herself in any of the mirrors lining the walls, all of them polished enough to sharpen her reflection like the edge of a knife. To whittle away any traces of softness or vulnerability. In this space, far from Lady Lilith's room with its jumble of animal prints and its cramped corners and its ghosts, Ruby could breathe. She could stand tall and unleash her full power.

Ruby shrugged off her coat, flung it over the sofa, and faced the back wall of the Enclave, where red curtains hid the floor-to-ceiling windows and the dismal alley beyond. If this building had been a house, there might have been a garden; but Lady Lilith's love for roses hadn't extended to the parts of her dungeon not visible to the clients.

Or perhaps she would have planted some rosebushes back here, eventually, if she'd lived long enough.

Now, when Ruby raised the lights, she saw the velvet curtains rising and falling as if battered by the rain. But that had to be an illusion—the glass was thick and the windows never opened.

Ruby glanced away from that mirage, and straight into another: on the long mirror on the adjacent wall, a line of red letters dripped downwards. *D-E-V-I-L.*

Ruby willed her suddenly galloping heart to slow. Claire's warning about the mirrors, and the superstitions that followed Ruby like old pests—they were getting to her, worming their way into her territory. Making her see things, even here where she should be safe.

"Are you all right, Ruby?"

Ruby turned slowly in the direction of Mara's soft, slithery voice. The girl had removed her coat to reveal her pale skin and paler outfit; her head was tilted at an odd angle, like she was trying to look under Ruby's chin the way she had when they'd first met.

"*Mistress* Ruby," Ruby said. When she pivoted her gaze back to the mirror, the word was gone.

"*Mistress* Ruby," Mara agreed, as Ruby watched her small red lips move in the mirror. "I guess you'll have to punish me for forgetting."

"Yes, Mistress Ruby, punish the little schoolgirl for not addressing her teacher properly," Gregory added unhelpfully.

"You," Ruby whirled and pointed her finger at him, "sit on the sofa and be quiet."

Without waiting to see if he'd follow her command, Ruby grabbed Mara's hand—and almost dropped it, it was so cold and wet from the rain outside. Even though Mara had been huddled under the umbrella. Ruby kept a slippery grip on Mara and pulled her to the leather spanking bench in the middle of the room, the one that looked like a hulking beast. "Climb up," she ordered.

Once Mara had rested her knees on the bench and wrapped herself around its monstrous central hump, the girl looked even tinier, and Ruby almost felt bad about what she was about to do. Still, she lifted the scrap of white lace that passed for Mara's skirt, and slapped her bare bottom. It was as cold as her hands had been, half-frozen, like marble. Mara was going to make Ruby work hard to warm her up.

Ruby tapped her cupped palms against one ass cheek and then the other, faster and faster, bringing Mara's blood to the surface. She could see in the mirror ahead of them, where letters had appeared and then vanished, that the girl's head had lifted. Her lips opened as though she were yelping, but Ruby heard nothing. She rubbed Mara's icy skin and whispered, "Louder. Guys like to hear you scream, even if it's fake." *And I know you can*, she thought but didn't say, remembering the squeals from Mara's tickling session.

Ruby returned to spanking, but Mara's flesh remained cold and her cries quiet. Ruby, on the other hand, was getting warmer—the warmth of frustration edging into anger, the warmth of pink ripening to red. Why wasn't Mara responding? Ruby was about to give up and do something different when Mara arched her back, pressing her ass right into Ruby's hand.

Finally. Ruby hit harder, and each strike stirred up the worry and irritation that had built inside her all morning. Irritation at this girl looking under her chin, searching out her scar—but no, that wasn't it at all. Irritation at another girl, a girl who was taken in by handsome older gentlemen with dubious intent, as much as she was by young smooth-talking musicians—because Ruby had overheard Claire mentioning her boyfriend a few times, and she could picture him down to his Led Zeppelin T-shirt and the wayward lock of brown hair on his forehead, even though she'd never met him.

That was why Claire had planned to quit—was still planning to, probably. Because of that man—that *boy*—who wanted to keep Claire in a cage while he went out and stuck his dick wherever he liked. And Claire would keep trusting and trusting, giving and giving, no matter how many times she got hurt—

Isn't that what you like about her? a voice whispered. *How sweet and trusting she is?*

But now that her angry thoughts had been unleashed, Ruby could do nothing to contain them.

Minutes passed before Ruby stopped spanking, suddenly aware that her palm was hot and throbbing. She looked down at Mara's bare skin and saw it blushing with warmth now, a perfect shade of pink. The girl lifted her shoulders, flipped her dark hair back, and spoke loud enough for both Ruby and their client to hear:

"Please, Mistress Ruby, spank me harder. I love it."

Well, that was unexpected.

A part of Ruby wanted to oblige, but at the same time, she reminded herself she was working, performing a role. The client behind them was paying for this session, and he was probably starting to feel left out.

"If you love it," Ruby told Mara, "then it's not an appropriate punishment, is it? Get down and kneel on the floor. You're going to watch while I show you what a dominatrix does to a naughty boy." She turned to Gregory where he sat lazily back on the leather couch, and beckoned him to stand. In his interminable interview, he'd mentioned he wanted cock-and-ball torture, so as Gregory waddled turtle-like toward the spanking bench, Ruby darted into the hall to grab a few slender pieces of rope. When she returned he stood above a kneeling Mara, running his fingers through her hair as though mesmerized by the dark pool of it. "Gregory!" she snapped. "I didn't give you permission to touch her."

She led Gregory away from Mara, leaned him against the spanking bench and tugged his pants and boxers down, exposing his shriveled genitals to the long mirror in front of them. Gregory could watch the entire process in the glass as Ruby crouched down in her corset and thigh-highs and stilettos, wrapping the rope around his balls until they bulged blue and veiny. Mara watched too, from her place kneeling behind them—Ruby could see it all in the mirror. And if she happened to glance behind her, toward the wall at the opposite end of the room, she spied another Mara, her folded form captured in miniature in the ornate oval mirror that reflected a reflection.

She hoped all those Maras were paying careful attention to what she could do.

"*Oaah,*" Gregory groaned as Ruby secured the string around his balls and wrapped more rope around his cock, which had stiffened into life. Clutching the end of the rope in one hand

and a riding crop she'd stashed near the spanking bench with the other, she led Gregory toward the mirror by the leash attached to his cock. He shuffled forward and she tapped his testicles with the crop to speed him up, saying, "This is what happens when you touch beautiful girls without permission."

"But Mistress, Mara is *so* beautiful"—Ruby rapped his balls again—"and I was hoping to see if *all* of her skin is so white and smooth beneath my hands. I don't think that's too much to ask, before the end of the session—"

Gregory looked up at her with eyes yellowed by age and greed. The eyes of a man who might be asking for another helping of pudding at the nursing home, and sneaking a peek at the nurse's cleavage at the same time. A rush of heat washed over Ruby, and she grabbed his balls and squeezed. She leaned in toward his face, close enough to see tiny red tracks crawl from the corners of those eyes. Yet his moan, when it came, was more pleasure than pain.

"You like that, huh?" Ruby said, and his lips rose into a lazy smile. She tightened her grip, but it was no use—the second she let go, he would beg to touch every inch of Mara again; he would believe everything he wanted, he deserved to get, regardless of what his desires took from anyone else.

Out of the corner of her eye, in the mirror before her, a sliver of red slipped downward. The coppery taste of blood crept into Ruby's mouth.

Ruby knew she should give his balls a break, if only for safety's sake, but instead she clenched harder. She wanted the pleasure to slide right off his face, his lips to contort to a grimace; she wanted him to feel the way women did when men demanded their bodies and their devotion and—

In the mirror, the red line had expanded to form an entire letter. Another *D*.

"Hey," Gregory said, too calmly to be suffering the amount of pain she hoped to inflict, "ease off a little, will you?"

Horizontal lines sliced across the mirror, cutting right through the glass like cane marks. The beginnings of an *E*. Ruby squeezed and squeezed, and past the air rushing through her ears came Gregory's grumbles and a distant gasp that might have been Mara, or the red curtains rising and falling, or maybe just Ruby herself. She dug her nails in and twisted until she might tear his testicles right off—

The curtain thumped like a dead weight against the wall.

NO. What was she doing? She didn't truly want to hurt this man. This man she didn't know at all, this man who'd done nothing to her. She had to let go. She tried to relax her grip, but her hand held fast, every tendon in her fingers clenching, Gregory's flesh swollen and pulsing beneath her palm. The stench of his arousal turning acrid with fear.

Fighting what felt like a force constraining her own flesh, she wrenched and wrenched her wrist until finally, her hand flew back.

"Jesus," Gregory let his hands fall heavily to his thighs, "are you trying to kill me? Get this rope off."

Ruby knelt to untie him, avoiding the sight of the red lines creeping further across the mirror, like the red tracks she'd seen in Gregory's eyes. But her fingers had turned thick and clumsy and though she'd tied and untied hundreds of cocks and balls in her life, she could not unravel this knot. "Hey," Gregory said just as she drew her hands back so she wasn't touching the rope at all. "Ow! You're pulling it too tight!"

"I'm not pulling—"

He jerked his pelvis from side to side, his cock going flaccid so the ropes slackened, even as he insisted, "Stop tugging! You're yanking my cock off!"

"Mara," Ruby barked, "get me the safety scissors from that table by the sofa."

In the mirror Ruby saw Mara rising slowly to her feet, her movements languid as a meandering stream. At the same time, Gregory writhed as though his genitals were aflame. It was no use—Ruby would have to take care of this herself. She rushed toward the table as more crimson lines rose like welts in the mirror, urging her on—

The scissors weren't there. "*Ahh,*" Gregory groaned across the room. "Get it off me, or I'm never coming back in this dungeon again. I'll tell your boss, I'll tell everyone, you're a pack of crazy bitches here."

Ruby's heart pulsed red in her throat, her ears, no longer beating in anger but in fear. She looked to the floor, the sofa cushions, between the sofa and the wall...

There. Behind the sofa, a promise of silver. Ruby wrestled her arm into the tiny space, clutching the metal so hard it pierced her skin, and rose to turn back toward her client—

Who was sitting calmly on the chair in the corner, Mara kneeling before him as he stroked her hair. "I apologize, Mistress

Ruby," he said in a sleepy voice. "I must have had a spell or something. Old bodies, you know. These ropes feel just fine."

Ruby dropped the scissors and for first time registered the sting in her palm.

And then she saw it, in the mirror, the entire word:

D-E-M-O-N, red letters hovering above Gregory and an unmoving, silent Mara.

Ruby went to the supply closet down the hall to grab a Band-Aid for her palm, and when she returned, she bent beside Mara, took a deep breath, and once more tackled the knots restraining Gregory's cock and balls. This time, they slid right out. The task done, she looked tentatively up at her client; he was a little paler, the contours of his collarbones and ribs prominent under his aged flesh, but otherwise he appeared no worse for the wear. Lady Eva's voice came through the intercom to tell them the session was over, and Gregory, his earlier threats forgotten, made his sluggish way out.

Mara stayed quiet, wiping down the spanking bench and sofa with Lysol as if she'd been sessioning in this room for years. Ruby considered asking her about the scissors, but she didn't feel like talking—and to tell the truth, she was still spooked, still recovering.

Just before they left, Mara peeked behind the velvet curtain, to the asphalt beyond. A hint of color brightened her cheeks, as if she were coming to life the way she had earlier, beneath Ruby's hands, and she pronounced: "The sun's coming out!"

Ruby had almost convinced herself the session hadn't been so awful, until she stepped through the door of the Enclave and turned to pull it closed behind her.

That red velvet curtain, the one resting against panes of glass that never opened, was dripping, releasing fat drops of water onto the carpet below it.

The dungeon grew busier as the day continued and the sun showed itself, and Ruby never got a chance to ask Claire again for her opinion on ghosts. When her shift ended, Ruby climbed into her rain-soaked Fiat Spider thinking about the super-natural, about ghosts and demons and creatures that walked the line between this world and another, darker one. She remembered, as a child, reading with a fear that became fascination about the Nephilim, the monstrously large and strong children of Lucifer. She had asked her mother about them and been berated for her obsession with the "wrong parts" of the Bible, the parts that described rebellion and evil, when she should be focused on Christian charity. "The devil will get you if you fall in love with him," her mother had said. "If you let him seduce you."

It seemed that Ruby couldn't do anything right, that she was destined to be cast out of her home like those angels from Heaven, and since her parents already had two perfect children who planned to become a teacher and a minister, they wouldn't miss her. So while a part of Ruby feared the devil, another part— the part that didn't *want* to be good—was enthralled, and welcomed him in.

Ruby drove past palm trees limp from the rain, past organic cafés with patrons sipping smoothies, and her thoughts fell back into the empty desert expanse of her childhood. The small town with one church, one diner, and one school, where every tale of Ruby's troublemaking made it back to her parents. The town surrounded by sand that snuck dry and gritty under her tongue and her fingernails, clinging to her until she feared she could run forever and find only more sand before her.

So Ruby sought a different escape. While her mother held her children close as birds in a nest, checking their homework every evening and their report cards every term, signing them up for every church activity, Ruby plotted. When she was finally old enough to leave their modest middle-class home on her own, and Ruby's mother pleaded with wide eyes for her to *be safe*, *be good*, Ruby always went out and did something unsafe. Something that wasn't good. She walked all the way to the train tracks and danced on the rails. She stole a pack of cigarettes and let the smoke simmer in her lungs. She slept with one boy in her high school, then another, and another, though their dicks tasted like rubbery foul fish in her mouth. By the time she realized she might prefer the sweet softness of a woman's lips against her own, she knew it was time to go.

Once she finished high school, with no college acceptances like her older siblings had flaunted, Ruby didn't wait to be cast out the way she imagined she would. She didn't walk or run through the endless sand surrounding her small town; she took a bus that rattled her right past it, toward the glittering city named for the angels and the salty relief of the ocean. She didn't spare a thought for her mother, didn't bother to return the messages she left on Ruby's phone. At first those messages were like the plaintive call of a bird whose fledgling had flown, but disbelief and fury swept in as her father's voice joined. They raged to find their daughter had no intention to confess her sins, to repent, to return. At last they stopped calling, and Ruby no longer had to imagine her parents' eyes breaking through her flesh to find the wrongness inside her, seeing all the unforgivable acts she'd performed.

And even now, Ruby was still like that little girl her mother had chastised: fascinated by the dark things, the evil things. Letting her imagination run away from her, letting her anger consume her until she was bound to hurt someone, and hurt the dungeon too. How had she gotten so carried away—caning Jack, forgetting he'd asked her not to leave marks, and then today, she could have ripped Gregory's balls right off. And no, nothing had actually happened to either man, but didn't that only make it worse—didn't it mean Ruby was losing track entirely of what was and wasn't real?

Claire might still be planning to quit, but maybe Ruby was the one who should go. Though if she left, she couldn't protect Claire or any of the other girls—

No. Ruby caught sight of the stoplight turning red and braked at the last possible moment. This wasn't about protecting anyone—or at least, that wasn't the main reason she was so desperate to stay.

The truth was that now she'd held floggers and canes in her hands, now that she'd seen men cower beneath her stiletto heels, Ruby couldn't bear to return to the weaker woman she'd been before. She couldn't abandon this power even if it destroyed her, because Mara wasn't the demon, no matter what those red letters looming over her in the mirror said.

Ruby was.

There was a certain kind of girl who bloomed at the dungeon, under the gaze of men's eyes and the touch of their hands. A type of girl who, when she realized men would pay hundreds of dollars they might not be able to afford to come back and see her again and again, would blossom into her power like a bud opening after it's soaked up all the rainwater, and the sun has finally emerged.

Mara was one of those girls, and as the days following her arrival turned into weeks, we watched Mara bloom.

She no longer tiptoed from session to session in too-big pink heels she nearly walked out of. Instead, she showed up one morning with a pair of white peep toes she kept spotless despite the rain. In those shoes, in her white thigh-highs and corset or her little bleached-out sailor suit with blue piping, Mara stepped assuredly up and down the stairs to the session rooms. Clients trailed after her with expressions of adoration edged with confusion on their faces, as if they couldn't quite remember where they were going, but they weren't too bothered about it.

Lady Eva also wore a glazed sort of smile whenever Mara was around—because business for Mara meant business for the Briars, too. Even if it was only more old business, the same clients who'd been coming to the dungeon for decades, making more frequent appearances than they had for other new girls. Not even Mara had the power to draw fresh clients in and bring the Briars back to its glory days, when the dungeon was so busy they had to hold sessions in the parlor and gazebo. When it seemed the flow of cash and desire would never subside.

Once Mara had floated out of the lobby with another client plodding behind, Lady Eva would reminisce about those old days, telling Nadia or Claire or whoever would listen, "Back then, pretty girls like you would have been in session all day and night." But then another client would call and cancel with a last-minute excuse, and we would look at each other, remembering an entry in The Book, how that client had remarked upon an eerie noise or dodged a falling object in Lady Lilith's room. And while we tried to keep the gossip far from Lady Eva's ears, the smile would still fall from her lips, the blue of her eyes sharpening as if she could see all we attempted to conceal.

Mara was like some rare hothouse flower, drawing the clients' attention to her within the dungeon walls; and so it seemed only natural that those clients were curious about where she'd come from, how she'd sprung so suddenly into bloom. Gunther remarked more than once on her "gypsy eyes," and one client liked to double with Mara and Nadia—or, as he put it, "the two Eastern European girls." Nadia played the sweet, blonde Ukrainian farmgirl while Mara was the dark-haired Romanian with her long, lacy shawl. It was all a ruse, a case of letting the client run away with his own assumptions—because on the rare occasions when Mara did talk about herself, it was only to say that she didn't remember her parents, and had no idea of her heritage at all.

But the truth was, most of us didn't pay enough attention to Mara. We each had our own problems to worry about, our own ghosts trailing behind us, quieter and easier to push aside than the one in Lady Lilith's room. Yet perhaps all that looking away—away from Mara, away from the strange machinations of the ghost, away from our own private hauntings—was a mistake.

Just because you're not watching out for something, just because you can't see it clearly, or even say for certain it's there at all—

Just because you don't believe something is real, doesn't mean it can't hurt you.

SEVEN: CLAIRE

It was the day after Claire's session with Jack that the true deception began. She couldn't keep going on imaginary job interviews forever, especially not ones that lasted a six-hour dungeon shift, so she sidled up behind Danny where he sat on the sofa with his guitar. She whispered right in his ear: "I got a job."

Danny turned to grin at her, switching from the melancholy melody he was picking out to a jauntier one. "You did? That's great! What is it?"

Claire swallowed and remembered Nadia's words. "Server for a catering company. So the hours will be kind of random. Days and nights..."

"You don't sound too excited about it." Danny reached out to squeeze her hand, but she only managed to hold her palm limply against his.

"Well, it's not my dream job."

"But it's better than having your ass beat by a bunch of weirdos." Danny turned toward the window before adding, "I didn't want to say anything while you were still there, but was it really that different from being a who—"

Claire pulled her hand back and dropped it with a slap to her thigh. "Escort." Danny swallowed. "From being an escort." And as Claire tried to ignore the nerves sparking where she'd smacked her own skin, Danny kept strumming his guitar.

That night, Danny left the bedside lamp on as he rolled over to kiss Claire, threading his hands through her hair with the same tenderness he'd offered the guitar strings. His fingers trailed down her spine, over her ass to the spot where Jack had spanked her, and Claire held her breath. "Those damn bruises," Danny said, as she dug her nails into her palms. "That was more than a week ago, wasn't it? At least they're almost gone." His lips hovered over her skin, where Jack's hand had been, and she forced herself to exhale as he kissed her with what felt like love. She'd dodged a bullet—at least for now.

Claire could barely sleep, after that, and the next morning she awoke to a heavy haze in the air. When she disentangled herself from Danny's sleeping body and peered between the window blinds, she saw clouds spreading like smoke across the sky. Just in time for a shift at her "new" job. She moved sluggishly, the weight of subterfuge holding her down, and pulled in to the Briars' parking lot fifteen minutes late. Hefting her duffle of outfits over one shoulder, she walked through the gate so quickly she pierced her palm on a thorn.

And entered the lobby to find what seemed like half the staff of the Briars gathered around the front desk, sitting in the leather chairs and overflowing onto the floor. "Claire," Lady Eva said from behind the desk, looking particularly regal with her lacy collar, "I see you've decided to join us."

"I'm sorry," Claire huffed between breaths, "I had a rough mor—"

"Sit down," Lady Eva interrupted, "we're having a meeting."

Nadia scooted to make a place for Claire on the floor, and Claire carefully lowered her duffle—slamming it would add insult to injury—and perched on top of it. At least the other ladies were still in street clothes, and it felt strange to see them all that way at once. Luna in a Blondie T-shirt; Mara wrapped in a lacy white skirt that looked long enough for her to trip over. Ruby in an oversized hoodie, leaning against the wall with arms crossed, one bent knee poking through the rip in her jeans. The sight disrupted the illusion of the Briars as a fantasy world lined in velvet and leather, where women always wore corsets and lipstick; it reminded her that all her coworkers had lives she'd only peeked into the edges of.

"As I was saying," Lady Eva went on, "I'm aware there has been some gossip about our...*resident ghost* making her presence known." Perhaps Claire only imagined it, but an edge of uncertainty seemed to creep into her boss's voice. "I know how you girls love to talk, yet the more our clients overhear, the less likely they are to return..." She paused and tapped her manicured fingers on the desk, and Claire took a moment to glance toward Ruby. She appeared unaffected. Bored.

"So I've decided to share something with all of you, something I hold very sacred," Lady Eva went on. "I hope this will show you why we must keep any ghost stories to ourselves." She lifted a few sheets of paper from the desk, and Claire could see the bold cursive covering both sides. "This is the letter Lady Lilith wrote to me a few days before she died in that awful car crash. It was so sudden..." She sighed and shook her head.

Claire thought she saw Lady Eva's hands trembling as she smoothed the papers with their faded edges down on the desk.

She withdrew a pair of glasses from the desk drawer, perched them on the edge of her nose, and read aloud:

"My Dearest Eva:

I fear I am writing this letter sooner than I'd hoped, but as you know, I've always had an ability to commune with the other side. I can sense when the veil between worlds is thin, and though I'm younger than I wished I would be, I can feel that veil thinning for me now. Fate has something terrible in store for me, and it's not something I can frighten away with the flick of a whip or riding crop.

Since the day you came to work in my dungeon, Eva, I knew you would be the one I'd trust to run the Briars after I was gone. The Briars, my life's work, my greatest achievement and my greatest love. When you walked into the lobby for the first time all those years ago, a little blonde submissive dressed in pink—"

Lady Eva broke off suddenly and cleared her throat. "You girls don't need to hear this part." She sat up straighter, all traces of shakiness and hesitation gone. "Let's see... Ah, here we are.

"...But I promise you, when I've departed from this world, I will not abandon the Briars. It's not easy for women like us, women who choose to wander off the narrow path society has laid out for us. I won't let any harm befall the ladies who have the courage to step through the front gate of my dungeon and take on an identity so many in this world would judge us for. We can't always count on the protection, or the understanding, of those outside these walls—but my protection, you can always count on. So if any of the ladies sense an invisible presence observing them, or hear a voice when they're alone in the room I've always loved best, tucked beneath the gables and the roses—

"Tell them not to be frightened. I'm simply letting them know I'm watching over them."

Lady Eva plucked off her glasses, and when she placed them on the desk the impact of their wire frames against the wood echoed through the absolute silence in the building.

Well, Claire thought, Lady Lilith certainly had a flair for the dramatic. It made sense, for a woman who'd founded her own S&M dungeon and named it after the blossoms and thorns she coaxed into climbing all the way from the building's front gate to the peaked roof.

"So you see," Lady Eva's eyes roamed the room as if to ensure every one of her employees was listening, "there is absolutely no reason to fear Lady Lilith's ghost." If Claire wasn't mistaken, her boss's gaze lingered longest on Ruby; but the red-tinged waves of Ruby's hair fell forward and hid her response. "That is," she went on, "there is no reason to fear Lady Lilith's ghost, as long as we all show her the respect she deserves. No silly gossip or dramatic stories; no reluctance to session in her room, the room she loved best." She paused. "No doubting that her intentions are good."

Lady Eva looked meaningfully at Luna, and Claire wondered if their boss had found The Book and read Luna's entries—she always wrote the longest and, well, most dramatic ones. They would have to start hiding The Book, if Lady Eva remained as suspicious as she seemed to be now.

At that moment the doorknob rattled, and the ladies jumped in unison. "Oh," Lady Eva said, "that's Kenny to see you, Mara." She glanced at the old-fashioned clock hanging on the wall to the left of the desk. 10:55, five minutes before opening time. "He called begging to session with you today, and I told him you were completely booked, but I could squeeze him in if he got here right when we opened."

As she finished, Kenny managed to force the door open, and it burst inward and smacked Emilie. "Meeting dismissed," Lady Eva said quickly, "go get dressed." All the women high-tailed it out of the lobby as if spurred on by Cupcake Kenny's big-bellied, lumbering intrusion into the building. He stopped to lean on his cane after every step, and Claire wondered, as she always did, how he managed to become so much more sprightly once he had a tied-up girl underneath him.

The dressing room buzzed with the manic energy of nine women packing in at once, chattering about the morning's revelations. It reminded Claire of the mood in the Dancers' Institute dressing room before an audition: anticipation with an undertone of fear. Wanting to escape quickly, she huddled into a corner and chose the outfit that would be quickest to put on, her old standby crop top and skirt. She hadn't slipped on her heels yet when a hand tapped her shoulder: Ruby, who had already managed to trade out her hoodie for a perfectly laced black corset. "Can we talk for a second?" She inclined her head toward the back door.

Claire stepped outside to see that puddles had collected through all the grassy patches, the soggy remnants of a week of off-and-on rainfall. Without her heels to hold her back, she impulsively leapt right over the biggest puddle, landing on the dry concrete beneath the gazebo canopy. It felt good to stretch her legs, to take up space for a moment.

She turned back to see Ruby on the other side of the puddle, her mouth caught in an *O*. "What?" Claire asked.

"Did you just do a split in the air?" Ruby asked. "How did I not know you could do that?"

"That wasn't a split." Claire laughed to hide her discomfort. She had forgotten where she was for a minute, and probably made a fool of herself. "I can do a split on the floor, but definitely not while floating in the air."

"Well, it looked like one to me," Ruby said, watching her own feet as she threaded her way across the puddles. "Shit." She coaxed one of her stilettos out of a mud clump. "You're much more graceful than I am, anyway."

"I went to school for dance," Claire said, "but I wasn't that graceful. I dropped out." Even before she'd finished speaking, she wondered why she'd mentioned it. None of it mattered anymore.

"I should have known you were a dancer." Ruby smiled. "I can't believe I didn't see it before."

"*Were* is the operative word," Claire responded. "What did you want to ask me, anyway?"

Ruby's mouth flattened. She must not have had time for lipstick yet; her lips didn't flash, flame-like, the way they usually did, but they were still beautiful. "I keep thinking about the vase," Ruby said. "In Lady Lilith's room. You said it fell over on its own?"

"Yeah," Claire said. Like the St. Andrew's Cross, but she didn't want to remind Ruby of that and worry her even more.

Ruby bit her lip and looked down at her muddy shoe, then up to meet Claire's gaze. An edge of wildness lurked behind the green of her eyes. She seemed miles away from the woman in the black hoodie who'd leaned against the lobby wall, acting as though she couldn't care less about ghosts and hauntings. "I think the ghost pushed the vase over," she said quickly. "I think she—*Lady Lilith*—was trying to keep you out of the attic."

"But I wasn't going in the attic." Even as Claire spoke, she remembered climbing the attic stairs, disturbing the dust under her palms and the soles of her stiletto heels. It had almost felt as if she'd lost control of her own limbs, as if some unseen force drew her upward—

But a ghost wouldn't beckon her to its lair and then chase her away. That didn't make sense.

"Well, maybe the ghost thought you were," Ruby went on. "I think there's something more going on—something Lady Eva didn't tell us. I think..."

"That Lady Eva's working with the ghost."

They turned to see Luna, still lacing her corset, and Alice following close behind.

"Well," Claire caught Ruby's fists clenching behind her back, where the other girls couldn't see, "yes."

"Do you think we can trust her?" Alice asked.

"Lady Eva, or the ghost?" Luna asked.

"Are we sure there *is* a ghost?" Claire didn't expect to find herself the most rational person in this situation, but...she still wasn't sure something supernatural was to blame here. "Minds can play tricks..."

A melody sounded from the pocket of the schoolgirl skirt where she'd stashed her phone. The opening notes of Joni Mitchell's "Circle Game."

"It's my mom." Claire pulled the phone from her pocket. "Something might be wrong, I have to take this."

The others nodded and headed to the other side of the gazebo. "Maybe the ghost can take care of my client," Luna was saying. "Peter booked a three-hour session with me today, and he keeps trying to guess where I live and which car is mine in the parking lot. It's getting creep—"

"Can you keep it down?" Claire hissed, then blocked the voices out to answer: "Hey, Mom, is everything okay?"

"Yes, I'm fine, dear." Her mom's voice slipped tentatively through the phone line. "I just— I was worried when you didn't call. I should have texted, but...I wanted to hear your voice."

Oh no. Last week had been the end of February, and Claire always called her mom on the last weekend of the month. It was the least Claire could do for the mother she'd left behind, but with all the recent drama, she'd completely forgotten.

"Anna?" Claire's mom asked, when the silence went on too long. The sound of those two round, open syllables always made her cringe. Her real name, the one no one else used, the one she refused to think about anymore.

"I'm here." Claire glanced around to check on the other women, but they must have gone back inside. "I'm sorry I forgot, I've just been...distracted. And I might have to go in a minute. I'm at work and—"

"But it's Saturday."

Shit. Claire was really screwing this up.

"They called me in to finish some paperwork." As far as her mom knew, Claire had worked as a receptionist since quitting first the Dancers' Institute, then her clothing-store job. Danny wasn't the only one Claire had hidden the truth from—though in her mother's case, physical distance made the deception an easier one.

Now, though, Claire wished that she could ask her mother for advice. Her mom believed in ghosts—she'd told stories of the Irish banshees, the spirits with wild hair who mourned deaths before they occurred. In high school, whenever her mother hugged her and said "there's no need to wail like a banshee, no one's died, you know," Claire realized she was taking some teenage crisis too seriously, that everything would turn out all right.

But Claire was no longer a child, and her mother no longer knew anything about her life.

"Are you sure you're okay, Anna?" her mom asked again. "You sound sad."

"I'm fine."

"How are things with Danny?"

"Danny's great," Claire lied. She tried to imagine her boyfriend's warm, strong arms wrapped around her, the way she sometimes did during an unpleasant session, when she wanted to escape.

But somehow, all she could think of was Ruby trying to wrap that towel around her shoulders in Lady Lilith's room, when Claire had been soaking wet and shaking. And stupid Claire, she'd jumped away and probably hurt Ruby's feelings.

Claire just hadn't expected it—that Ruby would reach for her. That Ruby would care about her. That anything she did or didn't do might affect Ruby's feelings.

But Claire was starting to suspect that Ruby was much more sensitive than she let on.

"Anna?" Claire's mom said again. "It sounds like you're busy. I'm sorry, I shouldn't have called."

"No, it's okay, I—"

"Claire!" Nadia called from the dungeon's back door, and Claire winced and hoped her mom hadn't heard. "You have a ses—"

"My boss is here," Claire said quickly, "I have to go. I'll call you soon, okay?"

"Okay, sweetie," her mother said. "I love you."

"I love you too." And Claire told herself the lies didn't make it any less true.

As Claire walked back inside the wind fluttered the potted plants, and a fat raindrop landed on her shoulder. Couldn't the weather give them a break? She entered the parlor, wondering what she would do if someone wanted to spank her hard enough to leave bruises—but when she saw who was waiting her spirits lifted. "Yarik, you're back?"

He smiled and raised his large hands—empty of gifts this time. "I thought I would have to find a new lady to play with, so imagine my surprise when I called and asked if Claire was still working—and your boss said why wouldn't you be?"

"You didn't tell her..." Claire glanced to the lobby, where Lady Eva sat a few feet away.

Yarik winked and continued in a softer voice, "If you've changed your mind about leaving, your secret's safe with me."

Yarik paid at the desk, and the two of them were halfway up the stairs when a roar split the clouds, and rain lashed down like the blows of a whip. "A *thunderstorm*? In LA?" Claire said. Though the awning shielded them, she instinctively hurried the rest of the way into Lady Lilith's room—only to find a needle of water piercing the ceiling. She ran for the trash can and placed it under the leak. But wait—in the bottom of the can, was that...

The scissors. Again. Maybe she should talk to Mara.

Yarik peered at the ceiling. "A storm this heavy won't last long," he said, "but a leak like this should be taken care of. I can go upstairs and take a look—"

"No," Claire said quickly, "Lady Eva would never forgive me if I put a client to work."

Thunder cracked and the drip became an onslaught, hitting the bottom of the can with the force of a stone. Claire groaned. She was too exhausted to deal with this; too tired of lying and worrying and—

Red words shouted from the mirror above the bondage bed: *YOU CAN'T HIDE THE TRUTH.* And then, like a spat-out afterthought, *WHORE.*

Yarik glanced at the mirror too—his eyes narrowing, but probably just following Claire's—before he reached a finger toward the leak. Claire guessed they had fifteen minutes before the can would fill. "All this water reminds me of the poem I'm teaching this week," he said, his voice so calm and solid, he seemed capable of overcoming any possible threat. Claire could barely imagine how that kind of security might feel.

But all she said was, "A poem?" On the mirror, the words washed away as if water streamed down them too. "I thought you were a history professor—"

"Poetry is history, my dear." Yarik danced his hands around the water, his voice growing more animated as he spoke. "Especially when it's composed by a historical figure as great as Pushkin. And this poem is a story, too—a play, almost." He breathed in, gathering himself to begin his tale. "A wealthy man courts a peasant girl who lives by the river, the Dnieper, that flows all the way from Russia to the Black Sea."

Yarik's hands traced arcs that could be the path of the river, or the curves of the young woman's form. Claire leaned back against the bed, trying to lose herself in the words. Her favorite client could spend half a session telling stories, forgetting all about the BDSM activities he'd paid to do.

"The man abandons his lover," Yarik went on, "let's call her...Violet, for a more respectable match. During his wedding, he sees a woman with dripping-wet hair watching him from the corner of the room. Years pass, but that rushing river haunts his dreams, until some strange force drags him back to the Dnieper against his will..."

Thunder sounded again, and in its wake the cross that had so nearly fallen during the last rainstorm rattled, as if someone struggled against its metal rings. The mirror beside it glinted with lightning—

But that was impossible. There was no window, no way for the light to penetrate and—

It wasn't lightning, but the reflection of a flame. Claire whirled toward the attic stairs, and there sat a lit candle in a glass jar, wobbling as if buffeted by the wind of the storm. Such a small, precarious flame, yet it promised so much power. So much destruction. Claire stepped toward it as Yarik's unfinished tale slipped from her mind. Her thoughts shifting from the acquiescence of water to fire's raging tongues.

"Claire, get back." Yarik's voice had turned low with warning, but Claire took another step and then another, the flame pulling her closer with every flicker back and forth. The entire jar trembled, and then as Claire watched, spellbound, the candle tipped onto its side and fire spilled like liquid onto the black-painted wood. A vision filled Claire's mind of the entire staircase, the entire attic bleeding red, and desire ignited inside her. *Let it burn...*

A heavy arm pushed her aside; water spouted from the trash can and doused the tiny inferno. Something small and round and golden landed with a clink on the stair.

Claire shook herself from her stupor, as chilled as if she'd been soaked. Just like the last time she'd stood here with Yarik. "That whole staircase could have gone..."

"This whole room," Yarik said soberly as he replaced the trash can under the leak—which was already ebbing. In minutes the storm had spent itself. Claire pictured the drenched roses, hanging their heads on the dungeon's roof.

Heading warily toward the steps, Claire whispered, "Lady Eva must have put this candle here, where the vase was. She must have lit it too—" But her eye was drawn lower, to that golden object Yarik had thrown—a coin. His voice came behind her:

"Pick it up."

Claire bent to retrieve the coin, and Yarik's words became guttural whispers, a song in a foreign language, as he circled the room. The occasional hint of English shone through: *Dark*, she heard a few times, and *light; remove*, just once, and, she thought, *multiply*.

The moment he finished speaking, the last drips from the leak petered out. At the same time, Claire uprighted the soggy candle. Only a faint scar marred the wood.

Claire returned the coin and Yarik spanked her lightly, but she suspected his attention remained on the shadowy alcoves of the room. When they were done, he handed her a hundred-dollar bill—with that same coin wrapped inside. "It's brought me luck," he said, "and you might need that now." He opened his mouth and then closed it, before extending his strong hand to squeeze hers. "That candle was not lit when we entered the room." He swallowed. "Promise me you'll be careful, Claire."

She answered, "I will."

Claire spent the rest of the day wondering if she should take the candle away, but in the end she feared upsetting Lady Eva. The idea of a candle lighting itself seemed so ridiculous, she couldn't bring herself to describe it in The Book—which had been moved to a new hiding place, tucked between a table leg and the dressing-room wall. But before she went home, she did find Ruby and grab her hand.

"I wasn't sure I believed in ghosts," Claire said. "But now..."

Saying the words would mean the lipstick messages, the falling objects were more than manifestations of Claire's troubled mind. That they existed outside of her, beyond her control—as volatile as a flame, as liable to spread and destroy.

With Ruby's expectant eyes on her, Claire admitted:

"I think I do."

As the contents of Lady Lilith's letter passed through the grapevines—or rose vines—of dungeon gossip, we enjoyed a respite of sorts. The rain stopped, the sun emerged with a warmth it hadn't held all year, and no ghostly incidents occurred. A few entries in The Book noted the candle that had appeared on the attic stairs, black wax in a jar engraved with roses; we supposed it was Lady Eva's way of replacing her vase, and no one mentioned a flame mysteriously lighting itself.

The biggest drama of the week was Claire turning down a session with Gunther, after she'd played with him so many times before. She claimed it was because Gunther kept coughing in the lobby, and she didn't want to catch what he might be spreading. But Mara gave her a meaningful glance from under her curtain of hair, and Claire suspected at least one woman knew the truth.

Claire couldn't risk bruises, with Danny waiting for her at home.

Meanwhile, inside and out of the Briars, we found an uneasy sort of peace. Ruby did her best to keep her thoughts from dark places as she practiced flogging and caning and learned a fancy rope tie. Alice smoked a lot of cigarettes and got another lucky lotus flower tattoo. Luna started a new painting, a depiction of a ghostly presence floating through Lady Lilith's room. Nadia tried three different cookie recipes and brought the results in to the Briars to share.

We thought we could relax, and we failed to pay as much attention to those hidden things—the things we hid from each other, and the things the Briars hid from us—as we should.

But then there was Gabriella.

Gabriella hadn't told any of us about her younger years keeping her calorie count below a thousand a day, purging in the polished toilet of her parents' bathroom. "You've lost bone mass density," her doctor warned when her period disappeared for a year, and he ordered the bone scan. Yet Gabriella was willing to flush out all her insides, if only she could look the way the magazines and fashion runways told her a woman should.

A decade later, Gabriella had stopped kneeling before toilets as if they were altars; she'd thrown out her once-treasured copies of *Elle* and *Vogue*. She'd thought the worst of her disorder was behind her, that her past would never come back to haunt her—until the night she'd seen her waist shrinking in the mirror in Lady Lilith's room, and heard the faucet run.

Since then, it had become harder and harder for Gabriella to keep food down. She would wake in the middle of the night with an urge to vomit, and just like when she was a teenager, she would run the sink in the bathroom—this time to keep her boyfriend Remy from worrying. Then she'd lie in bed all day with her stomach simmering as if something red and hot and tight was coming to life inside her. When she dragged herself to the dungeon and clients complimented her slender silhouette, that simmer rose until she feared to open her mouth. She was sure all her years of pain would spill right out onto her clients and scorch them like bile. She told a few who wouldn't stop commenting about her weight that she couldn't session with them any longer—and then, when no new clients arrived to replace them, realized how foolish that was. Rent was due, and if her stomach didn't calm down she'd need to see a doctor, too.

So when Corset Henry booked a session with Gabriella, requesting she wear the ocean-blue corset he loved—the one Gabriella had paid too much for on Melrose Avenue—Gabriella couldn't say no. The corset, which had once fit snug, yawned an inch from her chest as she stood appraising herself in the long mirror in Lady Lilith's room. It wasn't possible to lose so much weight so quickly, but here she was.

Behind her, Henry trailed his finger down her neck until he reached the corset's stays, undoing the ribbon like he was unwrapping a precious gift. Then he worked his way from the bottom up, tugging tighter on each lace in turn, as if he wanted to make Gabriella's waist disappear. Groaning with his own release, each time he constrained her form.

Gabriella tried not to think, not to feel, but she couldn't ignore that red bud sitting inside her, so hot and heavy it was too much to hold. And then, she saw it: that same crimson coil of heat but now outside of her, wavering in the mirror.

Was that a flame? A flame, rising from the candle Lady Eva had placed on the stairs.

Gabriella slowly turned toward the stairs, toward the attic, toward that flame. "Where are you going?" came from behind her, but Henry's words didn't penetrate. All that mattered was connecting the fire inside her to the one out here, making up for the time she'd wasted trying to keep herself small. She stepped forward until her hand hovered an inch from the candle, so close she could feel its dangerous warmth, and a voice that was half air whispered:

Burn it all down.

Wind rushed down from the attic like water and blew the flame out, and flew into Gabriella's face cold and damp as a breeze off the ocean shore. She wobbled and tripped over her heels, onto the steps, bracing herself on her left forearm—

And because of the bone mass she'd lost so many years ago, that tiny tumble of only a foot, at most two, was enough to snap Gabriella's fragile ulna.

EIGHT: RUBY

Ruby had only been in love once—with a person.

Two years ago, after *it* had happened, and the wound under Ruby's chin had healed into a thick red scar, Ruby wanted to flee from everything she knew and everyone who knew her. The neighbors she smoked weed with occasionally, her kind landlord and the cashier who always rung her up at CVS; anyone who might ask questions she didn't want to answer. She was determined to leave Hollywood and go somewhere no one could find her.

Ruby wanted two things: One, to start over, somewhere she could keep from getting close to anyone. And two, to become a real dominatrix. So she rented the apartment in West LA, not far from the Briars, a few miles and an entire world away from the flashing billboards and late-night drug deals of East Hollywood. She used her last penny to pay the savings deposit and first month's rent, packed her meager belongings into her secondhand Honda—those were the pre-Spider days—and drove across town. And then she found Mistress Katrina.

Ruby had planned to train with a dominatrix for a long time. She'd looked into working at a dungeon, but if she didn't have domming expertise, she'd have to start as a submissive. The prospect of being that vulnerable was unthinkable. So she would have to convince a dominatrix to teach her privately, and that would require money. She'd found a hostessing job at a restaurant and taken on as many shifts as possible, but with the higher West LA rent, she had even less funds than before. Still, Ruby simply could not wait any longer, so she searched the internet for every dominatrix listing she could find. She called them all, offering to clean their space or run errands in exchange for lessons. Only Mistress Katrina agreed.

The first time Mistress Katrina opened the door of her little cottage on a residential street, Ruby wondered if she had made a mistake. A curvy blonde in her thirties looked up at Ruby, with pillowy lips and long-lashed eyes and the scent of vanilla perfume surrounding her. Katrina was gorgeous, yes, but even encased in black vinyl, she wasn't the commanding presence Ruby had hoped for. Still, for weeks Ruby arrived at midnight as Katrina's last client was leaving, and headed to the secret room behind the ordinary living space, where the St. Andrew's Cross and spanking bench waited to be cleaned. For weeks Ruby tried to imagine Katrina wielding the whips and chaining men to the cross, but she couldn't picture it. She worried she was wasting her time.

And then, after a month, Katrina let Ruby watch one of her sessions.

Ruby tucked herself into a corner as the solid-boned client strolled in, and she wondered how petite Mistress Katrina would possibly subdue him. She wondered as the man took off his clothes and revealed his hairy chest and belly; she wondered as he rested his torso on the spanking bench and Katrina slapped his spongy rear end; and then, Katrina grabbed the man, and threw him to the carpet, and placed her spiky stiletto in the middle of his back, and everything changed in an instant.

Mistress Katrina dug her heel in and the man groaned, a sound of anguish and surrender and desire. Ruby could still hear it in her mind, years later: the moment he transformed from a rational man to a needy animal. Katrina kicked him onto his back, and hovered that same heel right above his genitals, and he looked up at her with the glazed eyes of a worshipper gazing upon his god.

Ruby followed the man's eyes up to Katrina, and saw that she was in fact a goddess: her wholesome features transformed, eyes that could draw out pain and desire, mouth that could dispense kindness or cruelty.

Ruby would never worship anything or anyone, but the closest she ever came was with Mistress Katrina.

Over the months that followed, Katrina taught Ruby how to use floggers and riding crops; how to tie up a man's dick and testicles so the slightest sensation would be heightened; how to overpower a man using only words, rendering all those weapons unnecessary. And while Katrina never touched Ruby, and Ruby learned nothing of Katrina's life outside those midnight hours, Ruby fell in love. She fell in love with the experience of domming, truly domming, her own power awakening and the widening of men's eyes when they recognized it. She fell in love with the woman who had given her this power. And Katrina never seemed to notice Ruby's scar, which made Ruby love her more.

Then, one night, when she was high from the session she and Katrina had shared, whipping a man with a single tail until he kissed their feet in grateful agony, Ruby went too far. She tried to touch Katrina.

Katrina gently guided Ruby away from her, and offered her an achingly soft, vanilla-scented smile. Then she told Ruby she was getting too attached, and besides, she knew enough now, and it was time for her to go make money on her own.

So Ruby had fallen in love twice: with Katrina, and with domming. And she could only keep one.

In the weeks before she'd met Mistress Katrina, when the wound under Ruby's neck had first healed into a thick scar, she worried the blemish would always remain so prominent. She wondered if she should have gone to the ER and gotten stitches. But by the time Ruby stopped training with Katrina, the redness had begun to leach from her scar. So gradually that she barely realized it, that raised line of flesh had flattened more and more.

Now, Ruby couldn't remember the last time the scar had blazed like a flame. It was slowly, slowly dissolving into her skin along with the memories of that awful night. And Ruby had resolved, sometime over the past year, that she wouldn't fall in love with another person until the scar was so subtle it no longer seemed like a part of her at all.

It wasn't a resolution Ruby had to think about much. The few hookups she'd had after Katrina had been so far from love it was laughable.

But these past weeks, as the ghost's messages had risen in pitch and the world had begun to tilt sideways on its axis, leaving everything Ruby thought she knew in danger of tumbling, she had to remind herself—

Don't fall.

Ruby had spent her last few shifts lost in a private storm cloud, so this morning, it took her an hour to pick up on the pall hanging over the Briars, the ladies whispering in worried voices. It wasn't until she realized Luna was sitting in the dressing room twiddling her thumbs, not simultaneously fixing her makeup and singing along to something on her headphones while writing her novel, that Ruby thought to ask: "Did something happen?"

"Gabriella broke her arm last night," Luna said. "In Lady Lilith's room."

Ruby's first thought was, *Thank God it wasn't Claire.* But she immediately chastised herself. "Oh my God," she said, "is she okay? Well, obviously not, but—is she going to be?"

"She texted me an hour ago," Luna said, "told me she's home recuperating in a bright pink cast. I asked her what happened, exactly, and— She said she doesn't remember."

"Do you think it was...the ghost?"

The silence that followed was more than enough to answer. And Ruby knew, right away, that *this* disaster was behind the Briars' gloomy atmosphere. Not just Gabriella's broken arm, which was awful, but which she would recover from—but the fact that the ghost had actually hurt someone. And...

"Was she with a client?" Ruby asked.

Luna blew out a breath strong enough to raise one of her hot-roller curls. "Yeah, and Nadia was watching the front desk when he came downstairs. She said Corset Henry was so freaked out he'll probably never come back."

"Shit," Ruby said. He was a good tipper and, when *he* was the one wearing the corset, an easy session. But she had something more than lost business on her mind.

Ruby had to find Claire and beg her to be careful.

She started by heading outside, where Alice was passing her lighter to a few girls huddled around the smokers' table.

"I don't get it," said a soft voice Ruby couldn't quite place. "I've never noticed anything strange in Lady Lilith's room. Or any of the rooms, for that matter." Alice and Emilie shifted and revealed the smaller girl behind them: Mara. Ruby had never heard her speak that much, at least when she wasn't responding to a direct question.

"You've only been here...what, a month?" Emilie asked Mara. "You don't notice the strange things because the entire dungeon still seems strange to you."

Mara shook her head, brushing her black hair behind one bony shoulder. The locks looked longer and thicker than Ruby remembered. "Actually, the Briars seems kind of...familiar, somehow. Like home, almost?"

Ruby wondered what kind of home Mara had grown up in, if crosses and cages reminded her of it. At least the girl seemed to have lost that frustratingly slow, stumbling way of speaking she'd had when she first arrived at the dungeon. Her voice, though still quiet, rang clearer and more confident now.

"Anyway," Alice said, "a bunch of us are visiting Gabriella later. I can drive anyone who doesn't have a car—you don't, do you, Mara?"

She shook her head no. "Thanks. I...I might be busy after work, though." She let her hair fall into her face again, as if reluctant to make eye contact with anyone.

"Do you take the bus?" Emilie asked. "I've never seen you at the bus stop. Or Uber? But that gets expensive..."

"Uh— Sometimes. I..."

This conversation was clearly a waste of Ruby's time.

"You can come too, Ruby," Alice called as Ruby turned to go back inside.

"I'll think about it," Ruby said without any sincerity. She wasn't good enough friends with Gabriella—with anyone at the dungeon—to show up at their home without it being painfully awkward. She didn't even know what part of town Gabriella lived in.

She didn't even know what part of town *Claire* lived in.

Before Ruby could continue her search, she got called into a foot worship session in one of the smaller rooms next door. There she encountered no ghostly messages, just the sliminess of her client's tongue as he sucked her toes. Once he left and she'd cleaned off his slobber, she returned to the lobby where Lady Eva appeared unusually scattered, searching for something on her desk, an entire lock of hair fallen loose from her chignon. She looked up at Ruby and said, "Stuart is coming to see you in fifteen minutes. And Jack will be here for Claire in half an hour—can you tell her, if you see her?"

Ruby's heartbeat picked up. "What room are Jack and Claire—"

"Lady Lilith's," Lady Eva cut in. Her voice was as stern as always, but fatigue crept around the edges. "It's the only one available, and I don't want to hear another word about it."

Ruby sighed and headed to the dressing room where, hearing Claire's voice, she paused outside.

"I can't understand why he hates it so much," Claire spoke urgently. "Professional submissive seems like a cool job for a future rock star's girlfriend. Right?"

"To us it does," came a soothing voice—Nadia—"but you have to remember, our boyfriends are picturing dirty, smelly men doing all kinds of sketchy things to us. Or maybe they're imagining gorgeous clients who will steal us away from them.

Anyway, I've seen it happen a million times: a guy starts to really care about his girlfriend, and he doesn't want her working here anymore." A pause. "It means he loves you."

"But he called me—he almost called me—a *whore*."

Ruby couldn't listen to this anymore. How could Claire waste two seconds of emotional energy on a man—a *boy*—who used that vile word, that word that was so clearly the opposite of everything Claire was?

Ruby cleared her throat and walked with clicking heels into the room. Two pairs of startled blue eyes looked up at her. Both women wore pink, and despite her frustration, Ruby couldn't help noticing how the rosy shade of Claire's corset brought out the flush to her cheeks.

"Ruby, I—"

"Jack's coming to see you," Ruby interrupted Claire. "In Lady Lilith's room. I think you should refuse to play with him."

"But why?"

"Oh, I don't know, maybe because you were almost crushed to death during his last session!"

"I'm going outside for a minute," Nadia muttered. "Come with me, Mara?" Ruby noticed Mara's presence for the first time—she was perched on the couch arm, running her fingers through her hair—and then both girls were gone, and it was just her and Claire.

"That wasn't Jack's fault." Claire's eyes darted as if looking for somewhere to escape to. "I can't just *not* see him."

"Why not? I do it all the time. A client grabs my ass or keeps pushing me to take my top off, and he's out. There's other mistresses he can see—and there's other submissives Jack can see. Any of whom would be *thrilled* with such a gorgeous client."

"Yeah, you can refuse to see clients," Claire's voice rose to a whine, "because you're…you're Ruby. You don't care what people think. Not all of us are like that."

"Clearly." Ruby crossed her arms over the stiff fabric of her corset. She knew she was being unfair, but she couldn't stop herself.

"Claire," Lady Eva's voice intruded, "Jack's here for you now. He's early."

"Oh— I— I'm coming." Claire jumped up and grabbed her lip gloss from the vanity table. She turned her head from side to side in the mirror, checking her makeup, painting her lips until they matched her cheeks and her corset. She was going to

106

session with Jack, in Lady Lilith's room, and Ruby couldn't do anything to stop her.

Ruby turned and left the room before Claire said anything more.

Outside, Luna, Alice and Nadia exchanged whispers while Mara stood on the other side of the gazebo, reaching her arms toward the clouds. Just stretching, Ruby supposed, though she almost appeared to be casting some spell. Her fisted hands unfurled as, above her, the smog scattered and the blood-orange sky broke through.

"Ruby," Alice hissed and beckoned her over with fingers that white-knuckled a cigarette. "I didn't want to say this in front of those new girls earlier"—she glanced back at Mara—"but we've got to start working together. Reading The Book every day, comparing notes..."

"Coming up with some kind of emergency plan..." Nadia tugged on her ponytail until she'd half pulled it out.

"This ghost, or whatever it is, has already done some serious damage." Luna cleared her throat. "I mean, I'm not worried for myself, but for the submissive girls who are in vulnerable situations and..."

An image of Claire, her ankles and wrists bound, pierced through Luna's words.

"Ruby...?"

"Yeah," Ruby muttered, "that's a good idea."

"And," Nadia said, "we're collecting a fund for Gabriella. That broken arm has to be expensive."

"Of course, I'll pitch in." Ruby's thoughts weren't on Gabriella, though, but stuck on that image of another blue-eyed girl.

A quarter-hour later, Ruby was no less distracted as she stomped her way next door. Stuart, her timid young client with his buttoned-up shirt and bow tie, tiptoed in her stormy wake. Ruby had sessioned with Stuart before, and she knew a few minutes into the session he wouldn't be so shy. She stopped in the hallway closet to grab a few dresses, a handful of oversized lingerie and the Caboodles-style makeup case, then clomped the rest of the way into the Enclave.

"Is something the matter, Mistress Ruby?" Stuart asked, fiddling with his bow tie.

"Only the fact that you're wearing the wrong sort of clothes," Ruby spat. "You're not showing nearly enough skin for the *slut* I know you are."

Stuart was nice enough, but Ruby was not in the mood to follow his script today. It was one of the things they didn't tell you when you applied to work at a dungeon, and she was sure it was even worse for submissives like Claire: you would have to act sexy and seductive on days you felt bloated and unattractive; you would have to suffer through silly tickling sessions when you were in the mood to hit something; and you would have to hear—and speak—words like *slut* and *skank* at moments you wanted to erase those combinations of letters from your brain entirely.

One thing you shouldn't have to do, though, was session in a haunted room where a coworker had broken her arm the night before. But Claire had made her choice. "Put on your party dress." Ruby threw a gown at Stuart. "I'm going to show you off to all my friends tonight."

The moment Stuart's hands closed around the tulle and lace, his fingers twitched and his eyes brightened. Another minute or two, and he'd fall far enough into his fantasies that he'd forget all about Ruby's own bad mood.

Ruby flung the remaining costumes on the sofa and rooted through the makeup kit until she located a tube of lipstick. Clinique Black Honey, a bee-stung color that must have been there since the '90s. She turned to find Stuart and make his face match his new outfit, but instead her gaze caught on the oval mirror in the corner.

With her chin lifted her scar was visible, monstrously thick, looking so much like a slash of lipstick that she dropped the tube in her hand and placed her fingers to her skin.

She felt no waxy substance, only the faint scrawl of the scar and her pulse picking up beneath it, and when she drew her hand away no residue stained her fingers.

Her eyes darted to check the other mirrors, while she called out to Stuart: "Do your runway walk."

"Shouldn't I put my heels on first, Mistress?"

She tried to breathe. "Yes, Stuart." Finally, she caught her reflection in the mirror on the back of the door. No lipstick line along her throat. With her chin lowered, her scar was nearly invisible.

It's all in my head.

Stuart had found the blood-red heels she'd abandoned with the rest of the supplies, and he squeezed his feet into them to perform what looked like a very uncomfortable strut across the room. His beaming face suggested he didn't mind the pain, but Ruby thought of a story her mother had made her read: a fairy tale about a girl who wore red shoes to church and forgot to pray. A girl whose punishment was to dance in those red shoes until her feet were chopped off.

Ruby remembered it all: how the girl with the red shoes feared she'd dance until she shriveled to a skeleton; how she begged the executioner to hack off her feet with his axe, and the executioner told her to confess her s—

Her eyes followed Stuart toward the mirror, and atop his reflection and her own she saw the red letters:

SINS

Again those ghostly words had pressed past the confines of Lady Lilith's room, invading the space Ruby thought of as her own. Would they follow her out of the dungeon, even, stick to her like that line of lipstick on her throat? Would they know just what to say, as if they could see her secrets—as if they knew exactly how to destroy her?

Ruby gulped, and closed her eyes, and tried to act like everything was normal. What else could she do? She plucked up the lipstick and sauntered toward Stuart. "I'm going to take you out tonight," she met his bright eyes to keep her own away from the rest of the room, "and I'm going to introduce you to all my friends, and tell them what a little *slut* you are."

Her gaze flicked to the mirror despite herself, and she watched the letters rearranging themselves, the *I* and *N* and *S* dissolving to create the new word she'd spoken. She wanted to scream at the ghost, to chase it out, but she could only speak to Stuart:

"I'm going to sell you to the highest bidder, like the..." She swallowed. "Like the little sissy boy you are."

She grabbed a tuft of his hair—damn it, she'd forgotten to grab a wig—and tugged him closer. She swiped the lipstick on and he pressed his lips together, clearly fighting the impulse to lick or bite them in his desire. Out of the corner of her eye, *SISSY* flashed in the mirror, and she dropped Stuart to turn toward it. The letters filled the glass now: *TRAMP, HOOKER, HARLOT. SLUT, SLAG, CUNT.* Ugly words coming to life. Infecting her brain. She had to erase them, replace them with her own. She gripped the lipstick like a weapon and scrawled words on the glass, a message she might have written on Stuart's own body in a past session:

SHOW ME WHAT A SLUT YOU ARE

"*Slut?*" Stuart's voice went as limp as his dick probably had under the tulle. "Just a slut? That's all I am?"

She'd stuck to the soft words for too long. *Slut* and *sissy*. She whirled toward Stuart. Toward the animal need in his eyes, the red creeping in from their corners. His messy lipsticked mouth making warped noises. Half-nonsense sounds, until they cleared:

"*Am I a slut, or am I a wh—*"

Something shifted on the couch. A feather boa, a fiery color, blood-orange. Slinking, snakelike. Ruby grabbed it and, before she could consider what she was doing, slung it around Stuart's neck like a noose.

The word caught, unfinished, in his throat.

"Shut up, Stuart." Ruby pulled the boa tighter and his eyes bulged. "*I* decide what you are. And yes, you are a—" She gulped, but she had to say it, just like she had to let the boa go.

"You're a whore."

It was as if the word had unleashed something. Ruby stepped away from Stuart and the very walls seemed to shudder. A low, heavy *thump* came from the back of the room. Ruby froze, and waited, and a second thump sounded. "Did you hear that?" she asked Stuart before she could stop herself.

"Hear what?" Stuart crossed his hairy arms over the dress's lacy bodice. "Actually, you forgot to turn on the music. What's with you today?"

Shit. Ruby pivoted toward the ancient CD player next to the sofa, and then she saw it: that thick red curtain, beating a bass rhythm against the back windows.

She turned away from the curtain and now the lipstick words were dripping, dissolving into red muck. Her mind spun like a crimson whirlpool; her gaze darted from one mirror to the next without her volition. All leaking storms of red raindrops. In the center of the room Stuart twirled, swaying his hips to some soundtrack only he could hear. "Turn it up!" he said. "I'll dance all night to Britney Spears! I'm a slave for you...no, I'm a *whore* for you."

110

He giggled, high and girlish, and Ruby lunged forward to grab the ends of the boa and pull the length of it across his throat. She couldn't stand to hear that word, that word...but as her gaze darted it screamed at her from every mirror, those five letters, that cruel song. His clown lips opened to expel the hard *wh*, the open *o*, and she yanked the boa tighter. In the back of her mind she knew what she was doing was wrong, so wrong, more wrong than the little girl in the red shoes who had her feet hacked off, but she couldn't stop. She would hack off his words like the girl's feet—

Whore, Ruby heard, not Stuart's voice but a little girl's voice, echoing from the oval mirror in the corner where those five red letters grew larger, dripping blood. She dragged Stuart toward that mirror by the boa around his neck, muttering, "I want you to see yourself." She turned him to face the glass, stood behind him and wrenched the strand of feathers like a tourniquet.

Stuart sputtered and spit; his hands flailed; the boa shed red feathers like petals into the air. This makeshift noose wasn't strong enough. Ruby would have to use her hands. She dropped the boa and reached from behind to grab his neck.

Stuart's eyes widened and he spoke into the mirror, "Hey, I'm not into this," but Ruby didn't care. She had to stop him from saying that word again. Her fingers hovered an inch from the bulge of his Adam's apple, so masculine and yet so vulnerable beneath the snappable birdcage bones of his neck. Just a little closer...

A cold metallic sensation like handcuffs, like scissors, bit into her wrists, and she dropped her arms. For just a second, clarity cut like a knife through her thoughts. What was she doing? She had to hurt something, but it couldn't be Stuart, it couldn't...

Crimson soaked her mind and her hands extended toward his neck again, until with the last sliver of rational thought she had left, she pushed his shoulders so he half-fell to the side.

Now it was only her and the mirror and that word. She reached out and swiped at those five red letters. If she could get rid of them, she could regain control of the situation, of herself. But the more frantically she scrubbed, the thicker and darker they grew. That word she never wanted to see or hear again, glaring at her, mocking her. She was powerless in the moment, powerless to help herself, much less some other girl in another room only a building away. So close they were within shouting distance, but Ruby wasn't sure her voice would work anymore.

There was only one way out of this. Ruby pulled her hand away and clenched her fingers into a fist. She drew back her arm and punched the mirror, once, twice, three times, until those five letters were annihilated in a torrent of broken glass, and the blood ran down her hand and over her arm like an outpouring of violence that, once let loose, could never be taken back.

NINE: CLAIRE

As soon as Claire entered Lady Lilith's room with Jack beside her, the mirrors started talking to her. *Slut*, they said, *whore, skank, harlot, traitor—*

That was a new one.

And Claire had let so many people down lately, she didn't want to consider who that last word might refer to. Who she might have disappointed.

Who she might have betrayed.

As she placed the paddles she was carrying on the bed, her heart beat hard enough to warm the metal of the coin Yarik had given her. The good-luck charm now rested under the bodice of her corset, where she'd impulsively tucked it moments before the session.

"Don't worry," Jack said, his voice so light Claire imagined the heaviness of the room might snatch it up and absorb it. "I'll keep you far from the St. Andrew's Cross."

Claire didn't find his words that reassuring.

"I can't promise, however," Jack went on, "that your ass will be safe from me. I hope you weren't planning on sitting for the rest of the afternoon."

Claire tried to giggle, but it came out hollow. Jack was looking extra handsome today, in a navy-blue sweater that deepened the shade of his eyes, but she could barely bring herself to look at him. His banter seemed off-key, and her thoughts returned to the way she'd caught Ruby looking at her, while Claire had pretended to focus on her lip gloss. Ruby's eyes in the dressing-room mirror had flashed with irritation, even anger. But beneath that lay something else—a sort of haunting, as if she were losing something she'd never had in the first place. And Claire couldn't escape the thought that *she* was to blame for Ruby's turmoil.

Why had Ruby had to walk in when Claire was rambling about Danny? That made it the second time, at least, that Ruby had overheard her whining about her boyfriend.

And why was a part of Claire starting to worry more about what Ruby was thinking, and feeling, than what Danny was? Why was a part of her—an unpredictable, slowly simmering part that frightened her—questioning whether she truly cared what Danny thought at all?

"Claire?" Jack's voice intruded, a hint of impatience deflating his usual buoyancy. "Why don't you take that pretty corset and skirt off so I can spank you. Or would you prefer that I do it for you?"

Claire quickly unlaced her corset, palming the coin before Jack could see it. The moment she touched the metal, the words on the mirrors vanished, and she began to have hope she could get through this session.

Claire hid the coin under her clothes on the edge of the bed while Jack was busy examining the paddles. He grabbed them and said, "Let's go over to that little sofa in the corner. It's about as far as we can get from the cross, isn't it?"

It was, but it was also closer to the stairs to the attic—where Lady Eva had attached a makeshift sign to the chain at the top of the six steps, above that temperamental candle. NO ENTRY, in red Sharpie letters. A response to Gabriella's broken arm, no doubt, which all the girls had been whispering about that morning.

Claire followed Jack until she stood where rain had leaked through the ceiling a week ago. Yarik's strange story came to mind—the woman with dripping hair, a haunting sort of wedding crasher—and she shivered. She opened her mouth to suggest moving elsewhere, but Jack had already pushed aside the leopard and tiger-print pillows and was sitting on the sofa's low cushions, which made a squelching sound as if they were sucking him in. Claire had no choice but to arrange herself over his lap, her bare thighs against the coarse fabric of his jeans, and clutch the slick leather of the sofa before her. *Meat room.* Room full of dead animal parts. Room that could swallow you up.

And then Jack was spanking her, and each swat carried her into the realm of the physical, just as her classes at the Dancers' Institute once had. When she was focusing on the transition from an arabesque on her right leg, to a *developée* on her left; when she was anticipating the next sting of palm or paddle against her flesh, and still smarting from the previous one; when she was simply a body, there was no room for fear or regret or the type of pain that struck too deep.

Claire raised her ass in the air, urging Jack without words to hit her harder. Forgetting how important it was not to get bruised. She worked her fingers into a tear in the sofa, into the soft insides spilling out of it, as each impact rolled through her. The force of Jack's blows would exorcise all the confusion and

114

the conflicting desires within her. It would leave her as still and empty as the room now seemed to be.

The trouble with this sort of exorcism was that when it ended, when Jack stopped spanking her, nothing had changed. She hadn't split open, and nothing had spilled out from inside of her. Those sparks still burned under her flesh, the ones that made her want to tell Danny off, to walk into the Briars and describe the gobsmacked expression on her boyfriend's face when she told him to go fuck himself. To see Ruby laugh and smile, really smile, the way she had after she helped Claire clean up the broken vase and concocted the crazy story for Lady Eva. Claire knew if she stood up to Danny, it would make Ruby smile. And then—

And then, Claire had no idea.

"Claire?" Jack said. "Is something wrong? You seem preoccupied."

He sounded like he actually cared. "Well, I—"

A noise came from above their heads. A creak that sounded distinctly like a footstep.

"Claire?"

"Did you hear that? It sounded like—"

There it was again. *Creak, creak,* each sound a hot coal rolling across her spine. She wished she could jump up and run out of there, drive home without bothering to change out of her dungeon outfit, and show Danny that he couldn't tell her what to do.

"No," Jack said, "I don't hear anything. And you're trembling. Here, sit up, I'll get you a blanket."

"No, thank you, but just—just spank me some more. Please, sir? That will warm me up." And shut off those crazy urges filling her mind, the ones that might destroy everything she'd fought so hard to preserve.

Jack did spank her again, but more lightly now, so that she could still hear the groaning of the floorboards above her, echoing through her bones.

"You wore my hand out, young lady!" Jack said after a minute. In the mirror ahead of her, Claire watched him shake and stretch his hands theatrically. "I'm not as resilient as I used to be. When I came here twenty years ago, I could punish naughty girls for hours."

"Oh really?" Claire said. She wanted to keep him talking. Maybe it would frighten the other noises—and thoughts—away.

"My girlfriend and I came here together," Jack said, as he slapped her backside again. "She loved to watch me spank other girls, and I loved to watch them spank her." As he spoke, his hand regained its firmness.

"Your girlfriend liked it when you spanked other girls? That's kind of unusual," she grasped on to the distraction he offered.

"Oh, Claire, she was *so* much fun," Jack said. "Sweet and sexy, just like you. Don't tell your boss, but we used to pick up girls here and take them home."

"Seriously?" Claire couldn't help asking. The creaking grew fainter above her, until she was almost sure she'd imagined it. That heat no longer crackled along her spine.

"Have you ever had a threesome, Claire? The only thing better than spanking and doing...other things, things that aren't allowed here, to one girl, is having two of them at once."

Well, this conversation was taking a turn Claire hadn't expected. Maybe a little dirty talk would keep the ghost, and the rebellious embers inside her, at bay. Besides, she was always game to hear about the dungeon in its earlier years—rumor had it the rules had been looser then, the sessions wilder.

"No," she answered honestly, "*I've* never had a threesome, but I've always fantasized about them. What was the craziest thing you did?" It was easier to ask these questions in the position she was in—still looking down at the split in the sofa's stuffing, with no need to make eye contact.

"Oh... I don't know..." He stopped talking to spank her, and probably think a little. But the answer, when it came, was a letdown. "I could watch my girlfriend make out with a girl almost as hot as she was all night long."

"I'm sure you did a lot more than watch."

"I used to tie her up and have the other girls go down on her."

"At the dungeon?"

He laughed. "No, but I could have gotten away with it here too."

"Well, these days you wouldn't," Claire thought it necessary to remind him. She didn't mind talking about this, but it would break her heart a little if gentlemanly Jack turned into a Gunther or a Cupcake Kenny, worming his fingers under her panties.

116

"No," he agreed, "but you know what we could do... Do you still do cameos?"

"We do. Would you like me to call someone in?" Cameos were when another lady joined the session for ten minutes in exchange for a tip. It was a good idea—she always felt safer with another woman's company.

"Why don't you call up another submissive?" Claire looked up at the mirror, and Jack's reflection winked at her. "I'll see if I can still handle two girls at once, the way my younger self used to."

Claire hopped up and made her way over to the intercom, listening for suspicious sounds and hearing nothing. She pressed the button and called down: "Excuse me, Lady Eva, we'd like to have a submissive come in for a cameo?"

"Let's see..." Some rustling followed, then Lady Eva went on, "Mara is the only submissive available. I'll send her up."

That was odd—Mara was usually in session all day. But Claire didn't have time to consider it, as Jack came to capture her hand and twirled her toward the bondage bed, with a finesse that made her wonder if he'd studied ballroom dancing. It wouldn't surprise her.

She did her best to come to a graceful landing and Jack said, "Did you just pirouette? I knew you were a better dancer than you made yourself out to be."

"You remembered?"

"The Hollywood Dancers' Institute didn't deserve you," he said, and his smile made him look as young as Danny in the dim light. "Claire"—he clutched her hand again—"will you let me take you out to dinner?"

She laughed, sure he was joking, but he only tightened his grasp.

Oh no.

"I'm—I'm sorry, sir," she wriggled her fingers and managed to extricate her hand, "but it's against the rules to see clients outside of here." That light, dizzy feeling left over from spinning across the room plummeted into disappointment. This wasn't as bad as if Jack had yanked her panties down or groped her, but it wasn't much better, either.

"Oh, come on, Claire." Jack's eyes remained bright, but a hint of steel tightened his tone. "I know how you girls treat the *rules*—"

The door creaked open, and Mara entered in her tiny white top and matching skirt with blue piping, stepping so lightly that her heels barely made contact with the carpet. Jack went rigid, and Claire couldn't decide if Mara had entered at the best possible moment, or the worst one.

"Hello, sir," the girl said quietly. Her wide eyes and willowy limbs made her appear so much like a skittish deer, Claire almost grabbed her to keep her from fleeing. "I'm Mara."

Jack stood up straighter and said, "Well, Mara, why don't you come get next to Claire so I can spank you." Yet he pushed his hands into his jeans pockets and stepped back from the bed, as if he wasn't that interested in touching either of them any longer.

Mara leaned over the bed, her dark hair falling like a curtain so Claire could no longer see her face, though she did notice the ghosts of ropes, faint imprints around Mara's wrists and ankles. At the same time, Jack slowly pulled his hands from his pockets. The tendons stood above his knuckles as he reached forward to flip up Mara's skirt and, finally, he spanked her.

And with each echo of hand against flesh, Claire wondered if the other two could feel the tension growing, thick enough to cut through with a knife—or a pair of scissors.

If Mara had left them any scissors.

On the mirror above Jack's reflection, something *did* cut through the tension, so sharply Claire almost gasped:

CHOP OUT THE LIES

Each letter a slash, more blood than lipstick.

FIND THE TRUTH

Claire wanted to scream at the mirror to shut up, or if it insisted on telling her *what* to do, to also tell her *how.* She bit her lip and forced her eyes away from the words, down to where Jack's mouth tightened into a frown. With the line of his lips exposing the wrinkles to either side, his age became fully visible for the first time.

After less than a minute, Jack stepped back and reached into his pocket to pull out his phone. He glanced at it and said, "I'm sorry, ladies, I'm afraid I'll have to cut this session short. A bit of an emergency." He took out his wallet and handed a bill to Mara and another to Claire—a hundred. Then, before Claire could ask what was wrong, he was gone.

That tension hung lower than ever until Mara straightened and stretched, and said, "There wasn't really anything on his phone, was there?"

"I...I doubt it," Claire answered.

"He just didn't like me."

"No!" Claire answered automatically, "It wasn't that." She should explain about Jack asking her out, though she wasn't certain that was why he'd run off, either.

"Well," Mara headed toward the far side of the room and returned with a towel and Lysol, "the least I can do is help you clean." Claire breathed in the scent of lemon and chemicals, hoping it would clear her head, as Mara wiped down the bondage bed. "I think I know why Jack didn't like me," Mara said, after a moment. "I'm too *exotic*."

The way she spat the word told Claire more than one client had called her that already. And Claire couldn't help thinking of all the men—and, well, Lady Eva and their coworkers—asking Mara where she was from. Trying to define her, to make her into something they could understand. And Claire wasn't immune. She had wondered where Mara came from too.

But offering Mara false comfort wouldn't help. "Look," Claire said, "you're gorgeous. You walk like you're floating, and those eyes and that hair—it's something else." It really was, a black waterfall flowing all the way to Mara's waist when Claire could have sworn a week ago, it only reached halfway down her back. "A lot of the clients are in love with you, but—"

"The same thing that draws so many of them turns others off. The ones who want the blonde or brown-haired girl next door."

Claire didn't know what to say, so she settled for, "You're right." She sprayed a paddle with Lysol. "It's not fair, but it's true."

The dungeon was a murky place, a place where men could reveal the parts of themselves they hid elsewhere. Sometimes, the fantasies they let free were sweet or simple or exciting; but sometimes, these dark rooms with their crosses and cages brought out the worst in people.

"The more I think about it, though," Mara startled Claire out of her thoughts, "the less I think that's what's going on with Jack." Her gaze rested on the mirror above the bed, as though she were studying her own image, but Claire had the sense she was looking beyond it. "I think he just reminded me of someone— I mean, I reminded him of someone—

"You know what?" Mara turned away from the mirror and looked into Claire's eyes. "You remind me of someone too."

Claire shook her head and finished wiping clean the spanking paddle. "You're the second person to tell me that today."

"Someone...I just wish I could remember who." A cloud passed over Mara's face, and for an instant, her expression revealed a pain strong enough to penetrate inside of Claire. A cold little hand, clutching at her heart.

Claire shivered, realizing all at once that she was naked aside from her G-string, and entirely overexposed. "Hey," she asked Mara, "can you hand me my clothes? On the edge of the bed there."

Mara grabbed Claire's corset, and something slipped from beneath it and landed on the zebra stripes of the carpet. Yarik's coin. Mara bent to retrieve it and above her head, in the long, thin mirror, words appeared that made even less sense than the earlier ones.

LET'S CALL HER VI—

Where had Claire heard that before? Forgetting her nakedness again, she stepped toward the mirror, and she wasn't even surprised when the reflection of the candle on the stairs ignited into fiery life. Claire reached toward the image of that flame, toward the promise of illumination, answers, an end to this dark limbo—

Something cold and insistent clasped bonelike around Claire's arms and slammed her down. She landed on her left hip, the impact throbbing through to the bone, and looked up to see Mara's eyes like two whirlpools above her. For a moment, Mara's gaze felt like something Claire could fall into and never climb her way out of; her head spun and the St. Andrew's Cross above her lurched back and forth.

The room settled, and Mara released her grip on Claire's forearms. "The cross," she half gasped, "it was about to fall on you. I called out for you to move, but you didn't hear..."

Claire was gasping too, trying desperately to catch her breath. She looked away from Mara, toward the mirror, but there was that flame, drawing her in again. And the cross...so it really had been falling, like last time, with Jack? Or was that an excuse...

120

No. Mara wouldn't push Claire for no reason. But where had such a tiny girl found so much strength?

Claire caught the glint of Yarik's coin in front of her—Mara never had picked it up. When Claire wrapped her fingers around it the pain in her hip eased, and she stood shakily.

"What is that, anyway?" Mara asked in a calmer voice.

"Oh, it's...a good-luck charm," Claire said. "We've got to get that candle—"

She turned toward the attic, where the candle stood small and innocuous and snuffed out.

A twanging echoed from the bed, from underneath Claire's clothes. She jumped, then realized it was only her phone. Playing the opening to Nirvana's "Come As You Are." Of all times, Danny had to call then?

Claire turned away from Mara and tried to sound casual as she answered, "What's up?"

On the other end, Danny cleared his throat. "Hey, babe, I'm sorry to bug you at work, but band practice was canceled tonight, and I want to take you out to dinner. Celebrate your new job."

Danny's sweet, hopeful voice flowed over her like water, flushing away her fear and anger, extinguishing it like the candle on the staircase. So strange and yet so natural, how quickly that fire could be doused. "Of course," she said, "I should be home by seven?"

"I'll plan on it," Danny said. She hung up, letting Danny's eagerness infect her, reminding herself in only a minute or two she'd be out of this haunted room.

But then Claire turned and saw Mara glowering at her. "Your boyfriend?"

"Yeah." Claire shrugged.

"If you ask me," Mara said, "he sounds like kind of a jerk."

Claire remembered that Mara had sat beside her and Nadia earlier that morning, probably listening in on their entire conversation. "He's—he's got his issues, but I know he's trying."

"Well, if you picked that song on your phone for him, maybe he's not that bad. It's a good song." Mara turned and flipped her hair over one shoulder—and Claire caught a flash of red. "Hey," Claire's pulse picked up, "what is that? I think there's something on your shirt."

Mara craned her neck to see her backside in the mirror, and there it was, unmistakable: a slash of crimson, bleeding down the fabric. Mara touched her collar and gazed, wide-eyed once more, at the stain blooming over her pale fingers. Lipstick, or blood?

Claire thought she might throw up. It was all coming back at once, piling in on her, crowding the room. What was next—another fire? Something—or some*one*—breaking, their bones splitting apart?

She'd been foolish to let thoughts of Danny distract her. And now Claire feared this would keep happening, over and over, until she understood what she was meant to learn. What part she played in this drama—because if the mirror's messages were any indication, this all had something to do with her.

As if the mirror had heard her thoughts, new letters formed. Answers, Claire dared to hope, but it was only more nonsense. *CALL HER VIO*—

"Violet," Claire remembered the name Yarik had used, twice now.

Mara grabbed Claire's wrist, her grip biting as the too-small handcuffs Bondage Brian liked to use. "What did you say?" she whispered, her voice so demanding, she seemed to have become an entirely different girl.

"Nothing, just—something a client told me. I'm probably remembering it wrong. We'd better go downstairs, I think Lady Eva has some bleach we can use on your shirt. That outfit's too cute to give up on…" As Claire rambled, Mara slowly, slowly let go, and Claire rushed for her clothes. She didn't want to stay in this room for a second longer than she had to.

Mara left Lady Lilith's room first, and as Claire pulled the door shut she saw red staining her skin, right where Mara's fingers had been, circling her wrist like rope. She brushed her other hand against it and felt only her own flesh, colder than usual but clean and soft.

By the time she'd descended the stairs, the color had evaporated, another mirage.

Claire trailed Mara through the front door of the dungeon—and straight into a madhouse. Lady Eva was talking over a man in a half-buttoned shirt, his bow tie swerving to one side as he gestured wildly. Claire noted the lipstick smeared clownlike across his face as she slipped past them; she caught the words "Ruby" and "crazy" from the man and "reasonable explanation" from Lady Eva. Claire's corset constricted, cutting off her breath as she sidestepped a few whispering girls and hurried to the dressing room. She stepped over a blood-spotted towel to find Ruby herself on the sofa, with Nadia wrapping Ruby's right hand in an Ace bandage.

"Oh my God," Claire said, "what happened?"

"It's okay," Ruby said, her voice tight as Claire's corset. "I just hit the mirror in the Enclave. It was an accident."

"She *punched* the mirror," Nadia clarified.

"No, I—"

"Ruby, I saw the slashes on your knuckles. You weren't slapping away a spider like you told Lady Eva."

"Yes I was!" Now Ruby sounded petulant and strangely childlike. "You can't tell me you haven't seen those spiderwebs in the Enclave. There's—"

"Don't worry," Nadia said, "I'm not going to tell the boss." She finished wrapping the bandage, which squeezed all of Ruby's fingers together so her hand look like a foreign appendage, and held the remainder of the fabric in one hand while she rooted around on the vanity table with the other. "I know we had some scissors around here..."

"All the scissors are missing," Ruby muttered; then she shook Nadia's hand away, brought the loose Ace bandage to her teeth and tugged.

"Ruby!" Nadia said as Claire wished she could help, instead of standing there looking stupid. "I still think you should go to urgent care," Nadia went on while she taped the bandage closed, "in case you need stitches."

"Don't be ridiculous! I'm not spending my savings on that. You know they'll take an arm and a leg if you don't have insurance."

"Okay, okay," Nadia said. "You can't drive, though. You'll have to get someone to—"

"I'll take you home," Claire interrupted, and Ruby looked up with doubt on her face, and that made Claire's heart wrench

"That's okay," Ruby said, "you don't have to help me. I guess you made it through Jack's session?"

Claire gulped and nodded. "The *session* was fine." It was Mara's behavior that unsettled her, but she didn't want to burden Ruby with that right then. "Please, let me help—"

"Don't you want to visit Gabriella with the other girls?" Ruby spat the question.

Claire hadn't heard about any plan to visit Gabriella, but it didn't matter. She struggled to make her voice as firm as—well, as Ruby's, and told her:

"No. I want to make sure *you* get home safe."

TEN: RUBY

Ruby couldn't believe she was actually there, heading along the I-10 in the passenger's seat of Claire's secondhand Toyota, which desperately needed a new coat of paint and—well, a good cleaning. It surprised Ruby that Claire wasn't a neat freak, and she had to stop herself from picking up the empty Starbucks cups and candy wrappers scattered below her seat, but she appreciated this glimpse into Claire's life outside the dungeon. She remembered Claire's chipped nail polish when she'd taken her hand, the day the vase had broken, and what Ruby had thought of her—*endearingly imperfect.*

Unlike Ruby herself, who had passed far beyond imperfect to *complete and hopeless mess.* She felt the strap of her tank top slipping and reached for it with her right hand—and ended up flailing around with a fabric-wrapped flipper. She lifted her injured hand to her face and inspected the bandage, counting the tiny drops of blood that had seeped through it.

Claire glanced over at her. "Does it hurt a lot?" She had pulled her curls into a loose, messy bun, a style she never wore at the dungeon, and a few locks had slipped free to dance around her face in the breeze from the open window.

"Nah," Ruby said, "it only stings a little. I'm sure it's not as bad as one of Gunther's spankings."

Claire laughed, but the sound was hollow. She was wearing one of those sweatshirts with the cut-out collar that fell below one shoulder, and it made her look like the actress from *Flashdance.* Ruby wanted to pull the shirt up and watch it fall again—but that was the last kind of thought she should be having right now. "You can take the next exit," she said, and could no longer stop herself from grabbing one of the coffee cups with her good hand and scooping up the scattered wrappers.

"Sorry about the mess," Claire said. "I have this bad habit of ignoring it until I can't stand it any longer, and then cleaning it all in a fit. Usually when I'm already late for work."

Silence followed as Claire exited onto Sepulveda Boulevard, and then Ruby had to direct her along the winding residential streets where the jacarandas had begun to bloom in shades of purple. When April arrived in a matter of days, a riot of violet petals would coat car roofs and sidewalks.

"So…" Claire spoke up again, "What happened, anyway? Did you really punch the mirror?"

"I don't want to talk about it." Ruby looked out the passenger's side window and saw red raindrops running down the rearview mirror, so she turned to face front again.

"Okay." Claire sighed. "Should I turn right or left here?"

"Actually, you can let me off here," Ruby said. "I'm half a block away."

"I'm not letting you carry your stuff in by yourself!" Claire said. "Besides, you need help getting settled for the night. Should I take this parking spot?"

"It's not like I broke a bone." Ruby winced as she thought of Gabriella. "I can handle it from here." But she didn't stop Claire from pulling into the empty space; it was a miracle to get one this close to her apartment.

Claire hopped out, opened the back door and grabbed the big bag of outfits before Ruby could stop her. "Which way?" she asked, as Ruby tried to take her bag back and Claire hugged it closer to her. "Let me help you."

"Fine," Ruby said, thinking how small Claire looked with the duffle slung over her shoulder, in that falling-off sweatshirt with her sundress fluttering underneath it. "Follow me."

It wasn't until they stood in front of her building that Ruby realized this was really going to happen: Claire was going to come inside. Aside from a few one-night stands and the maintenance man, this place hadn't seen a single visitor since she'd moved in.

She unlocked the door and said, "Um, it's kind of small," as she flicked the lights on—and became painfully aware of how depressing the space must look. Not a single picture hung on the walls; no colorful rugs or potted plants sat near the curtained windows. For God's sake, there was barely any furniture—just the bed and the end table and a beanbag chair in the corner. "You don't have to stay," she told Claire.

"Well, if you don't want me to…" Claire actually sounded wistful, as if she wanted to stick around. And she also looked like she was about to keel over if she didn't put down the duffle.

"Here—" Ruby rushed forward and tried to grab the bag's handles, but she'd forgotten, again, about her injury and ended up fumbling and dropping the duffle. "Ow." She clutched her

126

right hand which, despite what she'd told Claire earlier, was causing her quite a bit of discomfort. Especially when she tried to use it.

"See," Claire said with too much satisfaction in her voice, "you do need help. Can I fix you something to eat?"

"Uh... I'm not hungry," Ruby said truthfully, thinking of blood running down broken mirrors, down her knuckles. "I might have a drink, though. Do you want one?" She walked into the miniscule kitchen with Claire behind her, opened a cabinet with her left hand and rooted around at the back of it. "Aha!" She pulled out the almost full bottle of vodka. "I don't drink much, but I knew I'd stashed this for an emergency. Nature's pain reliever."

Claire raised her eyebrows but grabbed the bottle away from Ruby. "Don't you dare try to open that by yourself." She fussed with the cap while Ruby cracked the fridge door and, to her relief, found a bottle of tonic water inside. She hoped that stuff didn't go bad.

"I can make you a vodka tonic," she said. "There's glasses in that cabinet I opened."

"Okay," Claire agreed, "but just one."

Ruby made a valiant attempt to open the water herself, but it became clear Claire would have to prepare the vodka tonic. Ruby tried to ignore the prickling at the back of her hand, the residue of dripping blood in her mind, and most of all, the sight of Claire's slim shoulder peeking out of that sweatshirt, her messy hair, her sweet half-smile. Before Claire could grab a second glass, Ruby reached for the vodka bottle with her left hand and took a long, fiery swig.

"Ruby!" Claire said.

"What?" Ruby tried her best to look innocent. "Saved you the trouble."

Claire picked up her glass and took delicate sips as Ruby wondered what they should do now. The kitchen was far too small for the two of them; they were so close that Ruby could practically taste the sweetness of Claire's cherry blossom perfume, chasing away the sting of the vodka. She walked back into the bed-slash-living-room with Claire following, and said, "Um...you can sit on the beanbag chair if you want. Or the bed."

"There's some joke about a romance novel here," Claire said. "You know—the hero and heroine have to spend the night together somewhere, and there's only one bed? It's a classic setup."

Ruby forced a laugh. "I've never read a romance novel." She perched awkwardly on the edge of the bed, wishing the black comforter was newer and softer, and Claire sat just as stiffly beside her.

"You really can go now," Ruby said. "I'm not going to punch any more mirrors tonight, I promise."

Claire glanced around as if searching for mirrors she might have to take down and hide, but instead she asked, "Do you have a TV? We could watch a stupid sitcom or something. Take our minds off everything for a while."

Ruby grabbed her laptop off the bedside table. "I watch stuff on here, mostly *Law & Order*. I bought, like, a hundred episodes on Amazon."

"*Law & Order*?" Claire scrunched her face up like she'd swallowed something sour, but it only made her look adorable. "That doesn't sound very relaxing."

"It's my comfort show. I like to see the bad guys found out and punished in under an hour." Ruby knew she should be forcing Claire out by now, but instead she was opening the laptop, pulling up her browser.

"Makes sense." Claire had slipped her flip-flops off and crossed her legs on the bed. Ruby took the empty glass from her hand and set it on the end table, then she followed Claire's lead and kicked off her own sandals. "Do you like *SVU*," Claire went on, "or is that too close to home, considering what we do for a living?"

"Of course I like *SVU*. Olivia Benson is a goddess. And so is Mariska Hargitay."

"And Christopher Meloni is smoking hot...half noble protector, and half lit fuse about to go off." Claire looked dreamily into the distance.

"You would say that." Ruby rolled her eyes.

"Well, Mariska Hargitay is smoking hot too," Claire added.

"Okay, I guess you're forgiven."

Ruby found an *SVU* episode and leaned back against the pillows, allowing herself to sink into them. The vodka was starting to kick in. "Here," she told Claire, "come next to me so you can see." Claire crawled up the bed, and Ruby had to remind herself not to get *too* comfortable.

They watched stone-faced detectives examine the evidence around a bloodstained woman's body, all of it at a safe distance behind the computer screen, but then Claire asked softly, "Are you sure you don't want to talk about it?"

Ruby was already shaking her head when Claire went on: "Tell me what happened, and I'll answer anything you ask me. A secret for a secret."

The offer was tempting. "Fine," Ruby agreed before she could stop herself.

"You first," Claire prompted, and Ruby had to look away from her expectant blue eyes, back to the screen where Detectives Benson and Stabler exchanged smoldering glances.

"I was seeing things in the mirrors," she spoke mechanically, trying to keep her mind on the TV show. "Words and...and things that weren't there, like you warned me about. So I punched the mirror to make them stop." She turned back toward Claire. "Okay, my turn."

"But that was barely an answer! You di—"

Ruby racked her brain for a good question and spoke over Claire: "You said you dropped out of dance school. Why?"

Claire's gaze darkened and Ruby almost regretted asking; but at the same time, she wanted to know the truth even more now. Maybe she could somehow make Claire feel better.

Or maybe she was only kidding herself.

"I had no business being there in the first place," Claire said, looking down and playing with her nails. The polish—pink this time, ballet-slipper pink—was chipped again. "We'd never had money for dance lessons growing up. I'd only had a few community college ballet classes for training, and technically speaking, I was the worst dancer there. I can't believe they let me in."

"But they did," Ruby said, "so they must have seen some potential in you. You were probably better than you think."

"No, I was awful. I could barely balance on pointe." Claire grimaced, an expression painfully close to disgust. "But anyway, I was determined to stick it out. I thought if I stayed late at the studio and practiced every night, if I worked until my muscles were throbbing and I was tired enough to collapse, if I wanted it badly enough"—and Ruby could hear in Claire's voice how much she had wanted it, still wanted it, maybe—"if I just suffered through it for as long as it took, I could overcome all that I lacked. But real life doesn't work that way." She swallowed, glanced briefly up at Ruby and back down again. "I was halfway through the program when the choreographer of the second-year student showcase, Mr. Rivers, said he would give me a solo. No one had *ever* given me a solo."

Claire paused and looked at the computer screen. Ruby had completely lost track of the plot, but some handcuffed murderer appeared to be in the midst of a confession.

"Anyway, Mr. Rivers said he would teach me to *seduce* the audience." She laughed, a dry rattle. "Turns out he only wanted to seduce me. As soon as I started refusing him, he reassigned the solo and told me I would never make it as a dancer."

"But he was a bitter old asshole! You can't give up on your dreams because of someone like that. You could go back. You could—"

Claire shook her head. "He was an asshole, but he was also telling the truth. That was what made it so much worse. Once he gave the solo to another girl, he made the steps twice as difficult. That was the choreography he'd wanted to use in the first place, but he knew I couldn't handle it." With those last words, her shoulders slumped, her body hunching into itself.

Ruby didn't know what to say. She looked down and ran her fingers over the bandage that masked the damage to her knuckles. The torn skin stung again, despite the vodka. "I bet we could find an episode of *SVU* about a Mr. Rivers. We could watch him go to jail for propositioning his students in under an hour."

"But like I said earlier—the real world doesn't work that way."

"So you quit the dance school—"

"Dancers' Institute," she clarified, "in Hollywood."

"You quit the Dancers' Institute," Ruby corrected herself, "and you became a professional submissive?"

"Basically, yes. I worked at a clothing store for a while, and then I...I escorted for about a year." Claire sat up and looked straight at Ruby, her eyes open and untroubled, as if that part of her past didn't bother her nearly as much as what had happened with her dance teacher. "Made enough money to pay off almost all my student loans. Then I found the Briars and liked it much better."

"I'm glad you found the Briars," Ruby said. "Escorting can be dangerous. And besides, if you weren't at the Briars, I would never have met you."

Claire smiled, just a little, and Ruby was relieved to see the weight of the memories lifting. She wasn't too surprised Claire had escorted—more than one woman who worked at the dungeon had, at one point or another—and she couldn't judge her for it. She was just happy Claire had trusted her enough to tell her.

"And that was a second secret," Claire's grin grew wider, "so that means you owe me one now."

Ruby's mouth fell open. "You little... Did you just trick me?"

Claire shrugged. "Maybe. Let me think of the perfect question..." She tapped her finger against her temple.

"I didn't agree to this!"

"When you were a kid, what did you want to be when you grew up?"

Well, that Ruby could answer. "A dominatrix," she said quickly.

Claire raised an eyebrow.

"I might not have known what to call it," Ruby went on, "but for as long as I can remember, I was fighting with any boy who called me a name or tugged my hair. And when I say fighting, I mean fighting—like wrestling him to the ground and stomping on him and even kicking him in the balls a time or two."

Claire giggled. "Oh my God, Ruby, I can totally see it."

"I drove my parents up the walls, and it was worse because my family was so religious. My mother always said"—Ruby took on a dismayed tone, exaggerated to ridiculous proportions by the vodka—"'Chastity, you have the devil inside you.'"

Claire's giggle turned into full-blown laughter. If she was still drinking her vodka tonic, she would have spit it all over the bed.

"*Chastity?* Your parents named you *Chastity?*"

"Hey." Ruby couldn't help herself; she pulled Claire to her and spanked her a few times over her dress. "You think because I'm injured you can get away with disrespecting me? You think I don't know how to spank with my left hand? That's *Mistress* Chastity to you."

Claire's laughter overflowed as she flipped onto her back to escape Ruby's hand, and then their faces were so close that Ruby could lean down just an inch or two and kiss her. It would be so easy. And it seemed like Claire wanted her to, the way she was looking up with her lips parted, expectant.

Ruby darted back and sat up against the pillows, putting some distance between them. What was she thinking? The strap of her tank top had slipped again, and this time she was careful to use her left hand to guide it back into place. Claire, too, was sitting up and rearranging herself. The messy bun had fallen, and her curls hung loose against her shoulders.

"It's only fair that I know your real name too, now," Ruby pointed out.

"It's Anna," Claire twisted her lips, as if the word tasted bitter, "but I think of Claire as my real name."

"Me too," Ruby said. "I mean—I think of myself as Ruby."

"It's perfect for you." Claire smoothed the hem of her dress as she re-crossed her legs. "So, it was your childhood dream to become a dominatrix," she went on. "I imagine there's not a college major for that..."

"I skipped college," Ruby said. "Skipped town, too, the day I graduated high school. I came to Los Angeles and went a little wild... About the time I should have been graduating college, I was trying to become a domme by answering Craigslist ads, and that went about as badly as you can imagine."

Claire winced, and Ruby quickly added, "I wised up soon enough and found a mentor. Mistress Katrina. I should have done that in the first place—it would have saved me a lot of trouble." She forced herself to concentrate on Katrina, and not on what had come before, and the words slipped out before she could stop them: "Except I fell for my mentor, and that was its own sort of trouble. It hurt when I realized she was only interested in me as a student." Shit—had she really said that? The vodka was loosening her lips too much. "I guess it was the opposite of what happened with you and Mr. Rivers," she added. "When Katrina rejected me, I—"

The staccato rhythm of a guitar interrupted her from the floor—the beginning of some old Nirvana song. Claire's eyes widened like a startled animal's. "Oh no," she said, "oh no oh no oh no," as she jumped off the bed and picked up her phone from where it lay beside Ruby's duffle. "I totally forgot. Danny was going to take me out to dinner to celebrate my new job."

That name, coming from Claire's pink lips, made the aftertaste of vodka rise acrid in Ruby's mouth. And that last thing she'd said... "Your new what?"

"I—I told Danny I quit working at the dungeon, since he hates it so much. He thinks I'm with some catering company..."

Claire kept her gaze on the phone as the panicked words tumbled out. "I've got to take this."

"I have to go to the bathroom anyway." Ruby slammed the laptop closed. "I'll give you some privacy." As Claire raised the phone to her ear, Ruby's stomach was already sinking; the moment she made it into the bathroom and closed the door, she slid all the way down it and landed on the cold tile floor. She told herself not to listen, to get up and run the sink full blast, but instead she just sat there and allowed Claire's panicked "*What?*" and "*I'm sorry*" and "*I'll be there as soon as I can*" to punch right into her.

She had been so stupid, allowing herself to think this past hour meant something. Thinking Claire was pouring her heart out to Ruby, when clearly, she still had so many secrets to hide.

A soft knock sounded on the door, and Ruby stood and opened it. Claire was off the phone now, but the color had faded from her cheeks, and shadows crept ghostlike under her eyes. "Danny got a DUI," she said. "I have to go pick him up. You'll be okay now, right?"

A DUI? The asshole kept getting worse and worse. But Ruby swallowed her thoughts and answered automatically, "Oh, of course, but will you? Driving, I mean. We were drinking..."

"I had one drink," Claire said. "I'll be fine."

"Okay, well, um, thanks for helping me," Ruby said. She tried to hold on to her frustration, yet no matter how questionable Claire's choices were, anger slipped away and longing took its place. Claire was already slipping her flip-flops back on and heading toward the door. Ruby knew she should step forward and open it for her, walk her to her car, even, but her own feet seemed rooted to the floor.

Claire turned back toward Ruby and lifted her hand with those chipped pink nails, then dropped it again. "See you," she said, and she was gone.

Ruby squeezed her eyes shut, tried to clench her hands into fists, but with the stupid bandage she could only manage one of them. She opened her eyes and looked around at the rumpled bedcovers, the bare, dark walls. Her apartment had never seemed so empty and so quiet. Claire had brought new life to it, just for an hour, and now Ruby would forever feel her absence.

Ruby squeezed her fist again, felt the sweet sting of her nails against her palm. "Fuck it," she said, and without bothering to put her shoes on, she marched to the door, opened it and stepped outside into the twilight. She hurried to the sidewalk and, seeing Claire's small, graceful silhouette had almost disappeared, she started to run. "Wait!" she called, but Claire didn't seem to hear her. "Wait!" she yelled again.

This time, Claire stopped, and turned, and Ruby ran the rest of the way to her, ignoring the pebbles that dug into her bare feet along the way. When she finally reached her, she grabbed Claire's hand with her good one.

"I wanted to tell you..." Ruby started. "I wanted to..."

Words failed her, and she pulled Claire to her, and wrapped her arm around Claire's shoulders, and kissed her.

Claire's lips were just as soft as Ruby had imagined they would be. Her body was just as small and perfect in Ruby's arms. Ruby felt it the moment Claire started to kiss her back, the moment those soft lips yielded and Claire's hands found their way to the sliver of bare skin between Ruby's jeans and her tank top. She did everything she could to memorize that moment, so that even if Claire never spoke to her again, she could hold on to this feeling forever.

And then Claire was pulling back, and looking up at Ruby with the moon's glow spilling over her face, etching out planes of light and shadow and regret. "I'm sorry," she said, "I have to go."

Claire turned and walked away, leaving Ruby alone in the growing darkness.

As March turned to April and our dungeon's ghost progressed from threats to acts of violence, memories were emerging; our secrets were slipping loose as if shaken from the rafters of an old room no one had entered in years. Some came purposefully, like the story Claire offered up to Ruby; some had to be coaxed out, like the tidbits Ruby surrendered to Claire in return; and still others were stuck, jammed into a tiny crawl space, like the threads of her past Mara struggled to tug free and untangle.

But those three women weren't the only ones among us with histories that haunted them. Every woman at the Briars had secrets, and every secret held a kernel of danger within it.

For instance: while Ruby and Claire were trading memories, and the other girls visited Gabriella after her own tussle with the past, Nadia, who often worked the desk at night, was left alone in the dungeon. To make matters worse, she'd worked herself into a frenzy reading The Book, where women now recounted strange horrors in both Lady Lilith's room and the Enclave. She pictured those blood-red curtains beating against the Enclave wall, beating their way into the ladies' minds, until they wanted to hurt the clients, twist their dicks off or—

Or break a mirror, like Ruby had done. And now here Nadia was in the Enclave, searching through exhausted eyes for any last slivers of glass, racking her brain for any way the women could work together to make this all stop. If only they could ask Lady Eva for help, but after that letter and the candle and...

Nadia looked up to the fractured reflection of her face in the mirror, her spray tan unable to mask the shadows under her eyes, and her thoughts all ran off. How long had she been breaking herself into pieces for everyone else? She spotted another glass fragment on the floor, and crouched down to reach for it, and when she stood again the mirror was whole, unbroken, and the image of a boy she hadn't seen in years looked back at her.

She gasped, and dropped the piece of glass, and lifted her fingers, tracing the face of her dead little brother in the mirror's surface. "Dmitri?" she whispered, but of course no answer came. Just the cherubic face surrounded by curly blond hair, the face of a boy Nadia had taken care of throughout both their childhoods. Her brother had had epilepsy, and Nadia had been the one to make sure he took his medicine, to lower him to the floor and turn him on his side whenever he had a seizure, and to hold him afterward and tell him he was safe. But she hadn't been able to stop the seizure that killed him, and no matter how many other people she'd tried to care for and comfort in the years that followed, she could never make up for that first failure.

Nadia stroked the image in the mirror with greater and greater fervor, as if she could reach through and touch Dmitri's velvet-soft hair, and when she lifted her hand her palm dripped with blood. She looked down at her flesh in confusion, then back at the mirror where the shards were jagged again, edged with red liquid where she'd run her hand against them, over and over. She shook in fear—no, in fury—how dare the ghost trick her? Make her believe her brother could come back, if only for a moment; stir up that aching and longing that transformed into the urge to rip the curtains, crash through the windows, set fire to it all—

NO. She wouldn't let the ghost control her. She told herself to stop shaking, it was just a few scratches, just a long night.

But she didn't stop shaking.

Nadia had told a few women at the Briars about her brother, but she had another secret, one she'd never revealed: that epilepsy ran in families, and she had it too. She'd only had two seizures in her life, just enough to diagnose her, and the risk of another seemed so low that she didn't think it necessary to worry anyone. But now, as her limbs trembled and her vision fractured like the glass of the mirror, she knew her past had come back for her.

Nadia had just enough time to stumble over to the sofa where she'd left her phone and dial 911, before she collapsed to the floor.

ELEVEN: CLAIRE

Claire drove to the police station to pick up Danny with the ghost of Ruby's lips buzzing against her own. She tasted Ruby on her tongue, bitter from the vodka and so sweet underneath; she breathed in the after-scent of Ruby's arms around her, a tangle of longing and smoke. No kiss from Danny, from anyone, had made her feel like this. She felt like she'd been half-asleep her entire life, and only now had she finally woken. She felt like she'd done thirty-two *fouetté* turns without falling, and the world was spinning around her.

The world spun her all the way to the Hollywood police station, where she plummeted down to earth when she heard how much the bail was: a thousand bucks. "I put it on my credit card," Danny told her. He was already free when she walked in, slouched in a plastic chair in the lobby, head in his hands. Claire was glad she didn't have to cover it, but she knew Danny would never be able to pay that bill off. Add in the rise in his car insurance—and all the Ubers if he lost his license—and she might be handling the rent by herself for the next year.

She didn't want to think that far ahead.

Two officers walked by with a cuffed man between them, and Claire reminded herself to be thankful she hadn't seen Danny like that. He had the nerve to still look handsome, the dreamy brown of his eyes darkened by the shadows beneath them. But Claire couldn't muster much emotion beyond sympathy for him at the moment.

"Come on." She turned to walk back to her car.

In the Toyota, tension pulled them apart and together at once like a rope strained to its breaking point. Danny stared out the passenger window, and Claire guessed he was wondering, like her, who had committed the greater transgression here, who should be apologizing and who should beg forgiveness.

"You know I only started drinking because you didn't show up," Danny finally mumbled.

Claire turned off Sunset Boulevard onto a quieter street, where a few clumps of club kids stood smoking. "One of my coworkers got hurt," she said. "I had to drive her home."

"And you couldn't have texted to let me know?" His voice twisted tighter with every word.

She gripped the steering wheel. She could have. She should have. "There was a lot of commotion. I just forgot."

"Really? You 'just forgot'?" Danny hurled the words out like he was performing one of those old-school punk songs. She'd never liked those, but Danny said he had to do at least one per set, or it would seem like he was selling out. He turned to look at her and went on, more softly: "Is there someone else?"

Claire wished he would keep spitting the words, blurring them into each other so she wouldn't feel obligated to decipher them, but instead his voice turned slow and halting. "Are you seeing another man?"

It was so far from the truth Claire had to laugh. Which made Danny smack the dashboard so hard she flinched. "I'm sorry," she said, "it's just...believe me, another man is the last thing on my mind."

"Well there's *something* on your fucking mind. It feels like you don't tell me anything anymore. *Fuck!*"

That last catapulted curse tipped Claire's guilt and confusion over the edge, and it morphed into anger. A strange surge that, when she truly allowed herself to feel it, changed her entire world. It shaded everything red outside the car windows, the palm trees and the billboards and the lines of band posters stuck to every wall, the same image over and over until it stamped itself into her brain like a song she couldn't turn off. All of it washed with crimson, transformed into a foreign, feral landscape, and she had to pull over to make it stop. "I don't tell you anything," she finally said, "because you forced me to leave the place where all my friends are, the place where I belong, where"—lipstick words imprinted themselves in her mind, red over red, *WE NEED YOU HERE*—"where I'm supposed to be. You said this would fix us, but no matter what I do for you, it's not enough."

With those final words, the red around her faded, the guilt returning along with the starless blankness of the night. Danny was right not to trust her. But even if Claire hadn't left the dungeon, the rest was a truth she needed to say aloud. Needed to hear Danny answer, as she pulled back onto the street: "I'm sorry. I never want you to be afraid of me."

They drove in silence, and Claire let her mind wander back to a time she'd been anything but afraid of Danny. Back to the night they'd met, a few blocks west of where they were now. Up on the side of Sunset where a hotel perched like a castle on a hillside, and a saddle ranch stood like a relic of another time and place, with statues of saloon girls forever frozen in its windows.

Claire had known it was a mistake, hanging out with her old crew from the Dancers' Institute, almost the moment she'd met up with them in front of the Roxy. They invited her out once a month or so, but it had been two months since the last time, and Claire suspected they had started to forget her. It had also been two months since Claire had chosen her new name and begun working at the Briars, and in the glow of the Sunset Strip, as they waited to get into the club, Claire felt the difference between herself and her old classmates like the contrast between the neon and the shadows.

"Could you believe how hard that audition was?" Anthony was saying. "Warner's choreography is all throwing yourself around on the floor and jumping up like a bomb exploded. It's like he wants us to walk away with our bodies covered in bruises."

Claire thought about the bruises on her ass from Gunther's and Mike's paddles, the stripes on her back from John's heavy hand with the flogger.

"As long as I walk away with the part," Missie answered, sucking on a cigarette like it would offer her sustenance. She'd lost weight since the last time Claire had seen her—the stress of preparing for the senior showcase, Claire was sure.

"Easy for you to say," Anthony answered, "Warner isn't as hard on girls."

"Well, Rivers is," Bethany said, and Claire's muscles tightened until she wished she had her own cigarette to distract her. "His solo is murdering my toes." She must have felt Claire tense beside her—there was no hiding your body language from another dancer—and she turned and said, "Hope you're not feeling left out, Anna. But believe me, you're lucky to miss this piece. It's, like, twenty arabesques on pointe. All on the same leg."

Claire didn't know what bothered her more: hearing that old name, *Anna*, like something that had been chewed up and spit out, or the reminder that she could barely do a single arabesque on pointe, much less twenty of them. "How's the receptionist job?" Bethany went on.

Claire wondered how they'd react if she told them what she'd really been doing. How she'd spent the past year staring up at stained motel ceilings while strange men thrust their cocks into her. How she'd spent the past two months with her wrists tied above her head or cuffed to a bondage bed, while more men struck her with their hands or riding crops or paddles, and how the force and the pain and the violence of it brought her closer to freedom than dancing ever had.

"The job's fine," Claire mumbled.

And then the bouncers were letting them into the club and Claire lost herself in the mass of bodies, she let herself become one more anonymous floating figure, she unmoored herself for the last time from the group who had known her as Anna, and she looked up to the stage and saw a brown-haired boy stroking his guitar like a lover and singing as if the lyrics were so raw and so true, he had to scrape them from his throat.

When Claire had been Anna, she'd never been bold enough to approach a man at a club without him showing interest first. But tonight she wanted to become someone else. So when she wandered outside between sets and saw that same brown-haired boy leaning against the building, smoking a cigarette, she walked right up to him and asked if she could bum a smoke. Danny told her later that he'd known all along she wasn't a smoker, that he could see her fighting not to cough and had to bite his lip to hold back his laughter; but it didn't matter. Claire had managed to be bold for one moment, and that was all it took for Danny to capture her.

When Danny asked her name, that night, when he took her hand and she felt those guitar-player callouses for the first time, she didn't even consider telling him about Anna.

"Claire," she said.

Now, nearly a year after that night, Danny reached across the car and put his rough hand on Claire's leg, and she jolted. She thought of Ruby's softer hand, a little higher up her body, spanking her over her dress an hour earlier.

"Don't do that, Claire," Danny said.

"Do what?"

"Act like you're scared of me." He lifted his hand, staring at the streetlights as he said, "I hate that you miss your friends. But I couldn't stand to see you letting all those men hurt you. I can't accept that you belonged there." They drew up to a red light and the color striped crimson across his face, and he placed his palm gently, so gently this time, on her bare thigh. The spot where she'd fallen—no, been pushed—a few hours ago, in a room that held a part of her Danny could never see. But so far, no bruises had risen to expose her.

"I want us to work." Danny turned toward her. "I want you to belong *here*. With me." And Claire knew, with a twist in the pit of her stomach, that he was telling the truth. She could see it in his eyes, which held that same earnestness they did when he stood on stage and sung lyrics he'd labored over.

And wasn't this what Claire had always wanted? From the time she was a little girl waiting for a father who never came back for her; from the years spent trying to tell stories with her body, to become the kind of dancer someone would look at and truly see; from the year after that, entering those hotel rooms with those strange men and knowing if something happened, days would pass before anyone would miss her. Knowing she could vanish as easily as a ghost. All she had wanted was for someone to worry about her, to care enough to go after her. And now that she had it, she wasn't sure it was what she wanted at all.

They'd finally made it back to their apartment building, but that twist in her stomach had turned to a weight that pinned Claire to the car seat. It felt as if the place she was about to enter wasn't her home at all. *This is what you chose*, she reminded herself. *This is good, this is safe. You'd be crazy to throw it away.*

Once she'd mustered the strength to open the car door, Danny took her hand in his, and she let him lead her inside. She let him guide her straight to the bed, let him lift her sweatshirt and her dress over her head, over the curls that had fallen loose on another girl's bed. She let him wrap her in his arms and she let herself fall into him. She clung to him as if he were some sort of salvation, as if by kissing every inch of his body and taking his cock into her mouth and telling him she was sorry, that things would be better from now on, she could make it true. She welcomed him inside of her and told herself he felt like home. Then he rolled over and his breath settled into a lullaby, steady and slow. And Claire lay awake in the darkness and forced herself to see the truth.

To look at Claire's life from the outside, to examine it clinically, as if it were a body splayed out on a gurney, anyone would say the escorting had been the lowest point. It was the worst way a woman could debase herself, wasn't it—to sell her own body? But after the way Mr. Rivers had humiliated her, escorting had been easy. Claire had already lost hold of her dream, had already been hollowed out inside; she didn't think a man was capable of hurting her more than she already was, even if he did push her beyond what she was willing to offer. But the truth was, while the men weren't Prince Charming, none of them *did* push her. Their desires were simple, simpler than the clients' at the dungeon, even. They were fine. The job was fine, a source of income like any other, and not the soul-selling enterprise the world made it out to be.

It turned out it wasn't whether you had sex with someone, or whether or not money was involved, that determined how much a person could hurt you.

Now, lying beside a man she'd thought she loved while she yearned for the taste of a woman who had crept in under her skin, Claire hurt. Her entire body pulsed with pain and regret, until she would have done anything to escape it, to leap endlessly across some imaginary stage and never come back down to earth. But she couldn't escape herself. She felt like more of a slut, and a whore, and a traitor, and everything else the mirrors at the Briars had told her, than she ever had before.

She just wasn't sure which lover she was betraying.

TWELVE: RUBY

Ruby sat in her Spider in the Briars' parking lot and looked down at the gashes running haphazardly across her right knuckles. They reminded her of those phantom cane marks on Jack's backside, a jumble of welts so chaotic they brought a bitter taste to her mouth. But the wounds on her hand wouldn't disappear if she squeezed her eyes shut and then opened them again. There would be no hiding these red stripes. And since she'd had yesterday off, she was sure the ladies had already concocted a dozen wild versions of what had happened, all of them tangling like the roses and thorns on the dungeon's roof.

Yesterday, after she'd unwrapped the bandage and washed the crusted blood off her hand, Ruby had taken an Uber to the Briars and retrieved her car from the parking lot before they opened. She loaded up on Neosporin and spent the day watching episode after episode of *Law & Order*. No *SVU,* though. She waited for a phone call from Lady Eva suggesting she take more time off, or never bother returning. But Lady Eva never contacted her, so she supposed everything would continue as normal.

As if that was remotely possible.

Ruby took a deep breath, tugged the sleeve of her hoodie as far down her hand as she could get it, slung her duffle over one shoulder and trudged her way to the front door.

In the lobby, Lady Eva held the desk phone away from her ear, her lips pursed in displeasure. Ruby focused on the black coils connecting the receiver to its cradle, a long, distorted umbilical cord, as a voice slithered from the speaker. Vague mumblings punctuated by "*sluts*" and "*bitches*" until Lady Eva firmly lowered the phone. Shaking her head with the same resigned disapproval she directed toward a lady's rumpled outfit, she muttered, "Phone freaks." The bad taste returned to Ruby's mouth at the reminder of those men who called to let loose a volley of expletives, or simply to expel their heaving breaths into the phone.

"In any case," Lady Eva stood and straightened her skirt, "I'm glad you're here early. Let's talk in the parlor before the others arrive."

Ruby shivered, but this time it wasn't the phone freaks that unsettled her. Maybe it would be better if Lady Eva fired her. At least that way Ruby would never have to face Claire again. But when they entered the parlor, her boss's words surprised her:

"I knew from the moment I met you you had the makings of a great dominatrix, Mistress Ruby."

Ruby was caught so off guard that she almost fell onto the little footstool. At the same time, Lady Eva perched on the edge of the low sofa, where clients usually sank much more clumsily down into the cushions.

"But, Ruby, you've got to get this—this anger of yours under control. A true dominatrix has power over her own emotions, above anything else."

Ruby gulped. "I know. I'm working on it."

"What really happened, Ruby?" Lady Eva asked. "And don't tell me any silly stories about a spider. Stuart said you tried to choke him, before you punched the mirror."

Ruby thought back to the warnings her boss had given her in the past, when the occasional client complained Ruby had been too heavy-handed with the implements. There were plenty of others who appreciated that same forcefulness, so it had never seemed like too much of a problem. She tried to tell herself what she might have a month ago: *I don't care what the clients think. I don't care what Lady Eva thinks, or the other girls, not even Claire—*

She couldn't fool herself any longer, so why should she hide the truth from Lady Eva?

"I..." She heard the front door open and the chatter of a few girls, their voices lowering when they realized a private meeting was taking place in the parlor. Once their whispers retreated toward the dressing room, Ruby went on: "I didn't mean to choke Stuart, I was just shocked by... by the messages in the mirror. Written in lipstick. Like the ghost was there and...like it knew exactly what to say to upset me."

Lady Eva's prim lips tightened. "Nadia mentioned some smeared lipstick on one of the mirrors when she went to clean up. But not the one you broke, I don't believe."

"Because it was a mirage! It was the ghost trying to..."

Any trace of sympathy faded from Lady Eva's eyes, her gaze going cold as she said, "Forgive me for speaking so bluntly, but that is bullshit." Ruby almost flinched—she'd never heard Lady Eva curse. "Lady Lilith was the strongest and kindest woman

I've ever known. She took me under her wing when I was a brand-new submissive; she guided me as I became a dominatrix. She taught me how to manage a dungeon full of women. And she would *never* want to scare any of the ladies here."

The thought came in a flash to Ruby: had Lady Eva ever felt about her boss and mentor the way Ruby had about Mistress Katrina? But the question faded in urgency as Lady Eva continued: "What happened is that your client made you angry. You wanted to choke him out, hit him, maybe, but since he isn't into that, you chose to hit the mirror instead. Does that sound right?"

"No!" Ruby nearly jumped to her feet, but reminded herself no good could come of arguing with her boss. Lady Eva never changed her mind once it was made up.

The dungeon owner sighed, then, and deflated into the sofa. "Ruby," she said, "we've lost Stuart as a client. We're lucky he doesn't want the rest of the world to know he likes to dress up in lingerie, or he would be suing us for reckless endanger-ment." She shook her head and gazed into the decorative mirror opposite the sofa, as if she wasn't speaking to Ruby any longer. "So many clients canceling, especially after dark. If this keeps up, I'll have to cut our hours…" She aimed her eyes at Ruby again, a glint of red creeping in behind the blue. "And it's not because of a ghost, it's because you girls can't stop telling wild stories, can't keep your emotions under control…"

Ruby bit her lip to keep from defending herself. At the moment, every inch of her felt controlled, each cell a tight coil of worry and indignation that she had to hold very, very carefully inside her flesh. "For the next few days," Lady Eva went on, "I'm not booking you any impact play clients—just foot worship and verbal humiliation. Show me I can trust you again. Now go get dressed."

Ruby nodded and turned to leave the parlor, when Lady Eva called out to her:

"I'm giving you one more chance, Ruby—don't screw this one up."

Ruby re-entered the lobby, and the morning got worse: she ran smack into Cupcake Kenny. He kept one hand on his cane and wrapped the other pudgy arm around her waist, so low he was almost squeezing her ass. God, he was repulsive. She made the mistake of looking up into his face; his skin had taken on a greenish tinge, as if some sort of mold were growing under his flesh, and his forehead dripped with sweat despite the coolness of the morning.

Ruby darted away from Kenny as Lady Eva emerged and said, "Kenny, are you here to see Mara?"

He nodded and inclined his head toward the cake box he'd placed on the front desk. "And to bring treats for all the lovely ladies."

"Ruby," Lady Eva said, "can you tell Mara her appointment's here?"

"Yes, Lady Eva," Ruby answered. She'd have to face her coworkers eventually; she might as well get it over with. She picked up the duffle she'd left by the desk, squared her shoulders and walked down the hallway like she didn't have a care in the world—though she kept her sleeve pulled firmly over her hand.

Ruby entered the dressing room to find every woman studying their outfit or phone, and very deliberately *not* looking at her. "Mara," she said, "Cupcake Kenny is here to see you. But he looks...sick. I'm afraid he'll throw up all over you while you're tied up."

Mara gazed into the vanity mirror as if she hadn't heard Ruby; she kept brushing and brushing her hair, though it was already gleaming. "Oh, I'm sure I can find something to settle his stomach," she finally singsonged, lowering the brush and playing with the charm bracelet that looked like it might slip right off her tiny wrist. Ruby noticed faint rope marks beneath the silver chain—the clients were tying her too tightly—as Alice sauntered up, rooting behind the makeup until she pulled out the beauty scissors. "I need to cut the loose threads off this dress," she pivoted toward Mara, "but maybe what I really need is a lock of your hair." Her voice remained light, joking, but Ruby caught the metallic edge behind it. "Is that how you cast your spell on all the clients?"

"Alice..." Claire whispered from her seat in the corner, but Alice grabbed a chunk of Mara's hair and brandished the scissors. Mara's eyes widened, darkened; her twiglike arms trembled. Ruby held her breath along with the rest of the room.

And Mara pushed Alice, who tripped over her platforms and fell with a smack onto the tiles. *"Ow."* She dropped the scissors with enough force to slide them forward.

Mara darted from the metal as if it were alive, a snake or a spider. "Don't *touch* my hair," she half-growled; then she shook her head until that hair streamed in long, languid waves again, and turned and floated out of the room.

"Jesus, Alice," Emilie muttered, "that was uncalled for."

"Oh, I was just kidding." Alice rose gingerly to her feet. "But Mara wasn't—she's *strong*. You know she's the one hiding all the scissors. And stealing the clients."

"Do you really want to session with Cupcake Kenny, Alice?" Ruby tried to sound nonchalant, though her mind darted to her eerie session with Mara, that panicked search for scissors in the Enclave.

"No," Alice brushed off her dress, "but I'd like to session with *someone*. I'm broke." She sighed. "But I'll have to apologize—that was too much, wasn't it?"

"Well..." Claire spoke as she laced up her pink corset, the one that matched her lip gloss. Despite the drama, Ruby couldn't help thinking of where those lips had been, two days earlier. "...Mara *does* give me the willies. Actually, she *reminds* me of the Wilis."

"The what-ies?" Ruby asked.

"The Wilis." Maybe Ruby was imagining it, but she thought Claire seemed reluctant to meet her eyes. "From the ballet *Giselle*. The spirits of women who perished of broken hearts."

Ruby shivered.

"And"—Claire stood and pointed toward her thigh, revealing purple swirls like handprints, or ghost prints—"Mara *is* strong."

"What the hell? *Mara* did that?" Ruby grasped on to the anger that filled her, more comfortable than her previous uncertainty.

"Not on purpose," Claire added quickly, "she was helping me. The..." Claire bit her lips and rushed the words: "...the cross almost fell again, up in Lady Lilith's room, and Mara pushed me out of the way and I landed on my hip."

The tension in Ruby's limbs twisted tighter. She had no idea what was really going on, but one thing was clear: the dangers just wouldn't stop coming.

"Okay, now *that* gives me the willies." Alice came closer to inspect Claire's thigh. "Do you think we should confront her? About the scissors, at least?"

Claire blew out a breath strong enough to raise a curl. "No. She's got a weird phobia. Making her self-conscious will only add to it." Ruby hoped Claire was right. "Besides, we've got bigger problems to deal with." As Alice shrugged and walked away again, Claire spoke softer, just to Ruby: "Can I get your number? I wanted to check on you yesterday, but I didn't even have it and—"

The door yawned open and Nadia walked into the dressing room, wearing her usual glitter but lacking the spring to her step. "You're back!" a few girls called out, and Ruby asked, "Back from where?"

"The emergency room," Nadia answered, her blue eyes hidden beneath cloud cover. "But I'm fine, no one needs to worry!"

"She had a seizure," Claire whispered. "In the Enclave."

The wounds on Ruby's right hand throbbed as if the revelation had awoken them. *What?*

Nadia, who hadn't missed a word of their whispers, looked right at Ruby and said softly, "I understand now. Why you punched the mirror. Something very wrong is happening here."

Ruby forgot about Mara, then, as a vision of bleeding glass and accusatory letters swam before her eyes, and she wondered what nightmare Nadia had lived through.

Nadia glanced around the room, which had thinned out until only Ruby, Alice, and Claire remained. "Lady Eva wanted me to take some time off," Nadia said, "but that would leave her with no one to cover my evening shifts on the desk. So I convinced her that returning to my normal routine would be the best thing for me." Nadia swallowed, and clasped her trembling hands, and Ruby tried not to imagine Nadia's entire body convulsing. "But that's not really why I wanted to come back. I'm taking over the desk when Lady Eva leaves tonight, and as soon as the clients clear out, I'm going up to the attic. I'm going to find out what's really going on here. I'm not going to let this ghost terrorize us any longer."

She paused and stretched her fingers, and the sequins studding her nails caught the light and flashed like a warning. "But I can't do it alone. Will you all come with me?"

"Are you sure we shouldn't have told Lady Eva about this?" Claire asked hours later, now in a little sundress rather than her

148

corset, as they climbed the stairs to Lady Lilith's room above the slumbering dungeon. "If she finds out she's going to flip her—"

"Better to ask forgiveness than permission," Ruby interrupted, hoping the darkness would hide the uncertainty in her expression. To tell the truth, she wasn't sure Lady Eva had any more forgiveness left to offer her. With Nadia in the lead, they all filed into the hallway—Ruby, Claire, Alice, and Luna, who let out a dramatic yawn.

"You all right?" Claire asked.

"Yeah," Luna said, "sessioning with Peter is just exhausting. He won't stop asking me where I live and what my hobbies are, and the only way to shut him up is to beat him so hard he can't talk."

"Sounds like fun," Alice said. "At least you had a session."

Luna yawned again in response—and she wasn't the only exhausted one. The day had already been one of the longest Ruby had ever spent at the dungeon, especially since *she*, unlike Luna, wasn't allowed to hit anyone. And with the memory of her hand reaching for Stuart's fragile throat, she wasn't sure she *should* hit anyone, no matter how willing her partner. She couldn't forget that crimson river washing over her mind, making her want to wring the words out of Stuart's voice box, the same way she'd wanted to wring off Gregory's cock and balls...

It was too dangerous. She never wanted to lose control like that again.

As Ruby's thoughts bled red, the ladies entered the black room to find a glow coming from the corner—from the candle on the attic stairs.

"Dammit." Nadia marched through the gloom and blew the candle out, leaving them all in darkness before Claire flicked the lights. "Lady Eva keeps lighting that candle before she leaves. I've told everyone who closes up in the evenings to make sure it's out, but..."

"Is she insane?" Alice interrupted. "She's going to burn the dungeon down."

"She says she's honoring Lady Lilith," Nadia's voice dripped with doubt, "and her spirit will keep us all safe in return."

"I liked it better when she just made us replace fake flowers every week," Claire muttered. Ruby gulped in the air that seemed in such short supply, and found herself breathing in Claire's cherry blossom perfume as well. Somehow, Claire's presence—after they'd avoided each other all day, as if neither knew how to act around the other—made her heart beat harder than the possibility of an unhinged dungeon owner and a violent ghost.

"All right," Nadia said, "let's do this." She clicked on the flashlight from the Briars' earthquake kit and stepped onto the bottom stair—

—and the thumping started. It sounded like the curtain hurling itself against the window in the Enclave, but came clearly from the room above them. Nadia headed up the stairs, undeterred, with Alice and Luna behind her, but Ruby could only stand still and try to stop her shoulders from trembling. She felt a whisper of a touch against her wrist and jumped a foot into the air.

"Ruby"—it was Claire, of course it was—"will you let me hold your hand? I'm scared."

Ruby knew what Claire was doing. She wasn't stupid. Still she said, "Okay," and Claire's hand stroked gently over her torn knuckles before coming to rest against her palm.

"Does it still hurt?" Claire asked.

What hurt was the questions they *weren't* asking— whether what happened two nights ago had meant anything; whether Claire would ever again allow Ruby to hold her.

"No," Ruby lied.

By the time the two of them climbed the stairs, passing the candle and stepping over the chain that barred the attic, the thumping had stopped. "It looks like someone's been up here," Luna was saying. Beyond the weak illumination of the flashlight, moonlight peeked through the tiny window that, unlike those below, hadn't been blotted behind black curtains. In that silvery light, Ruby studied the wood floor and saw only a shroud of dust before her. Except, there—on the other edge of the cramped space that seemed about to collapse in on her, far beyond her companions' footprints, she spotted them. Tracks that might be more footprints, carved out of the dust. A rickety-looking spanking bench stood in the center, and she wondered aloud, "Did they actually use this room for sessions?"

"Either that"—Alice stepped forward and touched the bench so a cloud of dust rose over the cracked leather—"or this was a dumping ground for old furniture." To the left, a rusty cage sat with its door yawning open, and a throne-like chair filled the opposite corner. On the wall beside it, a jagged diagonal crack split a dull mirror in two. Ruby found herself walking toward the chair in spite of herself; she thought she could make out snakelike lines where the dust had been disturbed across its velvet surface. Almost like something had been dragged across it. The sight dredged bile up to her throat.

Claire reached for Ruby's hand again, and this time, Ruby felt a circle of warm metal within Claire's palm. "What is that?" she whispered.

"It's—it's a lucky coin," Claire whispered.

Ruby squeezed Claire's hand as if they could share the coin's protection between them. Claire squeezed back...and then the jangling started. It came from the farthest corners of the room, behind the throne and the other lumps of old furniture. A sound like carabiners clinking, like a handcuffed prisoner desperate for freedom. It came from the walls and the ceiling, from above and below and, it somehow seemed to come from inside of Ruby, rattling around her chest and fighting to escape her. She clutched Claire's hand but then the floor quaked, knocking her away from Claire and to her knees. Nadia dropped the flashlight and its beam shook too, making shadows shudder from one wall to the next, until the light went out entirely. A message came to life in Ruby's mind, not a voice, exactly, but a certainty of what she must do, etched clear as red lipstick on a mirror:

Get out. Leave and never come back and let old corpses lie.

Ruby tried to steady herself on all fours and fumbled for Claire, ready to grab her and pull her down the stairs and do exactly what the warning had told her, when the shaking and the sounds stopped. A silhouette, slender-limbed and tender as a willow tree, wavered in the lone hint of moonlight before the window. Across the old mirror, a shadow outlined by moonglow curved like a torso, torn apart where the glass had broken. Something brushed Ruby's cheek, something like smooth strands of hair, and the fear within her softened. An empty aching bloomed in her chest; she couldn't keep from opening her mouth and welcoming the strands of hair inside her. They tasted like loss and longing, a clog that formed deep inside her throat.

"Ruby!" she heard Claire calling as if from a distance; the gold gleam of the coin arced through dust motes and landed with a clink on the floor. Warm yellow light danced through the air, and the silhouette separated into wisps that drifted into the darkest corners.

Ruby stood as Nadia grabbed the flashlight and flicked it back on. "Is everyone all right?" She circled the beam around four blood-leached faces. The room had gone dead quiet.

"My lucky coin," Claire broke through the silence, bending to pick it up again. "I think it actually worked. I think it chased the ghost away." Her voice raced with a frenzied kind of excitement.

"Did you see her?" Alice growled, sharp-nailed hands clenching. "That...that woman in the window... The way her face drooped, deformed, her hair falling out in clumps. Some man did that to her. She was an onryō, out for revenge..."

"What are you talking about?" Luna said. "She was beautiful. Her hair flowed like a river. But she was crying, like La Llorona."

"I didn't hear crying." Nadia sounded half-dazed, enthralled. "I heard singing, like the Vila—"

Claire, still crouching, interrupted: "What's that in the corner?"

She crawled forward, and Ruby couldn't help calling out, "You'll get splinters," as Claire darted a hand out and grabbed something from behind the throne. She dropped it in the middle of the floor, jumped to her feet and scuttled back.

It—the *thing* Claire had touched—looked like a dead bug. Ruby crept a little closer, and with the help of Nadia's flashlight it resolved into a clump of hair, dark and tangled, woven together with a few rusty bobby pins. Ruby bit her lip to keep from screaming. "What the fuck *is* that?"

"We've got to take it with us." Luna reached forward and plucked it up between two red nails, thrusting it into her jeans pocket. "We can't just leave it here. I'll take it home and burn it." She grimaced as she wiped her hand off on her jeans, and Ruby noticed the purple eyeshadow and mascara creeping beneath her eyes, as if a few tears had leaked from them.

"Oh no," Nadia said, "do you hear that?"

What now? Ruby thought she might throw up already, that it might be the only way to expel that bitter, lonesome taste the ghost had slipped through her open mouth. Then she heard it too, a torrent loud enough to rise from the room below: "The water's running."

They all turned and ran to the bathroom, where Alice arrived first. "Shit, the sink overflowed. The shower too. How is this possible?" She had shut off the faucets by the time Ruby looked over everyone's heads into the bathroom, but the damage had been done: water sloshed above the floor tiles, mirroring the queasy motion in her stomach.

"TOWELS!" Alice yelled, and they bolted for the supply closet and returned with half the dungeon's stock of bath towels. In moments those towels were soaked through on the floor, with water still seeping out around them. Luna and Alice pressed more towels into the tiles, while Ruby and Claire tilted the metal hamper between them as the others dumped the used towels into it until it grew too heavy to hold. Her arms aching, her thoughts descending into gloom, Ruby couldn't help concluding their current effort was as useless as the entire trip into the attic had been.

It took three of them to lug the hamper downstairs once it was full to bursting; it didn't seem possible that so much mass could come just from some water-logged cloth. Ruby couldn't shake the sense they were carrying something else, something with a much greater weight behind it. They emptied the towels into the washer and Nadia added detergent while Luna and Alice ran back upstairs with the hamper. They returned a minute later, and Luna rubbed her purple-streaked eyes and said, "It's as clean as it's going to get up there. I'm not going in that room again tonight."

"I don't blame you," Nadia said. The wonder had fled from her tone, her voice fissuring. "It was a stupid idea. I'm sorry I made you guys do this."

"It wasn't stupid!" Claire wrapped her arms around Nadia, her voice far too bright for the moment. Ruby shivered in the absence of anything other than cool, empty air around her own limbs. She was caught in that cold, cold feeling the ghost had awakened inside her, something like loss.

"I'm leaving the laundry for tomorrow," Nadia said. "I'll tell Lady Eva the flood happened while we were still open, that one of the clients left the water on."

"Good idea," Alice said. "Blame it on Gunther or Cupcake Kenny, and maybe she'll finally ban one of them."

They laughed more than the joke deserved as Nadia flicked off the last lamp in the dungeon lobby and they headed outside. Everyone hurried to their cars, fleeing from that attic and the willowy figure that might still be watching, but Ruby's feet dragged as if she were slogging through mud. Finally she reached the Spider and unlocked it—and glanced up to see that across the now-empty parking lot, only Claire's car remained. And there was Claire herself, standing in front of it, the street-lamp spotlighting the longing in her eyes.

The thought Ruby had pushed down all day came rising up in her: now that she knew how it felt to hold Claire in her arms, the distance between them would always haunt her.

"So." Ruby swallowed. "We're alone now. Maybe we should talk about—"

Claire was running then, across the moon-sprinkled as-phalt, until she had her arms around Ruby and her lips against hers. Claire stroked Ruby's hair, clutched it and tugged; her hands wandered down and grasped Ruby's arms, searing with a heat that matched the insistence of her tongue in Ruby's mouth. "God," Claire drew back and they both gasped for breath, "I've been dying to do this all day—"

Claire cut off her own words as she lowered her lips to Ruby's throat. She was like a wild animal, clawing and biting, piercing Ruby's flesh but somehow, that passion couldn't penetrate. Ruby wrenched away. "What about Danny?" she asked.

"Fuck Danny," Claire said, her breath fiery against Ruby's ear. "I'll break up with him. If I can go in that attic and come out stronger, I can tell him..."

She broke the words with another ravenous kiss. And Ruby should be soaring with relief, but even as she kissed Claire back, she couldn't trust what she said, couldn't believe this was real. Claire's bare arms were feverish beneath Ruby's hands, yet Ruby couldn't draw any of that warmth into her. The ghost had hollowed her out somehow, left an ice in her veins that wouldn't thaw. Where was the heat Ruby had felt with Stuart, with Gregory, and even, in a different sort of passion, with Claire the other night?

Fire and water. The candle on the attic stairs, taking the place of a vase that had doused Claire. Now it was as if Claire and Ruby had switched places, too. And as much as Ruby despised this frozen feeling, she couldn't shake it off.

"Ruby?" Claire pulled back and brushed a strand of hair off Ruby's face. "I lost you for a sec."

"It's been a long night," Ruby said. "We should get some rest."

Claire nodded, disappointment cooling the fire in her eyes, making Ruby ache even more. She walked back to her car, and Ruby impulsively called out: "No nightmares, right?"

Claire looked back and half-smiled and said, "No nightmares. The ghost can't follow us home."

In the days that followed our journey to the attic, we all sensed the turn in the air, the rising heat like the sun beaming brighter, coaxing some wild seedling into bloom. But there was no garden, yet, no growth outside ourselves. We were the ones transforming under our flesh, even if we were too disbelieving to admit it, too frightened by the possibilities of what we might become.

First, there were Ruby and Claire, their passion for each other expanding to fill every inch of the dungeon. They stole kisses in the gazebo corners, the supply closet, even the alcove of Lady Lilith's room where the vanity held cross-dressers' makeup. They attacked each other as if possessed, as if each needed to take the other's essence into themselves. Only Ruby's teeth on Claire's flesh was off limits, because despite her vow, Claire still hadn't let Danny go.

Then there was Nadia, fuming every time she closed up— at eight rather than midnight, because clients had stopped showing up after dark. Everyone lost business, but what really bothered Nadia was the lit candle guarding the entrance to the attic. That small but dangerous flame, lighting her own frustration up. She'd gently suggested to Lady Eva that burning a candle all night might be unwise, and replacing the old smoke detector wouldn't hurt either. Her boss's response had shifted from the insistence that "Lady Lilith will protect us" to "I'll stop lighting the candle, but *she* still will."

Nadia wasn't sure which worried her more: a crazed boss or a ghost with the power to kindle a flame. Either way, she prepared herself to arrive one morning and find the dungeon burned to a skeleton, the roses and thorns alchemized into ash that rained down upon the charred bones.

Though why would Lady Lilith want to destroy the dungeon she herself built?

Maybe Lady Lilith, like Nadia and so many of the ladies writing in The Book, thought it was time for some changes around here. Time to stop letting the oldest clients get away with their oldest tricks, even if that meant resorting to violence, burning it all down.

What Nadia needed was answers, but she lacked the courage to look for them on her own. And that was where Gabriella came in, when she stopped by one evening to pick up the funds the ladies had collected for her.

By the time Gabriella entered the lobby, Nadia had already blown out the candle upstairs, and was about to lock up the cash drawer and go home. But even after hours, men kept calling, and Nadia was foolish enough to answer the phone. Ugly words tumbled out, pummeling her eardrum and reaching Gabriella a few feet away. Deranged rasps from a voice distorter, mutterings of "SLUTS" and "WHORES."

"Fucking phone freak"—Nadia's burst of anger surprised her; the phone heated like a coal beneath her palm—"just leave us alone."

"Asshole," Gabriella shouted, then clamped a hand over her mouth.

"You sluts," the voice went on, "should ask yourself why a demon is haunting your dungeon. What sins have YOU done?"

Nadia banged the phone onto its cradle, and the mangled voice cut out. She tried to release the handle but found herself squeezing tighter, tighter, as the plastic grew hotter beneath her flesh. So much pressure, about to explode...

She raised the phone high and slam-slam-slammed it down.

The old-fashioned push buttons broke into pieces, the way she wanted to break that voice distorter, break that evil man's throat. He was a client, someone she'd smiled politely at from behind the desk—he had to be, if he knew about the ghost. She jammed one of her nails and pictured the black bruise that would rise behind the glitter, but that wasn't enough to make her stop.

From the back of her mind, reason crept in: What would Lady Eva say about a broken phone? Nadia used every ounce of control she had to hold the receiver wavering over the cradle, but then came Gabrielle's dark, determined voice:

"It's an old phone, for an old world that shouldn't exist anymore. Crush it."

That voice didn't sound like the sweet Gabriella Nadia knew. But did any of them know who they were anymore?

Gabriella reached out with her pink-plastered arm. "Be careful," Nadia warned—

Gabriella wrested the phone from Nadia's gasp and threw it onto its cradle so hard the plastic casing split.

Wires spilled out like innards.

Gabriella clutched her wrist and whispered, wide-eyed, "What did I do?"

Nadia looked down at the wires and circuits, a puzzle she couldn't unlock, an old system unsuited for a new world. Slowly, slowly she grabbed the key for the cash drawer and gripped the metal ridges against her palm. This key unlocked every drawer in the desk, including the one marked "Private," where Lady Eva kept fake flowers for a ghost. "It's time to get some answers," she said, and looked up in time to see Gabriella's certain nod.

Nadia bent down and inserted the key in the lock.

THIRTEEN: CLAIRE

After the venture into the attic, Claire had fully intended to break up with Danny the moment she came home, with the taste of Ruby still lingering on her tongue. Salt and longing, as if Ruby had held back tears. But the farther Claire drove from the dungeon, the more sparks flew away from her skin, snuffed out in the cool night air. By the time she entered her apartment and Danny met her with lips parted, as if he were about to sing lyrics he'd written just for her, the last embers were gone. The anger that had lit her up back in the dungeon parking lot felt silly, now, as impossible as a ghost who could bring dommes like Ruby and Luna to tears.

"What happened to your leg?" Danny asked, tracing his fingers tenderly across her bruised thigh. His voice held concern, not suspicion, as he lifted his hands into the notch of her waist, where they had always fit perfectly, and pressed his lips to hers.

"I fell at work," she pulled away to answer. "Luckily I didn't have any dishes or trays of food in my hands." She kept talking, not wanting his mouth where Ruby's had been. But away from The Briars, she was spineless, not ready to let him go.

A week passed, a week of being tugged back and forth like a fraying rope, before Claire entered the dressing room one morning to find only Ruby inside. She gripped a curling iron the way she might a flogger, shaping her hair into those cascading waves Claire liked so much. "Do you have a session with a special client?" Claire asked.

"Nah," Ruby said, "I figured if I put extra effort into my appearance, I'd be less likely to ruin it by going on a rampage and punching things."

Claire's gaze darted to the back of Ruby's right hand; the lacerations, though no longer red and vicious, still stood stark. "Well, I love it when you do your hair like that," Claire said. "It reminds me of this classic movie star... Ava Gardner?"

"Veronica Lake." Ruby released the curling iron and one lock of crimson-tinged hair tumbled downward. "She was blonde, though."

"Yes! You're like a dark-haired Veronica Lake. I've always thought so."

Ruby clamped the iron down on the next section of hair. "What do you want, Claire?"

"Is there something wrong with telling you you look nice?"

"Considering you claimed you would break up with Danny a week ago, and you haven't—yeah, maybe."

Claire sighed. "I'm sorry, Ruby, I—"

She had no good excuse, so Claire simply stepped closer and, careful to keep clear of the curling iron, lowered her lips toward Ruby's neck. Ruby's shoulders lifted and then softened, the first sign of surrender...until the door opened, and they jerked away from each other.

Nadia marched in, wearing a sequined blue corset that matched the determined glint to her eyes, and behind her trailed another figure with pink plaster encasing her forearm. "Gabriella," Claire said, "you're back!"

"Yeah." Gabriella shrugged. "I stopped by last night to get the money you ladies chipped in—I'm so grateful, by the way—and..." She snuck a glance at Nadia. "I thought you might need some support. It seems like the ghost has gotten worse. Besides," her tone rose with fake cheer, "gotta make that money, right?"

"Good luck with that," Nadia muttered. "The ghost has scared half our clients away. And," she added grimly, "she left another souvenir." She reached into her crystal-studded handbag, pulled out a plastic baggie, picked something out and flung it onto the vanity table.

Ruby screamed and dropped her curling iron onto the thing, and the smell of singed hair rose from the table. It didn't help the sudden upheaval in Claire's stomach. "Is that..."

"Just like in the attic. Torn hair and bobby pins." Nadia paused. "I found it under the desk last night, while Gabby and I were...snooping."

"Well why'd you bring it here?" Ruby's voice whined higher than Claire had ever heard it. "Get rid of it. Burn it!" But Claire was more intrigued by Nadia's last word.

"Snooping?" she asked.

"We found the deed to the dungeon, with Lady Lilith's real name, and a picture. And then used the internet to find the rest. I'm going to write it all in The Book"—Nadia spoke with assurance in her tone—"because every woman who works here deserves to know the truth about the Briars' founder, whether Lady Eva thinks we do or not."

"And the truth is...?" Luna had entered the room, with Alice following. Claire took the opportunity to slide the hairball as far as possible from Ruby, before she bludgeoned it with the curling iron.

While Nadia picked up The Book, Gabriella crossed her pink forearm over her brown one and took over the story. "We found an obituary in the *LA Times* archive online. Rose Lilith Garner, owner of a...*massage parlor*"—Claire supposed "massage parlor" was the closest a mainstream newspaper could come to conceptualizing a dungeon in the '90s—"perished in a tragic car accident on the Santa Monica Freeway, in 1995. A semi-truck rammed into her sportscar, and she died instantly. She was alone in the car."

Silence reigned for a moment, even the scribbling of Nadia's pen in The Book had gone mute, as they contemplated such a horrific end to the woman who had created their entire world. Yes, Lady Eva had mentioned the accident, but to hear it so bluntly...

Then urgency took over: "So what else?" Luna asked. "Why has her spirit hung around here so long, and what changed *now*? Why the sudden upheaval? There's got to be more—"

"Not in the obituary," Nadia said, "but that wasn't all we found."

"We started rooting around the lobby," Gabriella added, "we had so much energy last night, we couldn't stop." Her eyes widened with what might be remnants of fear, before she went on. "We found this stack of photo albums, at the back of the supply closet—"

Claire glanced at Ruby, wondering if she was thinking about the fifteen minutes they'd spent in that closet a few nights prior. Despite all that time, they still hadn't managed to replace the empty Lysol bottles in the Enclave.

"The albums were all dated," Gabriella went on, "from the '80s to the early 2000s. Full of pictures of the women who worked here, and tons of Lady Lilith. Lady Eva, too."

Ruby, who had calmed a little, peered at the cracked-open door. "Where is Lady Eva, anyway? Aren't you worried—"

"She went to get a new phone." Nadia wrote her final words with a flourish and placed the pen down decisively. "Don't you two notice anything besides each other?" She glanced meaningfully between Claire and Ruby, and Claire felt her cheeks warm.

"The desk phone broke last night—a complete accident, it's decades old—"

Claire sensed a story there—especially considering the Band-Aid wrapped around one of Nadia's fingers—but Gabriella interrupted:

"If we hurry, we can look at the albums now."

A collective inhale, then Luna demanded, "What are we waiting for?" and led the way to the lobby. Their group grew as they entered the parlor, every woman who wasn't in session drawn in by the lure of old secrets, finally exposed.

Claire craned her neck to see over the bodies, while Nadia emerged from the closet holding an oversized book, its black-embossed cover labeled "1984." She sank onto the sofa and, with seven women circling her, opened to the first photo: a woman with sleek tanned limbs, biceps and calf muscles etched into a promise of power, her zebra-striped corset matching the carpet below her towering heels. Claire wondered if Lady Lilith had had the corset made to match the room she must have designed herself. The dungeon's founder brandished a flogger in one hand while the other rested on the St. Andrew's Cross beside her, and in heels Lady Lilith almost matched the cross's height.

Lady Lilith looked out with defiance in her eyes, daring anyone to enter her domain and emerge unscathed, unaltered. Her hair rose in teased spikes from her head like an '80s rock star's; her hands on the cross and flogger ended in equally sharp, rose-red nails.

Nadia turned the page to reveal the same imposing figure with her arms around a group of women, all of them in heels and corsets, and more girls kneeling and gazing up with adoration. Next came Lady Lilith with her heel on a naked man's back, the force of her weight on his flesh so clear you could feel it through the photo, through the years. Claire looked up at Ruby, then, and she caught Alice and Luna's gazes as well. She was certain they all shared the same thought:

This woman, spiked and sturdy and sure of herself, was not the wavering silhouette they'd seen in the attic.

Could a ghost transform so completely, become something so utterly different from the living person she once had been? Perhaps, if her death had been as tragic as Lady Lilith's...

"What about the attic?" Luna asked. "Are there any pictures of—"

A trembling hand, too old to belong to any of the dungeon's employees, reached out and snatched the book away from Nadia.

"How dare you." Lady Eva's voice was a tiger's growl, as if she had absorbed the energy of that animal-print furniture up in the haunted room. "This isn't yours to gawk at"—she clutched the album tight to her heart, fingers rigid as claws—"you have no right. And Nadia, I never expected this of you."

The room hushed, silent and still as the eye of a storm. Claire wished she could flee but found her limbs so frozen, she might as well be tied to the cross. She waited for Nadia to apologize; to her astonishment her coworker only sat up straighter, looked Lady Eva right in the eye, and said: "I'm asking you to stop keeping secrets from us. We're in a dangerous situation—a potentially deadly one—and we deserve to know what's really going on."

"Deadly?" Lady Eva shook her head until blonde wisps escaped her chignon. "You're exaggerating, telling wild stories again..." The album wavered in her grip, but Nadia continued:

"Why was the attic closed off?"

Lady Eva clenched the album tighter, tighter, until her taut bones seemed about to snap. "I've been trying so long to keep everything the same, just the way she wanted it." Her voice shook along with her hands. "And if you girls would stop stirring everything up—"

A small, black-haired blur tumbled into the room, tugging at Lady Eva's arms. "The candle," Mara wheezed, "it tipped over and I think I beat all the fire out, but your rug—"

Lady Eva dropped the album onto the footstool behind her, and raced for the stairs.

By the time Lady Eva and Mara returned, most of the ladies had scattered into the corners of the dungeon. Only Claire, Ruby and Nadia remained in the parlor, staring at the closed album. The dungeon owner stepped calmly, purposefully into the room, picked up the album and returned it to its place in the closet. Her eyes shone blue and watery, with the slightest trace of crimson at the corners. "You girls will leave these alone," she said with frost in her tone, "and we won't speak of them again."

Claire was sure as soon as they left, Lady Eva would place the books under lock and key; or she might just take them home.

Either way, they'd have to look for answers somewhere else, now.

Everyone spent the afternoon tiptoeing through the dungeon as if avoiding broken glass. Claire was dusting some paddles, attempting to pacify Lady Eva, when a soft voice slipped into her ear: "Want to do a double with me and Kenny?"

Claire jumped and dropped a paddle, and Mara quickly knelt and handed it to her. "Oh, Mara," she said, "I didn't see you there. A double with Kenny...Cupcake Kenny? I didn't know he did doubles."

Mara smiled, a tentative half-smile rather than the showy red blossom Claire had seen her use with clients. "He doesn't, but I asked him if we could do a cameo with you—because you invited me in for a cameo, and I felt bad about making your client run out—and he said why don't we make it a double."

The last thing Claire wanted to do right now was session with Cupcake Kenny, but Mara looked so pleased with herself that Claire couldn't say no. Besides, it wasn't like there were many clients to choose from these days, and she'd chased Jack away by turning down his dinner invitation. The familiar refrain urged her on:

She needed the money.

Once she and Mara and Kenny had gathered, Claire wasn't even surprised when Lady Eva sent them up to that haunted, dead-animal room. Apparently one fire for the day wasn't enough reason to steer clear. Well, there was nothing to do but get through it.

Claire and Mara headed upstairs while Kenny returned to his car to retrieve his huge bag of bondage supplies. While they waited Claire paced the boundaries of Lady Lilith's room, looking out for any more of those bundles of hair and bobby pins, appraising the damage to the attic stairs. Burn marks had scattered like animal tracks, and a singed smell lingered, but that candle still taunted them. "What happened?" Claire finally asked. "Was the candle lit when you came in?"

Mara just tilted her head, that frustratingly placid look in her eyes, and played with her dangling charm bracelet. "I'm not sure," she said. "I didn't notice."

"You *didn't notice*?" Irritation swept over Claire, then, until she almost expected the candle to light up again in response. Half of her wanted to grip Mara's thin arms, throttle her until she understood the danger they were all in; the other half wondered if Mara knew exactly how dire their situation was. If she was a part of it somehow. She could have lit the candle, tipped it over—

No. That was paranoia, messing with her head. Mara was odd, but not malicious. Claire took a deep breath and tried to settle herself. "Look, you've got to be careful. Not just with the fire, but with guys like Kenny and Gunther who will take advantage of you."

Mara looked right at Claire with eyes so dark and inscrutable, Claire couldn't tell if they were accusatory or concerned. "How are things with your boyfriend, Claire? Have you broken up with him yet?"

Touché, Claire almost said aloud. "Well, no, it's comp..."

"I knew a girl like you once." Mara's voice grew even quieter, so Claire had to lean in until they were inches apart. "I forgot about her, but...it's starting to come back." Something else was creeping into Mara's eyes, glassy and liquid—something like loss. "She had a boyfriend who wasn't good enough for her, and just like you, she wouldn't let him g—"

A thumping cut off Mara's words. "The ghost," Claire said, and impulsively grabbed Mara's hand at the same time Mara reached for hers.

Mara's grip was tight, her flesh cold. Words flashed on the mirror behind her—

SHE STILL NEEDS YOU

—and faded before Claire could be sure they'd been there at all.

And then Kenny barged through the door. Of course—that was the noise. The strangest stench entered the room with him, sickly sweet, like the first hints of rot.

"Mara," Kenny said, as Claire tiptoed a few steps away from the man. He leaned heavily on his cane, catching his breath, and when he spoke again the words slunk out, serpentine. "My lovely courtesan," he gazed into Mara's eyes, "I see you've brought a friend with you today. Now I can seduce the both of you."

There it was—that word Claire hated. *Seduce.* She'd forgotten how Kenny claimed he would "seduce" submissives in session, the same way her dance teacher had once tried to seduce her. The two memories twined painfully together, like the ropes Kenny would wrap around her.

Kenny had never called her a *courtesan,* though.

Mara laughed, a bell-like sound, and tossed her hair over her shoulder. An actress gathering herself, preparing for her role. As the locks rose and fell Claire thought she caught a glimpse of red—another lipstick stain on Mara's collar? The streak stamped itself on Claire's eyes like an afterimage, and the sour smell expanded through the room until she could taste it. She tried to imagine a more pleasant smell—Ruby's scent, smoky and strong, cradling her until she felt safe again—but she couldn't stop the tendrils of dread from unfurling.

Kenny propped the cane in the corner and walked haltingly to the bondage bed, resting his ample weight against it. He reached an arm out and pulled Mara to him, and the second his doughy hand touched hers he stood straighter. Claire remembered that: the way he came to life when he fondled her, pulled her top off and tied her hands together, and suddenly he didn't need the cane any longer.

Kenny slipped his hand inside Mara's top and stroked her breast, and Claire saw her shoulders rising with tension. "My little concubine," he said, in a voice so dramatic he seemed to be re-enacting a Greek tragedy, "from a land far away. So enticing and exotic. Your body was made to please men. Now bring your friend over here, so I can see if she pleases me as much as you do."

Claire swallowed that rotten taste on her tongue. Kenny had always been vile, but at least with Claire he'd stuck to words that could as easily describe the cupcakes he brought to the dungeon. *Luscious*, he'd called her, and *scrumptious.* So *scrumptious* he'd claimed he was unable to keep his hands off her...and he hadn't.

Mara extricated herself from Kenny's clutches and walked over to Claire. "God, I'm sorry," Claire whispered under her breath. "I had no idea he was talking to you like that. It's not okay for..."

Mara's eyes darted back to Kenny, who looked rather dazed, his gaze clouding as he watched the two of them. Her lips curled up into a little sneer. "I can handle him," she said. "You don't need to worry about me."

A wave of shame rolled over Claire, combining with the sickly smell to turn her stomach. Mara was right. Claire was being patronizing, and trying to explain away something she, a blue-eyed, brown-haired girl who had slipped safely beneath the label of "girl next door" even before she'd ventured into sex work, would never have to deal with. Then, to her relief, Mara's lips settled into that half-smile. "Just watch," she whispered.

Mara guided Claire toward Kenny, close enough she could make out the beads of sweat erupting over his brow. His skin was wan and yellowed like old paper. God, what was wrong with him?

"Claire," he ran a damp finger across her cheek, "those curves of yours make my mouth water. Now..." He stumbled his way to his big bag and pulled out a length of rope. "It's time to tie you up together. Take off your clothes."

As Claire unlaced her corset, she realized with a lurch that she'd forgotten to tuck Yarik's coin inside her bodice. She caught, again, that flash of lipstick red as Mara took off her top, and then they were both naked aside from their underwear. Kenny turned them to face away from each other, so he could bind their wrists together behind their backs. Claire forced herself to focus on the chain of Mara's bracelet worrying against her forearm and not on the sensation of Kenny slowly, lasciviously wrapping the rope around them. She could look in the mirror in front of her and see him securing the knot behind her back; she could see Mara, too, could see Kenny's hand creeping to the inside of Mara's slim thigh and edging upward.

Claire watched as Kenny's pudgy hand inched higher, higher, and a red tinge seeped out from behind the mirror's surface and washed over the image. It washed over Claire, too; it crept into her heart and made it beat hot and fast until sparks danced through her. In that mirror image Kenny's hand curved firmly around and then under the triangle of Mara's underwear, and the blank stupor of his expression twisted into a smile, and Claire thought with sudden certainty:

He deserves everything that's coming to him.

And then the room exploded.

All the mirrors filled with red, no words, no letters, even, just slashes crisscrossing like welts until they covered every inch of the glass surface. The St. Andrew's Cross and the spanking bench shuddered; the metal rings attached to them tinkled like a little girl's laughter. The zebra stripes of the carpet swiveled and swam, competing currents in a river. The sweat droplets on Kenny's forehead multiplied, swarming and streaming down his cheeks and dripping off his chin. He drew back from Mara and clutched both hands to his heart, as if he were trying to dig his fingers beneath his skin, to reach in and protect the fragile muscle. The foul smell grew stronger; he wheezed and staggered and spluttered "Hel—"

"Oh my God, Mara." Claire tugged at the ropes that had become a vice around her wrists, tightening with every motion she made to escape them. "I think he's having a heart attack."

Claire watched with the blood draining from her own limbs, her anger falling into fear, the fight leaving her, as Kenny collapsed with a thud on the zebra-print carpet.

She turned to look in the mirror again, to discern Mara's response; but the girl's long, dark hair had fallen forward, and her expression was impossible to make out.

Ruby stepped behind Claire in the lobby and wrapped both her hoodie and her arms around Claire's shivering shoulders. "He'll be okay," she whispered in Claire's ear. "I heard the paramedic tell Lady Eva his vital signs were good." A pause. "Though I don't know why you care so much." Ruby trailed her hands down Claire's arms and rubbed the rope marks imprinted into her wrists.

"I know Kenny's not a saint," Claire pushed the words out past the sickness swimming in her stomach, "but... I thought he was dying. I've never seen someone die before, not like that, right in front of me."

A flash came to Claire: Gunther, clutching desperately at his throat. She *had* seen a man come close to dying. And though she'd tried to forget that day, this time she couldn't deny the truth: she'd wished something would happen to Kenny. Not with words, perhaps, but in a red spark that had lit up inside her chest. As if she had willed what had taken place into being.

And she wasn't the only one here who'd felt those sparks. She'd read the entries in The Book, couched in vague language of heated veins and whirlpooling thoughts. But the subtext was clear: The ladies were tired of sweetly saying "I'm sorry, sir, that's not allowed." Like Claire had with Gunther, with Kenny, they wanted their clients to feel as powerless as they did.

They wanted these men to hurt.

And now, as the paramedics gawked their way out of the dungeon with a body on a stretcher, and Lady Eva paced the lobby and pulled her hair out of its chignon, Claire feared how much damage that desire could cause.

The women had been right that morning: they *had* to figure out what was going on, and they had to do something about it, before some greater tragedy occurred. And Claire felt, somehow, that it had become her responsibility.

And she thought she knew of one person who could help her. Someone who had given her a coin that offered real protection, who had put out a fire and whispered words Claire had begun to suspect were more of a sorcerer's spell than a song.

When Yarik arrived for another appointment, he didn't even pretend to have a roleplay or spanking session in mind. Mara and a client were in Lady Lilith's room, so Claire and Yarik went to one of the small rooms next door. Once there, Yarik pulled out a few bags of herbs, unlikely stowaways in his suit jacket. "Protection," he explained, "against supernatural forces."

Claire peered from the dried leaves in Yarik's hands, so fragrant she could smell the woodsy aroma through the Ziploc, up to his serious eyes. "I guess you learn a lot as a Russian history professor?"

He smiled through his thick beard, though the concern never left his gaze. "Teaching, studying, traveling, well— I've seen some things in this world."

Claire took one of the bags, squeezed the herbs until they crinkled beneath her palm. She tried to remember the heat that had filled her back in the attic. Was there a way they could use that fiery energy, without burning it all down? "I'm not sure protection is enough," she said. She took a breath, and then:

"I think we need to go on the offensive."

As Claire prepared to harness a fire, the other ladies dealt with combustions of their own. Ruby continued to turn down impact play sessions, fearing what she might do with a flogger or cane in her hand; she tried to contain her passion like a tangle of roses in her chest, and wondered how long she had before the thorns pierced through.

Lady Eva struggled to set up the new desk phone, and Nadia and Gabriella helped—a peace offering their boss seemed to accept. Although Nadia was shocked by the burst of frustration that overwhelmed her when, while unwrapping the plastic around the phone parts, she couldn't locate a single pair of scissors to help her out.

Such a minor inconvenience shouldn't have awakened a boiling fury within her; but then, she considered, maybe all that anger was about something else.

And then, at the same time Claire spoke to Yarik, Luna was just down the hall in the Enclave, encountering an inferno of her own. It seemed like a typical session at first: Peter lay naked on the bondage bed, his chest and limbs constrained under an intricate arrangement of red and blue and purple ropes. Luna had spent an hour crafting that artwork, and she would never have expected her client still had the power to wound her from beneath it. She thought she could take a moment to rearrange her curls in the mirror, to admire the ombre eyeshadow which, unlike that night in the attic, remained firmly in place on her eyelids. But then Peter spoke:

"I saw your makeup tutorial, by the way. On YouTube."

Luna froze. She posted her YouTube videos as Modern-RenaissanceGirl, with no connection to the Briars or the name Luna. ModernRenaissanceGirl, the same name she used for...

"And I read your Tumblr," Peter added. "I love how you paired the portraits you drew of your ex-boyfriend with the poems about him. Sounds like he was a cheater and an asshole, but underneath that, you really loved him." He paused, and then added, "You loved him, Adriana Morrez, the way I love you."

"How the fuck did you find my real name?" Luna asked, turning from the mirror and toward her bound client. In her ears a ringing came to life—no, not a ringing. A weeping. A wailing. Like the sound she'd heard in the attic a week ago. Even as she asked, she knew it was far too easy for clients to use the smallest clue and uncover an entire life online. Just another danger of working at an old-fashioned dungeon in the digital age. But Luna would be damned if she'd let him get away with it. "None of this is any of your business," she spat.

"But it is my business." Peter's scrawny body squirmed beneath the ropes, his eyes shining with delusion. "Look how I'm telling you, Mistress: tied up, at your mercy. See how much I trust you. I can be your new boyfriend, your slave. I'll be loyal."

"You sick stalker piece of shit," Luna said—or yelled, it seemed, over the ghostly sobbing that had filled her mind. "You had no right to read any of that. No right."

Would he out her, she suddenly wondered? Would he write a comment on the YouTube video: "You can pay Modern-RenaissanceGirl by the hour to tie you up and kick you in the balls. Just call the Briars in Los Angeles and ask for Luna." Luna was going to be a respected artist one day. If she ever revealed her dominatrix self, it would be on her own terms.

She tried to think logically, to determine how best to handle this, but the wordless wails of the ghost had burrowed into her mind. She could no longer decide if those cries were desperately sad, or simply furious.

Luna glanced around the room and saw the black cloth hanging over the oval mirror Ruby had punched and broken, like a patch over a mutilated eye. Ignoring her client's pleas, Luna headed toward that cloth; she lifted the fabric and contemplated the shards of glass still beneath it. The crying in her mind turned so shrill, it might have come from behind the glass. She thought, as she had since that night in the attic, of the tales her grandmother told: stories of La Llorona, the Weeping Woman, a ghost cursed to wander the world for all of time, after she took revenge on a very bad man in the most horrific way possible.

Luna pulled a shard from the mirror with her naked palm, and marched back to Peter. She tugged the rope above his right wrist so it no longer touched his flesh, and she began to saw through it, slowly, back and forth. Her client had gone quiet. After a minute, he swallowed, and said, "This seems dangerous."

"Shut up." The glass dug into Luna's palm, liquid seeped out, but she ignored it until she'd severed the last thread. That blood on her flesh only mirrored the rush of red inside her, the heat she wanted to pour over this man. The pain of the cut was only an echo of what she wanted to make him feel.

Peter lifted his free wrist, and Luna jumped back before he could grab her. From the intercom a voice crackled: "Excuse me, your session has ended."

"Thanks, Lady Eva," Luna called out. "The cleanup might take a while." The wailing of La Llorona had become a dull throb as she crossed to the other side of the bed, out of Peter's reach. And then, too quick for him to stop her, she grazed the glass over his cock and balls until she saw the first bead of blood.

Peter dropped the hand to his side. "Please," he said, "don't. I'll do whatever you say."

"You'll delete my sites from your computer," Luna said, "and you'll never look at them again. You'll forget you ever knew my real name." She had lifted the glass from his genitals and prepared to saw free the rope around his left ankle. She hadn't determined how much farther she'd have to go before she could be sure he'd keep quiet.

A minute passed, the voice in her head keened, Peter's ankle was free and kicking but he'd stopped talking. Luna pointed the glass toward his balls again—

And the bed, the heavy, solid bondage bed, tilted toward her. She scrambled into the corner, out of the way of the tumbling black beast and Peter's writhing body. The woman's weeping slammed into silence as the bed thudded onto its side and Peter squirmed free, yelling, "What the fuck!"

"I didn't push it!" Luna said. "I don't know how it fell!" But she was becoming aware of what she almost *had* done. Did she want to go to jail? Did she truly want to hurt Peter that badly?

No, she didn't want to go to jail—but a part of her still sizzled, enraged that the bed had tipped over and stopped her, before she'd accomplished what she'd set out to do.

Peter rushed to his clothes in the corner. "I'm leaving," he said. "I'm leaving and I'll never bother you again, I promise." He ran out with his fly unzipped and his shirt half-buttoned, while Luna stared at the open door as her hand unclenched, and the glass fell to the carpet.

She bent to grab the shard, when she saw something behind it, beneath the wavering edge of the red velvet curtain. Something like a little hairball. Something she had seen before, in the attic, and had taken home and burned in her backyard.

The sounds of the wailing woman were gone, and now there was only Luna, unable to hold back her own cry of horror.

FOURTEEN: RUBY

Ruby studied the baggies of what looked like woodchips and black crystals in Claire's hand, and tried to shake the feeling she'd walked in on some New Age drug deal. "You say your client gave you these?"

"Yes," Claire said, her gaze painfully earnest as she met Ruby's eyes. "Wormwood and black salt. Yarik said they're the most powerful substances for banishing dangerous spirits."

"And you trust this guy?" Alice crossed her arms over her satin minidress and tapped one Lucite heel on the concrete.

"I do," Claire said. "I didn't even tell him about the ghost, he—he sensed it, and he brought these herbs because he thought I might need them. He's a Russian history professor, he travels through Europe doing research and..." She glanced around the gazebo and Ruby did too, making sure it was only the five of them out here: herself, Claire, Alice, Gabriella and Luna. "I think he's a *sorcerer.* Or something."

"Oh for God's sake." Alice threw her hands up and walked off to the smokers' table. But the other girls appeared interested. And Ruby was too. It wasn't like the rest of them had taken any initiative.

"Yarik gave me that coin I threw on the floor," Claire added, "when we were in the attic."

Alice turned slowly back toward Claire, and blew out a plume of smoke.

"You have to admit," Claire pulled the coin from the bodice of her corset and flipped it on her palm like a trump card, "the ghost did not like this coin."

Ruby enjoyed this version of Claire, this girl who was so sure of herself. She just wished she could pretend to steal the coin from her, make her chase after it, and grab her, and kiss her—

But they couldn't do that in front of the others. Because Claire still had a boyfriend.

"Well," Gabriella shivered, "we've got to do something. I don't want that fire in my veins again, that feeling like I can't control myself... So a séance. Why not?" She drummed her fingers over her plastered forearm as she spoke, both nails and cast shaded the same electric pink. But Ruby's thoughts had taken on a darker color.

Séance. Ruby hated that word. It made her think of Ouija boards and full-moon nights and malevolent spirits. And maybe Claire noticed Ruby's hands clenching, the red lines standing out on her right one, because she quickly corrected Gabriella: "Banishment. It's not a séance. We're trying to get rid of the ghost, not invite it over for a tea party."

Luna marched forward in her lace-up boots and grabbed the bag of herbs. "That's it, though. We shouldn't banish the ghost, we should raise it up, ask it—her—why she's doing this. How we can access her power..."

She curled her hand into a fist and Ruby thought, with mingling dread and desire, of her own hand curling around the cane that day she'd hit Jack. Her own fist punching the mirror.

"Luna's right about one thing—this ghost has power to spare." Nadia had joined them. "She's making us stronger. Angrier, and more willing to use that anger." Her voice wavered as if her own words frightened her. "You can't tell me you haven't felt it too."

"Nadia," Alice said and quickly stubbed out her cigarette. Who knew whether epilepsy could be aggravated by cigarette smoke, but they were all treating Nadia like an invalid these days. "Can you help us sneak into Lady Lilith's room again, after hours? We need to ask the ghost for help, not banish her."

"Wait a second." Claire snatched the bag back with what seemed like confidence, but Ruby heard the doubt creeping into her tone. "Yarik gave me instructions to *get rid of* a ghost. He said it's a dark energy, not something to play around with. Remember Kenny had a heart attack..."

"Because he's unhealthy, not because of a ghost!" Alice yelled. "Besides, he deserved it..."

Claire closed her eyes and went on, quieter now: "It was the ghost. The things I thought, before Kenny keeled over... The red river rushing through my mind..." She opened her eyes and looked at them all, eyes wide and blue even as Ruby knew they held fire inside. "It's too dangerous. We can change things around here—we should—but not through a ghost who doesn't care who she hurts." She looked meaningfully at Gabriella's arm.

"I'm with Claire," Gabriella said. "Séance was a poor choice of words."

"Wimps." Luna leveled her gaze on Nadia. "You're with me and Alice, right?"

Nadia's hands trembled, one of her nails blue-black with a bruise, and Ruby hoped they weren't driving her to another seizure. But her words, when they came, were steady and sure. "I can't say there isn't a part of me that likes that power, the way it felt when...well, when Gabby and I crushed the lobby phone, right after a phone freak called us all sluts and whores."

Ruby wasn't even surprised. "But," Nadia went on, "what did breaking the phone accomplish? What would hurting one man, or two, accomplish, aside from landing us in jail or getting the dungeon shut down? No, Claire is right—we need to change things a different way. We need to talk to Lady Eva, rewrite the rules, *after* the ghost is gone."

"And that's another thing," Claire jumped in. "Lady Eva's been acting strange, and you must have seen that red tinge in her eyes—"

"Banishing the ghost might help her too." Gabriella's voice rose with hope.

"Ruby," Claire turned to her, "you've been quiet. What do you think?"

Ruby's skin had grown uncomfortably warm; she had the impulse to raise her hands, hold them over her scar. But she kept her arms firmly at her sides, doing her best to stand tall, as her mind raced. With the ghost's help, they could frighten away Jack and Gunther and the other creeps, make sure they never hurt Claire. Claire would find the courage to break up with Danny, and Ruby herself would feel that dark energy racing through her veins. Like the heady, intoxicating rush of domming, but stronger still...

A part of Ruby wanted so badly to say yes, that they should call on the ghost's power. The words were already halfway out of her mouth. But another part of her remembered that cold, empty feeling from the attic. The abyss that waited on the far side of anger and destruction. She didn't want to get any closer to that sort of darkness.

"I'm with Claire," she finally said, and Claire's answering smile lit her up inside. "I want this ghost gone."

And so it was decided. While Luna and Alice stomped around and smoked too many cigarettes, grumpy at being overruled, every woman received an invitation to the banishment—even Mara. They needed the energy of the entire dungeon staff, or so Claire insisted.

Meanwhile, the ghost seemed grumpy too. Clumps of hair and bobby pins appeared in cages and behind bondage beds; the washing machine shredded an entire load of towels. But time marched forward and, finally, the night they'd chosen arrived. Claire sat beside Ruby on the dressing-room couch while Nadia was in the lobby, calling Lady Eva to make sure she was safe at home, that she'd taken one of her sleeping pills.

They would all feel better if they knew Lady Eva would sleep through this, no matter what happened.

Ruby glanced at the bag of crystals in Claire's hand; they looked like grains of sand that had been pummeled, over and over, by the waves of a black ocean.

"Black salt." Claire followed Ruby's gaze downward. "Salt and ash, Yarik told me. Salt for purity and ash for—well, for death, I guess."

Ruby pulled her hoodie tighter around her. "It's not from a corpse, is it?"

"No!" Claire actually laughed, and looked more relaxed than she had any right to. "It's a Russian tradition to burn a mixture of salt and rye flour on top of seven birch logs. The flour turns to ash, and it alters the chemical composition of the salt itself so it's—"

Ruby couldn't follow any of this. She was remembering, now—salt was part of any basic witchcraft ritual, like the one she and two other tenth-grade girls had copied from a Wicca book they found in the library. Salt could cleanse spaces and repel demons. "My high school friends and I tried to do a séance, once," she blurted. "With salt and candles and a Ouija board."

Claire laughed again. "Didn't every teenage girl? I mean, it's like a slumber party rite of pass—" Claire met Ruby's eyes. "You said your family was religious?" she asked, the words like halting footsteps into a room she wasn't sure she should enter.

Claire and Ruby had done a lot of kissing, but not so much talking. Especially not about their pasts.

"Yes," Ruby said, "they were very religious. And since I grew up in a small town, there was no hiding anything." She was taking an unsure footstep herself with each word, but she couldn't back up now. "I was afraid of ghosts—I couldn't help it, my parents had told me over and over how dangerous the occult could be—but I was drawn in at the same time. Like when someone warns you never to touch a hot pan on the stove, and all you want to do is try?"

Claire nodded that she understood, so Ruby went on. "I stupidly tried to conquer my fear, by suggesting we hold the séance at the graveyard. We tried to raise the ghost of someone's great-grandmother, and all we managed to do was start an inferno that would have burned half the cemetery down if the fire department hadn't shown up."

"Oh no." Claire clutched the salt tighter.

"When my parents found out, they sent me on a church retreat to 'get rid of the devil inside me.'" Ruby shook her head in disgust. "Two weeks of hikes in the blistering desert and nights shivering in our tents after the sun went down. Two weeks of the camp leaders screaming at us about our sins, commanding us to purge our impure thoughts and devote ourselves to prayer." She knew she should shut up now, but instead the memories tumbled out of her. "Well, I did pray, though I'd told myself I wouldn't—I prayed at night in that freezing tent that God would get me out of there and back in my warm house where the sand wasn't blowing everywhere, battering my skin and burning my eyes."

Ruby paused; she noticed Claire's hand had left the bag and was reaching halfway toward hers. But maybe Claire sensed, as Ruby herself did, that the slightest disturbance might make the story bury itself again and never re-emerge.

"That was the only time I prayed," Ruby went on. "And when the church bus finally dropped us off at home, I thought my prayers had worked. I told my parents how the retreat leaders made us hike all day in hundred-degree heat and called us worthless sinners. I thought they'd be horrified. But you know what my parents said?"

Ruby laughed, a dry, desert sound, and Claire did grab her hand this time. "What?"

"They said, *Good*. They said, *You deserved it*. They said they hoped it worked." Ruby shook her head. "Thank God—well, thank the universe—my parents never figured out I liked girls. I would have been sentenced to one long church retreat until I graduated."

"So...your parents don't know you're gay?" Claire asked.

"My parents don't know anything about me. After that retreat, I realized praying wouldn't get me anywhere. I had to get out by myself. So I left after high school and never spoke to them again." Ruby cut off the story there, and the feelings too; she wouldn't let herself sink back into that desert heat, those frigid nights. That last lost hope that her parents would see her as anything other than a monster.

"Wow," Claire said. "I can't imagine…"

The ache in Claire's voice snapped Ruby back to the present. "Sorry I laid all that on you." She was returning to herself, recognizing the contours of the dressing room around her.

"I'm glad you told me," Claire said. "I want to know everything about you."

Ruby would have expected her confession to weigh her down, to mire her in the past; but instead, at Claire's words Ruby felt something lifting. She studied the painting of a whip-wielding woman on one wall and said in a lighter tone, "I don't know what would bother my parents more—knowing their daughter was a lesbian, or a dominatrix."

Claire scooted closer, until Ruby could feel the warmth and the life radiating off of her. "How about you as a dominatrix, sitting in the S&M dungeon where you work, next to a girl you've kissed on…*many* parts of her body, and preparing to take part in a ritual, most likely of pagan origin, to banish a ghost?"

Ruby smiled. Claire had a way with words. "Well, I've never been the type to do things by halves." She paused. "So, what about your family. Do they know you…?"

"It's just my mom," Claire broke in. "She doesn't know about the dungeon, and certainly not the escorting. I know she would love me no matter what, but…there's some things parents shouldn't know."

"Agreed. But"—and Ruby wondered why this question suddenly seemed so important—"what if she found out you were dating a girl? What would she say about that?"

Claire looked away from Ruby, into a dusty corner. Ruby's stomach dropped; why had she asked something she might not like the answer to?

But when Claire turned her gaze back to Ruby again, she was smiling. "You know what?" she said. "I don't think my mom would care. I think she just wants me to be loved."

Loved. "I—" Ruby started.

"Claire, Ruby," a high-pitched voice broke in from the doorway—Nadia, in her sparkly hoodie that would probably glow upstairs, no matter how dark the room and how dark their task. "The girls are getting here. I think it's about time."

178

A few minutes later, Ruby stood squirming within the circle of twenty women in Lady Lilith's room, all of them chattering and giggling like they were at a—well, a slumber party. Apparently Claire's teenage experience of a séance had been more the norm than Ruby's. She picked up bits of dungeon gossip: Gunther had developed a coughing problem, and almost spit up on more than one unfortunate submissive; Jack was so dashing that many of the girls wished he would ask them out to dinner, the way he had Claire.

Ruby had read about that, in The Book, even if she hadn't heard it directly from Claire's lips. Just more proof that Jack was a total sleazeball, a wolf in cashmere.

Now, though, Ruby had other concerns on her mind. She wondered if these too-cheerful girls expected to exorcise an evil spirit and then paint each other's toenails. And to make matters worse, she had somehow managed to end up next to Mara, the only one quieter than she was. Mara tilted her head in that irritating way of hers, like she was trying to look under Ruby's chin, and Ruby wondered about the wisdom of including her. Not that she could do anything about it now, with Alice calling from the corner, "Sit down, everyone."

Ruby sat cross-legged on the floor as Claire came over holding an actual witch's cauldron, albeit a miniature one, filled with those balls of hair that left Ruby half-choking just to look at them. "Luna brought the cauldron," Claire explained, placing it on the carpet and setting out the salt and herbs beside it. "Apparently she went through a Wicca phase. Put hexes on a few ex-boyfriends."

The sound of deliberate throat-clearing drew their attention to the corner, where Alice stood by the light switch. "I'm going to light this candle—" She held up one of the thick white candles they used to drip melted wax on clients. "—and turn out the rest of the lights. Everyone make sure your phones are off. It has to be completely dark in here." Ruby had worried that Alice and Luna might stage some last-minute protest, insisting that Claire change the ritual; but they seemed to have accepted that this banishment was happening, so they might as well be a part of it.

Ruby watched the lighter come to life in Alice's hand, the blue-orange flicker catching hold of the candlewick and leaping upward, the room cast into darkness so that flame made a shadow play of the mirrors and the women's now-serious faces.

Alice walked carefully over to Claire and handed her the candle, and Claire stood and wrapped all ten fingers around it so that Ruby couldn't grab one of her hands the way she wanted to.

"Everyone hold hands," Claire said as if she'd read Ruby's mind—but that only meant Ruby had to take Mara's hand instead. It was tiny and bony and cold, of course. Freezing.

Claire closed her eyes in the flickering candlelight, took a deep breath and said, "I conjure thee, Lady Lilith, by the strength of the women gathered here tonight. By the strength of all the women who have worked at the Briars, for more than three decades; by the strength of this magical place you have created, a place where wishes are fulfilled and fantasies brought to life."

Ruby wondered if Claire had come up with all those words herself. It couldn't be easy, standing before so many women and one strong old spirit and speaking confidently and clearly. But Claire was doing it. Ruby didn't think she could have.

Claire opened her eyes, crouched close to Ruby and whispered, "Put the herbs in the cauldron."

Ruby disentangled her shaky fingers from Mara's to empty the bags into the cauldron. She smelled old wood and mineral-rich soil and, oddly enough, the slightest hint of fresh-baked bread.

"Lady Lilith," Claire stood straight and continued speaking, "we are thankful for everything you've done for us. You've given us a safe, beautiful place to work, a place where we can enter as timid girls and learn how to dominate any man, if that's what we wish. Or, a place where we can simply enjoy being spanked and tickled, if that's what we desire. A place where we can reveal ourselves to each other, and find true sisters."

Every woman in the circle took a collective inhale, as if they all recognized the truth of Claire's words. Even Mara reached her hand out for Ruby's again, and Ruby didn't hesitate to grab hold. And then Claire went on:

"You've created this place, Lady Lilith, you've watched over us for so long, and now—" Claire paused, and the candle flame wavered and cast a shadow like doubt over her features. Mara's fingers stiffened, little slivers of ice against Ruby's palm. "—now it's time for you to rest. To go on to whatever comes next for you. To a place where you can find peace."

Claire knelt and touched the flame to the wormwood chips in the cauldron until the fire took hold. She spoke again, slower this time, as though she needed to get these words exactly right.

"*Crimson fire, black salt, pure earth, remove everything dark, multiply everything light.*" Then she blew out the candle, and placed it on the carpet, and reached out for Ruby's free hand.

The warmth of Claire's hand only made Mara's on her opposite side feel colder. So cold her fingers leached heat out of Ruby's own body as they clung tighter, tighter, a vice she couldn't shake off. She wanted to tell Mara to stop clutching so hard, that she was hurting her, but the words caught in her throat. Smoke rose before her, forming faint specters above the firelight, emitting a scent of sweet sage and rosemary and sun-warmed earth. Not the putrid smell Ruby had expected, not at all, but on the underside of it lay the faintest hint of rot.

That smoke wrapped itself around Ruby and drew tears from her eyes until she closed them, but at the same time it coaxed open her lips, it slipped inside her. It tasted bitter and salty and dry, like a yearning for sweet liquid, for a relief that would never arrive. It carved a cold, empty aching through her, that same ache she'd felt in the attic, and a vision came of her mother and father, looking with disapproving eyes at her younger self, their gazes penetrating her skin to uncover the devil inside her. And then it was a different face, Claire's innocent face, peering into Ruby and finding the wrongness beneath the surface. Claire's sweet smile twisting into a grimace of repulsion.

Ruby tried to hold on to the warmth of Claire's palm against hers, but all she could feel was cold, cold, cold.

Then fluorescent light slipped through the corners of her closed eyes, and she opened them wide.

The fire was only a smolder, the contents of the cauldron reduced to a lump of metal and ashes. Around her the women stretched and whispered. Claire looked right at Ruby, lit up, wide-eyed. "Did you see it, Ruby? Did you see the smoke rising in the shape of a woman? Did you hear the way she sighed—like she was relieved—like she was thankful she could finally leave?"

Ruby didn't want to crack the hope in Claire's eyes, so she said, "Yes, I—I saw it. I heard it." And then, to add truth to the lie, "I'm proud of you."

As the other women stood to clean up, Ruby looked down at the hand Mara had held in the dim light. Blue lines tracked across her palms, like the phantoms of ropes someone had tied far too tight.

Somehow, it was just Ruby and Claire in the parking lot again; perhaps all the others had conspired to give them this time together, but Ruby wasn't sure she wanted it. What she wanted was to ask Claire to come over, to lie in bed with her so they could chase away the last echoes of the ghost. But she couldn't get the words past her lips. She couldn't bear to hear Claire turn her down. So all Ruby said was, "I'm tired. I'm going home."

Ruby was tired, but when she'd gotten home and showered the last remnants of smoke from her hair and her skin, she couldn't sleep. So she clicked the lamp on and rooted around in the end table drawer until she found it: an ad from an old *LA Weekly.* A picture of Mistress Katrina brandishing a whip, the words below promising she'd leave her clients "groveling in gratitude and desire."

Mistress Katrina had never commented on Ruby's scar, and Ruby had loved her for it. But Katrina had also never kissed Ruby, or tucked her head beneath Ruby's, or brushed her lips against that sensitive spot on the side of Ruby's neck. Claire had done all these things, over the past weeks, and Ruby had become certain: there was no way Claire hadn't noticed her scar. And yet Claire had said nothing.

Ruby shivered. Since the ritual at the dungeon had ended, she hadn't managed to get warm. She put the picture back in the drawer, switched off the lamp and curled herself into a ball under the covers, rubbing her legs to make the blood flow.

"*I want to know everything about you,*" Claire had told Ruby. But did Claire truly want to know? What would she say, if Ruby told her the story behind that scar?

Ruby closed her eyes and willed herself to sleep, to let questions she couldn't answer dissolve into the dark. But she couldn't stop thinking about wounds, about the visible one on her flesh and the subtler one Katrina had inflicted. Ruby had thought she'd loved Katrina, but now she wasn't so sure. Because over the years, the wound Katrina left had revealed itself to be nothing more than a surface scrape, an injury she could patch up and move on from, without leaking bits of blood anywhere she might go.

Claire was a submissive, a girl who, as far as Ruby knew, had never expressed any desire to wield a whip, to make marks on another person's flesh. But wounds were funny things. You could never tell when they might sneak up on you—

When what seemed like no more than a scratch might split wide open, and refuse to heal.

Later, we would all wonder: If we hadn't invited Mara to take part in the banishing, would things have turned out differently? But it was a useless question—we had to invite her, just like we invited every woman who worked at the Briars. Mara belonged with us in spite of her strangeness; perhaps because of her strangeness, her quietness and her secrets.

Every woman who ended up at the Briars, whether it was for a few weeks or a few years, was a woman who wouldn't settle for the ordinary. We were all women who saw the unseen, and reached for it—we were women who wanted impossible things. Women who left behind what we knew to be safe. Women who stepped outside of the expected and into a world of dreams and courage and transgressions, a garden of blossoms and thorns.

We made our choice even if, in doing so, we ran the risk of becoming ghosts.

We wanted the extraordinary, and in the days after Lady Lilith's spirit made her dramatic exit, we got it. In the alley beyond the Enclave, a place without fertile soil or access to sun, green tendrils emerged from patches of dried-out dirt. They grew faster than should have been possible, suggesting the shapes of bushes, promising briars and buds to come. Most of us barely noticed the new growth, only affording it the briefest glance as we passed between the parking lot and the dungeon's front gate. But it was there, taking strength from the magic of the dungeon and the women who believed in it.

And the rosebushes weren't the only extraordinary thing germinating beneath the surface, remaining mostly unseen. Our dungeon spirit had been banished, but perhaps, some of us suspected, the seed that had come to life around and inside us was not entirely the work of a ghost. Maybe it was simply what happened when you worked at a place where you changed your name, and lost or willfully abandoned the one you were born with; maybe it was the natural consequence of work where men saw you as a body, not a person, and let out the worst parts of themselves.

Maybe that seed existed in every woman, and it only needed the right circumstances—supernatural or very, very human—to take root and sprout.

184

FIFTEEN: CLAIRE

Claire couldn't wait for Yarik to come back and see her again, so she could tell him how well the banishment had gone. How the right words to say just came to her, channeled, almost, rushing through her insides and out of her as if her body had housed some unearthly power. Then as the smoky figure had dissipated, a subtle weight settled against her shoulder—like a hand resting there, a hand that was finally able to relax, to let go.

Since that night, both in the dungeon and out in the world, Claire's step was lighter, her mind clearer. The foul words had been wiped forever from the mirrors in Lady Lilith's room, and from her thoughts as well. In the week since they'd held the ritual, all evidence of the ghost had disappeared, and even if Claire hadn't managed to break up with Danny yet, her good mood still followed her home. She felt free enough to lift her leg in an arabesque as she tidied the bedroom, and who cared if her perfectly pointed toe hit the bedpost or the wall or—

"Ow," Danny whined, "you got my nuts."

"Oh, shit." Claire giggled as she lowered her leg to a possé and half-twirled to face him. "I didn't hear you come in. I didn't hurt you, did I?"

Danny smiled and pulled her closer and Claire caught a whiff of him, fresh sweat and marijuana, and it was so different from Ruby's comforting smell that she drew back before she could stop herself.

Danny jerked back, too, and crossed his arms over his Ramones T-shirt, and all the warmth melted out of him. "Who is he?"

"What?"

"I'm not stupid, Claire." His voice had taken on that punk-rock edge again, the words catapulted out like little stones. "I've seen how happy you are these past few weeks. Dancing around the apartment, with that secret smile on your face. And it sure as shit isn't because of me. Sex with me is just some chore you have to get through."

"No, Danny, that's not true." The instinct to fix, to soothe, rose up in Claire, and she reached for him. Despite everything, she hated the hurt in Danny's voice.

He accepted her hands on his shoulders, her arms wrapping around him until she felt the heat of his skin. The potential for passion or anger. His lips lowered toward hers and she told herself to open, open to him, just for now—

Then he whirled her around and yanked her skirt up, making her cry out.

"I fucking knew it."

"Knew what?" Claire asked over her shoulder, her heart beating double time.

"You've got bruises on your ass. Fresh ones. I thought I saw it the other night, but it was dark and I told myself I was just..."

His hands fisted at his sides as Claire forced herself to turn and meet his eyes. "It's not a man," Danny said slowly, deliberately, "at least, not *one* man." He gulped and his Adam's apple bulged. "You're still working at the dungeon, aren't you?"

"Yes," she whispered past the lump in her own throat. Where was that fire she'd felt after seeing the ghost in the attic, when she'd sworn she'd break up with Danny right there and then? Where had that courage gone, now that she needed it? "I'm sorry, I—"

Danny raised his fists and fear clenched its hands around her heart. But he only stood there, cold eyes aimed right at hers so she knew he meant the words. "I should have known never to trust a whore."

It turned out Danny didn't need to use his hands to hurt her; all he had to do was storm out of the room. Moments later, Claire heard the apartment door slam.

The aftershock rang through Claire's ears and made it hard to think, hard to do anything except mechanically strip and crawl under the covers, though the sky had barely gone dark outside the closed blinds.

A few hours later, Claire heard the door creak open, the careful footsteps in the hall. Next came the rustle of T-shirt and jeans slipped off, a gentle, tentative song. And then Danny was sliding into the bed and wrapping his warm arms around her, pressing his broad chest against her spine, surrounding her in a lullaby that ached and soothed and stung.

Despite what he'd said—because of what he'd said?—this apology was a comfort she wanted to burrow inside of. It wasn't everything she'd dreamed of; Danny wasn't some magician who could uncover Claire's true self and appreciate her for all that she was. But in the darkness, in the middle of the night, it was hard to disentangle herself from an embrace that felt so safe, and so much like love. It was hard not to think this was what she deserved.

In the morning, those murky midnight thoughts had faded, and Claire wanted nothing but to get up and shower and go to work. But Danny was determined to offer another sort of apology, whispering, "We'll talk about this later, okay? We'll work something out." Leaning over and kissing the spot behind her ear, brushing her curls back from her eyes. Finally rolling on top of her and thrusting as Claire lay back and stared at the cracks in the ceiling and felt nothing, just like the whore she had been only a year ago.

Just like the whore Danny said she was.

Parking at the Briars that afternoon, Claire still felt as raw as if she'd slept in a bed of rosebushes, so when she noticed the first flash of green she was sure she'd imagined it. But no, her eyes didn't deceive her: in the alley behind the annex, shoots were emerging from cracks in the asphalt. Strange, yes—impossible, even—but she would take this as a good sign. A hint that Lady Lilith was still with them, in her own way. A lone green leaf waved back and forth, and Claire told herself that things weren't so bad. The danger of the ghost had passed them over, and that was still something to celebrate.

She would find the courage to break up with Danny soon enough.

In the dressing room, the other girls made it easy for Claire to hold on to her sense of hope. They sang silly pop songs while they laced up corsets and brushed on eyeshadow, digging back decades and trading:

"I wanna ha—"

"I wanna ha—"

Until Mara finished off with a hair flip and a *"zigazig ah."*

"Mara!" Claire couldn't help giggling at the sight of Mara in her little white skirt, popping her hips and shaking her ass like Baby Spice.

"What?" Mara said. "You can't *not* sing along to the Spice Girls. Even if I am more of a Nirvana and Pearl Jam girl." She shrugged, picked up a comb and tugged it through her hair. Was that actually a tangle? She kept teasing the comb through it as if fighting her way down the locks.

Claire was glad Mara had finally started to fit in, to break out of her quiet shell. It must be easier now that the ghost was gone. But then Mara looked at Claire, looked into her, almost, as if she could see beyond her sunny surface. "Are things still okay with your boyfriend?" she asked.

The pop-song refrains had faded, most of the ladies were headed out to the lobby or gazebo, and Claire did her best to clutch on to a bright and breezy moment that was quickly dissipating. She glanced at Ruby, who was studying herself in the small mirror by the back door. Or was she actually studying Claire's reflection?

"We had a fight," Claire mumbled. "I...I've got to find a way to break up with him. And it's hard, since he lives with me and he doesn't have anywhere else to go, and..."

She looked at Mara's wide eyes, but she was actually speaking to the mirror by the back door.

Ruby picked up a brush and yanked it through her hair. Only the three of them lingered in the dressing room now.

"What happened?" Mara asked, her voice tinged with real concern. "What kind of fight?"

"Yeah," Ruby turned and crossed her arms over her chest, "what happened, Claire?"

Claire couldn't lie to Ruby. She just couldn't.

"He found out I'm still working here," Claire said. "He said...he said he should never have trusted a...a *whore*."

At that word, the blood drained from Ruby's cheeks. Her eyes flashed a brighter green. "And you told him to get out."

"Not yet," Claire said, "but I'm going to..."

She wanted Ruby to walk over and wrap her strong, sure arms around her, so she could nestle her head in the crook of Ruby's neck. But Ruby just said, "You're going to...

"What you're *going* to do is keep punishing yourself. And me." She whirled on her heels and stormed out the back door.

"Oh no," Mara whispered in the sudden quiet. "Sorry I—"

"It's not your fault," Claire mumbled, feeling suddenly dizzy and unanchored and lost. She searched for something to ground herself and found herself, perhaps unwisely, meeting Mara's eyes. And there it was, that darkness she'd caught a glimpse of once before, after Mara's cameo with Jack: that aching loss, empty and bottomless as an old well. Claire had the sense, then, that this girl could understand how she felt better than anyone else.

The door to the hallway creaked open, and Mara and Claire both jumped. "Oh," said Lady Eva, "you're just the two girls I'm looking for. Mara, Gregory is here for you, and Gunther wanted to see you too—but since Gregory made his appointment first, Gunther will session with Claire instead."

Good. A few smacks from Gunther, and Claire would get her blood flowing. Thaw out the ice that had crept into her bones. She'd lose herself for an hour and become nothing more than a naughty schoolgirl, punished by Principal Gunther as she had been so many times before.

A few minutes later, Lady Eva announced from the front desk: "Claire, you and Gunther can go in Lady Lilith's room." It was a relief to hear those words without a jolt of fear, to know the room wasn't a danger anymore. Claire followed Gunther to the equipment wall, where he cleared his throat with an alarming rattle, and she tried to put her finger on what seemed different about him. His smell, maybe? The falsely virtuous aroma of Ivory soap had been replaced by something stronger, almost minty.

While Gunther stacked Claire's arms with paddles and wrist and ankle cuffs, Mara and Gregory emerged from the parlor. Claire watched as Lady Eva's eyes narrowed on Mara's wrist, the silver chain and yet more rope marks beneath it. "What a lovely bracelet, dear," she said. "It looks like one I remember from..." She leaned closer. "That detail on the flower charms, and the little bits of...amethyst? So exquisite. Where did you get it?"

Mara's client shifted awkwardly behind her, waiting to pay for his session; an odd moment to start a discussion about jewelry. But though they'd hoped banishing the ghost might bring back the sharp-edged, clear-minded Lady Eva, the opposite seemed to have occurred—she didn't even appear aware that the threat was gone. Claire suspected her boss was still taking too many of those pills she'd seen her sneaking from the desk drawer.

"I..." Mara glanced down at the bracelet and back up, with that look of wide-eyed confusion. "It was a family heirloom."

But Mara always claimed she didn't know her family. Lady Eva didn't seem to remember that, though; she just shrugged and took the outstretched bills from Mara's client. Gregory's liver-spotted hands shook as he offered up the hundreds, as if he were jonesing for a fix. Claire couldn't help thinking the man looked older, the thin flesh stretched taut over his bones.

Meanwhile Gunther, who had already paid, shuffled past the desk—

And he didn't grab any peppermints from the bowl in the lobby, the way he always had before.

Claire entered Lady Lilith's room with Gunther right behind her; the moment he stepped inside, a cough erupted from his throat and echoed off the dark walls. Once it faded, Claire became aware of a noise coming from the bathroom. The water was dripping again, a steady *plink, plink* against the porcelain.

Claire threw the paddles onto the bondage bed, ran into the bathroom and wrenched the faucet handle with much greater force than it deserved. The water stopped.

Maybe the sink leaking never had anything to do with the ghost. Maybe it was just a plumbing problem.

So Claire told herself, as she stepped more slowly out onto the zebra-striped carpet, where a thick hacking made her startle and turn. Gunther stood in front of the St. Andrew's Cross, spitting into a handkerchief. "All right, Little Miss Claire," he said in that pedantic voice, "get over here and I'll give you the old strip search. I hear you've been a very naughty girl."

"Aren't you going to give me a peppermint—er, cigarette—to hide first, sir?"

Fifty or sixty sessions with Gunther, and he had never *not* handed her a peppermint, called it a cigarette, and told her to hide it in her bra or panties.

"You know what, Claire?" Gunther stuffed the handkerchief in his pocket, grabbed her with the same dirty hand he'd held it in and pulled her toward the bondage bed. "I can't stand the thought of peppermints these days. The smell makes me sick."

He pushed her down until her hands were braced on the bed, then reached around her ribcage and ripped upon her tie-front top. Claire's breath came out in a nervous rush.

"No bra, I see." Gunther clamped his fingers around her nipples. "Not surprising, for the *slut* who's been caught giving head to every member of the football team." He drew back from her, then, and let out another violent cough.

Claire stood and turned to face him, crossing her arms over her now bare chest, forcing her voice to come out light as a joke. "*Me?* Giving blow jobs to those gross, sweaty boys? Believe me,

190

sir, the worst thing I've *ever* done is smoke." Her mind whirled. As much as he liked copping a feel, Gunther wanted to spank and paddle an *innocent* schoolgirl. Or so she'd thought.

"Oh, don't you dare lie to me." Gunther's normally placid, if patronizing voice twisted into a raspy growl. It matched the ugliness contorting his features, casting a red haze over his eyes. "You *whore*."

The word sent tremors through her, smaller than yesterday's earthquake but disturbing the same fault lines. She wanted to tell Gunther to shut up so she could cling to the illusion of safety. But instead he grasped her arm, coughing into her hair as he fumbled for the cuffs they'd brought upstairs. He fastened them around her wrists and ankles with rough, rushing hands, yanked her to the St. Andrew's Cross, and attached the cuffs so her front side lay against the big black X. Then he tugged her schoolgirl skirt down.

"Wait!" Claire said. "Aren't you going to spank me over your lap first?" She couldn't take an entire hour of Gunther paddling her.

"Oh, Claire," Gunther spat, "you're a tough girl. You don't need a warm-up."

He snatched the thick wooden paddle off the bed, swung it like a baseball bat and hit her bare ass, full force. The shock was too great to register as pain; it reverberated through the room and made everything that wasn't bolted down rock back and forth, the spanking bench and stool and vanity table and even the huge, heavy cross Claire was bound to.

"Gunther!" Claire squeezed her eyes shut and red sparks danced behind them. "Stop!"

He did stop, and rubbed her ass cheeks with the same hand he'd been coughing into, and somehow that was even worse. "You know, Claire," he said, "I never realized how the smell and taste of peppermint is everywhere." He smacked her rear end with that filthy hand as he went on. "Toothpaste, aftershave, air fresheners. Even Starbucks and their goddamn peppermint mochas."

Claire watched in the droopy-eye mirror as Gunther stepped back from her and hacked into the handkerchief again. She thought she saw something fall from his mouth into the fabric, a tiny lump, striped white and red. "I haven't had a peppermint in months," Gunther paused to spit again, "but I can't get that taste out of my mouth. It's worse than cigarette smoke."

He picked up the paddle and swung, catching the tops of Claire's thighs. This time it did hurt, a throbbing, red and raw, as if something had burst inside her. The cross wobbled and the mirrors on the walls swayed back and forth. A second blow—a third—and Claire squeezed her fingers tight against the cuffs, every cell of her focused on surviving the pain that rushed like a crimson river through her.

The sensation passed, a wave that rose and fell, and then came the water in the bathroom again. Two faucets, the sink and the bathtub, both gutted wide open. "Gunther!" she yelled. "Go turn off the faucets and uncuff me. This session is over."

"You're"—*cough*—"crazy"—*cough*. "The faucets aren't running. I don't hear anything at all."

"*I'm* crazy? Gunther, get me off this cross right now."

He laughed, or maybe it was another spluttering cough. In the mirror she watched him expel something into the handkerchief. Was it red-and-white splinters, or was it drops of blood? He flung the red-stained cloth to the floor, picked up the paddle and walloped the side of her hip.

"Stop!" Claire screamed. "Stop!" The pain flowed through her until, at the moment it would have become too much to bear, it sharpened into something else. She had trusted Gunther, so many times, offering her bare ass to him with the understanding that he would never truly damage her. And now he kept slamming that paddle, again and again, as if he wanted to force his way beyond flesh and muscle and break her bones. The cross and the spanking bench, the stool and the mirrors all quaked, on the verge of implosion, and she didn't know if it was his blows or her own anger that stirred them.

The spanking bench tipped, then the stool, then the oval mirror she'd been looking into. It crashed to the floor and glass shards spilled out farther than they had any right to. Without the mirror, Claire could no longer see Gunther, but she heard him— the coughs had deepened into a clogged, desperate hacking. He kept hitting her, though, and with each blow the cross she was attached to rocked further. It flung her back and forth like a child on a carnival ride; she tugged her wrists and ankles until the carabiners attached to them cried out.

192

"Help!" Claire screamed as loud as she possibly could, hoping beyond hope that someone would hear her. "Help! Lady Eva! Ru—"

The word wouldn't leave her throat. Something was blocking it, a thick, foreign sensation in her mouth and her nose, keeping her from speaking, from breathing. Her heart raced like a wild animal; she had to get the words, the breath out, had to expel all this fire and fury inside her. And then the cross was falling further, careening toward the floor. She was about to land on her back, with the hundred pounds of wood she was chained to right on top of her.

"Claire!" The last trace of breath left her at the sound of the door opening, the voice that disappointed her: Nadia, not Ruby.

"Claire?" That was Luna, and another voice said, "What the fuck happened? Are you okay?" Alice.

"Where's—where's Ruby?"

"She's in session next door," Nadia's voice came closer. Claire had become aware that she was still standing against the cross, that it hadn't tipped over. Nadia uncuffed her as Luna said, "Someone call 911. Does anyone know CPR?"

Claire was about to assure them she was okay now, she didn't need CPR or to go to the hospital, when she allowed Nadia to guide her off the cross, and she turned to a scene of carnage before her.

Water seeped from the bathroom door. Glass glinted across the carpet. The spanking bench and stool lay like felled beasts on their sides. And in the midst of it all was Gunther, motionless, flat on his back, eyes bloodshot and unseeing, his hand still resting on the handle of that spanking paddle.

"I know CPR," Alice said, and she knelt and grimaced, tilted Gunther's head back and placed her hands on his broad chest.

Claire could barely watch as Alice lowered her lips to Gunther's, as she alternately blew into his mouth and pumped his chest for what might be seconds or hours, before she pulled away and shook her head. "Artificial respiration isn't working. That means asphyxiation...." She let out a heavy breath, wiped her mouth with one hand and stood. "He's dead."

Luna, who must have gone downstairs for a minute, barged back in. "Ambulance is on its way. And Lady Eva is too panicked to climb the stairs—probably for the best. She doesn't need to see this."

Claire shut her eyes, wishing she would wake up to discover this was only a nightmare. But when she opened them, Gunther's lifeless body remained. "I don't understand... The ghost was gone..."

Nadia emerged from the bathroom, her spray-tanned face gone pale as she stepped through glass shards. She held up a clump of something, dark and dripping, that made Claire gag as if her throat was still clogged. "Is that..." Claire trailed off, dread scraping its way along her tongue.

"One of those bundles of hair and bobby pins," Nadia said. "It was stopping up the shower drain."

"What?" Claire couldn't bear to look at the other girls, or at the thing in Nadia's hand; she flung her gaze around the ruined room as if it would resolve into some explanation she could understand.

"Lady Eva was right all along," Nadia went on. "Lady Lilith's ghost *was* on our side. She was trying to protect us. She was holding back this... this..." Nadia dropped the wet mass of hair on the floor, as if she couldn't bear to touch it a moment longer, and cast a glitter-tipped hand around the room. "This force of destruction. And then we chased her away."

She paused, and lowered her arm, and spoke the words they all dreaded, but that were suddenly undeniable.

"We banished the wrong ghost."

It's not your fault. Claire heard the words from every woman who passed her where she huddled on the dressing-room couch, while the ambulance came and went outside and Nadia did her best to calm Lady Eva in the lobby. Even Luna and Alice offered Claire comfort, rather than reminding her they'd been against this banishment in the first place. But Claire didn't hear the one voice she needed most. Of course Ruby had to be in the middle of a two-hour session next door, and Lady Eva didn't want to interrupt them and alert the client that something was wrong.

Claire knew, logically, that it *wasn't* her fault—any woman at the dungeon would have assumed Lady Lilith's ghost was the only one—but she suspected the full force of the guilt hadn't hit her yet, wrapped as she was in a blanket of shock.

By the time Ruby did emerge from session, all the ladies were remarkably composed. They seemed to have decided if they couldn't banish the right ghost, they would chase away emotion instead; they put their energy into cleaning Lady

Lilith's room until every trace of the damage was gone. Claire didn't have the strength to get up and help, but she soaked up whatever calm she could from the women around her, so by the time Ruby rushed back to the dressing room and enfolded Claire in her arms, Claire no longer felt the need to cling to her with every cell of her being.

"I'll be okay," Claire said.

"I can take you home," Ruby said, "or you can come to—"

"No," Claire said with sudden resolve, "that wouldn't be fair to you. I need to break up with Danny first."

Ruby drew back and, from the wide smile that parted her lips, Claire knew she had no real conception of the horror that had taken place in Lady Lilith's room. And hopefully she never would. "So you're going to do it," Ruby said.

"I'm going to do it," Claire said, ignoring the pinch of fear in her heart. She had messed up so many things, these past few weeks; it was her responsibility to be strong now.

But once Claire had put on her street clothes and driven home on autopilot, Danny was nowhere to be found. He didn't answer her calls or texts, and, like the night before, he didn't appear until she'd been in bed for hours, and he snuck in and wrapped himself around her exhausted body. Claire yearned for Ruby's gentle arms instead of Danny's coarser ones; she longed for the embrace of someone who truly understood her. But to get what she needed, she had to speak up first. And right now, she felt like she had when she was chained to the cross in Lady Lilith's room, when she was crying desperately for someone to save her, but the words died in her throat.

Claire couldn't tell Danny to get out, that she didn't love him. But she couldn't sleep in this bed beside him either. She couldn't go to work and face Ruby's wounded eyes, and the threats of a dark presence she'd foolishly believed she'd conquered. She couldn't, she couldn't, she couldn't...

Claire's entire life had been one long string of *couldn'ts*, and now here she was: lying in bed beside the wrong person, drained and depleted but with her eyes wide open.

Wondering what had brought her to this place, where she was bound by the sort of ropes she feared she could never unravel.

SIXTEEN: ANNA

Before she grew up and became Claire, Anna was a little girl who loved to dance in the park and at playgrounds and in every room of the small apartment she shared with her mother. When Anna first felt the urge to leap and stretch and twirl, she was too young to know about all the things she couldn't do. She thought, as almost all little girls do, that she could do anything. She thought she could shape her limbs into something beautiful; she thought she could create magic from every movement. She thought she could make the father she'd never known come back, just to watch her.

Anna didn't know that with every careless, swaybacked arabesque, with every wildly zigzagging chaîne turn, with every hour spent flinging herself into the air from her mother's mattress, she was training her body to do the opposite of what she would need to be a ballerina. There was no money for ballet lessons, and Anna didn't realize she needed them, so she never learned to force her back as straight as if she were laced into a corset, to nail her gaze onto one spot when she turned, to iron out the micro-bends in her limbs every time she lifted them. She had no idea her flights of freedom were embedding bad habits deep within her, habits that couldn't be undone.

The first of many couldn'ts.

By the time Anna was eight or nine, she'd learned that the dances she choreographed to her mother's favorite songs, Stevie Nicks and Joni Mitchell, couldn't keep the smile on her mother's face for long. There were too many things stealing that smile: the long hours at the restaurant or the receptionist's desk or wherever her mother currently worked; the cost of the American Girl dolls Anna wanted and the raincoat she needed; the dates her mother left for with the hopeful hum of those same songs on her lips, and returned from with her lipstick smeared and the hope drained, out of tune.

Deep inside, Anna understood that the biggest thing stealing her mother's smile was the same thing she tried so hard to dance away: her father's absence. No great leap could carry Anna across space and time to wherever her father was; no mesmerizing pirouette could bring him back home.

Once she became a teenager, Anna began to dance for a different reason: stretching her arms and legs was the only thing that lifted the misty, muddy fog that smothered their little town. Only dancing made Claire believe she could float away, defy gravity for a moment—but even dancing couldn't hold the fog back for long. Anna needed a plan, so after high school she enrolled in community college, majoring in business because it seemed practical, but mostly because they didn't have a dance major. She took every dance class they did have, though, and with each one she discovered more things she couldn't do:

Balance on pointe.

Execute a double pirouette, or a *fouetté* turn.

Anna lacked a *foundation*, her teachers told her, a strong skeleton to support her flights toward freedom. But she had spent so many years dancing that she didn't know how to stop. So she practiced for hours, she poured all her fire into her physical self until every inch of her ignited. She welcomed the pain and hoped it would burn off the fog that pushed her down.

Despite all the hard work and sacrifice, the *couldn'ts* still loomed. As Anna signed up for auditions at the Hollywood Dancers' Institute, as she hugged her mother goodbye and set off for the long drive down the coast, the refrain of *I can't, I can't* played through her mind. When she saw the other dancers warming up, their movements so practiced and fluid they seemed a different species from her, she thought, *I can't*, and almost walked out.

But she couldn't leave either, so she made it through the audition, and by some miracle of will and work, she was accepted into the program. Then she saw the tuition fees, and thought, *I can't*, and took out loans. She moved into student housing and took her first classes with her muscles beating the tense tattoo of *I can't*; she hid in the back and absorbed the teachers' yelled admonishments to "straighten that leg, Anna" and "keep up with the beat" as if each critique cracked her bones. She stayed after each class to practice and told herself the aching in her muscles would transform her, heavy sinew into buoyant ribbons that could float and soar.

And she thought her efforts were working—finally—when she saw the list of soloists for the second-year showcase, and her name was among them. A part of her still whispered, *It was a mistake*, and, *You don't deserve this.* But she silenced the chorus of *I can't* as she began her private rehearsals with Mr. Rivers, who had that permanent pinched expression on his face that too many of the teachers did—the lines that formed once they'd passed their performing years and found the only option left was to guide the next generation, a role they'd never wanted.

That crease of disappointment between Mr. Rivers' eyes only faded when he was guiding Anna into position with his own hands, lifting her leg or circling her waist to pull her spine straighter. At first, Anna tried to ignore the nigglings of doubt in her stomach. But when Mr. Rivers' hands rose higher, past her waist and up her ribcage to the breasts covered only by the thin fabric of a leotard; when he told her he wanted her to *seduce* the audience as she performed his choreography, she couldn't deny her misgivings any longer. She knew why she had gotten this solo. She knew what Mr. Rivers expected of her.

I can't, Anna thought, but she did. She kept showing up for each private rehearsal. She let Mr. Rivers run his hands over her thighs and up her ass, let him brush the hair back from her face and whisper in her ear: "*Seduce me.*" Then she performed the movements he had created for her. The series of *developpés* in which her leg rose higher each time, as though she were trying to fly away; the *grand jetés* across the floor, the leaps into desperate freedom.

Each time she struggled, he frowned and the wrinkles emerged between his brows. He expected her to open her mouth and her legs to him, soothe those worry lines away. *I can't*, she thought. He growled out, "You've got to leap like you're trying to split the world apart. Split your legs, split yourself apart, you're so reckless in your desire. Look—I know you have the range. You can do a split in the air, you can defy gravity and float, if you only believe in yourself."

He lifted her left leg behind her; he ran his fingers up the calf encased in pink tights, along the inside of her thigh; he guided her leg higher until it was parallel to the floor and she tipped like a wobbly doll. She had to reach out a hand and lean against him, close enough to smell the sweat pooling in the crook of his neck, musky and animal-like beneath his cologne. His hand arrived at the top of her thigh, grazed ever so softly over the fabric of her leotard, over her pussy, as Anna held her breath and found that she was, in fact, floating. But it was the wrong kind of floating, the bad kind that meant she couldn't bear to exist inside the body she had put through so much pain, not for a moment longer.

Mr. Rivers' hand kept moving, to the inside of her right thigh; he wanted her to lower her left leg and lift the right one, so he could guide it skyward. He was showing her she had the range to do a split, in the air; she had the range, but not the strength or the control. Not the foundation, the skeleton. He danced his fingers along her thigh to her calf and then her pointed toes. He lowered her leg and pulled her to him and said, "Come have a drink with me, Anna. We'll see where the night takes us."

"I can't," she said.

The next day, she discovered her solo had been reassigned to Sylvia Adams. A week later, the new soloist confided to Anna that she hated Rivers' choreography, that there were too many double and triple *fouettés*.

There hadn't been any double or triple or even single *fouettés* in the choreography Mr. Rivers had created for Anna, because Anna couldn't do them.

But even worse was the fact that Mr. Rivers still taught one of Anna's classes, a class she needed to graduate. After she'd lost the solo, he started calling her out for every misstep, barking, "A ten-year-old could do that turn without wobbling. If you can't even balance, Anna, you'll never make it as a dancer." Her classmates looked at her with pity, and the tattoo of *I can't, I can't* beat louder in her head until, once again, she found herself floating above her body. And then, in one class, he taught a combination of wild turns and *grand jetés*, so many it left all the dancers shaking their heads. "All of you should have the skill to split the air with your legs," Mr. Rivers said, and he turned his face with its accusatory lines right on Anna.

They were supposed to perform the combination across the floor in small groups, with all the others watching. They—and Mr. Rivers—would all see her fail to defy gravity, to leap into straight, soaring lines, the way the rest of them could. She couldn't. She didn't belong there. Her bones were breaking into pieces, so easily it seemed she had been patching them together with tape all this time, and no wonder her efforts had been wasted.

Anna floated out of her body and from her perch on the ceiling, she gazed at her pathetic, patched-together form waiting her turn. She couldn't do it. She couldn't become the dancer she'd always wanted to be, the one who deserved to be watched and admired.

From her spot on the ceiling, floating Anna looked on as her body walked out of the dance studio before she could humiliate herself any further. She never returned.

The *couldn'ts* didn't stop, though, once she'd abandoned the studio and entered the real world. There was the *couldn't* of working at the clothing store, the prospect of hours and months and years ahead of her, wasted waiting for shifts to end. There was the *couldn't* of answering her first Craiglist ad, the *I can't, I can't* as she made her body exit the Uber and walk around the exterior of the motel until she found the right room number.

But it turned out that she could, she could in those dimly lit motel rooms, because she was already adept at the wrong kind of floating.

And now, when she had left the motel rooms behind, had taken on a new name and found herself once again trapped in the wrong place, with the wrong person, Claire who had once been Anna conceded that none of the bad things that happened to her made her feel worse. None of them made her more broken. They only affirmed how broken she had always been, inside; they only fashioned that brokenness into a shape that others could understand. The way Mr. Rivers had propositioned her; the lonely, shameful hours with men she didn't know; the bruises clients like Gunther left on her body, and the cruel words Danny spoke; all these things were a relief, when it came down to it, because they offered reasons for the way she had always felt, since the first time she'd learned *couldn't*.

They offered hope that someone else would see what had always been true, that she was walking around with her bones rattling beneath her skin, barely fastened together, a skeleton of fractures.

They offered hope that someday, someone might come along and save her.

SEVENTEEN: RUBY

Four days had passed since Gunther's body left the dungeon in an ambulance with its lights and sirens off—because there was no need for it to rush. Four days of whispers winding like rose vines until they reached Ruby's ears. Apparently the session with Gunther had been much more horrific than Ruby had first realized, and all the women now believed that Lady Lilith's ghost had departed only to make way for a more sinister presence. Claire herself hadn't said much about the incident—maybe she didn't want to worry Ruby, though it was too late for that. All the ladies walked warily through the dungeon these days, even Alice and Luna. Ruby wondered if they felt the same cold she did, the ice that, since the banishment, had invaded her bones. Sapping her strength, leaving her with the sense of some impending doom.

A client's death was more than any of them had bargained for—

And it looked like the situation was about to get worse. As Ruby approached the dungeon, a glowering police officer marched out. Ruby flinched in time to the gate banging shut behind him; she instinctively darted back until he'd passed her, on his way to the cop car she now noticed by the sidewalk.

With tension growing in her limbs, Ruby reluctantly stepped inside. Lady Eva spoke low and urgently into the new desk phone as Ruby hurried to the dressing room, where she met an incongruously cheerful face: Gabriella's. She must have missed seeing the cop. She was belting some Beyoncé song about burning her tears away, waving her arms over her head, and in her vinyl outfit she might as well have been in a nightclub.

"Celebrating something?" Ruby asked, as a smaller form slipped through the back door.

"Gabby, you got your cast off!" Mara shook her hips in a tiny white cardigan and skirt that made her look like a spectral cheerleader.

"That's right," Gabriella said, "I'm celebrating my freedom from itchy skin I can't scratch, and having to do my makeup and tie up and flog guys with only one hand."

Oh.

"I'm *so* glad you don't have to deal with that anymore." Mara sounded as relieved as if she'd gotten her own cast off.

Then she flicked her hair behind her shoulder—but it must have been wet, and since it was so long and thick, the water drops traveled a few feet to smack Ruby's cheek.

"Hey!" she said on instinct, although she was too distracted to really care.

Nadia walked in, hands twitching at her sides, and Ruby had to stop herself from scanning her coworker for signs of another seizure. But all Nadia said was, "Lady Eva wants all the ladies to gather in the lobby."

It was a small group: Nadia, Gabriella, Alice, Mara, and Luna. Since Gunther's death more women were calling out or had even quit, and who could blame them? The dungeon had already been dying, in a business sense, and now they had the threat of real corpses to top it off.

Ruby leaned against the wall, fidgeting with the straps of the tank top she hadn't had time to change out of, trying not to reveal the worry that clawed inside her. Her boss's shoulders stood rigid beneath her silk blouse, her neck an erect column, by all appearances the same stern mistress who'd ruled this dungeon for so many years now. But she seemed like a puppet, her limbs held up only by a few strings, putting on a play even as the scenery crumbled.

Lady Eva cleared her throat. "We had an unexpected visitor this morning." She paused. "A police officer investigating Gunther's death."

A few stifled gasps followed.

"The cause of death was asphyxiation—choking," Lady Eva barely held her voice steady, "and since it took place here, the police wanted to check out our...business establishment." The dungeon owner looked up and out at each woman, and when her eyes rested on Ruby's a hint of Lady Eva's strong, icy will pierced through her. So that fortitude hadn't all vanished. "What we do here is entirely legal," she went on, "and the cop seemed satisfied that Gunther's death was an accident. But this can*not* happen again, especially with clients in the building. And if you girls keep causing chaos, dredging up matters that would be better left alone..." Her voice rose toward a crescendo, until Ruby pressed her back against the wall, preparing for an explosion—

But the opposite occurred, as Lady Eva crumpled inward. Tears carved tracks down her cheekbones; her head fell to her hands as if it were too heavy to keep upright. "What is happening to my dungeon?" she wondered, voice quaking. "To my girls?"

Nadia rushed to hug her, and Lady Eva continued from beneath Nadia's arms. "I tried so hard to keep everything the way she wanted it"—she stopped to gulp in air, her chest heaving—"but it was never enough. And now, I just want you all to be safe. Ruby—I want you to have the time and space to become a true domme, without punching mirrors. Gabriella—I don't want you to suffer through another broken bone. And Nadia—"

The words dissolved into sobs. Ruby was stunned. Lady Eva actually seemed to care about her, about all of them, with a depth Ruby had never witnessed before. A depth that could break through the dungeon owner's flawless glass surface, and leave it in shards. Ruby thought of the way Lady Eva spoke of Lady Lilith—her words colored with adoration, admiration, and something more. Again, she wondered if Lilith and Eva had been more than just boss and employee, mentor and student. Was Lady Eva now feeling the loss of Lady Lilith's spirit on top of everything else?

Perhaps that wasn't Ruby's secret to know.

The door creaked, a whisper that made everyone jump. Claire slipped inside, her cheeks flushed and curls rising in whirls. "I'm sorry I'm late, Lady Eva, I overslept and the apartment was a mess and—" She stopped short as she took in the scene before her.

"It's fine, Claire," Lady Eva said. "All of you, go get dressed. The clients will be here soon."

In the dressing room Nadia filled Claire in on the meeting, but Ruby was distracted by Alice playing with her packet of Camels, fingers twitching over the last cigarette. "Is everything okay?" she finally asked.

Alice squeezed the filter tight enough to crush it and whispered, "I don't know how I'm going to pay my rent. I really need one of Jimmy's three-hour sessions, but last time he took a shower in Lady Lilith's room, he heard some weird voice singing in the bathroom. He hasn't made an appointment since then."

"I can lend you some money," Ruby whispered. She still had savings, although she hadn't added much to them since the ghost began causing trouble.

"No," Alice said resolutely, flicking the ruined Camel into the trash, "I'll manage somehow."

Ruby wanted to offer some comfort—or get Claire or Nadia to do it instead—but before she could, Lady Eva appeared and called her up front. The dungeon owner's face was powdered white, the redness banished to the corners of her eyes, as she announced that a client was in the parlor. Already in her corset and thigh-highs, Ruby stepped up front and into the small room—and the cold rushed through her bones.

It was Jack, with those blue eyes and silver-tinged scruff and that way of leaning on one hip with his hands in his pockets, like he was waiting for every woman to fall all over themselves in their rush to sing his praises. Jack, who had taken the hardest caning she'd delivered in her life and hopped right up, untouched. Jack, who'd charmed Claire and then nearly crushed her beneath the St. Andrew's Cross—even if that wasn't the way Claire had told the story.

Ruby had to stop herself from walking back out.

"Jack." She crossed her arms. "I thought you weren't interested in seeing a domme again."

He didn't waste time on pleasantries. "I want to tie you up."

"I'm a dominatrix. Men don't tie me up."

"And that's precisely why I want to."

"No." She turned to walk out for real, when he added, "Then I guess I'll see a submissive. Lady Eva said Claire is here...?"

Ruby pivoted slowly back to face him. "Don't session with Claire again. Pick a different girl."

Jack raised one perfectly arched eyebrow. "Telling a client what to do? I don't think your boss would like that very much. And she already seems quite fragile this morning."

Ruby dug her nails into her palms. "You can tie my wrists together. That's it."

Jack's eyes lit up like hard little sapphires. "Excellent."

On their way to the annex, Jack made a detour toward the back of the building and crouched to examine something in the dirt. Ruby pulled the coat that concealed her corset tighter around her as she followed. "Is your boss trying to grow more roses?" Jack asked. He pointed a manicured finger toward the stalks climbing from the earth. "Not the most hospitable spot," Jack said, "but isn't that what you all are here?"

"Excuse me?" Ruby huffed. The frustration she'd tried to bury the past few days was rising back up.

"Roses and thorns," Jack said, "blooming from the most unlikely ground."

Oh, so he was a poet now. Ruby didn't respond as she led him toward the door.

In the annex hallway, Jack picked out a few bundles of maroon rope hanging from hooks. Ruby couldn't help shuddering as she went ahead into the Enclave and turned on the light—and breathed in smoke and salt, that scent from the attic, like longing and loss. Cold circled her limbs, threatening to constrain her, and she did her best to shake it off. She had to keep fear at bay if she wanted to get through this.

The door creaked behind her and Jack coughed. "It smells like incense in here," he said, and with his words that smoky odor dissolved.

Ruby turned to see the ropes coiled in his hand, sinister as those birds' nests of hair the ghost had taken to leaving everywhere. "Why don't I tie you up?" she said. "You have to be a true man to let a woman truss up your cock and balls."

"We had an agreement, Ruby. Come over to the bondage bed and put your wrists behind your back."

The cold swept through her until she thought of retreat, of telling Jack she couldn't go through with this session after all. But then Claire's face flashed into her mind. Flustered and red-cheeked, the way she'd rushed into work just now; or pale with those haunted eyes, the way she'd looked after Gunther died.

Claire was strong enough to do this every day. Ruby could get through it one time.

She walked slowly to the bondage bed, where Jack had dumped the mass of red rope. A pile of innards spilling out of the leather.

Jack placed his smooth hands on her shoulders, and Ruby tried not to flinch. He guided her so her side was to the bed and ran his hands down her arms until, behind her back, her wrists met. She could feel his knucklebones beneath the flesh as he gripped her forearms tightly in one hand, pressing her own flesh and bones together like the click of a lock. He picked up one of the ropes and let go of her for the barest moment, so he could wrap the cord around her wrists. He didn't give her enough time to pull her limbs apart.

"You know," Ruby forced herself to speak, to distract Jack as much as possible, "we're breaking the rules right now. Mistresses aren't allowed to let clients dominate them in session." She gazed into the mirror ahead of them and saw Jack inclining his head to one side. He'd now wrapped the red rope three times around her forearms, and she wiggled her wrists. Every millimeter of extra space would help. "I could get in trouble for this," she added.

"Don't worry." Jack tilted his head further to face her, grinning and flashing his blue eyes, and Ruby separated her wrists another half-inch. "I can keep a secret."

He returned his attention behind her to tie off the rope, and Ruby thought of locks again, of keys turning, clamps tightened, snares laid. Jack knew how to tie a knot.

The second he finished, he lifted his hands to her shoulders and flung her around to face him. His movements slowed and became more gentle, his fingers tracing up her neck, under her chin and across the raised line of her scar, back down and along the edge of her corset. She hoped he couldn't feel the panicked pulse of her heart.

His pointer finger landed at the hooks that held the corset closed and wormed its way under. "You can't take my top off." Ruby's own hands wriggled behind her, loosening the rope in imperceptibly small degrees, as she tried to block out Jack's touch. "We didn't agree on that."

"I think I can do just about anything I want right now," Jack said jauntily. "This is why I love tying women up."

"I can still walk out of this room," Ruby said. "I can tell Lady Eva you crossed my boundaries, and she'll ban you from ever sessioning here again."

Jack laughed and unclasped the corset's first hook. "Even though you're breaking her rules?"

"Yes." Ruby forced herself to inject her normal certainty into her voice, to sound like a mistress and not a scared little girl. "Lady Eva always protects the women who work for her." Secretly, though, Ruby wasn't sure what this new version of her boss would do. The woman she'd seen this morning had been a puppet with her strings snapped, capable of swaying whichever way the wind might take her. And Lady Eva had warned Ruby, only a few weeks ago—she had just *one more chance*.

Lady Eva had already chosen not to believe Ruby, when she was telling the truth.

Jack laughed again, the laugh of a man with money in his wallet and a smirk on his handsome face, sure in the knowledge that he could take what he wanted without fear of punishment. Ruby's bound hands burned with the desire to slap that self-satisfied smile right off him.

"Regardless," Jack said, "you won't walk out of here, Ruby."

He grabbed her wrists and prodded her toward the long mirror at the end of the room, the one where Ruby had seen SINS and DEVILS and WHORES but where, now, there was only the reflection of one woman. One woman, tall and sharp-edged but, with her wrists restrained by a carefree, confident man, she had become someone Ruby didn't recognize.

Jack stopped them before the hulking spanking bench, the rivets shining along its edges like a row of watching eyes.

"You won't stop this session—" Jack turned to face Ruby so only his broad back was visible in the mirror. He undid the second hook of Ruby's corset, and then the third. "—because you don't want me to play with your little friend. Claire. Maybe you didn't realize it, but your eyes sparked when I said her name." He looked up to Ruby's face, straight into her, and his own eyes flashed red. "You just did it again."

Jack finished unhooking the corset, and let it fall to the crimson carpet, and she stood with her breasts bare before a man for the first time since she didn't know whe—

No, she knew exactly when. Since the night she'd gotten her scar.

Ruby's gaze darted to the mirror in spite of herself, while Jack shifted to one side as if to give her a better view. Gooseflesh had risen over her pale chest, her nipples tightened in sharp points of fear. Fear she could do nothing to change, or to conceal.

"I like sessioning with Claire"—Jack drew closer, until Ruby smelled the hunger in his sweat and her heartbeat ran wild—"because she reminds me of the only woman I ever loved." His hands cupped her breasts and he leveled his eyes on hers. "That's a secret," he said. "Can you keep secrets as well as I can?"

Ruby nodded, while her hands worked at the knot behind her.

"Claire even looks like my old girlfriend." Jack pinched Ruby's nipples, hard. "The same curly hair; wide, innocent eyes; cute little body with a spankable ass like a cherry on top." He squeezed her breasts and Ruby's entire body throbbed. "*Violet.*"

Jack closed his eyes, lost in memory. "That was her name. I haven't seen her in twenty years now."

He opened his eyes and looked down at Ruby's breasts in his palms, before his fingers inched higher. "The trouble with girls like Violet—and like Claire—is that they're so friendly and sweet, they flirt with everyone—male *and* female—without realizing what they're doing. They leave a trail of broken hearts without even knowing it." His hand circled Ruby's neck, lingering on her scar until beneath it, her pulse ignited. "It's cute at first," Jack said, "but eventually it becomes a problem. That's why I started coming here, all those years ago. I needed to learn how to be a true dominant. I had to remind Violet who was in charge." His grip tightened around Ruby's throat, and she fought the urge to pull back as his voice turned dark. "I had to teach her to stay in her place."

Ruby looked straight at Jack then. That flash of red had vanished from his eyes, their blue shade as untroubled as a summer sky, and she saw it like ice dousing the fire inside her:

Jack was a truly evil man. The kind of man who only cared about his own power, about making himself big by making other people small. Ruby recognized it easily. She'd seen that kind of man before.

But Jack must have seen something in Ruby's eyes, too, because he dropped her throat and threw back his head and laughed. When he finally straightened, he said, "Oh, Ruby, you're in love with her, aren't you? You foolish girl."

It was returning to her, now—that crimson fury that had overcome her the first time she'd sessioned with Jack, when she'd caned him as if she could slice through his flesh, into his bones. That urge to rip Gregory's balls off, to silence Stuart's voice; that violent rage she'd tamped down but which, now, she could use.

In one quick movement, Ruby pushed her bare chest into Jack's front, surprising him enough so when she half-turned, he followed. She kneed him in the balls, hard, and his back smacked onto the spanking bench behind him.

"You little cunt—"

Behind her back, she worked the last of the knot free and her hands burst forward, landing on Jack's arms and pinning them to the bench's sides. He could fight her if he wanted, she could feel the muscles rising beneath his shirt, but for the moment he simply looked up at her, stunned. "If you ever touch

Claire again," she said slow and clear and certain, so he would hear every word, "I will kill you. That's a promise."

She released his arms and walked slowly backward as he sat up.

The man had the nerve to smile, yet she caught the waver in his voice. "Claire is one of those girls who has too much love to give." He smoothed his hands over his shirt, ironing out the creases. "She gives it to everyone, fools you into thinking you're special. But you'll lose her, just like I lost Violet. And tell me—"

Ruby had bent to pick her corset up off the floor, but she froze as Jack's gaze narrowed under her chin. As if he'd caught her in another trap. "Have you told Claire how you got that scar?"

"What do you know about that?" Ruby gritted out.

"It bothers you, and that tells me everything I need to know." He stood and straightened his jeans with a wince he couldn't quite conceal. "This was an interesting session. Thank you, Ruby."

He dug into his pocket, pulled out his wallet and tossed a hundred-dollar bill on the spanking bench, then turned and walked out.

Leaving Ruby thinking that, while the ghost hadn't shown her presence beyond those first moments, this was the most frightening session she'd ever had.

Ruby took a minute to fasten her corset and slow her galloping heart, before she walked back across the parking lot to the main building. She didn't want anyone to suspect she'd let a client get the better of her—again. Only Lady Eva sat in the lobby, talking on the phone and playing with a pill bottle in her free hand. She barely noticed as Ruby slipped by her to the dressing room—

And found Claire perched on the edge of the sofa, tapping her chipped nails against her thighs, jumping up the second she saw Ruby and asking, "Are you all right? I saw you heading next door with Jack."

It reminded Ruby of the way she'd worried during Claire's first session with Jack; in fact, she'd waited in the exact same spot, scratching at her scar. Despite everything, Ruby couldn't help but smile. "I'm fine," she lied. "Just...promise me you won't session with Jack again, all right?"

Claire shrugged. "I didn't want to anyway."

"Oh my *God*," Luna said from the far end of the couch, "I think that's the exact yellow skirt Alicia Silverstone wore in *Clueless*."

"But her top is all Gwen Stefani," Gabriella added. "Pre-Harajuku era." They were peering over each other's shoulders, gazing down at something.

"The '90s was all about bare midriffs," Nadia said.

"What are you guys looking at?" Ruby asked.

"Those photo albums," Alice said. "We're looking for pictures of Lady Lilith and her room. If we can figure out *why* her spirit returned after her death—if there was something here she needed to protect, or control—then maybe we can understand what's happening now that she's gone."

"But how did you get those?" Ruby asked, shocked. "I thought Lady Eva locked them up…"

"After you went into session," Luna said, "Lady Eva took a bunch of her pills to 'stay calm.' Seemed like an opportune moment, so Nadia brought her a glass of water and palmed the key right out from under her."

Nadia didn't look the least bit apologetic, and her hands didn't tremble as she traced the gold-embossed *1997* on the album's spine. "We still need answers," she said. "I did what I had to." Nadia had changed; they all had.

Meanwhile Luna flipped a page and paused. "Whoa. Claire"—Luna grabbed the book from Nadia—"this girl looks just like you."

"Let me see that." Ruby nearly pushed the others over in her rush to look at the old photos. A strange feeling was coming over her, a different kind of cold.

The girl *did* look like Claire; her hair was a little lighter, her eyes a little darker, but she had that same sweet smile, captured behind the plastic photo album slots. On her knees, with the zebra-striped carpet beneath her; leaning over the bondage bed, eyes wide in false fear; in the lobby with legs tucked under her like a mermaid, her arms around another girl who was almost entirely cropped out of view. Ruby scanned to the top of the page, where a name was written in flowery purple letters, and that icy feeling tightened around her throat.

Violet.

"Jack told me his girlfriend was named Violet," she whispered. "Twenty years ago."

"A coincidence, I'm sure," Alice scoffed. "Besides, Violet's probably not her real name—"

"Actually," Nadia jumped in, "I've heard girls used their real names here more often before the internet took off—there was less risk of stalkers. But that would still be quite a coi—"

Claire's curls, so much like those of the girl in the photos, brushed over Ruby's shoulders. "Jack told me about his girlfriend too," she said. "He didn't give a name, but he said he used to come here with her. They would pick up girls here and take them home."

Claire looked away from the pictures, gazing up at Ruby with wonderstruck eyes. "Jack didn't come here with his girlfriend," Claire said. "His girlfriend *worked* here."

Luna jumped off the couch and ran toward the lobby, as Nadia called, "Luna... Be careful."

"This is the perfect time to ask questions," Luna said, "while her defenses are down." The others followed until they all stopped short behind the front desk, where Lady Eva spoke into the phone. "...Mara tomorrow, at four? Perfect. We'll see you then, Kenny. Get some rest. Don't overexert yourself."

"Cupcake Kenny," Gabriella whispered. "It's got to be."

Lady Eva was going to let Kenny session with Mara again, let him tie her up, when he'd had a heart attack? She'd just warned them to be careful, and now she was inviting the possibility of another ambulance, more attention from the cops? Ruby barely had time to process this before Luna asked:

"Lady Eva, do you remember a girl named Violet who used to work here? In the '90s?"

Lady Eva's features pursed with annoyance, a more familiar expression than the despondency of this morning. "I've run this dungeon for twenty years, Luna, and I've hired hundreds of girls. You can't expect me to remember someone from that long ago."

"She was pretty," Luna said, as Ruby rolled her eyes—like that would narrow it down. "Curly dirty-blonde hair, dark blue eyes..."

Lady Eva closed her eyes. "I do remember her. She was the reason we had to close off the attic."

"*What?*" six voices said at once—a mistake, as Lady Eva's eyes flew wide open.

"There was an accident in the attic," Lady Eva spoke tersely, "and I barred the staircase off because it was never safe in the first place. That's it. It's really no concern of yours."

The front door opened and Mara entered, holding a riding crop. "Mara," Lady Eva said, "I booked you a session with Cupcake Kenny for tomorrow."

Mara nodded, her expression tranquil, free hand winding through her hair. Maybe Ruby was imagining things, but it still looked wet, the ends clumped together, shining a deep, glossy black.

Lady Eva turned to the rest of them. "If you're all going to stand around here twiddling your thumbs, I'm sure I can find tasks for you. The equipment wall needs dusting, and the sofa covers ought to be washed—"

The others were slinking away, but Ruby remained, imagining herself describing what had taken place during her session with Jack, and wondering how this stern, stiff woman before her might react. There was a good chance Ruby might find herself fired, and unable to protect Claire at all.

Ruby's boss must have had her reasons for becoming so brittle, for erecting her glassy armor. Before she'd become the Briars' owner, Lady Eva had worked here herself, in a time when men's bad behavior was considered the norm. A time when a romantic relationship between two women was, in many places, unthinkable.

Lady Eva had so much potential to understand what the women in her dungeon were going through, to truly support them, to change the things that needed changing. But instead, their boss had chosen to align herself with old spirits, old ways, and separate herself behind a wall of glass.

"Do you need something, Ruby?" Lady Eva finally snapped.

Ruby answered, simply:

"No."

We were all on edge now, not only at the dungeon but everywhere we went, in every part of our lives. We could no longer pretend that the world hadn't been peeled back at its edges, like a corpse dissected on a medical examiner's table, the skin sliced open to reveal the strange sinews of muscle and coiled organs. Reminding us we didn't know the true forms of anything, not even ourselves. There was another world out there, on the other side of a veil, as Lady Lilith's letter had said; a world of unseen forces, resting so precariously against our own that with the slightest misstep, it could all tumble down.

And when we banished Lady Lilith's ghost, our misstep had been more than a slight one.

Perhaps it was because Alice knew she was balancing on a knife's edge, dancing between two worlds, that she chose to walk home from the bar after midnight, alone. It was only two blocks to her apartment in WeHo, and days earlier, she'd pressed her lips against the mouth of a tall, solid man who'd perished at the hands of an incorporeal ghost. The threats of mere mortals, looking for easy prey on dark streets, seemed more worthy of laughter than concern.

And besides, Alice wasn't easy prey.

And she was angry, despite the cocktails she'd sipped and later chugged. She needed the walk in the cool night air, if she'd have any hope of sleeping that night.

She'd headed to the bar at ten, after a long talk with her father on the phone. She hadn't wanted to call him, but she still didn't have rent money, and she was just desperate enough to ask for a loan. Before she could, though, he launched into the familiar song—why hadn't she applied to med school yet? Her MCAT scores were so good, and she couldn't work as a waitress forever—

Alice had had enough of anatomy lessons as a biology major in college. She had no desire to spend years in white-tiled buildings, suffering sleep deprivation beneath fluorescent lights. She preferred the anatomy of cock-and-ball torture, the science of tying wrists and ankles together without cutting off blood flow for too long. But she could never tell her father that, and she couldn't ask him for money now—she would only be proving his point.

Alice was tired of all of it. Tired of worrying about money and haunted dungeon rooms, but more than that, tired of everyone telling her what to do: the college professors with their focus on grades and competition; her father, who cared about grades too, but only if they'd lead to stable employment; the dungeon clients who had no interest in her intelligence, but wanted her to wear pigtails and frills. She'd chopped her hair into its sharp bob just so she could deny them one part of their fantasy.

Even the bartender tonight said to slow down, she was too little to hold all that alcohol. She'd spent a precious few dollars trying to chase away her troubles for an hour, and it hadn't even worked.

And then, there it was again, as she turned off Santa Monica Boulevard onto the side street that led to her apartment: a man, telling her what to do. "Hey, little girl, stop," he blocked her way on the sidewalk. A skinny punk in a wifebeater and sweatpants. "Hand me your purse."

Oh, no. No way was Alice handing over her bank cards and the twenties left in her wallet. And she had kicked so many men in the balls at the dungeon, she didn't hesitate, or allow her anger to fizzle into fear. She lifted one pointy-toed boot and struck home, and as the man keeled over, groaning, she ran.

Exhilaration fizzed through her, frothy as the cocktails she'd drunk, until she half wanted to turn and land another blow. She laughed, a high, bell-like sound, and wondered if the stress had tipped her all the way over the edge—

And then something sharp touched the back of her neck, and she froze.

"Give me your purse, you little cunt." The same man—she recognized his voice—but his tone razor-edged. The metal dug into Alice's flesh until slippery strands of fear emerged.

She clutched her handbag tighter, slowly unzipping it, wondering if she could pull out a dollar or two. Throw it at the man and run.

His other hand tugged at her skirt, and the sound of satin ripping rent the air. "Give me your purse, or you won't like what happens instead."

Alice had dug into the bag, now, feeling for her wallet, but her hand grasped something else. Something like a tiny bird's nest, with metal ridges woven through torn tendrils. She almost dropped the thing in disgust, but some instinct, something

214

burning red inside her, made her clutch it and pull it out, and whip around to brandish it at the man.

He scuttled back, the knife tumbling from his hand as he stared wide-eyed at the thing. Alice looked down at it too, only half-visible in the darkness, but she knew what it was, even if she had no idea how it had wormed its way into her purse. The clump of hair and bobby pins writhed in her hand, and she saw what the thief saw:

A mass of moving black snakes.

A red coal burning inside a skull.

A woman's silhouette, turning to reveal a backside that was only a tree trunk. Hollow. Rotten.

The images sent sparks through Alice's veins. They made her invincible. She stepped forward, still holding the tangle of hair in front of her, and aimed her boot high enough to kick the man in the chest. He went down, and whether he was felled by her own strength or the shock of what he saw, Alice didn't care. She stood over his prone body and slammed her stiletto heel where she knew each of his organs was, as if an anatomy diagram was superimposed over his wifebeater. Liver. Kidneys. Gallbladder. Spleen. Finally, she stabbed her heel into his balls, again and again and again. She wouldn't stop until her stiletto ripped through the fabric of his pants, pierced his flesh and drew blood.

"That will teach you to tell women what to do," she said. "That will teach you to take things that don't belong to you."

She clutched the hair tighter, felt it wriggling against her palm, before some self-preserving part of her told her it was too much power to hold. So she threw it atop the man's heaving chest, and watched, her body buzzing, until he gradually grew still.

She should flee before he got back up, but instead she knelt and reached into his pants' pockets, pulling out a handful of crumpled bills. Stolen, dirty money, but better it go toward Alice's rent than whatever this piece of shit might spend it on.

Without waiting to see if he'd ever wake up again, she turned and walked away slowly, casually the rest of the way home.

EIGHTEEN: CLAIRE

After five days, the bruises Gunther's paddling had left on Claire's ass and thighs still blazed an angry red, and Claire accepted the discomfort as a punishment she deserved. After all, it had been *her* idea to banish the wrong ghost. She had been partially responsible for the death of a man. An awful man, at least the side of him she had known, but he hadn't deserved to die.

Since Danny was avoiding her, he hadn't seen the bruises—but she needed to confront him, to end things for good. She'd texted him that they had to talk, and he'd texted back that the band was close to a breakthrough on their new song. The last few nights he'd crept into the apartment after midnight and had still been asleep when she'd left for work, looking so innocent with his body curled under the covers that she wondered if she'd only imagined him speaking such cruel words.

And on top of everything else, it was also time for Claire's monthly check-in with her mom. A prospect that promised only more avoidance, more lies, as she sat cross-legged on the bed where she'd slept beside Danny so many times, and dialed the familiar number.

"How's work?" her mother asked.

"*Fine.*"

"How's the weather?" her mother asked.

"*Fine.*"

"How's Danny?"

There was so much Claire could say, but she was tired of thinking about Danny at all. She found herself saying instead: "I...I met someone else. Someone who's amazing, and loyal, and smart and so strong, and I really care about...about *her*."

The pause that followed made Claire bite her lip and grip the phone. "Well," her mom finally said, "if it's someone you really care about, then you shouldn't let...*her* get away."

Claire breathed out. "I know. I just have to break up with Danny first."

Another pause. Claire looked down at the chipping pink nail polish she desperately needed to touch up. "You'll do the right thing," her mother said. "You're strong too."

The next day, when Claire had once again slipped out before Danny woke, she found Ruby alone in the dungeon dressing room. Ruby sat on the sofa poring over one of those old photo albums, her dark hair falling over her shoulders, and Claire had the rare chance to just study her. She was so beautiful; Claire had thought so from the first time she'd seen her, but the more she got to know her, to peek beneath her gemlike surface and glimpse all the trials she'd been through, the more beautiful she'd become.

Ruby must have sensed her presence, then, because she looked up. "I told my mom about you," Claire blurted out. "She approves."

Ruby's lips tipped up into a smile, but only a small one. "And Danny..."

Claire looked down. "As soon as he comes home before two a.m.—"

Those crimson lips pursed. "You could always break up with him by text. Change the lock and leave his stuff outside."

Claire sighed and sank down on the couch. "I've lived with him for a year. He was the first one to...to make me feel hope again, after I left the Dancers' Institute. He may be a jerk, but I've got to tell him to his face. I owe him that much."

Ruby nodded, but Claire couldn't escape the disappointment in her eyes. So she changed the subject: "Anything interesting in those books?"

"Just figuring out what I can about Violet," Ruby's voice perked up. "I didn't see a trace of her in the 1996 or '98 albums—so she didn't even work at the Briars a full year. And I'm trying to find that girl she has her arm around in the one photo. I didn't find a match, but— Look at this..."

Ruby grabbed the *1997* album and flipped through it, pausing about halfway. A few spikes poked out, made of the same plastic material that encased the photos in the rest of the book. Claire brushed two fingers over one of the teethlike remnants and tugged. With a bit of force, it would rip right off. "Someone pulled a page out."

"In the middle of the *L*s. There's one page for every woman who worked here, in alphabetical order, and, well—" Ruby paused. "There was one girl that someone wanted to forget. To erase."

Claire's stomach lurched. She wondered if all this really mattered, if it could truly have anything to do with the ghost, and she was relieved when Alice walked into the dressing room and saved her having to respond. Well, not walked so much as strutted, as if she were a model on a runway and she knew all eyes were on her.

Nadia entered from the back door and stopped short. "Don't we have a Wonder Woman costume around here somewhere?" she asked. "Alice, you're giving off superhero vibes."

"I feel like a superheroine," Alice said. "I had an... interesting night. But anyway, I came back here for a reason. You have a session, Claire. And don't worry—it's not Jack."

It wasn't Jack, but another client Claire had hoped to see, though she feared he'd arrived too late: Yarik. His warm scent reminded her of the sage-and-baked-bread smell when they'd performed the banishment, and Claire was quick to offer him her usual hug. But she doubted she could find any real comfort there anymore.

And it seemed Yarik didn't expect her to. He broke the embrace and shook his head. "I could feel the darkness before I opened the dungeon gate, Claire," he said. "I've failed you."

"No, I failed. I didn't understand what we were dealing with..." The guilt ambushed her as she glanced toward the lobby. "We shouldn't talk about this here."

Mara and Kenny were about to go up to Lady Lilith's room, so she and Yarik once again sessioned in one of the small rooms next door. On their way through the parking lot, as the sun streaked across Yarik's face and lit up his eyes, he nodded toward the alley behind the Enclave. "I see the roses are growing there," he said. "That will offer you some protection, at least."

Back inside, Yarik's eyes darkened once more. He didn't suggest picking out any paddles from the equipment wall, and Claire led him to the small room at the front of the building, with just one mirror and a flower-patterned sofa and bondage art prints on the wall. Before she could even begin to explain what had happened, Yarik took off his suit jacket and threw it over the back of the couch and said, "Claire, I can't keep my secrets any longer.

"I haven't been entirely honest with you."

Dread crashed like a wave over Claire until she half fell onto the sofa. She couldn't take another disappointment, another betrayal. Not now. But when Yarik sat slowly beside her, his presence felt as solid as always.

Claire's instincts couldn't have steered her so wrong.

218

Yarik cleared his throat. "I'm not a Russian history professor, Claire."

Oh no.

"I'm a Russian *folklore* professor, with an emphasis on the supernatural. And...I'm a bit of a ghost hunter on the side." Despite the gravity of the moment, excitement crept into his tone. "I found the Briars—and Lady Lilith's room, in particular—through an online forum of haunted places."

"You're kidding me," Claire said, even as it started to make perfect sense. He'd always wanted to session in Lady Lilith's room, and seemed more interested in peering up the attic stairs than in spanking or tying her up. He told a story every session, and now that she thought about it, most of them *did* include ghosts. It was such a revelation that she couldn't be upset.

"So what does this forum say about our...supernatural residents?" Claire wondered if Lady Lilith would have appreciated the notoriety.

"Not much," Yarik said, "just a few rumors of a female spirit in the attic. And I didn't add any new details. I came back not only for the ghost, but to see you."

"You had to say that, or you would hurt my feelings." Still, Claire hoped his words were true.

"But then," the smile fell off Yarik's face, "a few months ago, something changed. Something dark came to life here, and I thought I could help you banish it, but—"

"It didn't work."

"It didn't," Yarik agreed and glanced around the small room. A space so silent and still, it was hard to imagine a ghost might linger on the other side of the mirror. "And if this spirit has survived the wormwood and the black salt that I gave you, if it's grown stronger, even, I can only think this darkness belongs here." He let out a breath. "Darkness is dangerous, but it's not always evil. It's here for a reason, and"—Yarik looked into Claire's eyes—"you'll find the truth. You're strong and smart enough. I know you will."

Claire thought of the mirrors' many messages, and hoped he was right.

"Should I spank you now?" Yarik asked in a lighter voice. "Here's another secret: I've started to like it."

Claire agreed, and soon enough Lady Eva called through the intercom that their session was over. "I'm sorry I muddled things up for you, Claire." Yarik stood and retrieved his suit jacket as Claire straightened the pillows on the couch. "The only advice I can give you is this: if it comes down to it—and I hope it doesn't—don't let go of her hair."

Claire didn't even try to make sense of that. "I have to leave on another long trip," Yarik finished. "Stay safe while I'm gone."

Claire said she would try, and as they left the room Yarik muttered something under his breath, something that might have been meant for Claire, and might not.

"When I recited lines from that Pushkin poem," he said, "I never thought I'd see her here myself."

Claire hadn't had time to process Yarik's words before she was back in the lobby, where Lady Eva looked up at her, calm if vacant-eyed, and said, "Kenny and Mara want you up in Lady Lilith's room for a cameo."

If Claire had been holding any paddles, she would have dropped them. "Cupcake Kenny? The one who just had a heart attack?"

"Yes, dear," Lady Eva said smoothly, "and they don't have too long left in their session, so you'd better get up there."

Claire glanced beyond the lobby to see a tall, corseted silhouette in the hallway. She could almost feel the tension in the crossed arms, the tapping toes. "Um...I just have to go to the bathroom real quick," she said, and rushed back to Ruby.

"You're not going up there, are you?" Ruby half-growled.

"It's a cameo," Claire said. "It's only ten minutes." She didn't want to do it either, but she'd rather not upset Lady Eva. "What could go wrong in ten minutes?"

Ruby leveled her green eyes right on Claire, like little knives. "Okay, okay," Claire said, "but what if Mara needs me? What if she wants me up there for support?"

"It's not your responsibility to take care of Mara, or to keep Lady Eva happy, or please all the clients, or..." Ruby's expression twisted; her eyes sharpened even more. "...or be nice to your fucking asshole boyfriend. Who should be your ex by now."

Claire flinched at the curse. She took in the lines of Ruby's body—the stiff stance, the clenched fingers—and wondered if something else was going on. Ruby looked right at her again, but this time her eyes were weary, no longer weapons, and Claire heard what she didn't say. *You care about all those other people—but what about me?*

"Claire?" Lady Eva called.

220

Claire looked at the wall lined with paddles and floggers, the floor tiles, anywhere except Ruby's eyes. "Ten minutes," she said. "Then we'll talk."

When Claire opened the door to Lady Lilith's room, she almost gagged on the smell. Like water and earth left stagnant for too long, like the sulfurous odor of a swamp. With the lights off, the scent darkened the air into a haze broken only by that candle flame on the stairs, wavering like a will o' the wisp on a bog. A fairy light, a ghost candle in the hands of an eternally lost, wandering soul.

Before even glancing at the rest of the room, Claire rushed toward that candle, though the thick air left her slogging as if through mud. She reached it, finally, and used all her strength to blow the flame out. Then she turned to make out Kenny's big-bellied form beside the bondage bed, and Mara lying on top of it. She was hog-tied, her wrists and ankles bound to each other behind her back, her long hair cocooned around her so Claire could think of nothing but one of those bundles of hair and bobby pins braided together. In the place of the metal, Mara's naked human limbs.

Claire remembered all the times she had been tied up and a strand of hair had fallen over her eyes or worse, her mouth, sticking to her lip gloss, clinging to her like some insect that wouldn't fly off. Without sparing a thought for Kenny's presence, Claire walked slowly to the bed and brushed the hair from Mara's face. It was wet, as though she'd soaked it with tears, and as Claire touched the strands she tasted salt on her tongue. She felt a tangle and teased her fingers gently through until it came loose.

"Isn't she," Kenny intruded, "so lovely"—*huh*—"all tied up and helpless, so I can do whatever I"—*huh, huh*—"want?" Kenny didn't seem capable of doing much of anything at the moment, as he struggled to talk and step closer to Claire at the same time, losing his breath with every other word. Claire wondered how he had managed to tie anyone up at all. He reached out a hand on which the sweat droplets burst like living creatures, and traced a finger over Mara's small breast as she shivered and shook. "See how she"—*huh*—"lusts for my touch?"

Claire looked into Kenny's glassy eyes and, before she could stop herself, she spat: "She's not lusting for you. She's crying. She's hurting. Can't you feel it, you sick fu—" She bit the last word off just in time, cutting it off as the taste of blood ran coppery and thick over the salt on her tongue.

But Kenny's thin lips only slunk upward into a smile, and without a single pant or huff, he said, "Yes, she *does* want me to touch her most precious parts."

Claire tried to look away from Kenny and his sweat-slicked skin, but instead she found her gaze trapped on his eyes, watching the pupils evaporate into a milky film. He wasn't hearing what she said. He wasn't seeing what was really here. A voice in Claire's mind, a voice of self-preservation that sounded almost like Ruby's, said: *Run.*

She lifted one foot, but Kenny had a coil of red rope in his hand—when had that happened?—and before Claire could step away from him, he had grasped her arms, turned her halfway around and was tying her wrists behind her back. The moment that smooth, seductive rope touched her flesh, all the fight sank out of her. The carpet beneath her feet turned to mud that sucked her down, down, down.

Kenny lifted her onto the bed beside Mara, his arms surprisingly strong. He pulled her ankles up behind her and fastened them to her bound wrists. The smell of rot had faded, replaced by a thick, murky nothing and the small but certain weight of Mara beside her. A cold crept over Claire, carving through her bones, until she yearned for the touch of any warm hands on hers. Even Kenny's would do. Maybe he *was* touching her, but she couldn't feel it through the numbing cold. It worked its way into her lungs, dark and liquid, stealing away the air and leaving her so sad, so empty, so alone.

Hours passed. Days. Years. She became aware of movement beside her, Mara stretching her limbs, sitting up. She heard the drip of Mara's wet hair against the leather bed. Had Kenny untied her, or had she slipped the ropes off on her own?

Mara stood atop the bondage bed, naked aside from her underwear, the slender curves of her form as insubstantial as moonlight in the dark room. Claire gazed up at Mara as Mara looked down at Kenny who, despite all his girth, now seemed small. "You see me," she whispered in a voice like smooth glass that broke off into shards, "a small, thin girl who always wears white. The color of innocence, of youth, of an unlived life. You see a girl who might as well be floating, a girl you can't pin down."

Mara looked up, then, toward the bare spot on the wall where that droopy-eye mirror once hung. Her hair lifted as if caught in a breeze and in the other mirror, the one behind her, her flesh dissolved until the luminous bones of her shoulders and spine jutted through. Superimposed over the tender triangles of her scapula, watercolor letters bled onto the mirror.

TRUTH

"A girl," Mara went on, "who might have come from some-place far from here. From another world. You see me, and your mind says, *Not a threat.* Your mind says, *Prey.*"

Mara's eyes sparked like coals kindled into fiery life.

"Your mind is wrong."

Claire waited, her arms and legs freezing like ice, swelling against the red rope, for the room to explode. For the mirrors to turn crimson, the furniture to shake, the pipes to burst. But all that happened was this:

Kenny opened his mouth as if to speak, but before he could, he crumpled to the carpet, all life fleeing his limbs at once. His last words stolen along with the last beat of his heart.

Mara turned up the lights and untied Claire before she buzzed down on the intercom and asked Lady Eva to call 911. Mara's hands against Claire's flesh were warm, warm as Claire's own skin in the room that no longer smelled like a swamp. Mara's hair was soft and dry as it brushed against her own. Everything might have taken place only in Claire's mind, aside from the body on the floor.

And soon Claire found herself once again wrapped in a blanket on the dressing-room couch, cocooning herself from the aftermath of an ambulance's arrival and a panicked group of girls. She grabbed the extra bottle of perfume she'd left on the dressing-room table and sprayed her wrists and ankles, everywhere Kenny's rope had touched. As she waited for Ruby, who was—of course—in session again, Claire played with her phone and thought back to what Yarik had mumbled as he left, what seemed like days ago. The Pushkin poem.

She googled "Pushkin poem ghost."

Too many results. She tried to remember the details—the river, the prince and his lover who, Claire suspected, had drowned herself.

She added more words. "River drowned maiden..."

A promising result popped up. A poem titled "Rusalka," with the subheading "The bank of the Dnieper." She remembered Yarik speaking that word.

Instead of clicking on the poem, Claire impulsively typed "rusalka" into the search bar. Wikipedia came up, and then a folklore website that looked trustworthy. *Rusalka. A Slavic female spirit or ghost. Usually malevolent. Associated with water. Takes the shape of a woman with long, dark hair, often dressed in white...*

She skimmed further. *While young girls traditionally wore braids, and married women kept their hair covered, the rusalka's wild, unbound hair was both a signal of her unnatural state and the source of her power.*

It was impossible. They'd all call her crazy. And what if she was wrong? She couldn't cast suspicion on her coworker, her friend.

And what if she was right? She still couldn't say anything, couldn't betray this girl she'd come to care about. This quiet girl with the depths of an ocean behind her eyes; this girl who couldn't truly want to hurt them.

Claire wasn't thinking clearly. She needed to wait, to reassess all this when she was back in her right mind. But one thing was certain:

She couldn't be alone tonight.

NINETEEN: MARA

The morning before she killed Kenny, Mara woke out of the liquid blackness and found herself in front of the Briars' gate, about to open the door.

It always started this way—with her coming back into consciousness, opening her eyes to a vision of red roses and barbarous thorns. She wondered, after she'd been back for a while, and had come to understand just how strange her condition was, why no one noticed her suddenly emerging into being on a palm-tree-lined street in Los Angeles, beneath the sun's sting if she was arriving for a day shift, or the bruised blanket of twilight for an evening one. But then, the longer Mara was back, the more she remembered that she had always been an unseen girl. The kind who floated around the periphery of other people's lives, the kind who could disappear without a single question or raised eye. Why should she expect anything to be different now?

Mara stepped through the gate in her white peep-toes, down the path lined with potted plants to the front door. In the lobby, she greeted Lady Eva and slipped past the front desk to the dressing room, where she smiled hello to Claire and Gabriella. She felt more comfortable around Gabriella now that the pink cast was gone, and she no longer had to watch the girl fumbling to apply her foundation using only one arm. Gabriella's struggles had niggled at Mara like a tangle of hair she couldn't unknot, a troublesome feeling she thought might be something called guilt.

Mara dropped her bag of outfits on the couch, unzipped it and perused the array of white costumes inside. "Wet hair again, Mara?" Gabriella asked. "Don't you have a blow-dryer?"

Mara flipped the damp locks over her shoulder and said lightly, "Hair this long takes a half hour to blow-dry. I've got better things to do."

It hadn't always been this easy. The first time Mara walked through the thorn-threaded gate of the Briars, even speaking had been a struggle. She'd had to expel each word with great force, as though they were trapped deep in her throat, yet her voice still came out almost too quiet to be heard. How strange Lady Eva must have found her, when she stepped into the lobby with no idea where or who she was, all her effort focused on trying not to walk right out of the too-big pink heels she wore. The dungeon owner had asked if Mara was the girl who had called and asked about working as a submissive, and the word "yes" had fallen from Mara's mouth like a stone.

In those early days, Mara barely understood the meaning of the words she spoke. She knew only a desire like a live coal in the center of her chest, where a living person's heart would be, and the certainty that she was here for a reason.

Back then, Mara had a hard time being in more than one place at once, remaining in the pale-skinned, black-haired human body she inhabited while a spectral part of her roamed the dungeon, following the other girls. She would get lost and confused, forget what she was doing, act in ways that made no sense at all. She would scrawl her frustration in red lipstick on the mirrors and pour it out the bathroom faucets, push it over like a piece of furniture, make it rattle the walls.

While Mara's body perched on the dressing-room sofa or writhed beneath a man's spanking or tickling hands, her spirit went wandering. She delved into her coworkers' and clients' heads, coloring their thoughts and actions the same crimson that burned from the coal in her chest. She dug out bits of memory and emotion, not knowing which were hers and which belonged to these others, and the mess that remained angered her. It made that coal blaze brighter in her chest, where her heart should have been.

And then there was the presence to deal with.

Mara immediately sensed the stern old presence that made its home in Lady Lilith's room, even if she couldn't see it, or speak to it; and at first that presence kept her from doing everything she wanted. On her very first day at the dungeon, Mara tried to choke that disgusting sadist named Gunther with a piece of candy and with his own greed, but that other ghostly presence knocked the peppermint right out of his throat.

Now, in the dressing room, Mara glanced at Claire's shadowed eyes in the mirror. She didn't want to think about Gunther anymore, and especially not about how Claire might have suffered during the last moments of the man's life. Those thoughts made the uncomfortable, tangled-hair feelings rise up in Mara again. She would rather focus on the women who shared her anger, the ones she could offer her darkness to. The ones like Ruby and Luna, who had just walked into the dressing room, texting with one hand and chugging from a Starbucks cup with the other, complaining that "some stupid asshole kept catcalling me on the street, he wouldn't leave me alone." Mara had helped Luna frighten her client, the one who'd threatened to expose all her secrets; she would have given Luna the courage and the fury to do more, but the old presence had pushed the bondage bed onto its side and freed the man before she could.

Worse than the way the old presence always interfered, though, was how it took over the old attic—a place that Mara felt should somehow be hers. In the attic, Mara could almost remember the living girl she might have been. Just thinking about it made her reach out and touch the bracelet on her arm, caress the flower charms. Those tiny blossoms cast water over the red flames of her coal heart; they cooled her anger to the blue-black of loss.

Mara had tried to lead the girls into the attic, to show them who she truly was. But every time, the old presence stopped her. First, when she lured Claire up the stairs, the presence knocked the vase over and woke Claire from her trance. Then she tempted Gabrielle toward the attic with the candle flame, and the presence pushed not an inanimate object, but Gabriella herself—likely not realizing how delicate the girl's bones had become. And when the six women came up together, and memory crashed over Mara like a wave of yearning and loss, the power of the old ghost and that old coin Claire had were enough to make Mara's spectral form dissolve.

Mara held on to those bits of memory, though, and wondered how she could grasp on to more. When the girls and the clients asked her where she was from, Mara wished she could tell them the truth. Did she once have parents, a family, a childhood—a home? Who had she been, before she became a submissive, a sex worker, a girl at the edges who could vanish and never be missed, never return? She wanted to go exploring, try to find answers beyond the dungeon; but every time she stepped past the gate, her consciousness blinked out. The liquid blackness surrounded her, and the next thing she knew she was dressed in a different outfit, carrying her bag of dungeon clothes, standing before the gate just in time for her next shift.

That bag of costumes changed, too, revealing new items over time: A pair of white peep toes. A colorless little sailor suit. A long, fringed cream shawl. Beyond the bleached-out surface of these clothes lay a hint of familiarity, a sense that Mara had known a version of these items once before. That the appearance of each one was a sign of excavation, of exhumation, and if she could just keep existing for long enough, she would find a way to dig it all up.

If Mara wanted to solve these mysteries, she would need enough strength to overcome the old presence; so she fed on the desires of the men she sessioned with, especially the ones who saw her as small and fragile and *other*. The ones who wanted her to be an innocent schoolgirl or a mysterious gypsy or a seductive concubine, or simply a girl who had chosen to work at a dungeon where she stripped and offered her naked ass to men for a spanking. In their minds, these things made her less of a human like them, and more of a blossom ripe for the plucking. The men lowered their defenses, thinking they could take what they wanted from her and fear nothing, and she sucked their lifeforce into her and grew stronger.

And then, the women she worked with, the ones who stood beside her in the dressing room, gave her an unexpected gift: they decided to banish the old presence. And they actually invited Mara along. By that point, Mara had become too powerful for their silly herbs and salt and incantations to affect her. She hid her spirit-self deep inside her human body, where no ritual purification could hurt her. She watched while the old presence, who had no human form to protect her, had her shadow-self ripped to shreds by coarse salt and bitter smoke.

With the old presence no longer thwarting her every effort, Mara started to remember how it felt to have human weight, to stand firmly on the ground. She began to joke with her coworkers, to laugh and smile with them and even, once or twice, to hurt when they hurt. But at the same time, she became messier and messier, as if she were beginning to unravel. Her hair grew long and thick and tangled into clumps no matter how much she brushed it. Sometimes the ends turned soaking wet, though she wasn't sure how they had gotten that way, and they dripped and dripped for hours.

Even as Mara was starting to feel more solid, more human; even as she began to recall the sensation of a living heart within her chest; it became harder to hide the fact that she no longer belonged in this world.

Mara was growing stronger, yes, but parts of her were fissuring, coming apart at the seams. She just had to hold on to her fragile girl's form for a little longer, so she looked for ways to increase her strength. She hid the scissors that could allow others to steal her hair, and when no one was watching she snipped just enough to make her bobby-pin talismans. Then she snuck them into the ladies' things so they'd carry them out into the world and maybe lose them there. So she could absorb more energy and perhaps, if she was very lucky, discover more clues to who she was and what had happened to her.

Because as long as Mara was trapped there, within the thorns of the Briars, she still had one problem. Beyond the coal heart that sparked inside her, that beat the tune of *wrong, wrong, wrong* that needed to be righted, she still didn't know why she'd come back here, to this place and time. She grasped at the strands of memory, hoping she could use them to mend her human form—strands like the blue-eyed man named Jack, and the name Claire had spoken, *Violet,* and another girl she thought was important. A girl she once might have been, a girl whose name began with the letter *L,* like loss. Back when she had a heart made of muscle, the kind that could bleed and be broken.

There was a reason Mara was here now. There was a reason the universe brought her back to this spot, a reason to resurrect this human form.

There was a reason, and as soon as she remembered it, she would finish what she came there to do.

TWENTY: RUBY

"**P**lease, Ruby, can I come over tonight?"

After all the times Ruby had offered, or wanted to offer—all the times Claire had insisted on waiting until she broke up with Danny, and yet she could never follow through—now, when Claire asked, a twisted part of Ruby wanted to say no.

Claire sat on the dressing-room sofa with a blanket pulled tight around her, as if she were desperate to shield herself from the world. Ruby couldn't blame her. Claire had seen two men die in front of her in less than a week; the most recent one, only a few hours ago. Ruby wanted to rip the blanket off and wrap her own arms around Claire instead, and warm them both up. She wanted to rip the blanket off and walk away, and leave Claire alone.

Ruby sighed, and crossed her arms over her tank top. She'd already changed out of her corset, and Claire was back in her sundress too. "Come on," Ruby said, "I'll drive."

Claire jumped up as if she couldn't wait another moment to escape the dungeon, now that she'd been given permission to. "I need to take my car too," she said. "I'll follow you."

"No," Ruby turned and walked toward the lobby, "you've had a shock. You shouldn't drive." She could sense that Claire wanted her to slow down, but instead Ruby walked faster, as though she were being pulled along by some force she couldn't control. It had been building in her all day, even before Kenny's death—a tightening within her mind, a tension wrapping round and round her like a red coil of rope.

They stepped out to the parking lot under a sun dying in shades of ruddy orange. As Ruby dumped her duffle in the back seat, opened the passenger's side for Claire, got behind the wheel of the Spider and drove, the feeling of *wrong* pressed down on her, abrasive as rope burn, crimson as the sunset sky.

"Is—is everything okay?" Claire whispered after a few minutes, when they were on the highway and unable to stop. A hint of her cherry-blossom scent, sweet and innocent, danced its way across the seats.

"Is everything okay?" Ruby laughed and gripped the steering wheel. "We work in a haunted dungeon. Two men are dead, and our boss is determined to keep going with business as usual. You're living with a boyfriend who says awful things to you. And I'm—I'm *trying* to be patient and wait for you." She gulped, and made a hopeless attempt to stop the words, but it was too late and they tumbled out. "I am trying to believe you want me as much as I want you. I'm trying to believe you won't keep putting yourself in danger. And you are making it very, very hard."

She pressed on the gas pedal, sped toward the Sepulveda exit and turned, squinting as the last rays of the sunset left her half-blind.

"Ruby, I—"

"Don't."

Ruby found a parking spot under a jacaranda that had lost almost all its violet blooms. She hopped out and grabbed her duffle, which seemed heavier than usual, an unreasonable weight that reminded her of all those wet towels they'd lugged downstairs after encountering the attic ghost. "Ruby," Claire said, taking a step and a half for each of Ruby's longer ones, "do you want me to go home? I can call an Ub—"

They reached her apartment, and Ruby unlocked the door, stepped into the small room and threw the duffle on the floor. "Come in," she said brusquely, "and take off your clothes."

Claire froze in the doorway, one foot inside and one out. Her eyes were wide and startled; her lips caught half-open, mid-word. "You can leave if you want," Ruby said. "Or you can stay here and take your clothes off like I told you to." A part of her felt as unsure as Claire looked; a part of Ruby was outside herself, watching herself standing straight and rigid and speaking those words. But she was speaking them. She had started something, and she couldn't stop it now.

Claire stepped all the way in and shut the door behind her. She slipped one strap of her sundress off her shoulder, then the other, and let it fall to the floor. She wasn't wearing a bra, and her nipples were perfect, beautiful little points. Ruby gestured to her G-string. "That too."

Claire lifted her hands, stretched her fingers with their chipped pink nails. She dropped them to her hips and pulled the G-string down.

"Get on the bed on all fours."

"Wh—what?" Claire just stood there, naked, and looked at Ruby with eyes like two drowning pools. Ruby stepped up to her, wrapped her arms around Claire's bare shoulders and pulled her close. She lowered her lips to Claire's, pried her mouth open and found the familiar comfort of Claire's tongue reaching out to answer hers. She trailed one hand down Claire's side, between her thighs, and teased her fingers featherlike against her pussy, just enough to awaken her.

She could do this for hours, but after less than a minute, she stopped.

"Up on the bed," she said again, her voice as stripped as Claire's slender form. "All fours."

Claire took two steps out of her flip-flops, toward the bed, then looked up at Ruby as if hoping she'd change her mind.

"I told you once already," Ruby said. "You're free to go. Or you can stay here and do what I tell you to."

Without waiting for a response, Ruby walked to her closet and rooted around in the back until she found it: her biggest strap-on. She took it into the bathroom to rinse off in the sink, but didn't bother looking for lube. Then she slipped out of her jeans and shoes, leaving her underwear and tank top on.

By the time she'd fastened the strap-on into place and turned back to the bed, Claire had followed her instructions and waited on all fours. Her hair fell forward to hide her face; her back arched, ass high in a longing curve.

Ruby climbed onto her knees on the bed and rested her hands on the hollows below Claire's ribs. Claire's muscles had gone taut, but she didn't flinch.

Without warning, Ruby entered and thrust.

Claire cried out and let her torso fall. Ruby followed her down and pressed her front side against Claire's back, wrapping her up in her arms, trying to hold every inch of her she could. Claire's body softened beneath her, soaking her in until they could almost be one. Ruby thrust and thrust and Claire screamed, muted by the pillow below her mouth.

Ruby grabbed Claire's hair and yanked her head up. "This is what you need, isn't it?" she said in a voice she barely recognized, but that was clearly her own. "Before you can truly care for someone." Another thrust, another answering cry. "You need them to hurt you."

"*Yes*," Claire said, as her pink-tipped fingers dug into the sheets. "Yes. Oh god, Ruby—Mistress—don't stop."

Ruby didn't stop. She slammed into Claire and beneath her, Claire's hips bucked. "This is who you are," Ruby said over

232

Claire's moans. "You're the girl who gives up on her dream because she never believed in herself, because she let one shitty guy scare her off. You're the girl who finds the worst piece of scum and gives him all your love. You're the girl who never, ever lets herself have something good, because you need so badly to be hurt."

Claire twisted the sheets beneath her palms and howled and howled. Ruby forced the wild movements of her body to a halt, though she couldn't stop her pounding heart, and she slowly, gently pulled out.

Ruby raised herself up and rested her hand softly where the silicone cock had been. Claire's pussy pulsed beneath her palm like the frenzied wings of a butterfly.

Ruby forced herself off the bed, just long enough to take off the strap-on and the rest of her clothes, before she climbed back up and folded herself around Claire. She brushed the damp hair back from Claire's face and traced the line of a tear down her cheek. Then Claire turned to face Ruby, she wrapped her arms around Ruby and Ruby sank into her warmth, and it was no longer clear who was holding whom.

The sun had long set and the room had gone dark. The outside world and its many other shades of darkness had disappeared for the moment. They were all that existed in the universe, just two girls, clutching on to one another for dear life. Then Claire whispered, "Do you know why Danny got so suspicious?"

Danny was the last person Ruby wanted to think about, but she was sapped, all anger drained out of her, so she said only, "Why?"

"Because I was dancing again." Claire snuggled closer, her chin tucked against Ruby's shoulder. "I thought I would never want to dance again, after what happened with Mr. Rivers, but these days I can't help myself. It's arabesques and *rond de jambes* all over the apartment, and I... I accidentally kicked Danny in the balls."

Ruby snorted. "I wish I'd seen that."

"Anyway," Claire wrapped her arm around Ruby's waist, "Danny wondered why I'm so happy, and— It's because of you. You make me want to dance again."

Ruby squeezed Claire tight. "I'd watch you dance anytime. I'd think you were perfect, no matter what those snotty teachers said."

"No dancing right now, though. I'm...worn out."

"Sorry."

"Don't be." Claire lifted her hand from Ruby's waist to stroke her hair, smoothing the strands off her neck and resting her fingers under Ruby's chin, against the raised line of her scar. "You know... I always wanted to ask you about this. It just never seemed like the right time."

Ruby gulped, her throat moving under Claire's palm. "It's never going to be the right time."

Claire pulled her hand back. "I'm sorry."

"—but if I'm going to tell you, I have to go further back first. Do you remember when I told you my real name?"

"Chastity," Claire said. She'd giggled the last time she'd spoken it, when they were both tipsy, but her voice held no humor now.

"Yes." Ruby swallowed. "If I'm going to tell you the story of the scar, I have to tell you about Chastity first."

TWENTY-ONE: CHASTITY

Before she grew up and became Ruby, Chastity was a little girl with sparks in her veins who did everything she was told she couldn't. When her teachers told her she couldn't yell at the boys and kick them and make them cry, she did it anyway. They deserved it—they made fun of her whether she was wearing the frilly dresses her mother forced her into for church, or the T-shirts and jeans they called "tomboy clothes." When Chastity's older siblings told her she couldn't beat them at tag or hide-and-go-seek, she fought as hard as she could to come out of every game on top. When her parents told her to stay in her room until she could be quiet and behave herself, she climbed out the window and howled at the moon.

Chastity didn't know where the sparks in her veins came from, the ones that made her oppose every restriction, every command. According to her parents and their church, people were born the way they were, and the ones like Chastity, the ones who yearned for freedom, had to work extra hard to be good. But Chastity wasn't interested in being good. *Good* meant sitting in church listening to the reverend drone on; it meant smiling at the boys no matter how mean they were; it meant doing endless homework, reading stories about well-behaved children whose lives in no way resembled her own.

Chastity knew there had to be more to life than *good*, just like there had to be more to the world than her little desert town, where the sand blew in everyone's eyes and kept them from seeing beyond what was right in front of them. Chastity wanted more, but what exactly this *more* consisted of, she wasn't sure. The closest she could come was those stories of Lucifer's rebellion she snuck peeks at in the Bible during church, when she was supposed to be listening to the sermons. Lucifer was the leader of the angels who defied God's orders, the ones "who did not keep their proper domain, but left their own abode." Chastity memorized that verse. *Proper domain* meant prison, she was sure; and if breaking free from her proper place meant rebelling, and rebelling meant falling, like Lucifer had, then that was what she'd have to do.

Chastity wasn't sure *how* to be like Lucifer, but still the sparks in her veins blazed hotter, the older she grew. She had to burn them off somehow, so by middle and high school she was rebelling in every way she could. She cut class to smoke cigarettes and pot, and wheedled her way out of detention with every possible excuse; she snuck out at night and met up with boys, just kissing and teasing at first, and then doing more. She liked to leave them begging, and she didn't enjoy their company enough to see any of them more than once or twice. The vast gulf between Chastity's name and the acts she was rumored to have performed became her high school's biggest joke. She suspected she might prefer girls, but the ones in this tiny sand-blinded town would never share her curiosity. Or so her young, yearning mind assumed.

The more Chastity beat against the walls of her cage, the more her parents disapproved. Her mother said the devil had seduced her; her father banished her to her room and raised his hand as if to slap her a time or two. But worse than anything her parents said or did, was the way they looked at her. They could see through her skin to where the sparks danced in her veins, and unless they succeeded in drowning those embers, they would never love her.

And then, by the end of high school, Chastity discovered it: the reason behind her rebellion, the true purpose of the sparks simmering under her skin. She was watching TV at a friend's house when she saw a scene of a dominatrix, her heel pressed atop the back of a naked man. Chastity really was seduced, like her mother had always warned. Using her friend's internet, she searched the word "dominatrix" online, and found a series of paintings of the pin-up model Bettie Page. The images reminded Chastity of old pictures of Lucifer she had seen: Bettie wore candy-apple-red boots and thigh-highs and gloves, and in one picture, tiny horns in her black hair. Her red lips parted around white teeth, biting down on a whip that ended in a forked crimson tongue. Here was the devil Chastity could love, and perhaps even become.

Chastity didn't know much about becoming a dominatrix, but one thing she was sure of: it would never happen in this little town, surrounded by endless sand. So she emptied the college fund her parents had prepared for her—her mom's fault for using J-E-S-U-S as her password—and with a few thousand dollars, more of a community college fund than a university one, she headed for the City of Angels and the coast. She got a job as a waitress, stayed in a hostel for a while before finding an apartment, made a wild group of friends. Those friends helped her figure out she was definitely into girls and not guys—but they couldn't help her become a dominatrix.

Months passed, then years, the ones her parents would have preferred she spend in college classrooms. Chastity found her niche as a high-end restaurant hostess—she was tall and thin enough that with the right makeup, she could pass for a model-actress and impress the customers. But it still wasn't enough money, in a city that sucked it all away, and besides, she hadn't forgotten the seduction of that word. *Dominatrix.* When some of the other waitresses talked about the odd jobs they got on Craigslist—modeling, some of it without clothes, and one girl went on and on about the guy who paid her to allow him to *suck her toes*—Chastity decided to give it a try.

Turned out, there were plenty of men asking to be dominated, and Chastity wondered if becoming powerful could be as easy as answering their call. She was quickly disavowed of that notion, quickly realized what an amateur she was: entering men's apartments or motel rooms in the fake corset she'd bought at Hot Topic, slapping their asses a few times, calling them pathetic losers and thrusting her feet in their mouths. She was like a child playing dress-up; no fear or even respect shone in the men's eyes, and when they called her "mistress," it never sounded real. But it was money, and if she saved enough, perhaps she could find a true dominatrix and pay her to train her.

But the money kept slipping through her fingers, lost on rent and food and Ubers, and right there, so simple, so easy, was a way to make more. Because even if the men posted ads asking to be spanked and humiliated, they usually wanted something else. The kind of thing Chastity used to do back in high school, when her name became a joke.

At first, when her clients asked for these things, she'd always said no. But after a few months, she started to reconsider. Since Chastity wasn't attracted to men, since there was no emotion behind her actions, she wouldn't truly be compromising herself. What was a hand job or two, or occasionally, if the man had an especially thick wallet—or even if he didn't, but rent was due—something more? She was the one using these men; she was the one in control.

And so, after a few months, Chastity became a prostitute without ever admitting to herself that was what she was.

She might never have admitted it—might have looked for the clients who wanted only to be teased and denied and, until she'd found enough of them, kept doing extras on the side—

If it hadn't been for that one night.

The client was an unremarkable thirty-something with a nice Hollywood apartment, so close to her own place they probably went to the same grocery store. The living room they passed on the way to the bedroom was well-furnished and clean. He was clean himself, too, not soaked in sweat or stinking of booze. Chastity's intuition didn't rise up to protect her, not when he sat on the edge of his bed and half unbuttoned his shirt, not when he smiled up at Chastity as she slipped off her coat. She didn't feel the ice behind his eyes as he looked over her body encased in corset and fishnets, as he nodded appreciatively and smiled. She was stupid enough to walk up to him, tug the shirt out of his pants and unbutton the rest of it herself.

Even when he stood and unzipped his jeans and said, "So tell me, Chastity, do you take it up the ass like a good little whore?", she wasn't smart enough to run. She only laughed, assuming he was egging her on, and said, "No, but I can give it to you. I have just the thing in my bag here—"

She was sure that was what he wanted. So many of them did.

One second she was bending over her bag, choosing the right dildo, and the next she was on her stomach on his bed, her cheap corset and boy shorts ripped off. "Get the fuck off me," she said, too shocked to be scared. Then she felt it, fleshy and foreign between her ass cheeks. Her heart started to run, now that her body could not.

"I'm a dominatrix," she said. "I don't do that."

"I've got news for you, sweetie," the man said from on top of her. "You're a whore."

Chastity used all her strength to shake his grip off, to lift herself up, as he growled, "Don't fight me, stupid girl."

She flung her arms and landed a wild blow across his face. She could see the ice behind his eyes now—the determination to claim what he wanted no matter what violence he inflicted, no matter who he hurt—in the moment before fear took over and the room blurred. "Fine, if that's how you want to do it," he said, and knelt to pull something from the pocket of his jeans, which had somehow ended up on the floor. Something that

238

shone candy-apple red through her warped vision. The handle of a Swiss army knife. He rose and flipped it open and held the blade against her neck, not cutting her, just letting her know he could, as he guided her back onto the bed on her stomach, and hovered over her.

Chastity wished she could float out of her body and watch what was happening from a distance, but the sharp edge of the knife held her within her skin. It forced her to feel every inch of him ripping inside her, forced her consciousness to remain right there as his hips moved and he thrust and grunted. She had to hold herself very still, her every cell alive and aware and throbbing, to keep from slipping on the edge of that knife.

Chastity had thought she could escape the devils of her childhood; she'd believed she could become a powerful goddess, rising high above everyone else. But here, now, the universe showed her what she was: a weak, human body capable of being torn apart, caught beneath the blade of a knife.

It wasn't until he was finished, and he slumped with his release and pushed her down with him, that the blade cut. An inch further back, and it would have hit an artery, and she might not have survived.

He lifted himself off her and got a washcloth from the bathroom, and she took it and pressed it against her throat. She held it there as she got dressed, trying her best to keep the torn corset closed around her, and he let her out. She held it as she called an Uber, and by the time she got home, it was soaked.

It took three more towels before the bleeding stopped, and when the wound closed, woven with scar tissue that was at once angry and fragile, Chastity was gone and Ruby had been born.

There was more to the story, of course—there was the move across the city, training under Mistress Katrina, becoming a true domme—but that was it: the defining moment of Ruby's life, even if it wasn't what she'd chosen, even if she'd tried so hard to block it out. The before and the after. And now, Ruby who had once been Chastity could only conclude that none of the bad things that happened to her made her feel worse. None of them broke her. Each one made her a little stronger, like a gemstone formed under great heat and pressure, showing her just how much she could live through. How much she could survive, without anyone coming to save her. How she could solidify, becoming whole within herself, needing nothing and no one.

How she could turn red as a beating heart, red as blood, red as a scar.

Red as a ruby.

TWENTY-TWO: CLAIRE

Ruby had moved away from Claire, as she told her story. She sat on the edge of the bed now, fingers clutching the sheets as if she wanted to pull them over her and curl into a ball, but she wouldn't allow herself to. Claire waited until Ruby was finished, until the apartment had closed around them, still and dark and silent, before she reached her hand toward Ruby's.

Claire wished she could say how sorry she was, but she feared it would come out too close to pity. "Did you...did you go to the hospital?"

"No hospital," Ruby said, as Claire worked her fingers into Ruby's fists until they began to unclench. "I didn't want to answer any questions. I thought about going to the cops, but... I couldn't tell them. What would I say, that I came to a man's apartment to perform sexual acts in exchange for money, and he raped me?" She breathed out. "I did think...that he'd do this to another girl. I should have done something."

"You were scared, and hurt, and alone." Claire slid closer to Ruby as she spoke. "You did the best you could."

Ruby turned to face the wall. "I've never told anyone about any of this...about the Craigslist guys. I try to forget I ever did those things, most of the time." Claire leaned into Ruby's body, usually so strong and certain, now trembling beneath Claire's arms. "I was... I was a *whore*." Ruby choked on the word.

"*Whore* is..." Claire swallowed, and tried to speak clearly, a difficult task after all she'd experienced tonight. "It's a violent, awful word. It's a word the world uses to punish us for something we have no reason to be ashamed of." Her thoughts sharpened as she went on, whittled as if by a knife, until she was speaking for herself as much as for Ruby. "The world has no right to tell us who we are, to make us into something ugly, because of what we choose to do with our own bodies." She squeezed her arms tighter around Ruby, drew her head close enough to smell the salt of dried tears and sweat on Ruby's skin. "I'm going to get you some water, okay?"

Claire fumbled to find the light switch, but remembered where the glasses were from last time. Ruby gulped the water all at once, as though she were quenching something more than thirst, and then said, "It wasn't just that I was a...a prostitute, though. It was that my parents were right."

Ruby turned her eyes on Claire, the watery green of them just visible in the kitchen light. "My mother always told me I'd be seduced by the devil, and I was. I was so desperate to feel powerful, that I didn't care how I got that power. And I still want it, now, even after I was punished for it. There's..." She tilted her head down. "There's something wrong inside of me."

Claire lifted her hand and tipped Ruby's chin back up, lowered her lips to Ruby's and tried to kiss away the words. When she pulled away she said, "What happened to you wasn't a punishment for anything you did or thought. You didn't deserve it. It wasn't your fault."

She reached out for Ruby's palm. "The devil isn't real, Ruby. You know that. The only real devils are the ones right here on earth." On top of the sheets, their fingers intertwined. "And you most certainly are not one of them."

"I know." Ruby swallowed, her voice still half-choked. "I know the devil isn't real, I know the Bible stories aren't true. But sometimes I think...I worry...there's a deep down part of us that can never stop believing the things we were told as children."

Claire didn't have an answer for that. So she just pulled Ruby under the covers, where they could forget that the world outside would never be as safe as the little space they'd created here.

After a while, Ruby spoke again. "There was a side of me," she said, "that wanted to go after him. I knew where he lived. I could have spied on him, figured out some way to hurt him..." Her hands tightened around Claire. "But I knew that would destroy me more than it would him. I'd be trapped, reliving what had happened... I'd be letting him win. So I decided on a different sort of revenge. I'd become the best dominatrix I possibly could."

"It worked. You're the best dominatrix I know," Claire said, burrowing into Ruby's warmth. "But..." She hesitated. If there was a time to speak the truth, even when it hurt, it was now. "Didn't you do that anyway?"

"Do what?"

"Let him win." Ruby tensed against Claire's arms, but she went on. "This..." Claire extended one hand from beneath the covers and gestured around the bare walls, the empty room. "This is not a life. You've given everything to your desire to be a dominatrix, until you have nothing else."

For the space of a held breath, Claire thought Ruby was going to pull away again. Jump out of bed and storm off. But then the taut lines of Ruby's muscles went slack. "*Had* nothing else," she said.

Now it was Claire's turn to say, "What?"

"I *had* nothing except being a dominatrix." She lowered her lips to Claire's neck and brushed them against her flesh. "But now I have you."

They both drifted into half-dreams, after that. It had been a long day, a long week, a long few months. When Claire opened her eyes, disentangled herself from Ruby's sleep-heavy limbs and made her way out of bed to find her phone, she was shocked to see it was only ten o'clock. She woke up, all at once, her heart pumping with the knowledge of what she could still do tonight. What she could offer Ruby, in return for all the trust she'd placed in her.

Claire cleaned herself up in the bathroom, slipped on her dress and called an Uber. Back in the bed Ruby's eyes were misty with sleep, but half-open.

Claire walked over to Ruby and smoothed a hand across her bare shoulder. "I'm going to go," she said. "There's something I have to do. I'll see you at work tomorrow, okay?"

"No, stay." Ruby tried to pull Claire back onto the mattress, but her phone dinged with the Uber's arrival, and Claire danced away from temptation and toward the door.

"I'll see you tomorrow," Claire said again. "Thank you for tonight. For everything. I—" She didn't know how to say what she felt, so she said only, "Sleep well."

Claire directed the Uber driver to the dungeon, where she picked up her car and texted Danny: "I'm on my way home and we need to talk—now." Then she drove back to Hollywood, past palm trees slumbering beneath their shroud-like fronds, and put Danny out of her mind to remember Ruby's words.

"*I'd watch you dance anytime.*" So much of what Ruby had said tonight was painful, a doorway into a past Claire wished she could help Ruby exorcise, as if it were only another demon, another ghost. But that one simple thing Ruby had said gave her hope.

Maybe Claire would never be a ballerina; maybe she'd never float across a stage like a swan or a fairy or a Wili in

Giselle; but she would have Ruby's eyes on her, appreciating her for who she was, and that would be enough.

When Claire entered the apartment with her bag of dungeon outfits over one shoulder, Danny was in the hallway, waiting, head lowered and hair falling over his eyes. His expression hidden from her.

Every time Claire had dared to picture this moment, she had imagined it going one of two ways. Either she would open her mouth and find it clogged, strands of hair scraping her throat, preventing her from freeing the words; or the fury would rush out of her, a crimson flood of destruction, drowning the bad but also the good.

But it turned out that she didn't need to scream and spew venom at Danny. There was strength in standing tall and straight and, with quiet certainty, speaking the truth.

"You've always claimed to want what's best for me," she began. "That was why you wanted me out of the dungeon, you said. And maybe you really do think you know what's right, but—"

Danny's hair still hid his gaze, and, with a hand that shook only a little, Claire reached out and brushed back the stray locks. She looked right at those eyes she'd once wanted to sink into, but this time she kept her distance and said, "I can't live the way someone else thinks is good for me. What matters is what I know is best for myself. And this—us—it's not going to work."

Danny sagged, collapsing into himself like a lost little boy. "I know. I've already packed my stuff."

She had expected an argument, and now she didn't know what to do with herself. She let her duffle slip to the floor as Danny shuffled to the bedroom and came back with a bag on each arm. "I left my guitar at the studio."

"Do you have somewhere to stay?" she asked.

"Ricky's friend's couch." Danny dropped the bags and Claire thought she saw shadows creep above his shoulders, like faint tendrils of smoke. She shook her head to clear the vision as he reached out to wrap his arms around her. But she pulled back. He hadn't earned that last comfort, and she didn't need it anymore.

Danny slung the bags back over his shoulders, and once more she spied that smoky shadow, circling his throat. He scratched his neck and frowned, tossed his head like he was trying to throw something off. "Take care of yourself, all right?"

Claire nodded. She didn't turn to watch as he walked out.

The second the door clicked shut, Claire's stomach let out a wild, alarming grumble. She laughed. She hadn't eaten all day, but she hadn't realized until then. Relief was coursing through her, reminding her she was, after all, a body with simple needs. She wanted to leap her way to the kitchen, but she happened to glance down at her duffle first. The corner of it had come unzipped, and something dark and metallic peeked out. She crouched down to look:

A clump of bobby pins, not rusty ones this time, but gleaming and new, wrapped up with a few locks of hair. Claire smiled, and felt no fear, and understood why breaking up with Danny had been so easy. And where that smoke had come from, too. She told herself she didn't want Danny to get hurt, but, well—if some supernatural force wanted to shake him up, make sure he treated the next girl better than he had Claire, it wasn't her place to stop it.

She placed her hand over the bundle, so the soft strands tickled her palm. "Thank you for the courage."

Her phone rang, and she glanced at the number. Ruby. She'd have to choose a song for when Ruby called, now that they would truly be girlfriends.

"Hey," Claire answered, "what's up?" She wanted to blurt out that she'd broken up with Danny, but stopped herself— better to wait until she could do it in person, and see Ruby smile.

"I— I found one of those...those *things*...in my duffle bag. It's been here all night!"

"Slow down, Ruby, it's okay. What thing?" Claire said, though she suspected she knew.

"The hair and the bobby pins." Ruby's voice wavered, ghostlike, as though the connection were bad—or more likely, as though she were panicked and shaking the phone.

"I found one too," Claire said. "I think it's a good thing. It's giving us the strength to—to do what we have to."

"But Claire, the—the way I treated you. I was so rough. You were crying. I—"

"It's okay, Ruby. I needed it." Claire hated to hear Ruby's agitation, but she was still floating, high on her new freedom. No true worry could pierce through.

245

"No! It was that—that thing." Ruby's words rushed out and tangled over themselves. "It twisted me, it made me hurt you..."

"Ruby," Claire said, "the ghost can't bring out something that's not already inside you." She paused, and thought through how best to put the words. "I want you, Ruby. *All* of you. You could never hurt me." Only Ruby's heavy breaths came through the phone. "We had a really long day. Get something to eat, get some sleep, and in just a few hours it will be tomorrow."

Nothing but silence. "Ruby? Are you there?"

Finally, a muffled, "Yeah. I've got to go."

Once more, Claire thought about telling Ruby she was free now. But she forced herself to wait, and said only, "Good night."

TWENTY-THREE: RUBY

"The ghost can't bring out something that's not already inside you." Claire kept speaking, offering platitudes, but Ruby could barely hear them. The feeling of wrongness that had crept behind her for most of the day, the one Claire had temporarily banished, had returned now. It shrieked through her ears like the howl of a demon. This was who Ruby was—someone rough and forceful, capable of violence and cruelty. *"You'd never hurt me,"* Claire was saying, but hadn't Ruby already hurt her? Ruby would never be able to shake off that dark, devil part of her. It was like she'd told Claire—you could never run away from the things you learned as a child.

Claire wouldn't be any better off with Ruby than she was with Danny, and now Ruby had no idea what to do. Once she'd thrown the phone down, she sat on the edge of her bed, the lights turned all the way up, now, and stared at her half-open duffle in the corner. She'd awoken about a half hour after Claire left, and had unzipped her bag, thinking to take out the corset that needed washing—but instead she found that *thing.* It was looser than the other bundles she'd seen, more of a ribbon of hair, slinking its way across her clothes. She wanted it gone, but she couldn't muster the strength to touch it. She couldn't do much of anything, after all the heavy words she'd spoken tonight.

Ruby had always heard that telling the truth was supposed to free you. But she felt only the beat of *wrong, wrong, wrong* pulsing from her heart. She'd turned herself inside out, and now all her muscles and bones were exposed, on the surface, so anyone could destroy her.

Ruby spent hours on the edge of the bed, trying to work up the courage to dispose of the thing. Finally, in the shadowy moments before the sun awoke, she wrapped it in a towel and took it outside to the dumpster. But it was too late—it had left behind a darkness, coiling around her like a rope.

Ruby thought about calling out of work the next morning, but she couldn't stay in this apartment, not now that it was infiltrated with the ghost's sinister energy as thoroughly as the dungeon. Nowhere was safe anymore. So she drove to the Briars, nodded to Lady Eva and headed to the dressing room in a daze, wondering if Claire would show up, what she would say.

The other girls were there, Mara and Gabriella were trading jokes, but to Ruby the words sounded like nonsense, like a foreign tongue. She kept looking down at her limbs as she changed into her corset, sure she'd see the red ropes she felt tightening around her.

And then, there was Claire, rushing in late with her cheeks rosy, eyes shining. "I cleaned the *entire* apartment this morning," she told the whole room, as she threw her duffle on the sofa and dug out a schoolgirl skirt. Her gaze landed on Ruby. "I had to clean it all, because I—"

The door opened and another woman entered—Nadia. "Claire, you'd better get dressed quick. A client's here for you." Nadia glanced at Ruby and hesitated before adding, "It's—it's Jack. He's in the parlor."

Claire and Ruby both froze; at the edge of her awareness, Ruby registered the others slipping out of the room, fleeing the impending explosion. "You can't session with him." Ruby used every ounce of control she possessed to speak the words slowly, calmly. "You promised me you wouldn't."

"I know, but"—Claire was shrugging out of her shirt and into her little tie-front top, and she was somehow, infuriatingly, *smiling*—"I feel invincible right now. Like I can do anything. I can get him to tell me more about Violet. That name, that girl—I just *know* she's important. We can solve this mystery, and—"

The invisible ropes around Ruby twisted tighter, slicing into the raw, exposed mess she'd become last night. Why was Claire being so obstinate? "You *promised*," she said again, "that you wouldn't session with him." No, Ruby hadn't had a chance to tell Claire how Jack had threatened her, but she didn't care in the moment. "I guess— I guess I just can't trust you."

Claire's hands faltered over the knot of her top. The smile fell from her face as if Ruby had slapped her. The twisting inside Ruby became an aching emptiness, that same desperate, hollow feeling that had washed over her in the attic and when they'd performed the banishment. The ghost's loneliness, burrowing inside her.

Ruby knew, then, that she would never have all of Claire. She would never deserve her. She couldn't decide which was worse—the blue-black loss, or the bright red anger.

"I can't trust you," Ruby said again, spitting the words like stones from some deep, ugly place inside her. "I poured my heart out to you last night, and you left me alone. You're too weak to say no to Jack or to Lady Eva. Too weak to ever break up with Danny."

Claire gasped, a strangled sound. She pressed her lips tight, then they parted. She would offer more excuses, more empty promises, and Ruby didn't want to hear it. "Go session with Jack," she said.

"Ruby, I—" Claire's eyes were so blue, so earnest, so open. They were everything Ruby wanted, and she couldn't bear to look at them.

Ruby turned away from Claire and said, "Go do what you want. Do the session. I don't care. I..." She breathed out. "I can't save you."

Ruby stormed out to the gazebo where the other girls had gathered around the smokers' table. She marched right past them all, to the fence that barred off the back of the dungeon from the outside world, and she fell to her knees and crumpled into herself. Everything hurt. The pain swept past all her fallen defenses, a red wave carving out her insides, and she could do nothing except let it roll through her.

By the time the onslaught had passed, the other women had left, and Ruby was alone. She raised herself slowly, unsteadily to her feet, and made her way back inside.

In the dressing room Mara sat on the couch, peering down at something, looking like a little girl with her legs tucked under her and her hair wrapped around her like a shawl. Ruby came closer and saw she was holding the photo album, the one with *1997* on the spine. "Violet," Mara murmured, one finger tracing a picture, eyes like whirlpools as if she were trying to pull the image into herself.

The truth hit Ruby like another wave, sudden and strange and undeniable.

Mara. The girl with skin so icy, a grip so demanding that her coldness lingered inside Ruby even now.

Mara, who, with those flower-stem arms, had pushed Claire hard enough to bruise her.

Mara, whose black hair grew faster and thicker than was possible—for a human.

Mara, who had appeared at the dungeon the same day as Jack.

"You knew her, didn't you?" Ruby spoke words that made no sense even to herself.

249

Mara looked up at Ruby with those eyes that so often appeared confused, but there was no question in them now. Only determination as she whispered, "I need your strength," and a dizzying cold wrapped around Ruby, a horror that consumed her until even the emotion was frozen, and she couldn't feel or move at all.

"I remember," Ruby heard through the haze, Mara's voice clear and certain. "I remember it all."

TWENTY-FOUR: CLAIRE

Claire had never been so furious in her life. What had gotten into Ruby? It was like last night had never happened, like she'd allowed some frenzied fear to take over and ruin it all. Was it because of that bundle of hair and bobby pins? Did Ruby think the ghost was that powerful, stronger than everything they had shared?

Or maybe it had never meant as much to Ruby as it had to Claire.

Claire barely heard a word Jack spoke in the parlor, could hardly see him as they headed up the stairs to Lady Lilith's room, because of course that was where Lady Eva had told them to session. Her vision pulsed red, her skin sparked with it until she knew only fire. She had broken up with Danny, she had believed Ruby truly cared, and now—what? It was all for nothing? She'd be left alone?

The stairs to Lady Lilith's room had never seemed so long. Inside Claire's chest her heart worked, the source of all that fire, a bellows expanding and contracting with each step, yet still they climbed. And then—

"Achoo!" Claire walked into a dust cloud, and the violent sneeze cleared her vision and her mind.

Jack laughed, a disarmingly normal, familiar sound. "It is dusty up here, isn't it?"

Beyond the dust sat the cracked-leather spanking bench, the rusty cage, the throne that had been tipped on its side. The attic. "How—"

"Didn't your father teach you not to follow blindly after strange men?" Jack asked, unfurling a loop of red rope Claire didn't remember him grabbing downstairs. "Oh, that's right—you didn't have one."

In one swift move, he pushed her torso into the spanking bench and yanked her wrists together behind her. He lassoed the rope around them as Claire struggled to keep her limbs apart, but he only pulled tighter. "Relax," he said. "Back in the '90s, I used to play up here all the time. I'm only indulging in a little nostalgia."

He tied off the rope in a knot that bulged against her wrist, then flipped up her skirt and spanked her. Each blow bit into her tender flesh with teeth, and none of his old warmth behind it.

"Stop!" she said. "We can't be up here." Oh God, why hadn't she listened to Ruby? She was still caught in a red rage, but now her anger had expanded to include herself, her own stupidity, and this man who'd become a stranger.

"Quiet, Claire," Jack gritted. "Do I have to gag you?" His hands clamped on her shoulders, and he forced her to the floor. Dust flurries rose as her knees hit the wood, the flesh ripping just over her bones. A crimson flash before her eyes—another rope—then he was wrapping it around her ankles. He was going to hog-tie her. She bucked and flailed, arms and legs scraping against the old wood, and each pierce of a splinter ignited more sparks inside her. Her gaze caught on a glint of light—the window, the one where the ghost had shown herself—but it wasn't a window anymore. It was a mirror now. The exact oval mirror, she would have sworn, that had hung downstairs and shattered moments before Gunther died.

Unlike the rest of the room, no dust coated the mirror's surface. It reflected, with painful clarity, the sneer on Jack's face as he wrenched her calves together and nearly twisted her ankles. She stabbed at his palms with her heels, and Jack gritted out, "You loved it when I tied you up before. Come on, Claire, be a good little gir—"

In the mirror, Claire saw another figure ascending the staircase, her every step so smooth she seemed to float. A small, slender figure, but with Jack and Claire both on the ground, she loomed over them. Her dark hair rose and fell like a wave, caught in a phantom wind tunnel. This morning, Claire could have sworn this girl wore a schoolgirl skirt like her own, but now her white slip fell to her knees, the edges jagged and shredded.

Mara.

"Jack," Mara said, her voice low and liquid.

Jack dropped Claire's ankles without tying off the knot. "You!" He jumped up and grabbed Mara's arm while Claire shuffled back, leaning on her bound wrists and kicking the ankle rope off. As Claire watched in the mirror, Jack raised one of Mara's hands to his face, his eyes widening.

Mara shook her wrist, and the charms on her bracelet tinkled like bells. "That's right," she said, "it's the one you gave Violet." She breathed in, and sucked all the air from the room as she did so. "The one she lost, twenty years ago."

"L—Laurel?" Jack asked, and Mara gave the slightest smile. Her red lips two rose petals, parting. "It *is* you," Jack said. His gaze darkened to the shade of a storm. "I thought, when you came up for that cameo, but— It's impossible—

"I killed you."

Claire gasped, an animal cry that brought Mara's attention to her. "Get out of here, Claire," she said in a razored tone. "This isn't about you. I don't want you to get hurt."

Claire stumbled to her feet as beneath her, the floor quaked, just as it had that night she'd stood there with the other girls, with Ruby's hand in hers. Oh, God, she needed Ruby now. Jack released Mara's wrist to clutch her throat; his eyes sparked, electric blue. "I saw the last breath leave your mouth. I watched the last light leave your eyes."

"I watched you hold my lifeless body." Mara's fingers closed around Jack's forearms, a grip so tight Claire saw only bone. She rocked him back and forth, and the furniture and the floor rocked too. "But a part of me didn't die."

Claire darted for the stairs, the floor lurching oceanlike beneath her, and made it to the top step. Another wave and she was falling, reaching out for the chain that had always barred the attic off, but the metal barrier had vanished. She tumbled over and over herself and landed with a flash of pain white as lightning, white as bone. Something had crunched and snapped, in her left arm. And then, a worse sight: the black candle tipped onto its side, in the middle of the carpet, spilling flames as it rolled.

The door swung on its hinges, and a familiar figure flung itself inside. "Ruby!" Claire called. She fought her way to her feet, her left forearm howling behind her back, as she struggled with her good hand to free herself from the bind.

Beyond the rising smoke Ruby took a few steps into the room, wobbling in her stilettos on what had become a twisting, flame-scattered floor. The door behind her slammed itself closed. "Claire!" she yelled. "We've got to get you out of he—" From overhead came a crack, then a slab of falling wood.

"Watch out!" Claire screamed, and looked up to see the ceiling opening itself like a mouth. The jagged ends of wood beams protruded, each one a rotting tooth. Two bodies tumbled down, one solid man and one sylphlike girl, limbs clasped around each other, intertwined, until Jack landed with a thud on his backside. Just missing the fire, which roared higher in response.

Mara held herself on top of Jack's body, clawing as if her fingers were thorns, while Ruby had half-fallen forward too. She caught herself on her arms and scuttled back on hands and knees, away from the spreading inferno, but also from Claire. "Behind you, Ruby!" Claire called. The St. Andrew's Cross was swaying, tilting further and further, as Claire tried to move her own shaky limbs forward. "Get out of the wa—"

It was too late. The cross tumbled, heavy and unstoppable, and forced Ruby flat onto her stomach, pinning her down. Crushing her entire left side. Crushing Claire's insides, too, where she watched helpless from across the room. Claire and Ruby screamed as one, and Mara stood and turned wide-eyed from one girl to the other, as if realizing she and Jack were not alone.

Mara's gaze landed on Claire's, the shadows of her eyes deeper than any in the dungeon, and for a moment Claire's panic dissolved. The fire in the room, the fire in her arm, faded to the edges of her mind. She knew only the empty ache of being completely lost, completely alone.

"I'm sorry," Mara whispered, her words slipping like small, desperate things into the hollows between Claire's bones. Claire forced herself back to awareness; Jack was pulling himself up, his strength seemed to return. Mara's red lips still moved. "I can't stop it no—"

The mirrors burst, every one. Glass shards consumed in a torrent of water that emerged from every frame, on every wall of the room. Water veined in red, as though even it could bleed, and the glass had sliced it open. Extinguishing the fire in a cloud of noxious smoke.

"Ruby!" Claire screamed through the ashen air, and she fought her way forward against the water swarming from her feet up to her ankles. Her desperation grew to a tidal wave, infusing her with power; she tugged again at the knot holding her wrists together, and this time the rope flew open. The water was rising fast, so fast, as Jack grabbed on to Mara and beyond them, Claire could barely make out the prone, struggling line of Ruby's body. And then, a memory came to her.

Her hair, Yarik had said. *If it comes down to it, don't let go of her hair.*

Claire stumbled her way over to Mara and, while all the girl's attention remained on Jack, she clutched on to the ends of her wild and tangled black hair. Despite the throbbing of her broken arm, Claire wove all ten fingers into the strands as if they were an anchor, and the room around her blurred. The red-tinged rush of water, the quavering floors and walls, Ruby fighting to keep her head afloat—it all disappeared. For a moment that was a lifetime, Claire saw all that Mara saw, knew all that Mara knew, and finally, she understood.

TWENTY-FIVE: LAUREL

Before she died and came back as a ghost named Mara, Laurel was a '90s grunge-rock princess who was head-over-heels in love...with a girl. A girl named Violet.

Laurel had long, luscious black hair and nail polish to match it, and while she was slender, she could hold her place in the mosh pits she liked to frequent. She was no willowy wraith who would be torn to shreds amid all those bodies. She wore ripped slip dresses—in black or white or purple satin, flowered prints or polka dots—or crop tops above low-rise jeans. Sometimes she held her hair back with a dozen miniature butterfly clips, a rainbow of shades, a multicolored girl.

Laurel was a wild tumbleweed of a girl who would try anything once, and that was how she found herself walking into a dungeon, at twenty-two years old, getting spanked and tied up and tickled, and making decent money at it too. But if Laurel arrived at the Briars for the thrill of it, she stayed for Violet.

Violet had shown Laurel around the dungeon on her first day, and Laurel had been stunned by her tour guide's beauty and sophistication. Violet floated through the rooms in her perfectly fitted corset and stilettos, her curls like a golden halo around her, while Laurel stumbled behind in too-big thrift store heels she kept tripping over. She was used to Doc Martens, and she could tell Violet's smile verged on laughter a few times. Still, the girl managed to hold her giggles back and remain patient with Laurel.

It wasn't until weeks later that Laurel learned Violet had only worked at the dungeon for a few months, and she'd once been as awed by the crosses and cages, whips and paddles, as Laurel now was. Violet spent hours going over the entire equipment wall with Laurel, telling her which straps were too mean to ever use, and which paddles made the most impressive noises without leaving bruises. No girl had ever spent so much time and effort on her. And such a lovely, lively girl too; a girl named after one flower, but who reminded Laurel of another. Violet was like a jacaranda, a riot of purple blossoms that scattered everywhere and transformed the world into some-place wonderful. She could leave anyone dazed and dizzy, their insides all a whirl. And yet she chose to pay attention to Laurel.

Violet was always asking Laurel to join her for double sessions; she came up with every excuse she could to touch Laurel, to straighten the blue bow on her little sailor suit, brush a hand against her arm and tease a tangle from her hair. Violet's own hair danced in fairy wisps as she said, "Laurel, you've got the eyes of an old soul. Has anyone ever told you that?"

No one ever had. Laurel was only interested in girls, not boys with their greasy hair and grabby hands. She'd talked one riot grrrl into giving her a few guitar lessons, but most women she'd met in the grunge scene were focused on one thing: the rock stars. *Male* ones.

Yes, Violet was kind to everyone, and yes, she did have a boyfriend she'd mentioned a few times, but Laurel and this magical girl had a special connection. For one thing, they were both named after wildflowers—and they both used their real names at the dungeon. Violet had proclaimed that all submissives should have flower names, and she certainly wouldn't bother to change hers; Laurel kept the same name because there was no one she needed to hide her dungeon life from, no reason to separate the two worlds. Outside of the Briars, Laurel was adrift, a petal on the breeze. She had no friends or family to speak of; no one to judge her or worry over her choices.

Laurel had had nothing, and that was why the messy despair of grunge rock appealed to her; but now she had Violet, and despite herself, she began humming pop songs. "Lovefool" by the Cardigans played in her mind on repeat. And then, one night, when Violet and Laurel had finished a session in the attic and were cleaning the furniture, it happened.

Violet flipped her curls so the slender line of her neck was exposed. "Kiss me, Laurel," she said, bending over the spanking bench, that tender spot between her ear and her hairline beckoning Laurel's lips closer. Laurel breathed in Violet's scent, summery and sweet as wildflowers. Her pulse grew wings and leapt into her throat. She could almost taste Violet's skin…

"Not there, silly." Violet giggled. "The top of my shirt. Get your lipstick on my collar."

"What?" Laurel forced the question past those butterflies in her throat. Violet and Laurel were both wearing white button-downs—their client had wanted a double dose of sexy secretaries—though Violet hadn't bothered with most of the buttons on hers, and had knotted it under her lacy bra. "This is a nice shirt. You don't want to ruin it."

"My boyfriend will buy me another one." Violet wiggled her hips in her black pencil skirt. "But first, I'll make sure he sees the stain on this one. He'll ask who was kissing me, and when I tell him how cute you are, we'll invite you over."

"S—seriously?" Laurel's heartbeat pulsed in her eardrums now. She couldn't have heard right.

"C'mon, Laurel." Violet arched her back into a luscious curve, and Laurel left a red lipstick kiss on her shirt, still disbelieving how lucky she was. Still disbelieving that next time, it might be Violet's skin her lips touched.

Soon enough, Laurel was in the passenger's seat of Violet's Honda, on the way to a Century City high-rise. "Shit," Laurel said as they rose ten floors in the elevator, her nerves climbing higher with each one, "your boyfriend's rich, huh?"

Violet giggled and offered Laurel a sip from the little flask hidden in her purse. "Just wait."

When Violet's boyfriend opened the door, Laurel barely spared a moment to take in the huge condo, the gleaming leather furniture, because she recognized the man in front of her. "You're..."

The young, blue-eyed man smiled with the charm she remembered; a grin that seemed warm but left ice crystallizing deep within her. "Yes, I'm Jack, Violet's client. You came up for a cameo with us once, right?"

Violet grinned at Laurel. "Don't tell Lady Eva?" *No dating the clients* was one of their boss's strictest rules.

"Oh, of course, I would ne—"

And then Violet's lips were on Laurel's, making her head spin twice as much as the contents of the flask, and she forgot all about Jack.

They did everything Laurel had dreamed of, on Jack's king-size bed atop slippery silk sheets, and Violet tasted sweeter than Laurel could possibly have imagined. Everywhere. Even Jack couldn't ruin it. "That's it, Laurel," he said in a slithery-smooth voice, as he watched Laurel go down on his girlfriend. "Show me what a good little whore you are."

Laurel hated Jack, but she loved Violet, so she went along with it all. She accompanied Violet to Jack's apartment a second time, then a third. But a week went by with no more invitations, until Laurel couldn't wait any longer, and she snuck up behind Violet and nibbled her neck in the dressing room.

Violet jolted as if she'd been slapped. She laughed, but her giggles no longer danced through the air as they always had before. "When can I come over again?" Laurel asked.

Violet's laughter died altogether. She wouldn't look at Laurel. "Jack...he doesn't want to do that anymore. He wants me to quit this job. He thinks I'm starting to like the girls here too much, and the clients too." Violet glanced up, then, and Laurel saw the bruise-blue shadows under her eyes.

Days and then weeks passed, and the shadows under Violet's eyes only grew. Her voice no longer filled the hall or the dressing room; she no longer found excuses to brush her arm against Laurel's or, for that matter, any of the girls'. Jack sessioned with Violet on almost all her shifts, but he never asked another lady to join them. He wanted Violet to himself, at the dungeon as well as at home, as if he were unwilling to leave her alone for a single moment.

"He's turning you into someone I don't recognize," Laurel said. "I don't care how rich and handsome he is, you deserve better."

But Violet only shook her head and insisted, "He loves me." One day, she showed off a silver bracelet Jack had had made specially for her, with amethysts inlaid into the flower charms, the color of the flowers she was named for. All the ladies oohed and aahed over it, and even Lady Eva joined in—though she never realized the gift giver was also one of the dungeon's clients. Only Laurel didn't admire the jewelry; she watched with her insides crumpling as, in the days that followed, Violet turned smaller and more fragile. Her limbs wilted, her wrists became so slim the bracelet could slip right off her. Laurel worried a gust of wind might break her.

They were cleaning the attic together again, after a session, when Violet told her. "I quit. It's my last day."

All the blood rushed out of Laurel's veins; she dropped the rag she was holding and found herself unable to kneel and retrieve it. "You can't," she said. "Violet, I—"

The moon peered in through the attic's small window, dancing across Violet's hair, lighting up the dark blue of her eyes. Laurel had to try, one more time. She found she could move her limbs again; she wrapped Violet up in her arms, lowered her head until Violet's lips met hers. Violet's rigid muscles yielded, and Laurel roved desperately across the curves of her body, unable to stop, unwilling to let go. She slipped her hands under Violet's skirt—

And Violet pushed her. The surprise of it sent Laurel skittering across the small room. "Jack was right," Violet said, her kiss-stung mouth twisting toward cruelty. "You are all whores here."

"Violet, no! You can't believe what that awful man tells you. Please, Violet, I—I love you."

She reached for Violet's wrist again and Violet pushed her, harder. Laurel slammed into the mirror behind her. The glass cried out, and split in two.

The longing inside Laurel became too much to hold, then, and it hardened into anger. She pushed back, and forgot how fragile Violet had become. Laurel pressed all her hurt and disappointment against Violet's chest and the girl tumbled, into the back of the throne-chair where her charm bracelet caught and slipped off; she tipped off the chair, and all the way onto the unforgiving wood floor. She wailed and rolled from her side onto her back, but her arm remained splayed out, her forearm bent backwards in a way that would have been impossible had her elbow not been broken.

The taste of regret bloomed in Laurel's mouth, bitter salt and bile. She rushed forward to hold Violet, to lift her up and assure her it had all been an accident, but Violet screamed, "Don't touch me! Go get help."

Still Laurel came closer, until she saw the pain withering Violet's wildflower beauty, and pulled back. She headed for the stairs as Violet whispered:

"Laurel? Don't tell them you were up here with me. We'll say I fell while I was cleaning, alone, and you heard me screaming from down in Lady Lilith's room. I—I don't want to get you in trouble."

It was the last kind thing Violet would ever do for her.

The break was bad enough that the girls were afraid to move her, and had to call an ambulance. The EMTs struggled with the stretcher in the cramped attic; they cast disapproving eyes over the crosses and cages and admonished, "You've got to establish some safety measures." And in the commotion Laurel found herself pushed behind the other women, on the edge, unnoticed, unwanted. Unable to catch one last glimpse of the girl she loved. All she had were the pictures of Violet in the dungeon

260

photo album, and she thought about taking Violet's page home. But she didn't deserve it. She didn't deserve to stay at the Briars herself, either, where the presence of the other women might comfort her. Laurel belonged where she had always been: alone, leaving no trace of herself behind, as if she were nothing more than a ghost.

So Laurel ripped her own page out of the album, tore each picture of herself into pieces. The one in the miniature blue sailor suit Violet had thought was so cute; the one with the rainbow gypsy shawl she'd found in a vintage store. Laurel threw the scraps of herself in the dumpster, and she quit her job as a professional submissive. With all the uproar over poor, sweet, beautiful Violet, no one would spare Laurel a thought; no one would remember her, not even Lady Eva.

But it turned out Laurel couldn't abandon her own past so easily. She couldn't go on without seeing Violet one last time, making sure she was all right, saying goodbye. So a few days later, Laurel left her tiny apartment and took the bus to Jack's condo. She had to give her name over the intercom at the door, and someone— Jack or Violet—buzzed her in and she rode the elevator ten floors, missing Violet's giddy presence beside her.

Jack answered the door, his handsome features creased into a frown. "Is Violet here? I need—"

"She doesn't want to see you." He nearly slammed the door on her, but she snuck her way in first. Red flashed in his hand— he was holding a rope, the kind he'd tied her and Violet together with before.

"Please, I just want to tell her—"

"Don't you think you've done enough?" Jack snapped, his eyes darkening. "Violet's elbow is held together with pins. She's in so much pain she can barely walk."

Laurel took a step toward the bedroom, determined to find Violet, but Jack grabbed her and headed the other way, through the half-open door to the bathroom. The bathwater was running, and Jack dropped Laurel's arm to wrench the taps closed. Laurel had noticed the huge marble tub on previous visits, wondered if it had hot-tub jets and thought it might be a fun place to share with Violet. Now, water sloshed almost to the top of it, heaving like Laurel's stomach had begun to.

"Look," Jack gritted out, "Violet can't even wash herself. Once I get rid of *you*, I'm going to bathe her."

Laurel turned to run, more certain than ever that she had to find Violet, get them both out of there. But Jack grasped her arm. "Vi—" Laurel called, and Jack swung his other hand to the back of her head, slammed her down and under the water. Her scream dissolved into the heavy warmth of it. Her heart bucked, her limbs thrashed, but she couldn't overcome the weight holding her under.

Jack yanked her up by her hair. The moment her lips met air she coughed and spluttered and cried, "Vi—"

Down she went again. Longer this time, until liquid fingers crept into her lungs and she thought she'd burst. When he pulled her back up, she tried to move her arms and found them bound behind her. Jack was tugging her Doc Martens off, twisting her ankles up and tying them to her wrists. "Vi—" Laurel tried again, but it came out only a waterlogged croak.

"You're a little witch, aren't you, Laurel, with those gypsy eyes of yours? You tried to steal my girlfriend away from me. Put crazy ideas in her head, said I was no good for her. She told me all about it." He scooped her bound body up, his hands rough and grasping, and with her white slip dress still on he threw her in the bathtub. She pressed against the ropes with every ounce of strength she possessed, fought to keep her head above the surface, her body transforming with every moment from a human's to a desperate, trapped animal's.

Jack held her under until stars danced before her, visions of the night sky she feared she'd already had her last glimpse of. He jerked her up by her hair and slapped her face and thrust her back under. On and on it went, until her limbs turned cold and unfeeling despite the warmth of the bathwater. Her hair was so drenched, such a heavy, hanging rope, that whenever Jack dropped it she fell back beneath the surface.

"Do you know what they used to do to witches like you, Laurel?" He growled into her ear, but the words were faint and distant. "The drowning test. They tied women up and threw them in the water, and if they died they weren't true witches."

Laurel knew, then, through the sting of Jack's hand cracking her cheek, through the all-consuming cold, that she would never survive this. Jack was a monster. For one last moment, her vision cleared and she saw him, eyes blue and soulless: a man whose only god was his own power. A man who believed he was entitled to everything he desired, and no punishment would ever touch him.

Then he pushed her down one last time, and her heart flailed against the walls of her ribcage and tried to save her, as living hearts always do, but Laurel couldn't feel it. Her spirit was above the bathtub, floating, witnessing the wild jerking of her body within its binds as the dark, liquid coldness caressed her. Seeped in through every crevice and possessed her.

Laurel watched her body fall into stillness, watched Jack stand and shake his head and regain control of himself, push the drain up and leave for a moment. The bathwater emptied and she looked down on her limbs cloaked in drenched hair and fabric, red rope that kissed her wrists and ankles. A last, loveless embrace, a final bondage.

Laurel took the bad things that had happened to her, and she used them. While her body lay lifeless and broken, she made her will stronger. Strong enough to survive while Jack wrapped her body in a sheet and took it down to the trunk of his car, then drove, beneath a moonless night sky, to the marina. A rich, powerful man who didn't have to worry about questions, about witnesses, as he carried that heavy sheet onto the yacht he must have owned. Laurel watched as the boat carved its way through the vast, empty ocean. She watched as her sheet-shrouded body fell over the side and below the dark surface, weighed down with bricks to sink it to the bottom. This cold, lonely liquid would hold her will while she waited.

No one had saved her, but as long as Laurel remembered the wrong that had been done to her, a part of her could never die. Outside the laws of the living universe, her spirit hovered. Her coal heart hardened, forged by the frigid water, the pulverizing pressure at the depths of the ocean, and waited for the day she would be resurrected.

The day that unbeating, inhuman heart could at last be kindled.

TWENTY-SIX: CLAIRE

Claire saw Mara's past, her purpose in a moment, and when the contours of Lady Lilith's room reformed around her, everything was frozen. The mirrors-turned-fountains had stopped flowing; the room no longer quaked; Mara and Jack stood immobile, and Ruby's mouth hovered just above the reach of the blood-veined water. A glass shard floated against Claire's ankle. She tried to lift her hands, still clutching Mara's hair, and found she could move them. She pulled tighter and felt the potential in each strand, the sparks buzzing against her fingers. The moment she let go, it would all explode.

And then, while Jack's body stayed still, his hands clasped on Mara's arms, his lips parted. "You never stopped haunting me, you know." His voice, once so charming and confident, had twisted into something ugly. "You little witch, you little *whore*. Violet, she—she never trusted me after what happened. She tried to find you... She always suspected...

"She left *me*." His eyes widened with the outrage of it, the disbelief that his will could be denied, despite all his power. The same wrath he seemed to feel now, as the tendons rose on his hands, yet his limbs remained unmoving.

"I had to move across the country." He spoke slowly and deliberately, every word a curse and condemnation. "I had to wait twenty years to come back here. I watched your body sink to the bottom of the ocean, but still, all that time, I felt your eyes on me. Still, after all these years, you found me."

With each of Jack's words pain wrenched into Claire, coursing through her broken arm like knives, like needles. It was a powerful pain, as all pain had the potential to be, if it could only transform into anger. It broke her open, scalding and crimson, until she couldn't distinguish what was hers and what was Mara's.

Claire knew, though, that it wasn't all Mara's. Those lipstick words had told her, back when Mara first arrived at the dungeon—*FIND THE TRUTH. TELL THE TRUTH*. And this was Claire's truth: not the unraveling of an old mystery; not the identity of a strange girl; but Claire's own anger. The emotion she'd buried so long but that had always simmered, a live coal deep within her. Waiting for her to claim it as her own.

Now, Claire had no choice but to let that fury fill her until she discovered, at the heart of all the rage, something smaller and lighter, but perhaps even stronger.

Violet looked for me, whispered a small, wondering voice. *She cared about me.*

Beneath Claire's shaking hands, Mara's hair thickened and lifted, trying to escape her. Claire thought again of the word Yarik had used: *Rusalka*. There must be a thousand names for what Mara had become. Perhaps even more. There were the Wilis, those wandering, vengeful spirits; there was La Llorona, the name Luna had whispered; there were the wailing banshees Claire's mother had sometimes called out to. So many names, spread out across time and space; as many as there were women wronged and abandoned, with nothing but their righteous fury to outlive them.

There were a thousand names for what Mara was, but before she had become this...this spirit bent on vengeance, she had been something else. A girl. A girl who had loved, and hurt, and lost; a girl who had deserved so much more than what the world had given her.

Claire could reach down for that broken glass by her foot with her good hand, and saw it through the strands of Mara's hair. She could wait for help to arrive and hope someone could find scissors. But Claire wouldn't do any of that, because it was time, at last, to tell the truth. To witness Mara's anger—all the women's anger—and give her the freedom to release it. Jack might not survive; *Claire* might not survive; but as long as she rescued Ruby, nothing else mattered.

Claire took one last, long breath, and gripped Mara's hair tighter, each strand a live wire beneath her palms.

And then she let go.

TWENTY-SEVEN: RUBY

The moment before Claire let go of Mara, her blue eyes landed on Ruby's, and Ruby knew, through the blinding pain and panic, through the throbbing in her smashed hip and shoulder under the weight of the cross, that Claire was coming for her.

And then the red flood poured from the walls again. Mara and Jack burst into motion and collided. Their every movement made the room tilt with them, the water sloshing and splashing and rising, rising. It grasped with slippery fingers against Ruby's neck, her chin, as she struggled to keep her head above the waterline. Claire was so small and so far away from her, her steps so slow against the writhing tide. Claire was fighting as hard as she could, but she would never make it in time. So this was how it would end, then—not in fire but in water, cold and insidious and all-consuming.

It was all over for Ruby, but she wished with all her might that Claire, at least, would get out alive.

That was Ruby's last thought, before the water rose up into her mouth and her nose. It rushed through her and over her, crept down into her lungs and above her eyes. It sucked her under. She tried for another moment to lift her head, to push up against the cross, to move her crumpled limbs beneath it. But the water soothed her pain, and along with the pain, the fight retreated. The liquid caressed away all her raw, exposed edges.

Here it was, so comforting, so familiar: that deep, numbing emptiness. The place where Mara had waited for twenty years, and where, now, Ruby could join her. A place where she was too cold to feel anything, where the ache of losing Claire faded. A place where she was completely alone, and no one could hurt her.

Ruby sank down, down, down into the relief of not breathing.

***

Flames dug into her crushed side. Something was worming its way in, needling the pain awake again, lifting the weight of the cross off her. She was being wrenched upward. Water flew from her lungs and air rushed in, burning like fire. She looked up and saw the wide pools of Claire's eyes, pulling her back to this world, to all the agony that awaited her. "Lean on me, Ruby," Claire gasped the words out. "You've got to stand up. The water's still rising."

Ruby's left hip screamed, she was sure it was breaking into pieces, but she grasped tight to Claire's arms and found her way up, until they both stood in the waist-deep water. In front of them Jack and Mara were grappling, their bodies tangled so tightly they might be wrestling or embracing.

While Ruby watched in wonder, Mara's hair lifted and flew behind her, twining and untwining, a hundred ropes so strong they could never be broken. Mara forced Jack's head under, he surfaced and spluttered and tried in vain to speak his anger, but Mara dragged him down again and again with a power borne from twenty years of grief and fury. At last, he stopped struggling, and only Mara's slender, soaked form remained standing.

She turned, then, and looked at the two girls. Ruby held tight to Claire, to the living warmth of her body. Mara's mouth opened, her lips moved; but the sparks in her eyes were fading, she was becoming more ghost than human, and no words were spoken. She sank lower, lower, into the rising water, until only her hair floated on the surface, and then it too was dissolving.

The mirrors stopped pouring. The water sloshed, gently, and fell into stillness. Ruby could see through the red veins of it, all the way down to the zebra-striped carpet. There were no bodies.

"She—she took him," Claire whispered. "She took him back to wherever she came from."

"Is it—" Ruby was afraid to speak the words. "Is it over?"

"It's over."

"You saved me, Claire." Ruby turned to look in Claire's eyes. Claire, drenched and shaking, so alive and so beautiful. The pain would be back, reminding Ruby her bones had broken, but for now there was only relief soaring through her.

Claire smiled, a small, tender thing. "We saved each other."

"Claire, I— The things I said this morning... I didn't mean any of it. I was just scared and—"

"Shh." Claire reached up and brushed the wet hair off Ruby's face. "I know. I love you."

"I love you," Ruby said, and lowered her lips to Claire's.

They kissed and they kissed in the room full of water, until gradually Ruby became aware of banging on the door. "Claire?" said a voice that sounded like Nadia. "Ruby?" That was Luna. "The door's locked from inside, we can't open it."

"The cavalry's here," Claire said.

"They can wait a minute," Ruby said, and kissed Claire again. But this time Claire pulled back.

"By the way," she said, "I broke up with Danny last night." Claire's lips tipped up into that sweet, sweet smile, and Ruby's insides swelled as she leaned down and kissed her one more time.

"Come on," Ruby said, and, hobbling and leaning on each other, they waded their way to the door.

"Watch out," Ruby called to the women on the other side, "stand back, there's a lot of water."

She reached out and turned the knob, and pushed the door open. And Ruby and Claire stepped out of Lady Lilith's room for the last time, together.

The entire second floor of the Briars had to be gutted, after all that water had seeped through the carpet and invaded the wood like rot. And the attic floor, of course, had already splintered into pieces. The skeleton of the building dismantled, destroyed, to make way for a new foundation. A stronger one, unburdened by years of old pain and old secrets. All that reconstruction was expensive, but we had some help: a generous anonymous donation, accompanied by a letter that deemed the dungeon to be of "historical and folkloric significance," a place worth preserving.

We worried that someone might come looking for Jack, but he had left no car in the parking lot, and always paid in cash; no record tied him to the dungeon. We heard no reports of his disappearance; perhaps despite his belief that he was so superior, he was, in the end, more like Laurel than he realized. Both alone and overlooked, but at least Laurel had Violet to worry about her, while no one cared enough to investigate Jack's disappearance.

While the dungeon was being resurrected, we all moved next door to the annex, which made for some cramped, crowded spaces. Our new lobby still held crosses and cages behind the desk, consigned to the corners; the little room with the flowered sofa became our dressing room. Whenever we doubted our abilities to adapt, to rebuild, we looked out to what had once been the bare alley behind the Enclave, where, by midsummer, a riot of red roses bloomed. An explosion in the colors of anger and love, demolition and passion, emerging from the earth and breaching the heavens.

We marveled to know that Lady Lilith had loved her dungeon, her remarkable community of women, so much that even now a part of that love lived on. And we marveled too, though only in our quietest moments, our wonder confined to whispers, as we considered a more shadowy sort of legacy. Claire and Ruby had shared enough, and while none of us knew the full story, we could all imagine the depth of longing and loss and fury that might upend the universe, defy every law of nature to bring a body back and correct a wrong that needed righting. We all wondered at the strength of one small girl who, despite a world that drowned her, found a way to complete her story.

And Claire, who knew more of the truth than anyone else, would sometimes catch sight of a pale, slender limb, a strand of dark hair wavering at the corner of her eye, in those moments

269

when, despite her happy new life with Ruby, a hint of melancholy intruded. But every time, when Claire looked closer, she discovered that she'd seen only a palm frond or a tree branch, silvered by moonlight. And each time she thought of Mara, or Laurel, and hoped that wherever the girl's spirit was now, she'd found what peace might be possible for her.

And as for Claire and Ruby? Well, they didn't have the option of dismantling their own skeletons, replacing the bones they'd broken during their final minutes in Lady Lilith's room. They had to wait for Claire's arm and Ruby's leg to repair themselves, for their wrist and thigh bones to stitch together again, even if they'd never be exactly as they once were. They had to learn to live with the old hurts, the memories that lingered like ghosts.

And even before those last moments, Claire had broken Ruby open, just a tiny bit, and Ruby had patched Claire up a little. Together they became something cracked, but whole; something imperfect, but worthy of saving.

And beneath the sun's rays and the moonlight, the roses of the Briars bloomed and withered and birthed new buds that opened once more, and the salt air blew in from the ocean, and the wide, wondrous world with all its mysteries continued to turn.

Stephanie Parent is an author of dark fiction and poetry. Born and raised in Baltimore, Maryland, Stephanie spent much of her adult life in Los Angeles, where she worked at a commercial dungeon as a professional submissive and dominatrix—an experience that inspired *The Briars*.

Stephanie's debut poetry collection *Every Poem a Potion, Every Song a Spell* was published by Querencia Press, and her short fiction and poetry has been published or is forthcoming in Cemetery Gates Media, Brigids Gate Press, Black Spot Books, and many other publications. Follow Stephanie on Twitter at @SC_Parent for the latest updates on her work.

www.ingramcontent.com/pod-product-compliance
Lightning Source LLC
LaVergne TN
LVHW052026161224
799254LV00007B/65

* 9 7 9 8 3 7 7 1 3 1 9 4 6 *